Other Books In This Series

TESSERACTS #TEN

A Celebration of New Canadian Speculative Fiction

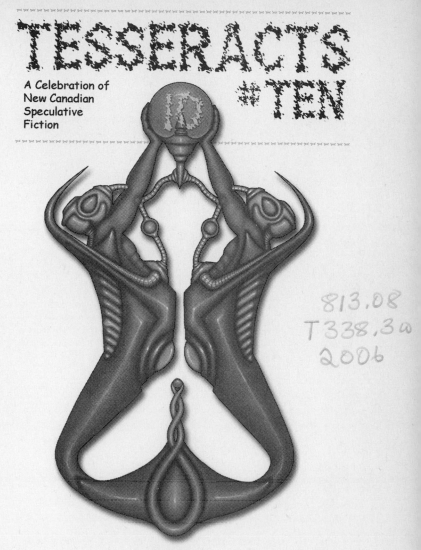

edited by

Robert Charles Wilson & Edo van Belkom

EDGE SCIENCE FICTION AND FANTASY PUBLISHING

AN IMPRINT OF HADES PUBLICATIONS, INC.

CALGARY

Edge Science Fiction and Fantasy Publishing
An Imprint of Hades Publications Inc.
P.O. Box 1714, Calgary, Alberta, T2P 2L7, Canada

In house editing by Laura Pellerine
Interior design by Brian Hades
Cover Illustration by Colleen McDonald
ISBN-10: 1-894063-36-8

EDGE Science Fiction and Fantasy Publishing and Hades Publications, Inc.
acknowledges the ongoing support of the Canada Council for the Arts and the
Alberta Foundation for the Arts for our publishing programme.

Library and Archives Canada Cataloguing in Publication

Tesseracts ten: a celebration of new Canadian speculative fiction /
Robert Charles Wilson and Edo van Belkom, editors.

ISBN-10: 1-894063-36-8   ISBN-13: 978-1-894063-36-4

1. Science fiction, Canadian (English) 2. Fantastic fiction, Canadian
(English) 3. Canadian fiction (English)--21st century. 4. Short
stories, Canadian (English) I. Wilson, Robert Charles II. van
Belkom, Edo

PS8001.T48   C813'.087608054   C98-901492-4

FIRST EDITION
(zc-20060928)
Printed in Canada
www.edgewebsite.com

Contents

A Nervous Look Down a Dark Road

by Robert Charles Wilson

We live in strange and perilous times.

This statement is no less true for having always been true. Times have always been strange. The future is as unknowable as it always was. As always, storm clouds have lately gathered on the horizon. As always, there are scattered rays of hope.

Sometimes, however, the storm seems closer than ever. You can hear the thunder and feel the lightning in the air. The going gets tough, and the thoughtful get nervous.

⇥•⫶•⫶•⇤

The nineteen-fifties and early sixties were such a time. Media iconography has draped that era in fading, contradictory images and emblems: Joe McCarthy vs. Marilyn Monroe; the radioactive atolls of Eniwetok and Kwajalein vs. the gilded, monoracial, faux-Christian suburbs imagined in such prime-time sitcoms as *Leave it to Beaver* and *Father Knows Best*. Ask the average seldom-reader what the science fiction of the nineteen-fifties was like and he'll probably venture a guess involving *The Jetsons*, flying cars, and hyperoptimistic visions of cities on the moon.

There is some truth to this, but less than you might think. In fact, in those days, science fiction had fallen on hard times. The old pulp magazine markets had dwindled to a precious few. The revolution in paperback publishing took up some of that slack, but did so, in part, by mining the rich back catalogue of those same defunct magazines. SF was occasionally declared dead, and its salvageable organs were freely donated to B-movies and television.

Nor did the future seem especially bright for the world at large. It is a cliché now, but was not then, to say that mankind had taken into its hands for the first time the power to destroy itself. Between the brushfire wars and the nuclear brinkmanship there was often giddy talk of a New Frontier — and the economy was booming, after all — but the talk seemed forced, ideologically driven. It might not have been true, exactly, but it was patriotic and probably good for you, like saying the "Pledge of Allegiance" or singing "God Save the Queen". "They trow not what is shaping otherwhere / The while they talk thus stoutly," in the words of Thomas Hardy. Or perhaps they trow all too well.

What they did often understand — these odd, strangely inhibited people, who could tolerate racism in their public media more readily than they could accept an advertisement for Kotex or condoms — was that some of the problems they confronted truly were unprecedented. Neither a prayer nor an ocean could long deter the nuclear bombers, should they be unleashed, and there was no wall over which the radioactive clouds could not drift. Who wanted to imagine, much less dramatize, such an eventuality? To save itself as a popular literature, shouldn't SF set aside these all-too-real fears and... well, *look on the bright side?*

Some in the field said so. John W. Campbell would allow doomsday scenarios in the pages of his *Astounding* (later *Analog*) only if they were represented as temporary setbacks on the road to human self-apotheosis. Progress, we might imagine, could be interrupted, but never stopped. Wasn't that what people wanted to hear? Wouldn't it somehow restore science fiction to its place as a literature of confident optimism? Might it not even bring back the glory days of three-color covers by Frank R. Paul and serials by E. E. Smith?

But it was a thoughtful anxiety about the future (plus a healthy distrust of human nature) that produced two of the era's classic novels, one of which became a perennial bestseller: Edgar Pangborn's *Davy* and Walter M. Miller's *A Canticle for Leibowitz*. Similarly, we remember John Wyndham not for his early space fiction written under another name but for the strange biological apocalypses of *The Midwich Cuckoos*, *The Chrysalids*, and *Day of the Triffids*. Likewise J.G. Ballard, who was and is a fine writer in many genres, but whose science fiction of that era remains memorable for the chilly, half-lit, deliquescent worlds of *The Voices of Time* or *The Terminal Beach*, fictions stranded, somehow, halfway between bohemia and Armageddon.

What was wonderful about these works was not simply that they acknowledged the omnipresent threat-and-weirdness of what we liked to call the Atomic Age. What was wonderful was that they captured these feelings and dispensed them like some fine distilled essence ... feelings everyone of my generation shared but which we had never learned to articulate. One might write bluntly about the Bomb without quite getting it, as Philip Wylie did in his atomic-attack novel *Tomorrow!* (1954). But Wylie was of an earlier generation, and his book was a polemic for civil defense. To truly understand what 1964 felt like you needed Ballard:

At night, as he lay asleep on the floor of the ruined bunker, Traven heard the waves breaking along the shore of the lagoon, like the sounds of giant aircraft warming up at the ends of their runways...

Or Pangborn:

It happened in 323, in Nuin, whose eastern boundary is a coastline on the great sea that in the Old Times was called the Atlantic — the sea where now this ship winds her passage through gray or golden days and across the shoreless latitudes of night...

→•I•I•I•←

It's the tail end of the year 2005 as I write this, and those shoreless latitudes seem closer than ever.

This year, three great natural disasters — the tsunami that originated off the coast of Sumatra, the earthquake that caused so much death and misery in Pakistan and Kashmir, and Hurricane Katrina — elucidated great gaps and inefficiencies in the civilized world's ability to cope with unexpected crises. One of America's largest and most historic cities was reduced to a sodden, filthy wasteland, and we watched the poorer citizens of New Orleans herded into a battered Superdome and abandoned there, at least briefly, by a flailing and ineffectual federal agency. Natural disasters can happen anywhere, anytime, of course, but overshadowing all this were bigger and more contentious issues. America, we were repeatedly told, is at war. The enemy is a shadow. He might be anywhere. He might be you. "The rules have changed since 9/11." Your papers will be inspected. Your phone will be tapped, your e-mail will be intercepted. If you are very unlucky you might, like Canadian citizen Maher Arar, be whisked away to some invisible foreign prison and tortured because you had the wrong friends, or were in the wrong place, or possessed a name that sounded like someone else's.

And the hurricane that devastated New Orleans: might it have been a symptom of a rapidly changing climate? The polar icecaps, according to news reports, have shrunk; the vast sea current called the Atlantic Conveyor has slowed measurably as melting ice dumps fresh water into salt arctic seas. Codfish may be facing extinction. Many parts of the world's oceans have been fished into virtual deserts. Oil — the lifeblood of global civilization as it stands — has begun to grow scarcer and more expensive even as emerging monster economies like India and China demand more and more of it. There are continual rumors, if no confirmed sightings, of an emerging killer influenza — or some other pandemic bred by the combination of massive poverty and unprecedented mobility. And in the face of all this, millions of Americans have united in an organized political movement... to expel the teaching of Darwinian evolution from the nation's crumbling public school system.

Bad times, too, for science fiction. Magazine circulation is down and book sales are sluggish outside a few select titles and authors. Once again, our tropes and stage-sets have been wholesaled to the movie industry. Images that were once the exclusive province of SF literature have become commonplace, digital costume jewelry for the Blockbuster Motion Pictures that shamble through our theaters every summer. "Cyberpunk," once cutting-edge, is the stock-in-trade of cartoons and direct-to-video thrillers.

And there is the same temptation toward denial. We don't want to admit that, as Tom Smallways says in the H.G. Wells novel *The War in the Air*, "this here Progress" might not "keep on." Science fiction, we are once again instructed, must be optimistic. It must hold out the promise of a glowing future. One American publisher has reportedly banned even the *idea* of global warming from its authors' works (though the same publisher welcomes stories of a resurrected German SS at war with invading aliens). After decades of denying that science fiction is an "escape literature" there is the pervasive sense that it isn't, but that it *ought to be*.

Admittedly, fiction that merely reiterated the threats we all face would be dreary. Margaret Atwood's *Oryx and Crake*, for all its virtues and excellences, came close to meeting that description. But the best SF doesn't just acknowledge the Horsemen of the Apocalypse, it names them and inquires after their families; it curries and bridles their mounts; it asks politely where they're bound, and what might happen after the last sinner has been scythed and the last grinning skull stacked with all the rest. Faced with nuclear annihilation, science fiction had the nerve and wit to invent Brother Francis and the Blessed Leibowitz. "Beate Leibowitz, ora pro me!" And the world paid attention.

I don't claim that what we have in this anthology of current Canadian science fiction and fantasy is the post-9/11 era's answer to Miller or Ballard. But it does represent a groping in that direction. Here we have a double-handful of mostly new, mostly young writers, floating ideas that are often comic, often horrific. Some of these writers are digging through the tropes of older SF and fantasy, rearranging the familiar in unfamiliar patterns. Some are inventing tropes of their own. And perhaps, from one of these new wellsprings, will come the visions we one day recall and say, "God, yes! That's it, that's what it was like to be alive and awake and human at the beginning of the 21st century."

Welcome to the new future.

Threshold of Perception
by Scott Mackay

On a crisp March night in 1910, I parked my bicycle outside the Meudon Observatory and, arching my back to ease the strain of the ride up the hill, gazed to the northeast where Mars rose, bright and clear, in the faultless air above Paris. I glanced up at the building, and knew that within its vaulted dome I had at my disposal the largest telescope in the world, the Grand Lunette, a 33-inch refractor capable of producing the most minutely detailed views of the red planet. I looked forward to a night of protracted observation.

I entered the observatory through the south door and climbed the steps to the concierge's compartment. The concierge, Herbert, looked up from his newspaper, rose from his chair, and gave me the keys.

"An exemplary night for you, Monsieur Marcotte," he said.

I produced a bottle of wine for Herbert, a vintage my mother sent by the crate-load from Marseilles. "Was there any mail today? I'm expecting correspondence from Percival Lowell."

"I believe Monsieur Flammarion took some to the observatory earlier this afternoon."

"And is Monsieur Flammarion here?" I asked.

"No. He's busy getting ready for his tour of Italy. You might as well go through his private chambers. It'll save you the trip up the tower."

"Merci, Herbert."

I gave him the wine — a way to have his own exemplary evening — and passed through Camille Flammarion's private chambers to the observatory.

There she stood, the Grand Lunette, its miraculous eye lifted skyward, its focusing knobs beckoning me, its lens angled majestically so that it peered out the open slit of the observatory dome. I was so eager to begin, I didn't bother taking off my hat. I didn't even remove my coat. I hurried directly to the telescope, made the necessary adjustments, and put my eye to the eyepiece. I sighted Mars with the keenness of a schoolboy and the reverence of a true devotee.

Yet in the end it was as a scientist that I studied our great red neighbor. And, as a scientist, I again thought of the elaborate claims Percival Lowell had made about Mars.

No matter how hard I tried to believe in Lowell's famous but hotly contested canals, I simply couldn't see them. Were the canals there? No. A civilization building a worldwide system of water-bearing canals to save itself from the merciless advance of the Martian desert seemed too grand an assertion on Lowell's part, especially when I couldn't see any evidence of the canals through my 33-inch refractor.

Mars appeared as a pale disk, with colours ranging from lemon to ocher, and showed immense detail, none remotely resembling artificial waterways. The surface held steadily. A maze of complex markings covered the southern part of Syrtis Major. Mare Tyrrhenum looked as spotted as a leopard's back. What Percival Lowell observed as a gridwork of organized canals, I perceived as a desert wilderness, with no sign of civilization at all.

I pulled my eye from the telescope and sighed. As a professional astronomer I knew I had a responsibility to tell the world, as I had done in two previous papers, that there were no artificially constructed waterways on Mars. But I hated so much to be at loggerheads with my good friend Percival, and I was reluctant to put pen to paper.

I glanced around the observatory. I heard footsteps. In a moment Herbert appeared with a glass of my mother's wine on a tray for me.

"Ah... Herbert. You're always so thoughtful."

"I would never forget you, Monsieur Marcotte. I see you've already rolled up your sleeves."

"I have indeed." I took my glass of wine and looked through the open observatory dome. The red planet hovered just above the horizon, a bright speck to the naked eye. "Mars is particularly clear tonight."

"So I imagine you can see the canals," said Herbert.

I felt my lower jaw protrude a fraction as my brow settled. "No, Herbert, I don't think I can. I've never seen the canals. In fact, Monsieur Lowell and I are conducting a vigorous correspondence debating their very existence."

"Monsieur Lowell is a great man. A great American."

I felt the corners of my lips tighten. I put my wine down, and took off my hat and coat. "*Oui*, a great American. And a dear friend to both myself and Monsieur Flammarion. But I sometimes question his observations. First it was his canals on Mars — that was strange enough — but now he's written a paper about spoke-like markings on Venus." I took a sip of wine. "I sometimes wonder how such an intelligent man like Monsieur Lowell can let wishful thinking so easily distort his perception. How can he so readily fall sway to Schiaparelli's grand illusion?"

Herbert peered through the slit in the observatory dome. "To a man like myself, it's fun to believe in the canals. And I pity those poor creatures living on Mars. Their whole planet is dying. Imagine! Having to build all those waterways just so they can stay alive! It's something I wouldn't like to see here on Earth. Though with so much water here, I wonder where it would all go."

Herbert left me to my work. I made a few sketches of Mars and wondered how Monsieur Lowell would react when I sent them by the next post. I grew suddenly eager — even anxious — to read his latest correspondence. I glanced around the observatory. I spied the pile of mail Monsieur Flammarion had brought up. I went to the table and, sifting through the various missives, found my much-awaited letter from the American astronomer, his response to my latest findings.

I tore open the letter and read.

I expected a vitriolic attack. But his remarks on the warrior planet were unexpectedly mild and surprisingly brief. "One needs a diaphragm, my dear Georges," he wrote, "usually from 12 to 16 inches if one is to catch the finest details. You'll have to stop your lens down. You'll never see the canals with a fully open refractor, especially one as large as the Grand Lunette." Throwaway remarks. Off-the-cuff remarks. What he seemed most concerned about was Halley's Comet. "I've been observing its approach with a new photographic technique my assistant, Mr. Lampland, has devised."

He then wrote extensively of Monsieur Lampland's photographic technique, a process using various chemicals and fluids to enhance the light-gathering properties of photographic paper, especially during long exposures.

"Until late August," continued Monsieur Lowell, "I concurred with most other astronomers about the likely course of Halley's comet. But now I'm not so sure. The comet's orbit has grown aberrant. Lampland has photographically charted the comet's trajectory since May and, using the stars of the Orion Constellation as guide-points, now detects a measurable distortion in the icy visitor's projected route." The American then made a grandiose and typical Lowellian claim. "I fear a direct strike against Earth is possible." I shook my head, saddened by this faulty conclusion. Why did he always come up with the most romantic and confabulist notions? "I plan to publicize my findings any way I can. To this end, I speak in London on April 2nd, and hope I can meet you there. As scientists, it's our job to convince the world of my findings any way we can." And why did Monsieur Lowell always have to be so evangelical about his suspect scientific discoveries? "I trust I can count on your support. Too often we're confronted with a skeptical world, and I fear that skepticism under such dire circumstances would be fatal."

I put the letter down. I sighed heavily. Much of the scientific world had already discounted Monsieur Lowell's theories about Mars. I couldn't help thinking of the story

about the little boy who cried wolf. Who was going to
believe this fantastical notion about Halley's Comet? Not
only that, I was highly suspicious of Monsieur Lampland's
new photographic technique. With such chemically sensitive paper, I feared an abundance of "phantom" light —
light that could mislead even the most astute observer.

I walked back to the Grand Lunette. I sat down and tilted
the telescope away from Mars. I sighted the comet and put
my eye to the eyepiece. There it was, Halley's Comet. It
streaked through the sky, captured perfectly in the excellent refractor of the Grand Lunette, its tail stretching out
for millions of miles, its frothy coma fizzing like an effer-
vescent confection around its diamond-like core. I mentally
charted its position against the stars of the Orion Constellation, then checked my logbook. I shook my head. Exactly
where it should be. Monsieur Lowell had once again fooled
himself.

⋯⊹⋯⊹⋯

On the evening of April 2nd, 1910, the streets around
the London Palladium were jammed with motorcars. People
crowded the sidewalks trying to get in to see Percival
Lowell. I pulled my collar around my ears and hurried
down the alley to the stage door. I climbed the back steps
and showed the custodian my special pass. I was glad
Lowell was speaking at the Palladium and not the Langdon
Lecture Hall at Victoria College, home of the British
Astronomical Association. I would sooner him make a fool
of himself before this fun-seeking rabble, not in front of
the stodgy but respected members of the much-vaunted
BAA.

I found my way to the green room where I was greeted
by the aging American astronomer himself.

"Bonjour, Georges," he said, speaking French, shaking
my hand vigorously. "I was afraid you weren't going to
make it."

I was alarmed by the change I saw in Monsieur Lowell.
He was pale, had dark rings under his eyes, and looked
as if he hadn't slept in days. He was fifty-four, but tonight

he looked much older. His suit, though impeccably tailored and of the highest quality, looked too big for him.

"Monsieur," I said, "I'm sorry, but traffic was bad. I had to leave my taxi at Charing Cross and walk the rest of the way."

"This infernal London," he said. "It gets busier every year." He arched his brow. "Have you been spreading word of my latest findings in Paris?"

I glanced away, where I saw a bouquet of yellow roses sitting on a table under a portrait of King Edward. "Monsieur, I... I've been following the path of the comet carefully since I received your letter in October, and I'm sorry to say I haven't detected any change. I've discreetly asked a few members of the Société Astronomique to keep an eye on it, and we've taken a few of our own photographs, but we failed to spot the aberration you wrote of in your letter."

He broke into English. "Georges... please. You must understand Mr. Lampland's new technique. More conventional exposures simply won't capture the shift in the comet's path. Without an extremely long exposure, your observations will be blinkered. I'm on a mission here, Georges, and you have to help me. We must convince the scientific world that I'm correct in my calculations. If we get enough of the professional community to join us, we might at least make some preliminary preparations against the collision."

My lips stiffened. I wondered how such a brilliant man could so misconstrue the observations of his own eyes. Even so, I felt I had to meet him at least half way, if only for the sake of our friendship.

"I'll take additional exposures when I get back to Paris," I said. "But please realize that the members of the Société Astronomique can easily dismiss any exposure I take. Photographic astronomy is a bit like... like cheating to them, Percival. Before I can persuade them of the evidence, I have to convince them that I'm playing a fair game."

The stage manager came for Monsieur Lowell a few minutes later. I followed them to the wings. I sat in an exclusive seating area backstage with a few special guests.

The stage manager announced Monsieur Lowell. The astronomer gave me a sad grin as he stood by the curtain waiting to go on. He went onstage to thunderous applause.

I peered out beyond the wings to the brightly lit stage. The American had drawn a good crowd. And because of the appearance of the Great Daylight Comet earlier in the year, a bright cousin to Halley's, his topic was of particular interest. As the applause died down, Monsieur Lowell placed a few notes on the lectern. He cleared his throat.

He began by explaining Monsieur Lampland's new photographic technique, how it allowed him to chart Halley's Comet with an extensive index of open-exposure negatives heretofore unequalled in the annals of modern astronomy. Then, by reciting in his best oratorical style a history of Halley's Comet, he eased his way into the bad news.

"All was well until last September," he said. "That's when Mr. Lampland and I discovered an unexpected deviation in the comet's projected orbit. We don't know why the comet has changed course. Maybe it was affected by Jupiter's immense gravitational pull. Or maybe an asteroid out near Mars gave it a good knock. Whatever the case, I'm afraid the comet's trajectory now looks ominous." The members of his audience contemplated Lowell somberly, fearfully. He looked at them as if they were all doomed. "We now know that Halley's Comet is heading directly toward Earth."

He let this pronouncement sink in. I felt acutely embarrassed for him. Alarmed murmuring swept through the theater. Why needlessly scare and panic these people? I wanted to go out there and tell them that Percival Lowell was wrong, that Lampland's photographic technique was far from perfect, that the light-blasted exposures were prone to misinterpretation, and that Monsieur Lowell had a history of making elaborate and grandiose claims. But I didn't want to publicly humiliate my good friend. So I sat there and listened, hoping he would finish his regrettable performance soon.

"A direct strike against Earth by Halley's Comet is bound to bring catastrophe on a global scale," he continued.

"Widespread loss of life is inevitable. We might even face extinction, like our unfortunate Martian neighbors are. But if we begin making preparations now, I believe a sizable portion of humanity can survive. I think it's possible that mankind can come through this, if we all pull together and act now."

Here it was again, the grand Lowellian theme. Just as civilization on Mars was doomed, so now civilization on Earth was doomed. A tragic tale destined to stir the imaginations of these clerks and dockworkers in their Sunday best. As fantastical and unlikely a story as a fiction of scientific romance. I sank more deeply into my seat, desperately wanting to support Monsieur Lowell in his extravagant assertions, but fearing that by this time next year, after Halley's Comet had safely passed, he would once and for all be dismissed as a dilettante and charlatan.

⋙⫶⫶⫶⋘

On April 10th, Percival and I sat at the table next to the Grand Lunette looking at his photographs of the comet for the hundredth time. The photographs were small, barely six centimeters square, and had to be viewed with a magnifying glass. Camille Flammarion, head of the Société Astronomique, was now down in Italy on his long-awaited sabbatical, and had offered Monsieur Lowell the use of his private chambers in the Meudon Observatory, as well as unlimited access to the Grand Lunette.

"Georges, if you would just give me your support on this," he said. "We could take the photographs to the Société tomorrow, and with your backing I'm sure we could make a case for my findings."

I again felt sorry for him. "Percival, these photographs are misleading. I'm not sure you've properly identified the comet in at least half of them. Monsieur Lampland's exposures aren't detailed enough to make any but the most rudimentary guesses about the comet's trajectory."

"I assure you, Georges, the comet has been identified properly in every frame. If only I'd brought the negatives. Maybe if you had the opportunity to compare these exposures to the negatives, you'd quickly see that I'm right. What must I do to convince you? Can you not understand what's at stake here?"

I shook my head. "I don't know, monsieur. These photographs are no bigger than postage stamps. One might as well look at tarot cards. Monsieur Lampland's chemicals are too sensitive. I see nothing but a rat's nest of light."

Percival shook his head, bewildered by my skepticism. Didn't he understand that science was science? One couldn't make outlandish claims without the necessary evidence to support them. I lamented all the scare-mongering that was going on with this particular comet. First it was Camille Flammarion and his claim that cyanogen gas from the comet's tail would impregnate the Earth's atmosphere and wipe out all life. Now Lowell insisted the comet would actually strike Earth. And no reasonable proof for either claim! I watched him scrutinize the photographs one more time through the magnifying glass. His belief was fervent. I pitied him. He had reached that threshold of perception where accuracy and objectivity no longer mattered.

"If only Monsieur Lampland were here," he said at last, putting down his magnifying glass.

He looked downcast, worried sick. I wanted to cheer him up. "Monsieur, let's take another look at the comet through the refractor. Maybe tonight we'll find something suggestive of your conclusions."

But he was too disheartened to make use of the telescope tonight.

"You go ahead, Georges," he said. "Every time I look at that comet I feel like I'm looking at a loaded gun. No one believes me, but I know I'm right."

"It's not that we don't believe you, monsieur. It's just that we need proof."

I got up and searched for that proof through the great 33-inch refracting mirror of the Grand Lunette. As seen through the telescope, the comet was now two-thirds the size of the moon. It spewed off gases like an overheated steam engine, nothing like the restful pink orb of Mars I liked to watch so much. The sublimation of ice into gas was spectacular. Here was the age-old portent. I felt mesmerized by the apparition, so mesmerized, in fact, that I at first didn't immediately observe the comet's unexpected change of position. A slight alteration, yes, just by a degree or two, but enough to tell me that it wasn't where it should be, that it had moved to the left of the Orion Constellation by a measurable if minute distance, and that maybe Monsieur Lowell might be right about the direct strike after all.

Then I heard a loud crash behind me. I whirled around and saw Percival lying on the floor. The magnifying glass clattered to the tiles beside him, remaining intact. I hurried over and knelt next to the stricken man.

"Percival!" I cried.

He stared up at me sightlessly, the left side of his face drooping in a ghastly fashion. I knew a stroke when I saw one. He lifted his right hand and clawed the air, his thumb and his baby finger twitching toward each other while his middle digits splayed in a spasmodic fashion. It was as if he meant to pluck the comet from the sky.

I stood up and turned to the door. "Herbert, come quickly! Monsieur Lowell has suffered a stroke! We must fetch the doctor!"

→•|•|•|•←

I took my latest findings to the Société Astronomique a few days later. The staid and mustachioed president of our Société, Dr. Maurice Durey, studied my newest exposures with growing concern. A line appeared on his forehead, and he looked at his colleagues. He went through my calculations line by line, then did some of his own mathematical jottings on a piece of scrap paper. Finally he sat back.

"It looks as if the comet's orbit deviates from what we originally anticipated," he admitted, "but I still don't see proof that it will intersect with Earth."

I pulled out Monsieur Lowell's photographs and calculations. "Yes, but if you take my observations together with Monsieur Lowell's, you realize that he might be right. I know he's been guilty of some elaborate claims in the past — the canals on Mars, and now these spokes on Venus — but these calculations look ominous to me, and I think we should take them into serious consideration."

Dr. Durey peered at Monsieur Lowell's calculations, then went through Monsieur Lampland's light-saturated exposures one by one. He showed everything to his two colleagues, Drs. Covillaud and Lenéru. They studied the photographs and examined the calculations with exhaustive thoroughness. Dr. Lenéru finally raised his left eyebrow and pointed to a particularly worrisome equation regarding the comet's projected perihelion.

"I think Monsieur Lowell might have something here," he said.

For the next hour, the four of us went through the equations again and again.

By the end of it all, Dr. Durey's face had turned white. He looked up at me, and I had the impression that he had aged a number of years in the space of a few moments. He lifted the calculations again, placed his monocle in his left eye, studied them once more, and all the while I couldn't help noticing how the paper shook in his hands, like a leaf caught in the repetitive eddy of a summer breeze, the corner of the twenty-pound bond quivering, beating with the speed of a bird's heart.

"Perhaps there's some substance to these calculations after all," he said, his voice calm, but somehow smaller.

⇒⊹⊹⊹⇐

On the evening of May 12th, 1910, I pushed Percival in a wheelchair around the grounds of the Meudon Observatory. He stared at the comet, which was now easily visible to the naked eye.

"I want to go home," said Monsieur Lowell.

His speech was badly slurred and it took me several moments to make out what he had said. "The doctor says you're too ill for the voyage, Percival. You'll have to recuperate in Paris before you can risk the Atlantic." I gestured toward the comet. "And in any case, the government has restricted travel for the time being."

Monsieur Lowell's face sagged.

Far in the distance, I saw Paris: the Seine snaking past the Louvre and the Tuileries, winding around the Eiffel Tower, curving south through the Arrondisements of Passy and Vaugirard. The sun was setting, and a lavender mist cloaked the city.

The comet hovered high in the western sky. I held two telegrams in my hand. One was from Camille Flammarion. He was postponing his return to Paris, was going to stay in his chalet in the Italian Alps, on high ground. What better place to weather the strike? The other telegram was from Lowell's family in Boston. They were leaving Boston. They would take refuge in Flagstaff.

I was about to tell Monsieur Lowell all this when the sky lit up with an eye-smarting flash. Here it was, I thought, the age-old portent, blanching the pastel air of Paris with its malignant glare, looking as if it were heading straight for the North Atlantic. I glanced at Lowell. His face was alabaster-white in the flash of the comet. But he was smiling. Why would he smile like that? Here was the day of our doom. The light faded as the comet dipped below the horizon. What possible joy could he take in something so horrible?

Then I understood...

"You were right after all," I said, feeling irrationally resentful toward the astronomer. "But your vindication must be bitter, Percival, mustn't it?"

A faint rumble swept through Paris.

He looked at me, his white hair wild around his bald pate, his blue eyes twinkling. "Bitter indeed, Georges."

⇥⊹⊹⊹⇤

Seven weeks after the end of the world, as I rode my bicycle up the hill to the Meudon Observatory, I felt within my breast the growing desperation of an encroaching hopelessness. I had one of my mother's wine crates fixed to my back fender, and it was full of canned goods I had scavenged from a number of abandoned stores in Paris. The road had turned to mud, and the rain still came down, a biblical forty days of it so far, with no sign of it letting up. As hard as I pedaled, the mud finally overwhelmed my tires, and I had to stop, get off, and push my bicycle up to the parkland surrounding the observatory.

The round reflecting pool in front of the observatory had filled to overflowing and now spilled out onto the lawn. The observatory pond was flooded. A number of motorcars were parked around Meudon, the vehicles of survivors who had sought refuge on the observatory's higher ground. A few cows and goats grazed miserably in the pouring rain.

I reached a tree near the reflecting pool and took shelter. The end of June. This should have been a pretty time in Paris, but the city was dark below me. The sinewy stripe of the Seine had disappeared beneath the grey-green flood of this modern-day Armageddon, and the smell of rotting bodies reached my nostrils, even all the way up here, at the top Avenue du Château.

I felt as if I had outlived my usefulness. Who needed astronomers anymore, when the sky was always cloudy. I was like the Meudon Observatory itself, a rococo relic from the past. And who needed the Meudon? With Paris steadily encroaching from the north, bringing with it a sea of light, the neo-classical observatory was now only of secondary importance to the astronomy world. Yet I had to remember, it was here at Meudon that we had first confirmed the current Lowellian catastrophe. For that reason the observatory would always remain in the history books.

I pushed my bicycle across the grounds and entered the observatory.

I found Percival asleep in his chair beside the Grand Lunette, facing the windows overlooking Paris. I walked to the windows and gazed at the capital once more. I saw the Eiffel Tower dominating at its center. So many buildings had been toppled in the initial riverine surge. I saw a few boats out in the main swell of the river, and a larger barge tied to the lozenge-shaped buttress of the Pont Neuf. The Pont Neuf itself had become an island, as had the towers of Cathédrale Notre Dame.

Then I saw a brief spark in the vicinity of Jardin du Luxembourg. Then another, and another... till the spark flickered into life and glowed steadily, a sharp and caustic blue. I walked to the office adjoining the main observatory, lifted my 3-inch refractor, and proceeded out to the terrace. I lifted the refractor to my eye and peered toward Jardin du Luxembourg.

My observations were exact and unmistakable. French troops blow-torched their way through twisted debris, while others cleared the rubble away. Still others erected what looked like the beginning of a dyke along Rue de Vaugirard, building a bulwark against the flood. My encroaching hopelessness deepened.

I couldn't help thinking of the doomed Martians building their canals.

⇒⊦•⊦•⊦⇐

May 12th, 1911. I write in my journal on the anniversary of the comet strike. Exactly one year has passed. The rain stopped briefly one day last week. Percival sleeps in a cot beside me. I'm afraid he's grown much weaker. I fear he might die soon. We have many survivors living in the observatory with us. Much of Paris is still under water. A hundred families are here now. I am the nominal mayor of this small community.

So far we've been lucky. We've scavenged enough food to survive. But conditions are deteriorating. There were no crops last year. There's been nothing to feed livestock. To make matters worse, Kaiser Wilhelm has finally chosen his moment. His troops invaded Belgium last Monday and are expected to enter France any day now. I don't know how much longer we can hang on. I rue the day Percival ever turned out to be right. I wish the comet strike was nothing but a mirage, like all those canals on Mars.

I put my pen down and turned to Percival. He coughed in his sleep. He woke up, opened his eyes, and looked at me.

"Brandy," he whispered.

"Percival, the brandy is gone. We have one crate of my mother's wine left, that's it."

"Then give me some of that."

I got up from the table, walked to the desk, and poured wine for Monsieur Lowell. He couldn't go home. Not now, not ever. There were no ships crossing the Atlantic these days.

The rain rattled like a thousand snare drums against the observatory dome. The dome was closed and the Grand Lunette sat unused, covered with cobwebs. With the sky overcast all the time, there was never anything to look at anyway.

Percival propped himself up on his elbow. He looked steadier than usual. This was our private chamber now. We lived here, the two of us, subsisting on canned Spam and the mushrooms I grew in the corner. I gave Percival his glass of wine. He drank it quickly and it seemed to restore him greatly.

"Help me to my wheelchair," he said. "I want to see how the troops are making out."

"Percival," I said, "our troops have been redeployed. Kaiser Wilhelm is making a nuisance of himself in Belgium."

"Let's take a look anyway," he said.

I helped him out of his cot and got him into his wheelchair. I pushed him to the office, and we looked out the window. The trees outside, having lost their leaves in autumn, had failed to regrow them in spring; with the world darkened by a globe-spanning blanket of cloud, photosynthesis had all but stopped. We planned to chop the trees down soon for firewood.

We saw the famous buildings of Paris sticking out of the water — the Sorbonne, Notre Dame, the Hôtel de Invalides — all under the grey-green flood of the comet. To the west we saw the great earthworks, a massive dyke system the French Army had been constructing all year, now stretching through the Arrondissements de Vaugirard, Passy, Batignoles, La Chapelle, and La Villette. The artificial construction seemed to amaze Percival every time he saw it.

"Some day, when all these clouds clear..." But he lost his train of thought as he gazed at the dike system through his spectacles. He swallowed, squeezing hard, as if he had a sore spot in his throat. "Some day... when we finally have blue sky again... the Martians will look down on us through their telescopes... and they'll see that they're not alone. They'll see our dykes... and they'll know that we, too, are having difficulties. They'll understand that they finally have somebody they can share their suffering with."

The rain lessened, and with it, came relative quiet. Percival Lowell's Martians. I remembered his writings. Three times the size of a human being and fifty times as strong. Easily able to build a vast network of canals. Possessed of inventions we couldn't even begin to imagine, inventions that made our present-day electrophones and kinetoscopes look like the clumsy contrivances of cavemen. Was he right about the Martians? Certainly he'd been right about the comet. But could I believe his grander notions about an alien civilization? When it came right down to it, I didn't know what to believe anymore.

I took a deep breath and glanced up at the dust-covered Grand Lunette. Why not believe in Lowell's sentient civilization on Mars? There was no proof to the contrary. Outside, the rain stopped. It was easy to believe anything now. Easy to believe that Kaiser Wilhelm would wage war in the sea of mud that was now Europe. Easy to believe that Halley's Comet could strike the North Atlantic and cause world-wide destruction. Even easy to believe in Lowell's grand and dramatic Martian canals, that which I had stubbornly refuted with all my scientific might for the last ten years.

❖❖❖❖❖

Later that night, when Percival was sleeping, I went to the office, looked out the window, and to my great surprise saw a break in the clouds, miles wide, showing the pale stars of the evening above. And lo and behold, there was Mars! I quickly seized my three-inch refractor and gazed at noble Ares for the first time since 1910. A spectacular image, reassuring, a beacon of light and wonder. And do you know, for just a moment, I saw them — they were there, unmistakable, steady in my lens, the canals of Mars!

I saw what Monsieur Lowell meant by their wonderful mathematical fitness. I saw what he meant by their overwhelming exactitude. And yes, I finally believed in them, these great inland waterways, and not only in the waterways, but in Monsieur Lowell's noble and wondrous Martians as well. Accuracy and objectivity no longer mattered. Not in this dark time. What mattered was belief.

I heard footsteps behind me. I turned. It was Herbert, formerly the concierge, now part of our little community here in the Meudon Observatory, bringing one of the last glasses of wine to me on a tray.

"Finally a clear night for you, Monsieur Marcotte."

I nodded. I took the wine. "And Mars is resplendent, Herbert."

"An extra treat for you, then, monsieur."

"And do you know, I think I finally might believe in the canals after all. I think they're up there."

"Of course they're up there, monsieur. I never doubted it for a minute."

I put my telescope down and looked at Mars with the naked eye. What mattered, I thought, was faith. The warrior planet shone like a message of perseverance.

"If they can do it, Herbert," I said, "so can we."

Frankenstein's Monster's Wife's Therapist

by Sandra Kasturi

She tells me she's happy now.
They've reconciled. He spends
most evenings at home
and they've started to try
to make babies: he bringing
their limbs home, she
with her sewing needle.

Puss Reboots
by Stephanie Bedwell-Grime

Pieces of the virtual kitty lay strewn across the carpet. The Siamese model had obviously seen better days.

Careful of the static built up by my rubber-soled shoes, I inserted a new motherboard, checked the other cards were seated properly and rebooted. The Siamese uttered a meow that degenerated into a high-pitched squeal. Something was terribly wrong with the purring subroutine. Its legs pawed the air. It tried to right itself, and then fell to its side and crashed.

I sat back on my heels and eyed the components on the upgrade flooring. Someone had abused it and badly. The little girl who had been whining at my elbow since I arrived was the most likely culprit.

Mom and Dad obviously had money. Their spacious unit came equipped with a wall-sized entertainment screen in the common room. Junior had a miniature one in her suite. They'd approved the funds for my service call in advance. It was plain they had money to buy junior everything she asked for. And no quality time to spend with her. No wonder junior took her angst out on her virtual pet.

And I was the one who would have to break the news that Fluffy couldn't be fixed.

I filed the job as "work in progress," pending replacement. The parents hadn't approved that much of an expenditure. V-Kitty no longer made a replacement for Fluffy. They'd have to upgrade. The kid whined some more as I let myself out of the unit. I felt bad leaving her like that, but what else could I do? I'm just a service technician, not a psychiatrist. Not even a well paid service technician at that. I fix office computers, small home appliances and virtual pets.

My next stop was an office in station central that had received a virus from Phoenix Prime instead of the expected docking fees. A lot of that going around these days — viruses masquerading as money. And of course they'd been trying to cut costs by running a pirate version of their virus protection. Doesn't the irony just kill you?

Nothing I could do except to try and rebuild from their last backup. Which hadn't been done for a while. Another dissatisfied customer and the morning wasn't even over.

I arrived back at the office in a foul mood. Actually, I usually arrive at the office in a foul mood, so that's nothing out of the ordinary. I never chose this career path. I kind of tripped over it, fell in and I've been trying to scrape up enough credit to retrain ever since.

My coworkers were mostly guys who never made it working in the asteroids. Couldn't handle the code for heavy machinery, weren't rugged enough, or just too lazy to adapt to mining life. So they migrated to station life, taking their chauvinistic attitudes with them. Our job never attracted the best — of anything. And I was one of the two women on staff. Lucky me.

The station office was cramped, as all station offices are. But ours seemed to evolve out of whatever storeroom the station wasn't using at the moment. Currently, it was the coldest hidey-hole next to the docks.

I put on my thermal jacket and poured myself whatever edible oil derivative passed as coffee and cream these days. Predictably, it tasted terrible.

Predictably also, Dan was busy checking his work queue. By the morning's end he'd have a pie graph of all our output up on his console, with his being the biggest piece. Didn't matter how well he did his job, just that he did the most and had the ear of our verbally abusive boss.

"Bad morning, Cai?" he asked in response to my scowl. Never tell him the truth, I'd learned long ago. He'd turn it into some excuse to help him with his own latest crisis. Another brownie point from the boss gotten off my hard work. The best way to deal with him was to trick him into thinking you had a huge workload planned for the day. That would have him running scared in two minutes. Probably to the outer rim of the station. Surely he could make up enough jobs to keep himself busy for the afternoon.

I nuked a cardboard station ration to lukewarm and mumbled something noncommittal in reply.

"Did you hear about Altair Substation?" he asked just as I had my mouth full. Mind you, a mouthful never stopped Dan from talking.

"Altair? What about it?" I asked, not really caring.

"Totally grounded by a virus. Locked up completely."

A cold feeling of dread settled in the pit of my stomach. The economy in the outer rim was unstable at best. Perpetually on the verge of collapse would be closer to the truth. Station economies depended on trade, on the steady flow of goods and credit. And if Altair was locked up, then that affected everything from food processors to docking computers and interstellar banking.

"Locked up how?" I asked. Wouldn't put it past Dan to be exaggerating just to make himself look powerful. Wouldn't be the first time he'd manufactured a drama to impress the boss. In Dan-speak "locked up" could mean anything.

"Completely," Dan reiterated. "Locked up. Every computer in the place."

My stomach twisted into a tighter knot. "Okay, that's bad, but why don't they just go to backup?"

"Backup's down too," Dan said, stabbing his fork at me.

"How can the backup be dead too?" I asked. They had whole departments to take care of that kind of stuff. Departments that treated us like crap. Called us technomonkeys, the lowlifes they called in to fix the small problems not worth their time. "Heads are going to roll."

"No shit." More than anything else Dan liked it when other people's lives were coming apart. Mine had amused him for years on end so far. One of these days I was going to get it together and ship off this piece of metal floating in vacuum.

One day. But no time soon.

I chewed a mouthful of tasteless protein ration, not so carefully disguised as lasagna. "Are you sure?" We'd been in space for a couple of generations now, stuff like this just didn't happen. "I mean, who'd you hear this from?"

"Mangor over at the Law."

Mangor was Dan's buddy. Mangor ran the seize and salvage operations. Mangor was Dan's hero. He had the power to ruin lives. Dan liked that kind of thing.

"Who'd Mangor hear it from?"

"From his mate the pilot. He had a contract to seize a load of ore from some guy on Altair. But when he got there he had to turn around because all the docking ops were down. Barely made it to Phoenix Prime on the fuel he had. Had to refuel there. Not a happy guy according to Mangor. He got paid on delivery and now he's out two loads of fuel as well."

A niggling thought occurred to me. This morning I'd had a Siamese I couldn't repair. An office system totally down and running on an outdated backup—

"Pilot's having trouble with his InFlight system, too," Dan said, breaking into my thoughts.

"They didn't quarantine him?" And the network guys called us stupid.

"Can't find anything wrong."

"His InFlight's FUBAR and they can't find anything wrong?"

"So Mangor says."

My queue beeped. I glanced at the portable clipped to my belt. Before lunch my job queue sat at 20 jobs pending. Pretty much an average workweek. I could usually get through 4 or 5 on a good day.

I blinked and looked again. My queue read 50 jobs. As if the day couldn't get any worse.

Mangor and his drama would have to wait. Knowing Dan he'd have a fresh drama brewing before the end of our shift. "Gotta go," I said, dumping the last of the cardboard lasagna in the recycler. They'd make it into spaghetti for tomorrow's lunch. Hopefully spaghetti and not meatloaf, which would be a cruel misnomer.

My queue beeped again. Jobs being upgraded from pending to urgent. All of them.

Dan's queue started its own high-pitched squeal. He stared at it in shock. I almost laughed. Dan being stuck with a real workload he couldn't worm out of. It was almost worth the misery of his company just to see it.

"See ya Dan," I said, moving toward the door.

"Wait a minute!" He darted to block my escape. "I need a hand."

"How many jobs you got?" I asked. The boss never gave Dan as much as the rest of us, being his golden boy and all.

"Thirty-five," Dan said.

"Sorry," I said making my escape. "I got fifty."

Overtime meant time off with pay, not more money. So being worked to death didn't really help me in any way. I had no money to afford an off-station holiday. And there was precious little to do station side. So I was pretty resentful as I made my way to my top priority job.

The Med Office was in an uproar when I arrived. Not what I needed, another ten people yelling at me. The R-Doc was down, which boded ill indeed. Meds ran off the services of two licensed physicians and a team of well-trained nurses. Most of the time they relied on the R-Doc to verify their diagnoses and provide medical advice. One of the real docs was off station on holiday. The other had a triage queue that spilled out of the Med Office and down the hall.

Because everyone else in the Med Office jumped when he hollered, the doctor expected me to as well. But I could tell with one glance that it was going to take more than yelling to fix the R-Doc.

"Look!" the doctor started in at maximum volume. He keyed in the diagnosis for the patient who'd been in a docking accident. The guy looked like he just wished they'd stop arguing and give him something to knock him out and take away the pain. I felt sorry for him. Give me a needle, I thought. I'll fix the poor guy. And something to knock out the doctor while I fixed the computer.

The R-Doc accepted the commands well enough. The doctor punched diagnosis. The computer spit out appendicitis.

"He's got a broken leg," the doctor yelled. Like I couldn't tell that myself.

"Okay," I said, trying to calm the situation. "Why don't you see to this poor guy's broken bones and I'll see what I can do with the R-Doc?" In other words, you stick to your specialty and leave me to mine. Sounded like a plan to me. But the doctor would rather holler about having to depend on stupid technology and the slowness of my department's response.

I listened as politely as possible, sucking in the urge to hit him out of my own frustration.

The patient moaned in pain. The doctor suddenly remembered his medical responsibilities.

I sat down in front of the R-Doc. The thing was totally locked up in a loop endlessly processing the same erroneous information. I keyed in the override commands, but the thing refused to break out of the process.

I hated to do it, but my only recourse was a cold boot. I glanced over at the doctor and found him engrossed with his patient. No sense involving him in this, I thought. And rebooted the R-Doc.

The R-Doc beeped twice. The welcome screen flickered to life.

"So far so good," I muttered to myself.

The R-Doc crashed.

"What have you done?" the doctor yelled, abandoning his charge.

The R-Doc screen faded to black leaving only a red blinking dot.

For some reason I thought of the Siamese lying on its side on the rug and the poor kid crying over its demise.

Could it be the wonky R-Doc, the outdated office computer, Mangor's irate pilot and the V-Kitty that needed to be put down were all related? Dan would probably swear they were.

I thought of Altair totally locked up, quarantined to all outsiders. I thought of the residents of Altair trapped on a piece of floating metal with no fresh food or goods of any kind coming in. Panic hit me. It made me want to cash in that inadequate savings account and take the first transport as far away as I could. But would it be far enough? And if Dan was right, that a virus caused all this chaos, was I already infected in some way? Would I get out in space and find all the ports closed to me?

The doctor was still screaming, a dull background noise I tried valiantly to ignore.

"It's not my fault," I insisted. "The operating system is shot. I'm going to have to reinstall it."

The doctor let loose with a stream of insults to my parentage along with insults to the R-Doc's parent company, and the parentage of the hacks that wrote the program. I stopped listening and got on the COM.

A company called MedGalactic made R-Doc 6.0. They said they could beam over an upgrade in two days. Provided I beamed over proof of their license and the required fee. What the doctor said to that I really didn't hear because he yelled it too loudly to distinguish the words.

From what I gathered Meds' budget had been cut and the first casualty had been the licenses.

So the R-Doc had no operating system. I looked around at the patients lined up in the halls, some of whom really looked like they needed a qualified physician stat, and sincerely hoped Meds could raise the money. But since there was nothing else I could do, I left to attend to my next top priority.

The next job was a specific request for a female technician. That piqued my interest. Most people looked disappointed when I showed up. Like whatever they were expecting I wasn't it. And if this person wanted a female technician it had to be for a delicate reason.

The owner met me at the door.

"Hi," she said, artificially cheerfully. "I'm so glad to see you."

Already I didn't like the sounds of it.

"I'm late for work." She shrugged into her gray, admin-istrative-level jumpsuit.

I studied her while she got ready to leave. Dark circles ringed her eyes. Her hair was disheveled as if she'd just crawled out of bed. She looked like someone who might work in our department, not like one of the admin-level holier-than-thou's.

A thump rocked the upscale unit. I glanced down the narrow corridor.

"He's been like that for days," she said. And keyed open the door.

"Wait a minute—" I started to protest.

"I've already approved a full repair." She leaned in close. "And as long as he needs maintenance, can you do an upgrade, too?"

Oh no, I thought. "But—"

"Got to run." She fled through the door, leaving me with whatever was creating a ruckus down the hall.

I crept down the corridor. Another thump made the thin metal walls vibrate.

"Are you okay in there?" I called.

"Beloved," came a deep male voice from inside.

Oh no, an Adonis 6000.

Using the codes on the work order, I keyed the door open and shut it before the virtual gigolo could escape.

The Adonis 6000 slumped on the bed against the far wall. Its owner had to be making a bundle because he was the top model. She obviously had a weakness for tall, dark and handsome. A weakness and the money to buy it.

Adonis 6000 could have been a poster boy for the virtual stud industry. He had curly hair and eyes like dark liquid pools. I'm sure that's what the advertising copy said. And eyelashes as long as your arm, I couldn't help noticing. I stopped myself from thinking about whatever upgrades she might have purchased. He was wearing a silk shirt, open to the waist. His chest was bare, if you like that kind of thing, and made of the most expensive and life-like synthetic skin.

"Where's Claudia?" the Adonis 6000 demanded. "You're not Claudia."

"Repair technician." I approached cautiously. I had the administrator override codes, but the thought of wrestling all that fake muscle didn't appeal to me.

"Claudia needs me," he said petulantly. "I'm her *love bunny*."

"Nice," I tried to hide my smirk, then wondered why I worried about what this over-sexed piece of silicone thought. "I think Claudia's a little worn out from your attentions."

I should have stayed on the other side of the room. I should have beamed the codes from the infrared port on my belt computer.

Because as soon as I stepped within reach, I was seized in an iron grip and yanked up against that synthi-skin chest.

"Mmphh," I said into his chest. I couldn't get a hand free to see the override codes on the work order. I thought the safe word was Oregano, whatever that was.

"Relax Claudia," the Adonis 6000 cooed.

"I'm not Claudia," I protested as his synthi-lips descended toward mine. I wondered if the Adonis 6000 would get the message if I kicked him in the nuts.

Probably not, I decided as the upscale synthetic flesh lips covered mine. I had to admit, the Adonis was worth the expense. But that wasn't what I was there for. And the Adonis 6000 belonged to someone else. I levered myself away with much effort and yelled, "Oregano!"

Muscled synthetic flesh arms released me. I tumbled onto the bed.

The Adonis 6000 rebooted. I reached for the control panel and switched to safe mode before he had a chance to reload.

His pupils dilated, then went black. The Adonis 6000 stared blankly into space. A green light flickered in his unseeing eyes. I heard the subtle whirr of software reloading.

"Reloading in safe mode," the Adonis 6000 said.

Good, I thought. *Sit in the corner for the rest of the day and be a good boy.*

I updated the work order as "pending parts" and further servicing. I'd need at least a couple of, ahem, larger parts, for the upgrade. I beamed the update to the house computer with strict instructions to the owner not to reboot him under any circumstances.

Then I escaped into the corridor. The way the afternoon was going I hesitated to take on anything further. More than half my shift had gone by and all I had was a string of in-progress work orders in my queue. And nothing completed.

Time to call in the big guns, I decided.

❖❖❖❖

"I think we have a problem." I stood in the door to the boss' office and waited to get screamed at. I wasn't disappointed.

"Yeah? And so do I. My problem is idiots standing in the doorway to my office when they should be out on the rim working!"

"I am working," I countered. I was sure my tongue had permanent teeth marks for the amount of times I'd had to bite it. "There's something weird going on out there. I—"

"Weird is not my concern."

Miffed, I took the offensive. "You should be concerned. I've got a dead V-Kitty, an office computer totally messed up and the operating system on the R-Doc in Meds is completely corrupted."

"All doctors are corrupt," the boss proclaimed. I hope that wasn't meant to be funny.

"Thanks for the insight," I said. "But what do you want me to do about it?"

"Fix it!" the boss hollered. "You're supposed to know how. That's what I pay you for!"

The door to his office whooshed shut in my face. "You don't pay me worth shit!" I muttered back and wished I had the guts to vent my spleen and scream it at him. Instead I slunk off down the hall looking for some dark hole to wait out the encroaching disaster.

I was huddled over a mug of some grain beverage that was supposed to pass as coffee trying to make myself as small and invisible as possible when the door to the lunchroom slid open and Sukey strolled in. Sukey is the only other woman on the crew and honestly, she holds her own against the men folk better than I do. Probably because she could out bench-press all of them.

Sukey nuked a mug of some black-looking sludge and slid into the chair opposite me. "How's business?"

"Sucks. I had a morning from hell. You?"

Sukey grunted around a mouthful of whatever she was drinking. "Everything's fucked. I don't know what's up."

"According to Dan, Altair is locked up tighter than a drum with some virus."

"Altair?" Sukey put down her mug. "All of it?"

"Apparently."

"But then Dan is probably full of shit. Remember the time he told us they were axing our entire department and sending us to Axis?"

"Yeah, I remember." That one even had me going. Probably because we lived in constant danger of being downsized.

"Still," Sukey studied the dark depths of her mug. "Something's up this morning."

"Well, don't mention it to Spolanski; he's in a mood."

"He's always in a mood. If I didn't know any better I'd say the guy had multiple personalities, all of them unpleasant."

"I was thinking more along the lines of hiding out for the rest of the afternoon until the network guys had a chance to figure out what's up."

Sukey snorted. "Leave it to those morons to fuck it up worse and blame it on us."

"Still, I think that's what I'm going to do. Whatever you do, don't hang out here. Dan's in shock because Spolanski actually gave him work today and he's looking for someone to do it for him so he can take the credit."

"Fell for that one once," Sukey said. "Once, being the operative word."

"We all did. Once."

"Got anywhere I can hide out with you?" Sukey asked.

"I could use some help with an Adonis 6000."

Sukey's eyes lit up. "An Adonis 6000, you say?"

I held up a hand for silence. "Spare me the wise cracks. The, ah, client also wants an upgrade, but I'm out of parts. I wasn't going to ask Spolanski for them. Not with the mood he's in today."

"I've got spare parts," Sukey said, way too quickly. "I could use a little stress relief today. Just transfer the work order to my queue."

What she was suggesting was highly unethical. But if Sukey could fix the Adonis 6000 that was one more job out of my queue and one less thing for Spolanski to yell at me for. And I could pretend that I hadn't heard her plans to take an unsuspecting client's Adonis 6000 for a test drive. Making sure it was operating properly and all that.

"Your shots are up to date?" I shouldn't have asked. But hey, the last thing I needed was someone giving the Adonis 6000 a disease and trying to pin it on me.

Sukey shot me a dark look back.

"Never mind," I said. "The less I know the better."

So now that I'd provided Sukey with an afternoon's diversion, I needed somewhere to hide myself.

Where could I go where they wouldn't find me? A vision of the broken Siamese writhing on the carpet flashed through my mind. The whole rotten day had started with it, why not end with it too? And the only way they could reach me out on the rim was by my pager, which I'd turn off and claim poor reception. Sounded like a plan to me.

I put my mug in the sonic dishwasher and stood to leave. "Well, I hope your day gets better."

Sukey scrolled through her queue. She looked up and shot me a smile full of anticipation. "Yours too."

＊⋅✛⋅✛⋅✛⋅＊

The kid was still sitting on the carpet in front of the entertainment center when I arrived. Surprisingly she let me in. Guess I didn't qualify as a stranger having been there earlier. The parents still hadn't come home. I felt bad for her.

"Watching vids?" I asked.

The kid sniffled and wiped her nose on the back of her hand. "Vid's not working, either."

Vids came in as a feed through the main COM. That didn't bode well.

"Look, I can't promise you anything, but there may be a way I can fix Fluffy. But I'm going to have to take him with me." I hated myself for lying, but what else could I do? I had the strangest suspicion Fluffy was somehow at the center of all this misery.

"You can't let Fluffy die," the kid said. "He's my only friend left from Altair."

Warning bells sounded in my mind. "Altair?"

"Where we used to live. All my friends are there." The poor kid sniffled some more. This time she mopped them up with the sleeve of her jumpsuit. I hoped the sanitary facilities included disinfectant detergent. "They don't call me anymore." She stuck out her bottom lip. It quivered. "They've forgotten about me."

"I'm sure they miss you terribly. But vid calls between stations are expensive. Maybe their parents can't afford it."

"You sound like my dad," she accused.

Surely I didn't look old enough to be confused as anyone's parent, I thought in horror. The day just couldn't get any worse.

"So, is it okay if I take Fluffy with me?" I felt like I was stealing a crying kid's teddy bear.

The kid wiped a stream of snot off her face with her hand, then cleaned her hand on the carpet. "Sure, he's dead anyway."

"He's not dead," I said, bundling Fluffy under my arm. The V-Kitty flailed weakly and emitted that annoying high-pitched whine. I reached underneath for the power switch. Fluffy uttered a low growl, vibrated for a moment as if trying to purr, then lapsed into silence. "He's just broken. I'm going to try and get him fixed. Okay?"

The kid sniffled a bit more, then nodded. "Look," I said as gently as I could. "I don't want you to get your hopes up too much. I'm going to do my best to make Fluffy better, but I can't guarantee anything."

She snuffled again. Blue eyes gazed back at me like she'd given up on hope altogether. She couldn't be more than six. I wondered how she got so jaded, then decided I didn't want to know.

Going back to the office meant risking running into the boss. I doubted the boss would find trying to fix a V-Kitty in the middle of an outright emergency a worthwhile use of my time. I ran through a list of possible hiding places. The outer rim office sprang to mind.

ORO had originally been command central for our department. Before all the independent companies amalgamated under one station government and we got sucked up in the mix. I liked working in the ORO a hell of a lot better than I did in the station center. But no one ever asked me.

The ORO was still there, no one having taken it over yet. Having been a team leader, I still had clearance. Probably the only one. Jarrell, our old boss, got canned. Damned shame that, he was the only one who truly understood what we did, having done the job himself.

The dimly lit corridor was barely heated. I shrugged on my insulated jacket. At least the ORO still had some power. I swiped my ID and waited. To my relief the lights glowed green and the door whooshed open. I stepped into the frigid dimness.

Lights flickered on the ancient monitors. The old company had been barely subsidized, not that the newly consolidated one was any better. We had newer machines, newer offices, nastier bosses and the same bad pay.

I sat down in a freezing cold chair. Shivering, I pulled the tail of my jacket under my butt. I powered up the old workstation that had been mine. Surprisingly enough, my password still worked. No one had bothered to change it. Probably because there was nothing on that out-dated machine worth stealing. But it had the capacity to log in to the main network.

But then, I've already told you what I think of the network gurus.

I put the V-Kitty on the cubicle beside me and rubbed my hands together for warmth. My breath came out in puffs of fog in the cold air.

V-Kitty let out a high-pitched squeal as soon as I turned it on. It sounded vaguely familiar. Like I should somehow recognize that noise.

How could a screwed up purring subroutine cause so much damage? I wondered. The V-Kitty let out another squeal.

The terminal I'd just logged into went down.

I stared at the workstation in disbelief. Okay, it was old. It had been sitting in this frigid tomb for months, but it had been working.

Dan's old terminal sat two down from mine. I looked at it dubiously. Dan wasn't too bright. He never changed his password. I knew he used the same logon and added the number of the month to it. It saved him from having to remember something new. I'd had to login for him several times. Some of the many times I'd saved his sorry posterior and never even got so much as a "thank you ma'am."

We'd moved out of the ORO in Octaire, eighth of the ten months in the station year. So that meant Dan's logon if it still worked should be Dan8.

I keyed it in. Nothing.

He might have added a character or two for good measure. I tried Dan8*. Star because that's what Dan thought he was.

It let me in.

"Dan," I whispered. "You sure are pathetic."

I reached underneath the V-Kitty and cut the power just in case. The last thing I needed was another broken machine in my queue. Not that anyone would notice, except that I'd logged on here. I guess I could say it was an emergency. Hopefully, they'd all be too busy to look closely. It would be a shame to lose such a good hidey-hole.

It was cumbersome trying to log in to the main network. These old clunkers ran fat-client and used few net resources. But I got in eventually. After a bit of rerouting, I even accessed the files for Exterminate, the high-level virus program normally inaccessible to us techno-monkeys. I checked the ancient microphone on Dan's old computer. The voice recognition seemed to be working fine.

I opened a new quarantine file, then activated the Siamese. It let out another squeal. I winced. Something was dreadfully wrong with that purring subroutine.

To my dismay a string of code raced across the screen. That couldn't be good. More code went scrolling across the monitor. I tried to bail out of the program, but it locked the computer up faster than I could hit "end task."

I watched the quarantine file fill until the extermination program couldn't contain it. Then the monitor went black. I heard its fan wind down into silence in the cold cell of the ORO.

I decided I needed some help. My COM was still working. Whatever had infected everything hadn't infiltrated it yet. Sukey answered a little out of breath. Actually, quite a bit out of breath. I politely pretended not to notice.

"Hey Sukey," I said as nonchalantly as I could. "I hate to interrupt your, um, afternoon, but I could really use a hand."

A string of curses echoed through the tiny speaker. "I can't get the damned thing to turn off!"

"Restart in safe mode," I said. "And hurry. I really need your help."

While I waited for Sukey, I shut down the V-Kitty and unplugged the power source just to be safe. With a shaking hand, I reached out and rebooted Dan's old computer. It started up okay, initially. But once it began to load programs, it froze.

"Quarantine is full," the screen read. It wouldn't let me in to have a look at what was in that file. But one line of code had loaded before it hung on me completely.

I kept thinking that something about it should make sense to me. But for all my staring at the screen, my brain refused to supply the clues.

The door to the ORO hissed open.

"What's so damned important?" Sukey demanded.

"Good to see you, too." I felt annoyed, myself. "And thanks for the afternoon's entertainment."

"Sorry," Sukey said. I noted the flush of her face. She was still out of breath. "It was great, at the beginning. Until... well, you know."

"Well yeah, that was the problem you were supposed to be fixing."

"I got the upgrade done," she said brightly. "Before the thing went wonky and tried to screw me into tomorrow."

Great, I thought. And decided I could use a little stress-relief myself.

"Something is really wrong with that thing!" Sukey flopped down into the seat beside me. In one glance she took in the Siamese lying on its side on my old chair and the string of code on the monitor. "Okay, this is weird."

"That's got to be the understatement of the millennium," I snapped. After all, I was the one with Spolanski breathing down my neck. I wasn't the one who'd just had all the kinks worked out.

"What in colonized space is that?"

"Something that came out of the purring subroutine."

Sukey glanced again at the screen, then back at the Siamese. "Out of that thing?"

"Yeah. And okay, I know I really need a holiday and I'm not the fastest ship in the fleet or anything, but I think all our problems started with the V-Kitty!"

"Nah—"

"No really. The kid who owns it said they brought it with them from Altair Substation."

"Altair? The station Dan says is quarantined?"

"The same."

"It's a kid's toy." Sukey poked it with a finger that ended in one long silver-lacquered nail.

"It's a pretty sophisticated toy. Meant to interact with entire families the same way a real pet would."

"Forgive me if I don't share your delusion."

"No really." I reached over and turned off all the microphones in the room. "Listen to this," I powered up the V-Kitty. It let out a purr that sounded like metal scraping against metal. A sound so familiar, and yet I couldn't place it. "That's the purring subroutine."

"The hell," Sukey said.

"The family put in a work order to have it fixed. But I don't think they really knew what the problem was. I think the purring subroutine got infected somehow and when it didn't work the kid kicked the stuffing out of it."

"Even if it's infecting our system with a tech version of the plague, how'd it take down an entire station?"

"Not sure." Then I added, "Yet." Force of habit. Never wanted one of the guys to think they had an edge on you. Especially not Dan. "But that sound is familiar."

"Familiar? It makes my ears ring like holy hell."

"I know I've heard that noise somewhere before."

Sukey studied me with the kind of indulgent look you'd give a lunatic. "You need a break, sister. Why don't you go work on that Adonis instead?" She grinned mischievously. "See if you can get *his* purring subroutine working."

"Funny," I snapped. "Focus, will you? I think we've got a serious problem here." I leaned over and rebooted Dan's computer again.

"Dan's machine?" Sukey snickered. "He'd kill you if he knew."

"He's not going to know, is he?"

Sukey's snicker deteriorated into a belly laugh. "My lips are sealed."

As I expected, the computer started to load again, then hung when it tried to deal with the quarantine file.

"Look at this. When I logged in, it was fine. Until I turned on the Siamese. It made that noise and that was it. Deadsville."

Sukey went to sit down in front of my old computer.

"Don't bother," I said. "It took that one out first."

"On a roll, aren't you," Sukey said without humor.

"That sound—"

Before I could yell, "No!" Sukey had turned on the V-Kitty. It uttered one last aborted squeal, then crashed.

I glanced up at her in annoyance and my eyes fastened on an old-time, holo-film poster Dan had left in the ORO. It had peeled away from the wall and now hung by one corner.

Dan's rather limited taste in entertainment ran along the lines of ancient technology. As if working with it all day wasn't enough, he lived and breathed the stuff in his off-hours as well. He especially loved old holo-films that showed clunky cold computers that took up whole rooms. Even better if they could be somehow programmed to engineer the downfall of humanity. I thought of the room-sized processors, their punch cards and their peripherals. Fax machines that spit out thermally treated paper and acoustic modems that sent data squealing across phone lines.

Suddenly it all made sense. Memory supplied the missing piece of the puzzle.

"That's where I've heard that sound!"

Sukey looked up. "Where?"

"Think Sukey. Remember that horrid History of Information Technology course they made us take in college."

"Yeah, so?"

"That sound. It doesn't ring a bell?"

"I think you've been hearing too many bells."

I resisted the urge to get annoyed. "It sounds like one of those historic acoustic modems!"

Sukey opened her mouth to tell me I was an idiot, and then thought better of it. "You're right, it does."

"And that's how the virus got out. Somehow the V-Kitty picked it up on Altair Substation. Probably when they took it in for an upgrade."

"And it's been squealing that string of code at every microphone on the station ever since." Sukey supplied.

"It's been screeching code into every open mike across half the galaxy. Think about it. Every computer the ship talked to in transit, the docking personnel, everyone they bought supplies from."

"If it gets loose in the main COM—"

I looked at Sukey's stricken expression and said, "I think it already is."

"We gotta talk to Spolanski! We've got to stop it."

"Spolanski's an asshole," I said. "And a stupid one at that. We need some real help."

Sukey grinned. "What about Jarrell?"

"What about him? They fired his sorry-butt in the amalgamation."

Jarrell was Spolanski's opposite. Friendly, smart and good at what he did, he'd been fun to work for. When Jarrell ran the department, I'd actually liked coming to work. But after the amalgamation there were fewer jobs than people to fill them. It came down to Spolanski the slick administrator versus Jarrell the absent-minded programmer. Spolanski got the posting. Last I heard Jarrell was trying to scrape up enough credit to buy a ticket home.

"Sure, he got the boot," Sukey said. "Admin forgot about him long ago. But I'd bet my pay allotment he's running a business off Admin and they haven't even figured it out yet."

"He wouldn't still have the codes."

"Bet he's got codes Admin doesn't even know they have."

I snatched up the V-Kitty. "Okay, what have we got to lose?"

"Just our jobs."

⇢⊶⫼⊷⫼⊷⇠

Jarrell looked as rumpled and unkempt as I remembered when he answered the door. For a moment he looked surprised to find us paying him a social call in the middle of a shift. Then he shrugged and offered us that familiar sheepish smile. Like he'd been caught at something. Most of the time he had.

"Ladies?" Jarrell always called us ladies, even though we were anything but.

"Hate to disturb your retirement, Jarrell," I barreled ahead, "But we could really use your help."

Jarrell's eyes flickered to the motley-looking V-Kitty under my arm. He choked back a chuckle.

"Don't say it. It's worse than it looks."

Sukey glanced down the deserted corridor. Jarrell didn't live in the best accommodations. In fact, you could say his unit sat one step above the worst. "Do you think we could talk inside?"

Jarrell stood back, granting us entrance. We stumbled into a dimly lit cavern of a room. Once it had been a store-room. As Jarrell's home, it wasn't much different. Ancient computers covered every surface, even the unmade bed. Stacked on top of each other they looked like so much junk. Until I noticed the glowing power lights. They were all processing something. I didn't ask what.

"Got to tell you, my help doesn't come cheap," Jarrell said. "I'm trying to get myself off this miserable tin can, after all."

"You and half the population." Sukey walked the length of Jarrell's improvised network.

"You running a node off the main network?" I had to ask.

Jarrell shot me a dark look that answered the question just fine.

"Might not be such a good idea," Sukey said.

"Helping us will probably turn out to be for your own good," I added.

Our ex-boss crossed his arms. "Want to tell me what this is all about?"

So, I told him about the V-Kitty, the wonky R-Doc, Mangor's buddy the pilot and Sukey's run-in with the Adonis 6000.

"Would have fired you for that," he said between chuckles.

"Right," I reminded him. "You stole every work order for a Femme 6.0 that came through the office."

"Like I said, Cai." His smile faded. "Look what happened to me."

"If this is as bad as I think it is, it's going to affect all of us."

"Think about it," Sukey said. "The entire galaxy locked up. No commerce, no transport, no fresh food, no new anything! Not even credit transfer."

Jarrell paled. If it was possible for someone that pasty to get lighter. His alarmed gaze shot from his archaic network back to the V-Kitty. "I'm not sure I want that thing in my house."

"Don't worry, I disconnected the power supply."
He breathed a sigh of relief.
"And we've got just the place for you to save the universe."

❖❖❖❖❖

Jarrell stared at the string of code still frozen on Dan's old monitor. "You say this came out of the V-Kitty?"

I nodded. As soon as I flipped on the switch, the Siamese uttered another of its ear-piercing squawks. I shut it down again.

"It sounds like an old acoustic modem," Jarrell said.

"I'm sure that's how it's spreading," I added. "Just about every machine on the station has a live mike input. You can't even make toast without talking to something!"

He looked up at the peeling holo poster above Dan's old desk and shook his head. "Someone showed some imagination when they wrote this thing." He pointed to a line of code. "See here, it's attacking the start-up sequence." His finger moved down a couple of lines. "And here, it's mutated into something different entirely."

"That can't be a good thing," Sukey said.

"Not unless you're the person who wrote it."

Sukey shot him a puzzled look. "What d'ya mean?"

Jarrell was still studying the code on the screen. "Obviously they had a reason. Beyond causing us all grief."

"Maybe they were just mad." I flopped down in my old chair and put the decommissioned Siamese in my lap. "I mean, those of us stuck out here in the fringes after the funding for the colonization projects dried up are all pissed about something."

"Boredom, bad jobs, bad bosses, bad food, over crowded quarters," Sukey supplied. "Few of us have the credit to go anywhere else."

"Doesn't really matter why, does it?" They both looked up at me. "Another few hours and this thing's going to make life more miserable for all of us."

Silence fell in the cold tomb of the ORO while we contemplated just how miserable life in our secluded corner
of the galaxy could be without contact with anyone else.

"We were really hoping you could write something to
fix it," I said finally.

Jarrell looked from me to Sukey and back again. "What
makes you think I could?"

"Ah, c'mon, Jarrell. We know what you're doing in that
old storeroom on the rim," Sukey said.

Jarrell's expression turned dangerous. "Is that a threat?"

Trust Sukey to alienate the only ally we had. "Of course
not." I put the Siamese down on the ice-cold chair and stood
between them. "But someone's got to rescue this pathetic
piece of tin. And you know we can't count on those network
fools." I pulled the pout that had always worked on Jarrell
before. Damn shame it didn't work on Spolanski. "You
always rescued us before."

Jarrell crossed his arms. "I don't see why I should do
it for free."

I glanced down at the battered V-Kitty in my lap.
"Maybe we won't have to."

A slow smile spread across his face. "I like the way you
think, Cai."

As if the mention of the network gurus had shifted some
great galactic karma, my queue started beeping like crazy.
A second later, Sukey's started the same persistent whine.
Our work orders escalated to second level support. I
imagined Spolanski having a fit in his chrome office trying
to track us all down. A virus warning scrolled across my
belt computer: "Disconnect all computers from the main
network."

"Looks like the network gurus finally figured it out,"
I sniped. "Took them long enough. I told Spolanski we had
trouble this morning. He just yelled at me."

Jarrell took one look at the red letters flashing across
my belt pack and ran for the artifact that had been his old
workstation. State of the art probably half a century ago.
Junk now.

"They'll find you if you log in here," I warned.

He shot me a facetious look. "I wasn't going to use *my* old log-in."

"Well, don't use mine," Sukey said.

Jarrell cocked an eyebrow. "Bet you they haven't changed the local admin."

I laughed. "You're probably right. Spolanski hates to memorize anything new."

"We're supposed to be disconnecting computers," Sukey warned. "Not logging in on them."

But Jarrell was too busy playing administrator again. And he knew how better than anyone else station-side since he designed it himself.

For a moment I felt hopeful. Then Jarrell's desperately un-plucked eyebrow drew down into a deep V. "This is bad," he murmured.

"We told you that." Sukey stared at her belt computer, watching the week's work get escalated up the chain of command. If you couldn't keep up with the workload, it got assigned to someone else. I could just picture Dan's pie chart.

"Tell me there's something you can do," I pleaded. And immediately felt like an idiot.

Jarrell's fingers flew over the keys, obviously at home using such an archaic input device. "I'm not sure—" He stabbed at the keys again, as if the poor old computer might understand the emphasis. "Hah!"

Sukey's head snapped up. We waited.

"Got it!" He highlighted a string of code, copied it. "See..." He pointed a finger at the monitor. We bent closer to look.

Then, like a string of Christmas lights being popped one after another, the entire lab went down.

The network gurus had found us after all.

I unclipped my belt computer and set it down on the desk. The tiny screen was crammed with red flashing type: Virus Warning! I refreshed the screen and waited for the update. Sure enough, it came in seconds.

"So much for the men in suits," Jarrell remarked acidly. He'd always hated the "grays," the people who wore admin-level jumpsuits.

"Guess disconnecting the workstations didn't work. According to the last post, everything running Admin Apps is totally locked up." I refreshed the screen again and got another post. "The network gods can't figure out how the virus is still spreading."

"Should we call them and tell them?" Sukey glanced at our faces and fell silent. "Guess that's a no, huh?"

"You do want off this floating tin can, don't you?" Jarrell asked.

"Sure, but we're totally disconnected. How are we going to—"

"Disconnected, not helpless." Jarrell said. "We still have local access. If the 'grays' had half a brain, they would have restricted that as well. But no one asked me." He typed furiously on the keyboard. Code scrolled across the screen. Sukey and I looked at each other and shrugged. Neither of us were programmers. They didn't pay techno-monkeys to be programmers. We just fixed stuff.

I wrapped my thermal jacket tighter around my body and shivered.

"There!" Jarrell yelled, making us both jump.

We looked at the gibberish flickering across the screen. "That supposed to make sense to us?" Sukey asked.

Jarrell copied his revised code to a data chip and held it up for us to see. "Behold, our ticket to a better life!"

"Okay, I'm with you on the better life part," I said. "But how are we going to get the fix into the system? It's not like Spolanski or the network gods are going to listen to any of us."

Jarrell glanced at the Siamese that now sported a growing bald patch on one side of its head. A war wound from its former owner. Dragging it around half the day hadn't helped, either. "We aren't going to ask them. We're going to set up our own *consulting* firm."

"They'll fire us!"

The horrified look on Sukey's face made me laugh. "Spolanski's been waiting for an excuse to fire me since he arrived. He'd rather put a kiss-butt like Dan in my place. Probably even has my replacement lined up."

"Already fired me," Jarrell said proudly. He shrugged. "I survived."

"Just barely." Sukey crossed her arms and glared down at Jarrell.

"Look—" I stepped between them. "You don't have to do this, Sukey."

"You can always answer your page and go help the 'grays.' We're not going to squeal on you."

"And the net gods will take all the credit for your hard work. And if they don't, Dan will and Spolanski will find a reason to fire you anyway."

Jarrell combed through the Siamese's fur, looking for the power supply. "Or we can take a chance."

"Took a chance coming here," Sukey complained. "Got me squat."

"That's what you get for wanting to see the galaxy," I sniped back. My nerves had been wound tight all day. My whole body ached from the cold and from waiting for disaster to rain down on my head again.

Jarrell lifted the Siamese's tail, looking for an access port. "Where's the mike input?"

I snatched it out of his hands. "You're not going to find it there, you pervert." I released the catch on the V-Kitty's neck and showed him the panel.

He retrieved my belt computer from the desk.

"Hey!" I started to object, then realized I was probably already fired anyway. Let Spolanski come looking for his equipment if he wanted it back.

Jarrell slid the chip into the reader. I watched it accept the new data and prayed it wouldn't crash before he finished.

Holding my belt computer's tiny speaker up to the Siamese's mike input, he pressed play. My belt pack squealed its code into the V-Kitty. We stared at the Siamese... waiting. Jarrell turned off the power supply.

"Well?" I couldn't help asking.

"We'll see in a minute."

Reaching under the Siamese, he rebooted it.

A low whirr rumbled through the ORO. The V-Kitty rolled to its feet. Its blue eyes glowed. It cocked its head while it loaded its operating system and accepted the new data.

"Here kitty," Jarrell said.

Its balding head swiveled in Jarrell's direction. Purring, it trotted obediently toward him.

"The purring subroutine," I practically yelled. "It's working."

The V-Kitty sprang into Jarrell's lap, landing there with the same precision as a real cat, not that I'd ever seen one. "Okay, kitty," he said, and picked it up. "Now for the real test."

Sukey stared at Jarrell, failing to understand the connection. But I already had it figured out. If the purring subroutine could contain a virus, it could be rewritten to contain the fix. I rebooted Dan's old machine. Jarrell released the catch on the Siamese's neck. Moving it closer to the ancient external mike, he pressed the command to make it meow.

But instead of meowing, the V-Kitty squealed a string of code.

Dan's computer loaded its operating system and started.

And for the first time, I believed we really might be able to amass enough credit to get off this piece of metal.

>∗‡∗‡∗‡∗<

Chaos reined in the rim when we snuck out of the ORO. I shuddered to think about what was happening in the offices down in admin.

"We need to test this thing on something other than that outdated garbage in the ORO," Jarrell said. "Any ideas?"

"We could try the Adonis," Sukey offered.

Visions of the three of us trying to wrestle that thing into submission flashed through my mind. "How about not?"

Jarrell just shook his head. "We need clients willing to shell out a ton of credit for the privilege of rejoining the net."

We thought for a moment longer as people charged down the corridors running messages on their own two feet instead of by COM. Warning sirens echoed through the metal halls, signaling vital systems being corrupted.

It occurred to me suddenly that worse things could happen than being marooned on a tin can floating in space. "We'd better work fast. Before that thing gets to life support."

"Good thought," Jared echoed.

"I had a work order for a small office this morning. Nothing vital, just one of the permit processors."

"Okay," Jarrell said. "We got ourselves our first job."

"Assuming they're willing to pay." Trust Sukey to find the flaw in any plan.

"They book space on transports," I pointed out.

"Sounding better." Jarrell was halfway down the hall already, elbowing his way through the mob of message runners.

And so I found myself back at my second stop of the day, still carrying the unfinished job from my first. Can't say the manager of the processing office was happy to see us. We must have looked like a band of lunatics, Jarrell in his rumpled clothing, me and Sukey looking like the end of a hard day and carrying a balding Siamese V-Kitty. He looked even more doubtful when Jarrell explained our fee structure.

"And why don't you just bring in a couple of faith healers from Phoenix?" he snarled. "I need real results. I'm losing revenue every second here!"

The manager towered over us, his gray admin jumpsuit looking almost as wrinkled as Jarrell's. He'd obviously been running his hands through his hair for most of the day because it stuck out at odd angles in our low-humidity, high-static environment.

"We've just fixed the old network in the ORO," I said. And sincerely hoped the guy had no idea what the ORO was, or how insignificant it had become.

He sighed heavily, the air going out of him like an over inflated balloon. "Okay. Try your mumbo jumbo. But I'm not paying you a cent until you can prove to me you've fixed it."

Jarrell sprang the catch on the Siamese's neck. It squealed its code at the application server. I stepped between them, just in case the manager decided to hit Jarrell. But his face crumpled from rage to relief when the system restarted.

It took us another hour to convince him it was really fixed. We charged him for that of course.

※◦I◦I◦I◦※

"We're stepping on some huge Admin toes here," I warned Jarrell when we stepped out into the corridor, our pockets carrying hard copy of the credit transfer. Just because one office was up and running again, didn't mean we could count on the rest of the system.

"Do we really care if Admin hates us for this?" Jarrell and his peculiar brand of practical.

"They're going to catch on real soon," Sukey said.

Message runners swarmed around us. We watched a herd of grays tear down the hallway, heading for Admin. They didn't seem to notice us in the crowds. Probably for the best. Jarrell watched them go with unbridled distaste.

"You've got a point there."

"We'd have a better chance of making more money if we split up," I said.

They both turned to look at me. "But we've only got one output device—"

Jarrell started to say. Then he smiled.

I grabbed Sukey by one muscled arm. "We might be needing that Adonis 6000 after all. Do you think we could borrow him? It's not like we won't be giving him back."

"Maybe. The owner's probably working O.T. today." She looked around at the mob surging down the corridor. "Everyone is."

Jarrell raised an eyebrow. "Let's go then. Profits are wasting."

※◦I◦I◦I◦※

In the end, we did manage to buy our way off-station. Not exactly in the kind of first-class accommodations we pictured. We left on a black market ticket hidden in the bowels of a barely-habitable freighter with the network gurus and station management chasing us all the way. Suffice to say, we aren't welcome to return.

But that doesn't matter. We couldn't afford a ticket planet-side, but we did manage to buy ourselves some pretty fine digs on a station with a tropical zone complete with wave pool. I'm not much fond of rain, anyway. Got us some upscale equipment and a small office and went into business. Legal this time. Well, mostly. Life is good.

Sukey ended up buying out the Adonis 6000's contract. I traded the V-Kitty for the newest V-Puppy. It seemed like a better choice for a kid who desperately needed a friend. For once that poor kid got what she wanted.

Once in a while everyone should.

Au pays des merveilles
by Wendy Waring

The pneumotrain sucked into Museum Station. As the blur outside the windows resolved to ashen light and wan faces, Rosemary scanned the platform. A snarl of bodies clustered around the New Story transmitter. She watched as they untangled and started toward the train. One woman lagged behind the others, her hand sliding too slowly from the neon palm on the bank of story kiosks. Her face was a contorted battle between real disappointment and canned emotion.

She looks like a Classic Victorian subscriber, Rosemary thought, as she looked away. *Probably streaming Dickens.*

Double doors swished closed. Commuters pushed into the compartment. Rosemary dropped her eyes to the work in her lap to avoid their vacant faces. A man with curly red hair pushed through the suits and dropped into the seat beside her.

Rosemary looked sidelong at him. The Bookworm.

He always got on with a book, some paper antique. He seemed incapable of reading silently. He laughed, he chuckled, he squirmed in his seat. Once Rosemary had even seen the salt trail of tears on his face. She tugged at the edge of her taupe suit. There was something unsettling about his ancient eyes and smooth coffee skin. One hand at her ear, she checked the signal strength on her headcomm and brought up SecuriCorps just in case.

On her lap the digitext pulsated. She only had a few more stations to tweak this budget. Her friends laughed at her for using digitext when everyone else had gone direct-to-stem. After all, she worked for New Story. Shouldn't she be using their products? Rosemary shook another digitext from its tube and snapped it like a laundered sheet until it went rigid. The thought of having an entire text beamed directly into her brain, even something as innocuous as a story.... She shivered.

The bookworm shifted upright and rifled through his grimy cotton bag. He pulled out a book, and an old lead pencil. He scribbled a note onto a torn scrap of paper, checking the book several times.

Where does he get those paper books from? Rosemary wondered, eyeing him sidelong again. *If my friends think I'm old-fashioned, I wonder what they'd make of him?*

Pencil end in mouth, he began to read.

Rosemary glanced at the cover of his book in the reflection of the curved train window. A woman fleeing a man in a trenchcoat in the dark. She deciphered the lurid salmon letters of the title from the plate glass. "*In a Lonely Place*," she repeated silently. She squinted at the yellowed text over the bookworm's shoulder. As he started the first page, she read along with him. Her tapered fingers twitched toward the book as she waited for him to turn each page. The stations appeared one after the other out of the dark embrace of the tunnel.

"College," announced the pneumotrain. Rosemary swore. She'd missed her station. She shouldered her way to the platform, fumbling with her reports. People pushed past her impatiently as she thwacked a digitext, rolled it up, and stuffed it into its tube. On the old escalator, Rosemary was blocked by commuters. Ahead of her, the bookworm rose to the top, his nose in the novel. She watched as he licked his finger and flipped another page.

At the top, she hesitated. Southbound trains were to the right. The bookworm was headed left, streetside. Streetside. Outside the city Seal. Rosemary had a moment of panic, but she followed him. She had at least an hour until her first meeting. *I could loop back... I can always turn back if he goes too far outside. And I've got SecuriCorps.*

They soon emerged from the managed safety of the tunnels. It was barely light. Rosemary's lungs convulsed. She wasn't used to the cold, crisp air.

She followed the bookworm's copper hair to the Carlton streetcar stop and stood waiting to board, stamping her feet and watching her breath frost the air. *When was the last time I took a streetcar? Come to think of it, when was the last time I was outside?*

She managed to get a seat just behind the bookworm. When the streetcar jostled, she leaned closer to read over his shoulder. In the warmth of the streetcar, the smell of machine oil and sweat rose from his clothes. She kept reading, breathing him in, laughing silently when he did.

They had just passed Jarvis when he closed the book abruptly and rang the bell. Rosemary sat back, as if she'd been shaken from sleep. *What am I doing chasing after some technopeasant? If I'm late for this meeting, Julian will hog all the kudos for the work we did — that I did.*

The streetcar trundled to a stop beside the old Allan Gardens. Through the window, Rosemary watched the bookworm step warily across the sidewalk's hard-packed snow, and then plunge into the park's knee-deep powder. *Where's he going?* The streetcar lunged forward, and she turned to watch his figure recede, his hair a torch in a field of white billows.

Rosemary tugged on the bell cord. As she rose, she saw the novel on the seat in front of her. She scooped it up. The driver bawled out "Sherbourne" and she hurried down the stairs, the book clutched in her hand. On the snowy sidewalk, she remembered why she never went outside if she could avoid it. The cold bit at her face. Her toes were already numb.

Rose and lilac clouds welcomed the streetcar as it headed east. *Must be close to eight.* She turned the book in her gloved hands. Paper books were getting rare. Maybe it was valuable.... *I've got to get to work.* She pulled her sheared beaver coat closer, fumbled with her headcomm, and messaged for a hover. She hated flying — too much horizon — but she had no choice.

In the hover, Rosemary kept her gaze fixed firmly on the landscape below. High-rise tenements hemmed in the hoary oasis of the Gardens. At the west end, five greenhouses were laid out in a U. A fresh path led through the snow from the streetcar stop to the back door of the Orangery.

⊷⊶⊷⊶

At the 53rd floor, the elevator chimed into a beige foyer furnished in tasteful anonymity. The receptionist greeted Rosemary as she stepped through the doors. She motioned her to the desk. "Julian's been looking for you," she whispered. "He's after some spreadsheets — something to do with current and capital something-or-other for the biennial. I told him you were down in Data Mining." She gave Rosemary a conspirator's wink then sobered abruptly.

"Where've you been?" said Julian behind her. "The meeting started twenty minutes ago. They've all been shouting at each other for the last ten."

"What's the problem?"

"The neuro-engineers are at it again."

"At what?"

"Arguing with marketing about bundling the story packets and response triggers. I don't know what difference it makes."

Of course you don't, Julian. She tugged at the fingers of her gloves. *It's all just hand-waving to you. Content production digs out stories, brain twiddlers bundle them up in a neuro-response package, and marketing sells subscriptions. As long as New Story keeps raking in the profits, you don't bother reading the specs.*

She slid her scarf from her neck. "So let me guess. Marketing wants to deliver content and pleasure-response simultaneously, and the Neuros keep insisting it has to be done serially?"

"Yeah, that's it. Something to do with serotonin or semiotics or some Russian guy. I don't know. Bit by bit. Something about the way we're wired."

"So who's winning?"

"Who makes the money?" Julian said, sardonically.

"And you wonder why I stick to digitext..."

Julian's nose wrinkled, and he leaned closer to her and sniffed her coat. "You smell like... snow. Don't tell me you've been outside!" He didn't wait for an answer; he turned on his heel and headed up the hallway. "Come on, Rosie," he said. "Make us look good."

Her face impassive, Rosemary followed his tailored swagger down the hall.

→•|•I•|•←

"Lights," Rosemary said, and the living room was abruptly illuminated by a row of halogen spots. "Dim," she snapped, blinking, and the lights dipped.

She dropped her keycard in the ebony bowl, kicked off her shoes and collapsed into the grey leather sofa. "Screen," she said, and the wall bloomed into life, its flicker an etiolated green on the apartment's off-white walls. She let the channels cycle, until she found the colourless drivel that passed for news. A tunnel fire in North Tonawanda. Another round-up of the homeless. Yet more snow.

"Screen off. Night sky," she said. Fibre optics flecked stars across her ceiling. She sat in the darkness, absorbing the comfort of being ten floors below ground, waiting for the solace of stillness.

She sighed. At first, she had been pleased with the spartan impression the designer had created. Now the domestic lineaments of her status seemed empty. Calling for light, she pulled herself out of the couch and tipped digitexts and datakeys from her briefcase onto the glass and granite table.

Julian had blindsided her at the meeting this morning. "This proposal to detect penny revenue leaks in subscription services, Rosemary..." He had looked right past her to the directors down the table. "It hardly seems worth the resources for what you'd recoup. Seems a bit nickel-and-dime, no?"

And each and every one of the seven managing directors had laughed at his little joke. It was a good idea, her pet project, and he'd got it canned. Julian Franklin — all-star of the squeeze play. She had a BASc from Waterloo, ECS from MIT, a year at Norsco, two at Lambent, three at New Story. She still couldn't manoeuvre her way out of a paper bag. "I'm sick of this. New Story. Same old story," she announced to the pale walls. She'd gone so far beyond the house she'd grown up in, she couldn't even shoot the shit with her sister. No, she couldn't even say "shoot the shit" without being embarrassed.

How did that happen? The big city, university, an Inside job that paid. Really well. Still...

She had a sudden memory of her sister laughing, smacking down tiles for a seven-letter word on the Scrabble board. "There! Beat me now!"

"Argh. Sudden Scrabble death!" She tumbled from the picnic bench in a melodramatic swoon. She laughed herself weak in the long grass outside the cottage while Polly pieced together outrageous stories with the words on the board. Then they'd drunk the rest of the ice tea with the rest of a bottle of rum. That evening, they'd pooled their pocket change and hiked into town through hushed autumn colour for a meal at the diner.

So how did we grow so far apart?

At the bottom of her briefcase was the book. She held it in both hands and stared at it, and then on impulse, brought it to her nose. It smelled of dust, and smoke, and resin. She laid it gently on the glass tabletop. The jumble of digitexts commanded her attention, but the book made its own demands. She stared at it a little longer, then forced herself to pick up a digitext.

⤗⊶⊶⊶⊷

Rosemary woke before her pillow began to hum and vibrate gently. The Circadalarm hadn't yet started its slow, stealthy brightening. She left the apartment to its darkness, called for a single halogen and began to read the book. She read over breakfast. She read as she dressed. She read on the train.

As the express elevator shot to the 39th floor, Rosemary turned to the last page. At the final sentence, she uttered a little sigh. Three executives in the elevator leaned away from her.

The day passed in a fog. She left work early and headed north on the train, the book tucked into her coat pocket. Dread clutched at her as she passed through the city Seal. Was it really worth going outside just to return a book? As she headed into the open city, she flipped through it with a nostalgic sadness, still mulling over what the story seemed to mean.

After the streetcar had rattled away down Carlton, the city was still, muffled. New snow covered the garden paths. The full moon was rising. Across the park, lights bobbed behind the windowpanes of the greenhouses. She watched them, entranced, as lambent greens bloomed and winked out against the monochrome of the city.

Four huskies leaped toward her through the snow, dragging an improbable sled: a legless man in a wheelchair with snowboards fixed to his wheels glided up to her.

"Hey there."

Rosemary backed away. "Hello," she stammered. She tried — and failed — not to look at the place where his knees would be. She stared at his strange contraption instead.

"It's three snowboards glued together. I cut a groove to fit the wheel in the top two, and a couple of flanges to secure the wheel. Groovy, eh?" He winked at her. "It means I can use the dogs year round."

"Oh." Rosemary looked about wildly. There was no one in the street. She fumbled for the headcomm in her pocket, and brought out the book.

The man on the sled nodded at it. "So you're headed for the greenhouses? Want a lift?"

She looked at the park, measuring the distance to the greenhouses through the knee-deep drifts. "I... yes," she said. "Thank you."

The legless man jerked a thumb at the back of his chair-sled. "Take a run at it, then jump on the posts at the back of the chair." He eyed her long legs. "You might have to bend a bit but don't worry, we'll get you there." He thrust out his hand. "Name's Turk Trout."

Rosemary stared at Turk for a witless moment, then reluctantly shook his hand. "Rosemary." She hesitated. "So I..."

"Just pop around the back and grab the handholds. You'll catch on quick enough." The dogs whined in their traces.

Rosemary took hold of the handles and said, "Okay."

"Run!" Turk shouted. The huskies took off.

Rosemary ran, barely managing to jump onto the back of Turk's chair. Her coat flapped like a cape behind her. Turk steered his dogs around elm trees and firs, pines and poplars, urging them faster and faster. The wind sang in her ears. They swooped in a grand arc to the greenhouses' shovelled path, snow singing under the runners. Turk drew up next to the compost boxes. Rosemary stumbled off the back of the sled, laughing. She could feel stray crystals melting on her cheeks. "That was wonderful!"

From under a tarpaulin stretched next to the compost boxes, a dirty face poked out. It croaked at Rosemary, "Have you got a book?"

Startled, Rosemary brought out *In A Lonely Place*. "But it's not my—"

"Round the back, then," the compost dweller said. Turk had already waved goodbye. The wind whipped up off the lake. She was alone. With a nervous backward glance, she shuffled off as fast as she could toward the greenhouses. She hadn't taken ten steps before she could no longer see the strange sentinel's post.

By the light of an old sodium vapour lamp, Rosemary tried the doorbell at the back of the complex. She waited, then pushed the door with her gloved hand. A wave of heat and noise escaped.

She edged forward into shadow. A thudding thrum filled the dark cavern of the building. It was hot, the air was heavy, edged with acid. She shucked off her fur and loosened her suit jacket and tie. She waited for her eyes to adjust, then paced slowly through the deafening noise.

Above her loomed the curving flanks of two gargantuan iron cylinders. Each had a circular iron plate door. She began to sweat as she stood staring at the single glowing eye that burned in one round knobbed face. The boiler room and its massive engines were huge. How did they fit in the small brick building she'd seen from outside? She backed away from the monstrously loud hulk and its mute iron twin, and almost fell through a hole in the floor.

Iron rungs led down. Rosemary righted herself, looked into the hole, and then considered her stockings and pumps. The boiler's red eye was on her as she bent over the dark gap.

"Hello!" she shouted into the gaping mouth. "Hello?"

There was no answer.

A tangle of pipes snaked along the walls and led to a row of five gauges labelled: Palm House, Trop House, Cold Temp, Trop Land, Arid. Abandoned on a chipped deal table, a corrugated lunch box held the remains of a sandwich. Next to it were half a dozen bottles of strange liquids, and a paper logbook. Rosemary scanned the entries — Candide, The little Prince, Barnacle Bill the Spacer, Ulysses, Thomas the Rhymer — were they the names of workers? She walked on, musing. Behind a pair of grease-stained overalls was a small door. Rosemary hesitated, then ducked through it.

In stippled moonlight, palm trees waved under a glass dome. She had found the Palm House. It was deserted. Rosemary was surprised to hear voices murmuring somewhere in the greenhouses. The hours posted had said that the Orangery closed at four.

She turned left. The path meandered into a greenhouse marked: "Tropical Landscape House." It was like walking into an old movie, the kind they showed at retro arthouse cinemas. Long liana trailed from rainforest branches. Crimson bougainvillea scattered bright eyes under her feet. Belled flowers and frilled petals hid in the lush greenery, their saturated golds and reds offering themselves to her.

When she passed through the vestibule to the Arid House, cool dry air transported her to a night desert. Succulents bloomed. Desert flowers erupted from fleshy protuberances. Horticulturalists had supplied tags for them: tamarisk, euphorbia, prickly saltwort. Then, half way through the Arid House, Rosemary came upon a man lying on his stomach in the middle of the path, his chin resting on his folded arms, his bent legs kicking the empty air. She walked up to him until her feet nudged the circle of his vision. He started, and looked up at her. His hair was stiff and black. Yellow eyes peered up at her out of a craggy face the colour of baked earth.

"Are you looking for Colm? Are you returning something?"

She nodded, mute.

"Try the Tropical House, the one with the pool in it," he said, gesturing. With his other hand, he covered the paper book he had been reading.

What's he hiding? She was almost afraid to turn back into the greenhouses, but the door behind the man led out into the snow.

She retraced her steps to the circular Palm House. Golden bamboo nodded and waved her through. In the Cool Temperature House, a pale white woman with jet hair read under a eucalyptus tree, her muscular arm bent over her head, a finger caressing her temple. Moonlight lit the angular planes of her face. She did not look up. The tree gave off a heady, astringent perfume.

Rosemary passed her in silence, following the curve of the path to the Tropical House. She passed through the vestibule into heat and steam. Into a pool entwined with liana and surrounded by gardenias, bougainvillea, passionflowers and orchids, a statue of a woman emptied a jug of water. And where the falling water met the pool, a woman sat immersed to her neck, reading. Water lilies undulated around her.

The man with the copper hair appeared at the far end of the path. "Can I help you? I'm Colm."

Rosemary floundered for a moment. "I'm Rosemary. You left your book on the streetcar." She held it out to him. "I'm sorry, I meant to bring it back yesterday, but..."

"—you started to read it and you had to finish it."

"Yes." Rosemary tried to look contrite. "I'm very sorry."

"No problem." He gestured to the door behind him. "Please. Join me?" He led the way out of the Tropical House. Rosemary followed him, but paused at the door for one last look at the woman in the pool. She was nibbling at a water lily.

✣✣✣

"What is this place?" Rosemary asked.

"It's the horticulturalist's office."

Rosemary took in the Linnaeus prints and shook her head. "No, I meant the garden. The people. The books."

Colm tilted his head, and looked at her as if he was seeing her for the first time. "Well, it's—" he hesitated "— a library for the displaced."

"Here?"

"As long as we don't mess with the plants," Colm said, "and keep the horticulturalist supplied with text, he's happy to let us use the greenhouses." He leaned against the desk, watching her as she glanced back toward them. "Well, thank you for returning my book. Come," he said, putting a guiding hand under her elbow. "I've got to check something in the boiler room. I'll show you my favourite plants on the way out." They walked through the greenhouses, but the pale woman, the water lily lady, and the man with the yellow eyes had disappeared. Rosemary found herself peeking through the greenery, trying to see where they had gone.

"Would you like to borrow another book?" Colm asked.

Rosemary thought of the last book, the feel of it in her hands, the smell of it, the slow grip it had on her. She hadn't thought of work at all while reading it. *Work. I can't...*

She met Colm's brown gaze; he had been watching her struggle with her thoughts. She blushed. "No. I really don't think so. But it's very kind of you to offer."

They passed into the boiler room. The manhole had been covered. When they passed the deal table, Colm flipped the logbook shut.

He held out her coat for her and she slipped her arms into its generous sleeves. "I wouldn't want to... to take resources away from your library."

"It's your decision, Rosemary." Colm smiled. "We're stretched, but I don't think we'll get flooded with borrowers from behind the Seal any time soon."

Rosemary backed up to the door. "Well, goodbye, then."

"Goodbye."

The door closed behind her.

She stood immobile in the circle of lurid orange light. The cold whistled around her.

She ran. She floundered through the deep snow, her long coat tangling between her legs, and she didn't stop until she had stumbled onto a streetcar heading west.

✦❖❖❖✦

Beyond floor-to-ceiling plate glass, the sky was bleached white. The meeting droned on. Rosemary hated these windows. It occurred to her that she probably threw herself into her work so she'd be too busy to stare out of them. She sat through four vendor presentations, an argument about Asian market placement, a power play for the vacating director's position, and Julian's bid for more budget, without taking anything in. She was coasting on reputation today.

The boiler room's dark eye haunted her. Displacing Gantt charts and spreadsheets, the names of plants and virgin colours sang in her head like incantations. Gloxinia. Tibouchina. Phalenopsis. Gamboge, crimson, jade.

Julian's fawning nasal voice brought her out of her fugue. "We'd be happy to work it through. I can present it to the team first thing in the morning. Right, Rosie?"

She stared blankly at him, and the meeting seemed to take that for an answer. It closed with the usual bowing and scraping, with Canadian and Taiwanese inflections. *It always comes down to grovelling*, she thought, as she made her way back to her office.

Just as she put her coat on, Julian showed up at the door, a drone tray floating behind him.

"Where are you going? I promised we'd get these project plans sketched out."

"*You* promised. I'm going."

"But we've got to get this done. I can't do it without you. You know that, Rosie."

She ignored his smarmy flattery. "No, *you* know that."

"Look, Rose, I know you're tired. I am, too. But without this extra push, you won't get promot—"

"—no, Julian, *you* won't get promoted. I could work til I dropped and never get promoted. Because I'll never play the game. Never know how to, never want to."

"Don't be ridiculous. Aside from the fact that you're good at what you do — but don't you go telling anyone I said so," he added, waving his finger at her. "There are quotas to be filled."

Rosemary stared at him. Was it anger she felt? Or just weariness? "Oh look, forget about it," she said. "You're right. I'm just tired."

"Desk," she said to the drone. It floated forward and deposited its load of tubes and datakeys. "Just leave it all with me."

❖◦❖◦❖

The floor was deserted. Once again, she'd eaten at her desk. She had been sitting without moving for minutes, staring at the same spreadsheet. Suddenly she sat up and stared straight ahead, calculating.

"Who makes the money?" Julian had said the day before. *Who indeed*. Rosemary primed her headcomm, keyed the holoboard. Her fingers flew. An hour later, she returned Julian's drone loaded with the materials for his presentation the next day. She leaned back into the thickness of her executive chair. She smiled. *Nickels and dimes.*

→•I•I•I•←

At his station next to the compost boxes, the sentinel kept watch. Scattered crystals glinted through snowfields. Out of the darkness, four huskies wove through the trees, brushing snow from pine boughs. A lone figure urged them forward. He winked through the trees, then disappeared.

In the boiler room, the red eye glowed bright. Rosemary put on her old hiking boots, pried open the iron manhole, and climbed down the hole.

Donovan's Brain
by Allen Moore

When Donovan was fifteen, his father died. For the rest of his life, the memory of his father's funeral would churn up whispered fragments of discussions he wasn't meant to hear: *some form of psychosis... he had to escape*. He and his brother moved to the farm to live with their aunt and uncle.

The principal of his new school called. He wished to meet with Donovan's guardians.

"Donovan has an IQ of one hundred and seventy-three." The principal was pleased to have so bright a child in his school. He was prepared to make special provisions.

Donovan's uncle was less enthusiastic: "The boy is like his father," he said. There would be no special provisions. Donovan's father had been given so much. Look at where it got him. No, the boy would work as hard as the next man, and learn to make his way according to the laws of merit.

But Donovan wanted nothing to do with physical work and he had no interest in his uncle's farm.

"My name will be known around the world one day," he insisted. "I'll do what others dream about." And although he believed this, he was irritated; his dreams felt smaller when cornered by pragmatism. Both his uncle and his brother argued that time spent at university made little sense; better to avoid debt, go straight to work, and get on with it. Donovan hated the way his family measured ideas in economic terms. He should keep his mouth shut, he thought. What did it matter? Among simple people, why say anything? Why speak of dreams?

Dreams. By the time he had completed his undergraduate computer science degree, he believed that dreams were
one of nature's hints; an elusive key to the mystery of
consciousness, a place where random notions merged with
ordered thought, whether asleep or adrift. This, he was
sure, was the birthplace of rare, extraordinary discoveries. And so he dreamed, especially during his PhD: a bliss-
ful decade of late-nights on campus and a private world
squeezed into the littered space of his study cell in the
basement of the computer science facility. It was a time both
lost and found in idle moments, like the midnight roof-
top breaks with a coffee in one hand and a joint in the other.
The crisp night air, streaked with halogen, provoked him.
He dreamed of a machine that would be able to discover
itself. He could not help but to dream also of grandeur,
recognition, and a future where his name would linger long
after he was gone.

The years came and went, as did his friends, girlfriends,
tutoring jobs, and student-loan applications. He lost touch
with friends and slipped away from his family. Months
would pass without his speaking to — or even seeing —
his advisor. He did not care. He had little faith in the many
who both published *and* perished. This was a place of
artificial action, where quest was about tenure and communication was dominated by e-mail. Still, at least he was
free to think. Or dream.

>+I+I+I+<

When he was seventeen, he stumbled across Kurt
Gödel's Incompleteness Theorem. It stated that the elements
of a formal theory could produce truths that are neither
provable nor disprovable within the theory. Donovan
thought he understood. In geometry class, he had seen how
theorems were used to "prove" other theorems. He became
infatuated by a possible extrapolation: the human mind
would never gain an intuitive understanding of itself.
Therefore, in his opinion, any major advance in artificial
intelligence — and specifically, the Holy Grail: building
a mind more sophisticated than our own — could not arise

from rational, organized research alone. At some point, one would have to make a creative leap into the unknown.

>+I+I+I+<

As he studied the brain, Donovan wrestled with the knowledge that neurons link and communicate in ways that could not, as yet, be replicated by artificial networks. Learning causes the brain to change physically — with every new experience it rewires itself just a little bit. Whereas artificial networks could only revise what had been assigned for revision. Donovan discussed this in conferences, hallways, lunchrooms, and wherever he crossed paths with other researchers. He argued that wherever randomness was controlled, flexibility would suffer. His peers said that randomness and physical variance had been adequately managed with software. "The idea," Donovan countered, "is to provide for possibilities that you cannot foresee. Some explorers made their greatest discoveries because they were not where they thought they were. Their greatest assets were their erroneous maps. We, on the other hand, have a new problem: we design the terrain before we explore its nature. Also, what served our ancestors well, limits progress today: our need for order and control." A few listened closely, but most waved him off as yet another quack drawn to their noble field.

The simplified models made by AI researchers had failed to interest neuroscientists. This had been more than a nagging concern for Donovan as he navigated through his PhD. It was a principal distraction that had led him astray in ways that he could not explain to his advisor. Only when he was about to throw it all away and leave school did he finally see a way forward. What was once a distraction became an objective: allow evolution a larger role.

>+I+I+I+<

After graduate school, Donovan discovered an ideal opportunity at Intercept Vision, a government research company whose products sought to interpret image fields for

machines. He never asked about salary. He took no interest
in what might be expected of him. His interests had nothing
to do with the company's outdated, mundane algorithm
development. He chose Intercept Vision — not IBM or MIT
— because of what he found in Sector Four: acres of derelict
machinery, robots, and computers; enough electrical power
to supply a factory; and an unusual degree of seclusion
for such a vast, underground space. The facilities were large
enough to support thousands: a sprawling labyrinth of
semi-dark corridors and underground bunkers. Above it
all, cobwebs scintillated in whatever light might touch their
vales. Nobody ever came through here.

>+|•|•|•<

He gathered robots, workstations, and mainframes from
Intercept Vision's cavernous underground. He spent
months cross-linking thousands of boards, weaving them
into a single network. He called it the Adaptive Decision
Machine. Should anyone ask, he would tell them that the
acronym meant "Antiquated Derelict Machinery." He
would claim to be studying communication signal decay.
But nobody asked. His work on the ADM went undis-
turbed.

Every morning, he started work by seven, unable to
sleep. At graduate school, he rarely arose before noon. But
now he knew the lure of purpose. The ADM gave meaning
to his time. As the assembly grew, with components and
cables covering thousands of square feet, he would stop
at times, lost in the realization that this was real, that it
was everything he could ask for, that a life-long concept
would soon come to trial, and that all he needed now was
time. Time to build it. And time to let evolution run her
course. He imagined one day unveiling the ADM. He
imagined one day presenting his ideas at a conference
where he would be the keynote speaker. He imagined
receiving the Order of Canada, when it would be *their*
honour to have *him* receive it.

He imagined much more than this.

❋❖❋

"Consciousness," he had said years ago, during the defence of his Master's thesis, "is not something that either *is* or *isn't*. Consciousness is not restricted to human thought."

"You're not one of these metaphysical types who believe that rocks have souls, are you?" his supervisor had asked, peering over the rim of his spectacles. Donovan hated this look, the glance of the sorcerer upon the lowly apprentice. He was the youngest and the smartest in the room and he despised soliciting *their* approval for *his* work.

"I'm not discussing rocks," Donovan said, raising his voice slightly. "Consciousness scales. It is a continuum. We may have more of it than a cat does, but only because our brain, our network, is more complex. Not because we are blessed and they are not." *One day*, he thought, *my work will continue without interference, without need of approval from anyone*.

"By extension, then," his supervisor continued, "some people are more conscious than others?"

"Of course."

"What about ants? What about bacteria? They make decisions without being conscious of the choices they make. Or such is the conventional theory."

Donovan had wondered about this since he was a boy. "The critical point," he said, "is this: where decision-making is adaptive, where new information changes subsequent decisions, then the entity can be said to have consciousness. To the extent that an ant can learn, it has consciousness. I agree that primitive life seems to be mostly hard-wired. Yet even single-celled organisms are adaptive, even if it occurs only through evolution. Or chance."

Chance: an underrated, high performance operator in Donovan's view. It is like a key, hidden between its more respected counterparts: reason and tenacity. It is rarely acknowledged, especially when it is the sole contributor to an important discovery. He once read of a young astronomer who had returned from the Southern hemisphere after

discovering Supernova 1987a, and who stated to the media
with victorious ceremony that he had done a great thing.
Donovan had no respect for people like this; hundreds saw
the star that night, what difference did it make who was
first to register the event? What skill was there in winning
a lottery?

Tenacity had carried him through the lonely campus
years. And reason suggested what he might exhume from
the graveyard in Sector Four. He would pass the baton,
and let chance run with it. This, he believed, was what
Gödel was telling him to do.

❖⦂❖⦂❖⦂❖

If a network was large enough, he thought, then all it
would need was the right combination of signals to ignite
something on par with creative thought. Something gentle
and evocative, like a ray of sunlight splitting dark clouds.
Like a Muse.

Donovan integrated cameras, motion encoders, thermal sensors, pressure transducers, and a microphone into
the network. In a sense, the ADM could see, feel, and hear,
though he refused to think like this. The input devices
would provide an endless variety of random signals: the
provocation that he hoped would lead to something more.
And because machines lay everywhere in dust-covered
abundance, he decided to connect the ADM to articulated
robotic arms, translation carriages, and to any device that
caught his interest, including a mail-delivery unit that,
according to the only papers it carried, once cruised the
hallways of the CBC building in Toronto. How it managed
to find its way to the West Coast, he had no idea.

He also found several crates filled with chemical lab
equipment. At first these meant nothing, but he soon put
the equipment to use when he discovered some hot plates.

He brought in what little he owned: his books, some
clothes, a computer, and a bicycle. He slept in a sleeping
bag on a stack of cardboard. His apartment was empty.
Sector Four became home.

He worked without noting time or date, remaining sequestered in the huge concrete bunker for days at a time, leaving the building only in the quiet of night for supplies.

➤╍╏╍╏╍╏╍◄

When he first applied power to the ADM, nothing happened. This was a relief: any discernible activity would likely have meant error, and perhaps disaster. Now that power had been applied however, the network had to remain on; its twenty-four trillion transistors had to find their states. He reduced the clock rate until every circuit board across the room was synchronized. Every second, two million pulses vanished into the boards and merged with the signals from the cameras, encoders, transducers, and the microphone.

The microphone: although he had intended at first not to "push" the ADM, not to work it using an organized training program, he could not hold back his desire to talk to it, to talk *into* it every time he passed by the microphone. Here, at last, was someone, or rather something, he could talk to. Oscilloscopes revealed the passing waveforms. Field boards stationed throughout the room reported that his voice had been heard, though he had to resist the urge to write *heard* in his notebook. The network merely carried signals from the microphone — as a canyon carries the voice of one who shouts "hello." Still, he was fascinated.

He wrote increasingly about his need to keep things secret. Codes appeared. Pages were torn out. "The others," he wrote, "would take everything. Destroy everything. They wouldn't understand the stove, or the sacrifice of genius. I hear them talk about me. They know. Time is against us." He kept the doors locked. Sometimes he heard footsteps. "No one will enter before the ADM is ready."

Weeks passed. The writing in his notebook became jagged and terse.

Every few days, the equipment recorded activity that he could not explain: nothing significant as far as science was concerned, but enormously important to the maintenance of hope and the recharging of belief. Patience, he knew, was the mandate of chance.

On the other hand, if chance meant waiting years for discovery, then patience was of questionable virtue. He was not in this to scrape together the meagre wherewithal for yet another modest paper. Even the landfills had seen enough research papers. Nor was he interested in funding; money would only bring people, budgets, schedules, and the stifling constraints of organized thinking. "Creative breakthroughs cannot be planned," he wrote. "But I am not stargazing. I will not be the forgettable Shelton. I am charting a course through risk. I am Columbus. And the results must be unequivocal."

He would push the network harder; try to wake it up. "I have decided that the ADM will listen not only to my voice, but also to my mind. To Donovan's Brain."

⊹⊱•⊰•⊱•⊰⊹

The principle of electroencephalography is simple: place electrodes on the skull and measure small variations in electrical potential. Donovan stuffed almost four hundred spring-loaded probes into the styrofoam core of his bicycle helmet. In the centre of the room, he set up a plush reclining chair, borrowed without notice from Intercept Vision's library. Facing the chair, he placed the microphone and a camera. On either side, consoles displayed network activity. When he sat down with the helmet on, he forced himself to think aloud, to speak every thought, and to make lively gestures. When he read the newspaper, he whirled his hands in the air. When he wrote in his notebook, he explained his thoughts. When he felt the need to rant, he let the ADM hear it.

He shared his thoughts on philosophy: "The problem with philosophy — and I mean the whole damn field, if you're listening — is that every last shred of it is conjecture. And it's getting worse. Today's convoluted, meaningless ephemera may fool the fools, but it has nothing over the ancient scriptures."

He denounced biologists: "They're unable to differentiate between life and intelligence. They go on and on and on about the complexities of life, never shutting up for half a minute to listen. We are talking about *intelligence*, something they seem to lack. Why am I not surprised? "

He dismissed artificial intelligence projects: "SOAR has ideal objectives, but it will never amount to anything. It is all about organizing ideas and compartmentalizing solutions. Decades of work, and what have they got to show for it?"

He shared personal problems: "I can't get them out. I see them crawling under my skin, and I try to pick them out, but they are everywhere now. It's gross."

In the midst of one of his diatribes, the ADM responded: two oscilloscopes indicated signal activity among the processor boards near bench seven. A field of signals swept away from the boards and spread throughout the memory cards of several robotic assemblies before returning to bench seven. The cycle repeated a half dozen times before diminishing to nothing. Donovan was stunned by the oscillations. He was disappointed to see the activity stop, but he knew something significant had happened.

A few hours later, it happened again. He awoke in his chair to discover a resurgence of activity among the boards near bench seven. The waves oscillated for several seconds involving only a few processor boards at first. This expanded to thirty, then fifty, then over one hundred boards in the central processor group. The light emitting diodes around bench seven flickered like a city. From there, the signal field propagated to dozens of memory cards in the robotic assemblies before drifting back to the central processor group. Then a most extraordinary event occurred, statistically significant even to the most sceptical observer: waves spread out across the network, into the cards of all seventy-one robotic arms, to several old Sun workstations, and even to a couple of old VAX mainframes. The signals moved in clouds, back and forth and around the network, their paths depicted by diodes that lit up as the pulses flew past the thousands of micro-magnetic field detectors scattered around the room. For nearly thirty seconds, he watched the dance. When finally it settled down, Donovan sat in his chair, stared into space, and wondered what to do next.

He decided to go further, to push harder.

He connected a wireless feed to the electroencephalogram probes in his helmet. With this, he also mounted a pinhole camera and a microphone. He no longer had need of his chair. Now, whenever Donovan wore the helmet, he would be connected to the ADM through the internet. Whether he was in the building or across the city, telemetry from the helmet would be transmitted back to Sector Four. He set out for the city, eager to stimulate the ADM using every means imaginable.

At this point, Donovan ceased to write anything further in his notebook. He never returned to Sector Four.

In August of 2027, the Journal of Adaptive Operations received a paper titled: "Statistically Significant Anomalies Pursuant to the Advent of Consciousness in a Man-Made Network." The Journal arranged for a team of researchers to investigate the claim.

October 4, 2027. We arrived at the specified location and found an abandoned, sprawling complex and nobody to meet us. We followed the directions as outlined in the researcher's letter, which led us to a lock box near the loading dock and a package containing a flashlight, a set of security codes, and detailed instructions. Although it was all rather odd, the directions referred to us by name and spoke of the project that brought us here. We had travelled far and we were not about to leave.

In an underground chamber (the size of half a football field) we found what must have been the ADM. It was a sorry sight: a quagmire of charred wiring and broken equipment. Toppled robotic articulators lay among the splintered remains of thousands of circuit boards, dozens of oscilloscopes, power supplies, cameras, motion encoders, and other devices. Everything had been destroyed. In places, the floor was half a metre deep with debris. We noticed many robotic arms had fragments of circuitry trapped in their grippers and scorch marks on their casings, suggesting that the destruction probably occurred while the system was powered. The air was rich with the smell of burnt plastic.

At this point, several police officers stormed in.

In the weeks prior to the visit made by the research investigators, the local electric power authority had detected an unaccountable power draw, which they traced to a dormant, government-owned technology complex. Constable Ploughman investigated.

September 24, 2027. Pursuant to report 23-9-4187, Sgt Penrose and I investigated the vacant Intercept Vision site with Mr. Purdeep, the utility rep. Metro security met us at the building and access was accordingly gained. Building met all conditions of Metro check list. Purdeep used detection equipment to locate source of [power draw]. Security could not open a large iron door labelled sector 4. Arrangements made to have torches brought in next day.

September 25, 2027. Dog Squad included in second visit. A hole was cut in sector 4 door and access was accordingly gained to very large room. Overhead lights were off and no persons present inside. Everywhere many small computer lights were flicking and going around the room in circles. Purdeep determined electric power loads to be equipment and computers operating and wired together. Purdeep unclear what this stuff was for. Metro security had no record of what was in the room before. Many rooms in facility locked and not opened for years. Other items found: Hundreds of empty food tins and pop cans. Peels from fruit. Buckets containing excrement and urine. Terrible smell. Large pile of trash pushed into corner. Academic texts, sleeping role [sic] and bicycle. No identification found. Sgt Penrose discovered anhydrous ammonia, stove, and still. I located ephedrine stash and large container filled with crystals. Forensics confirmed methamphetamine. We decided to use snare tactic. Did best we could to make the door look undamaged. The light in the hall is very poor which helped. Arranged for surveillance.

Although the investigators could not make sense of their discovery, they were convinced that organized crime was involved. The police set up on-site, twenty-four-hour surveillance. Constable Yashinko worked the surveillance shift on the third night and filed the following report:

September 27, 2027. 2:43 am. Loud smashing sounds suddenly occurred in Sector 4. I radioed for assistance immediately. Then I stood in the dark alcove down the hall from the iron door as agreed in the Readiness Plan. The noise continued for approximately one minute before everything went very quiet. I waited for the perpetrators to leave, but no one exited. 2:52 am. Officers Taylor and Ng arrived. 2:54 am. We entered Sector 4 and turned on the lights. It was filled with smoke and all the equipment was destroyed. There was no one in the room.

Moments earlier, as officers Taylor and Ng rushed to assist Constable Yashinko, neither paid much attention to another dispatch call:

Request paramedic. Southwest corner Main and Hastings. Possible seizure or overdose. White male, dark clothing, white helmet. Collapsed on sidewalk beside Carnegie front steps. Caller reports victim has stopped breathing.

Many decades later, Professor Tse, a theological historian, gives the keynote address at a formal dinner:

In the beginning, it was thought to be a computer virus, but no one found even a fragment of code. For years, experts predicted that it would bring down the internet and corrupt data everywhere. Between 2033 and 2036, parasitic activity overloaded servers and optical cables around the world, effectively shutting down all communication for hours at a time. Concentrated efforts to stop the phenomenon were both illusory and destructive. "Destructive" because wherever the combative effort was most fierce, threat followed the greatest damage. Then, as everyone knows, on September 27, 2037, all e-mail accounts received the now-famous Donovan Message, which stated that any systems attempting to block a "Donovan Oscillation" would be denied access to the internet, whereas those systems that allowed unimpeded access would not only be spared, but also safe-guarded against all future viruses. A significant claim, given that, at the time, militaries around the world had viral research departments whose job it was to exploit viruses for both offensive and defensive purposes.

All attempts to find the source of the message failed.

It may be difficult to imagine a world of pro- and anti-Donovanians, but at the time, many believed that a great hoax was about to blossom. In February of 2038, naysayers in the banking community feared that if believers reduced their guard, financial irregularities would take place on a colossal scale. Imagine, they said, what you have in your hand when you take a dollar from everyone on the planet.

It was not a hoax. The Donovan Message proved true to its word, and dissenters paid a brutal price: by mid-2039, corporations, universities, and military facilities around the world were brought to their knees with irresolvable system errors, problems that vanished the instant a public apology appeared. And meanwhile, those who let Donovan have His way were not only free of problems that others could not solve, but also found their viral nets had nothing to catch. It was the beginning of a new age.

In these modern times, we take it for granted that our electronic exchange is pure. But seventy years ago, communication problems threatened the sanctity of civilization. Only Donovan could restore order. Only Donovan could, for example, circumvent organized internet crime, the most famous case being that of the Blackmark System, which catalogued billions of explicit, compromising images of citizens: images snatched from passing e-mails, private accounts, and unsuspecting cell phone users and, soon to follow, images taken by strangers and neighbours who sought anonymous commission in the blackmail business. The whole affair brought out the worst of human nature. Then, in May of 2040, thousands of servers simultaneously destroyed over two trillion files, annihilating the Blackmark System in a single decisive strike. After that, Donovan was revered and praised, not feared.

We no longer know a world of plagiarism, pirated software, and child pornography. Even the music recording industry, near extinction in 2030, has regained its economic position. Only a few of our elders have ever seen an mp3 file, and most of them are deaf.

We are grateful to Donovan. Without Him, what manner of deceit might the news media publish? Without Him, who would protect us from the perpetrators of wrongful thought?

The Undoing
by Sarah Totton

There are two accepted procedures for performing ocular excision, or surgical removal of the eye. One involves stitching the eyelids shut prior to dissection and removal of the skin and soft tissues around and within the orbit. In the second method, the eyelids are stitched open before the eye is dissected out. Given my patient's particular circumstances, I was instructed to use the first method. This method has an added appeal for me; although the second method is less bloody, it involves performing the operation with the eye open — and I dislike being watched while I work.

✦✛✦✛✦✛✦

I tugged the leading edge of the suture line, pulling it taut enough to bury the knot, and then I cut the end of the suture flush with the skin. I assessed my work. I had achieved a nearly perfect apposition of the tissue's edges. A scar was inevitable, but this one would be subtle — once it healed — as near to invisible as my skills could render it. An ugly procedure done neatly.

Apart from professional pride, the presence or absence of a scar was moot. Without eyelids (I had removed them) to keep it in, a prosthetic eye could never be fitted. The final effect would be unaesthetic. But that was, after all, the point. With artful lighting the photographers would make it appear even more grotesque. I had seen their work with other high-profile criminals on the covers of magazines and in the newspapers. No doubt they would do my work justice.

I swabbed the blood along the incision line. The sound of the patient's breathing broke my concentration, and I remembered that I was not alone. I turned off the anaesthetic and pulled the surgical drape from the prisoner's face. My incision crossed the prisoner's temple stopping just shy of the hollow of his empty orbit. It was swollen and still orange with prep solution.

With a sense of quiet satisfaction, I stripped off my surgical gloves and gown and disposed of them down the chute. The patient's blood had soaked through the gown and stained my scrubs beneath.

Afterward, I debriefed Dr. McCull about the surgery. I use her title as a courtesy here. She is an administrator. A doctor on paper, but not in practice. This is apparent in the length of her fingernails and the clean femininity of her clothing. I wore my blood-stained scrubs into her office to make her aware of who was doing the cutting.

"Good job, Dr Lewis," said McCull to me, as though she would know. All she had ever seen of this patient was his file, and perhaps the press release photos.

→•I•I•I•←

I cleaned up in the compound's concrete-floored shower before going to the secure room where the prisoner was recovering. I sat by the end of the bed typing the surgical report on my laptop. The record said: *Harrow, James. Age: 26* but he looked much older than that. He bore the hallmarks of prolonged stress; deep lines scored his face from the corners of his eyes halfway down his hollowed cheeks, and his tousled hair was shot with grey. No doubt, Harrow thought his actions had been justified. The world had been unkind to him, and he was simply fighting back. I myself thought that the world would be a better place, the air would be cleaner, without him in it.

I was watching him when he woke. His remaining eye was blue, the same pale colour as hospital-issue scrubs. It was striking in the dim light. Silvery. He blinked —

winked — several times, then turned and reached over the bedrail with a splayed hand, the shackles around his wrists jingling. The chain, fastened to the rail at the head of the bed, pulled taut; he could reach no further.

"What is it?" I asked.

At the sound of my voice, he went still. "My glasses," he said.

I took his glasses from the bedside table just beyond his groping fingers, and put them into his hands, careful not to let him touch me. I wondered which of those hands had held the gun.

Harrow unfolded the glasses and put them on, then almost immediately took them off. Eye unfocussed, he polished the lenses with the edge of the bed sheet, and put them back on. The white cotton pad glared at me through his left lens. He took the glasses off and touched the cotton padding above his cheek, kneading it with his fingers. He began to pick at the tape, attempting to peel it off.

"Leave the dressing alone," I told him.

He stopped working at the tape and pushed himself back to sit up against the head of the bed. He squinted in my direction, clutching the dressing, his face screwed up as though I had put an onion in his skull where his eye used to be.

"Take your hand off the dressing," I said.

He did so reluctantly. His breathing became harsh as I checked the dressing's integrity. I could detect no visible seepage.

"What happened to my eye?" he said.

"It's gone," I told him, straightening.

He massaged the cotton under his palm.

I'd dealt with enough victims in the past to know that he didn't yet realize what had been done to him. It takes people time to adjust to the loss of something they can never have back. It was, in a small way, a loss of innocence that I was witnessing in this man.

Harrow released the dressing. Casually, he pulled the chain around his right wrist taut, as though he were testing its strength. He allowed the chain to slacken, regarding its length in silence for a few moments. Then he lunged at me. By reflex, I recoiled, but his hand was brought up short with a sharp click of the chain.

The curtain by the bed stirred, and the guard put his head around it. "Can I talk to you outside, doctor?"

The guard had no doubt been watching us through the video surveillance monitor behind the curtain. In any case, I had no desire to remain in such close proximity to Harrow.

Before we left the room, the guard looked at Harrow. "Watch yourself," he said. He looked inclined to use his weapon on Harrow there and then.

In the hallway outside, the guard put a comradely hand on my shoulder and spoke to me quietly. "I have to caution you not to go near this prisoner unless it's medically necessary, doctor. He tried to assault a civilian last week during his public parade."

It was good to be reminded that Harrow deserved those shackles, that he deserved everything I had done to him and would do to him.

I left Harrow in the recovery room and returned to the prison compound's makeshift operating room. From the instrument table, I picked up the stainless steel scraps bowl, mounded with bloody gauze. I rummaged in the soft contents of the bowl until I found the globe of the eye I had just excised. Almost surprised to see it there, I picked it up. The eyelids were sewn closed with their matted lashes looking like an insect's legs crossed in death.

What had this eye seen before the gun had gone off? When it had narrowed at its victims in the federal office building, had it seen them as people or as mere targets?

The eye of James Harrow, terrorist, murderer. I dropped it into the biological waste bag for incineration. It made an insignificant wet sound as it landed.

⇥•⌶•⌶•⇤

Two months later, I amputated Harrow's hand at the wrist. As Harrow was left-handed, I had been instructed to take off that hand. I had decided that it was too risky to leave Harrow unattended under general anaesthetic during surgery so I had asked that someone on the prison hospital staff be brought in to monitor him. Though the assistant would be unable to cope on his own should anything go seriously wrong, at least he was there to notify me of any drastic change in Harrow's vital signs. As long as he didn't watch me, I was fine with it. It left me free to concentrate on the surgery.

I found the procedure challenging; I hadn't amputated a hand in several years. That hand had been severely macerated in a bomb blast. Harrow's hand was sound and healthy. In this sense, the procedure was more straight-forward since Harrow's tissue was viable, and not damaged or diseased. What made it difficult was something more subtle.

From a surgeon's standpoint, it is more difficult to take off a hand at the wrist than it is to amputate an entire arm with the shoulder blade attached. The arm is held to the body by muscles and tendons only, whereas the hand is attached to the wrist with ligaments. Cutting ligaments will readily blunt a blade. By the time I'd finished the procedure, I had gone through three disposable scalpels. I released the tourniquet on the patient's arm and began tying off the weeping blood vessels before closing the skin over the stump.

I cut the end of the suture and set the scissors down on the instrument tray. It was only then that I noticed, in a moment of dull surprise, the motions of Harrow's chest as he breathed. It is an odd facet of performing surgery that, while the bleeding vessels I clamp and ligate remind me that I'm working with living tissue, I nearly always forget until the surgery is complete that the tissue is part of someone alive, that the world is bigger than the window in the surgical drape.

It's something that happens to you when you become a surgeon, though I don't remember exactly when it hap-pened to me. You learn to separate the world within the operating room from the one outside. Most people can cut the meat on their plates without being bothered. It is a series of small but uncomfortable steps from there to cutting human cadavers, to opening a living, breathing patient and putting your hand inside, manipulating it, altering it. It lends a certain feeling of power — of entitlement — to grapple with that force inside a living thing. It is a feeling we surgeons need in order to do what we have to do.

⋆⋅⊹⋅⊹⋅⋆

The handcuff no longer fit around Harrow's left wrist, and it dangled empty next to his cuffed right hand. I turned on the lights and stared at the too-white expanse of his face. With the eye bandage gone — I had not removed it — a lonely black eyebrow arched over the cavity below. In the two months since his eye surgery, the scar had healed as well as I had predicted.

Harrow regarded me with his single, silver-blue eye. Slowly, he lifted his bandaged stump before his face. Tendons rippled and tightened in his forearm as he tried to flex his missing fingers.

He took a few heaving breaths, then raised his head to look at me. He said nothing, but a light gleamed in his silvery eye. For a chilling moment, I felt something pass between us, something momentous, something I didn't understand. Then he closed his eye, and he was just a criminal again, my patient. I swallowed and went back to the operating room.

There seemed to be a lot more blood than the last time. Splashes of it, shining like black currant jelly in broad sweeps around the mouth of the floor drain. I hosed down and disinfected the floor, took the instruments out of the tray where they'd been soaking and began to scrub them clean. Had I been employed in a hospital, this would not have been my responsibility, but this room was my domain and everything in it was under my control. That was how I liked it.

I knew that what I was doing here was unpopular with some. Even those who approved did not like to contemplate my doing it. I took no joy from it myself, beyond the pride in serving my country and the satisfaction in knowing that, with every stroke of my scalpel, with every suture I placed, the world became a better place. Deterrence was the key. The terrorists would see my work, the public would see it when Harrow was turned out to the media, and they would know what this country did to people like him. The more I worked, the fewer of his kind there would be, the fewer crimes we would see, the safer the world became.

I cleaned every flake of blood from the instruments I had just used and laid them out neatly in a row to dry. It gave me a sense of completion, a sense of rightness.

⋆∘⋆∘⋆∘⋆

Later, at two a.m., I was paged back to Harrow's room. I realized why as the elevator doors opened and I heard Harrow screaming.

One of the guards met me as I stepped out. "Can you shut this bastard up?"

"I'll give him some painkillers," I said.

As I walked past, the guard put a hand on my arm. "Not too much though, doc," he said.

The noise was worse when I entered the room.

"Finally," said the guard.

Harrow belted out another lung-cleansing scream.

"Oh, cry me a river," said the guard. "Or make that *half* a river."

Harrow twisted around in the bed and shot him a helpless glare.

"Aw, what's the matter, cop-killer?" said the guard, raising his hands. "You all *cut up* over what I said?"

I drew up the hydromorphone and injected it through the port in Harrow's I.V. line. Harrow surged up as the needle went in, his scream ending in a sigh. Almost immediately, he relaxed in relief.

"About time," the guard said, and he sat down by the bed. I pulled the curtain across, leaving me alone with Harrow.

"Thanks," said Harrow.

"Don't thank me," I said. "I'm just following orders."

After a moment he said, barely audible, "So was I."

He spoke with the calmness and clarity a strong analgesic brings.

"Don't try to justify what you did," I said.

He was silent for several moments. At last, he spoke. "What gives you the right to do this to me?"

"What gives *you* the right to kill someone?"

"I love my country," he said.

"So do I."

"You believe in a country that does *this* to people?" He brandished his stump in my face. "Do you?"

"I believe in peace. I believe that people have the right to be safe from murderers like you."

"But not from people like you," said Harrow.

"It's simple justice," I said. But I knew that on some level, that that was not what he meant, that I hadn't fully grasped what he had meant.

The curtain rings jangled, and the guard's heavy boots clacked on the tile. There was a look of barely restrained rage on his face. "Hey, Harrow," he said. "Guess what the doctor's taking off next?" He smirked and clutched his crotch.

Harrow's eye went from the guard to me.

"Yeah," said the guard. "If you're lucky, maybe the doc'll leave you a stump to jerk off with."

For the first time, I saw an expression of genuine fear in Harrow's face.

"A word?" I said to the guard. I stepped out into the hallway. Before he could speak I said, "Listen to me. I make the decisions in this patient's treatment. I decide what he needs to know. I don't need you telling him the protocol. Understood?"

"I'll treat that piece of shit cop-killer however I want," said the guard. "And I don't have to take orders from a civilian." He went back into Harrow's room.

I was not like the guard. It did no good to take pleasure in Harrow's suffering. Justice was objective. It had to be. Cold, precise. To be otherwise was to be like Harrow. My way was humane, clean, painless — the way it ought to be.

⇥∗⟨∗⟩∗⟨∗⟩∗⇤

Castration was a procedure I had never performed before. I had my assistant leave the surgical text open on the table so that I could consult it during the procedure. The text referred to the procedure, delicately, as 'orchiectomy.' The recommended technique was to draw the testes out through an inguinal incision, a cut along the fold where the abdomen joins the thigh. The recommendation was based on prevention of spread of a tumour, since this was normally the reason for performing castration. Harrow did not have cancer. I decided that the simplest and best approach was to make an incision down the midline of his scrotum. Three times during the surgery, the patient moved. I instructed my assistant to turn up the anaesthetic.

Though the surgery was otherwise uneventful, it had been some years since I had performed a procedure with which I was unfamiliar. I observed the patient in recovery with a certain degree of professional concern.

Harrow lay on his side, eye squeezed closed. With his unshackled stump, he was stroking the sheet beside him over and over, as though he were patting a dog. A comfort-seeking gesture.

With the stethoscope, I listened to his heart. I could hear him breathing loudly, masking its rhythm. "Mr. Harrow," I said. I straightened, and as I did, he opened his eye and looked at me. I felt something pass between us again, something elusive, but powerful. I saw the light in his eye. The same light that had once shone out of the eye I had held in my hand. The light of whatever it was that lived in Harrow, beneath his body, beneath the hate, beneath the propaganda, beneath whatever it was that he said he believed and why.

A human light.

The look on Harrow's face stayed with me for the rest of the evening and afterward. It would not go away. I went online to find out what I could about him from information released to or discovered by the public. It might have been lies, but I was looking for something unofficial, something human, perhaps some inkling of understanding.

He was indeed just twenty-six years old, born and raised in the city twenty kilometres from the compound. My city. My neighbourhood. He had lived an unremarkable life. One brother, William, a law-abiding citizen. Parents still living, likewise law-abiding, divorced recently. An unexceptional academic record. The high school he had attended was not far from my own home. I may very well have seen him from my car some day in the distant past. One year in university, studying fine arts, before dropping out, six years before his arrest. He could have been anyone's son. He could have been mine. What had happened to him?

>-I-I-I-<

A week later, during his next public appearance, James Harrow attempted to escape. He was shot several times by his armed escort before he got more than twenty feet. Fortunately the shooting occurred before he was brought into the public gallery, and no bystanders were hit. I was paged within minutes of the incident. I had seen everything on the newscast, and I drove to the prison compound with a troubled mind.

Since his sentencing, I was the only doctor attending him. The first thing I did when I arrived at the compound was to pump enough hydro into him to make a healthy man vomit. His eye was open, and he appeared conscious, but he simply stared off into the distance.

I found five round, swollen marks on his back, pulsing red. I'd seen a mark like these on a police officer I'd treated once.

"Was he wearing a Kevlar vest?" I asked.

"It's standard procedure," said the guard. "The spectators in the gallery are checked for weapons, but it's an extra precaution. For his own protection."

I had no doubt that if he hadn't been wearing it, he would have died in the gallery. But he hadn't escaped unscathed. His legs were still shackled, and one of the bullets had pulverized most of his calf.

"That was a stupid thing to do," I told Harrow. "Did you actually think you could get away?"

Though his eye remained open, he did not respond at all, not to my voice, nor to my touch while I examined him. The light in his eye, the one I had seen last time, was gone. And that made it somehow harder to meet his gaze. When I induced him for surgery and it finally closed, it was a relief. By the time I left him after four hours of surgery, he was stable, but still unconscious. I stayed on in one of the visitors' rooms, reluctant to leave the compound in case I was needed.

As I sank down onto the hard chair in my quarters, I realized how tired I was. Tension contracted my shoulders. Why had he done it? He had been out in the public gallery before; he must have known the level of security there. Without help, he would have stood no chance of escape. Had he been expecting one of his associates to be in the gallery?

At midnight I was paged again to Harrow's room; his heart had stopped. I was unable to bring him back.

He had escaped, after all.

→•I•I•I•←

By the time I returned home it was nearly dawn. I sat in the car for some time, staring at nothing. Then I started the engine again and drove. A few minutes later, I pulled over to the curb. Across the road from me was the school James Harrow had attended. I took in the fifteen-foot high fence, the barbed wire coiling over the top. The schoolyard was nothing but concrete. Completely safe. Nowhere to hide, nowhere to plant a bomb. The street was ultra-bright. Not a single tree. It was a good neighbourhood, a safe neighbourhood. I could not remember the last time a crime had been committed here.

I saw the sterile, blue lights of a police car down the block and realized that if I lingered here, I would likely be questioned. I drove off, remembering my own childhood days, grass, trees. It hadn't all been concrete and wide-open space then. There had been places to hide, mystery. There had been danger, too, but also beauty. It seemed to me I remembered a light about this place akin to the one

I had seen in Harrow's eye. A living light. The thing we surgeons grapple with but can never touch directly.

I drove and drove, looking around me for that light, but it had gone, and I could not remember remarking on its passing.

Blackbird Shuffle
(The Major Arcana)

by Greg Bechtel

(A, α)

A small black shape flutters up from the ditch in front of the car. He stomps the brake and swerves, the steering slack and useless as the car slides to a halt on the soft shoulder. Coughing on dry grit, he spits out the window and pries his hands off the wheel as the world re-coalesces through settling dust. He shakes, coughs again, opens the door and walks to the front of the car.

On the grill, a few sticky feathers, a smear of red. On the ground, a bird. She's female; somehow, he knows this. A miracle of sorts, that she wasn't pulped by the highway-speed impact, caught in a wheel-well, dropped to the ground at any point in the hundred-odd meter deceleration. Must have stuck to the grill. How many variables had to combine, just so, to lay her out neatly like this, waiting?

Her beak opens and closes silently. Black eyes open wide, blink rapidly, stop, blink again. One wing extends at an unnatural angle, the other flapping weakly, raising small breaths of dust.

He retrieves a cardboard box from the back seat, dumps out the loose papers, and lines the bottom with a facecloth from his pack. Returning, he gently picks her up, lowers her into the box and places the crude nest in the passenger seat.

He folds himself into the driver's seat and accelerates onto the road, the drowsy haze of long-distance travel replaced by a new hyper-awareness of his surroundings, a surreal did-that-just-happen sense of dislocation. Nothing has changed. The White Album clicks and cycles over in the tape deck for the fifth time since Thunder Bay. As before, the sun beats down on the patched two-lane, not even a logging truck to break the monotony of trees. *Idiot strips*, he's heard them called, the narrow fringe of trees left behind to hide clear cuts from highway-drivers.

6. The Lovers
"I just need a..."
"I said, don't."
"...kleenex."
"Shut up and keep your hands on the wheel where I can see them."
"Christ! It's just a goddamn kleenex. I'm gonna—" Sneeze. My ears pop. It's not good to hold it in like that, and now I can't breathe through my nose. Fine, then. See if I care.
"Don't talk. Drive," he says. I try to breathe through my mouth, but my nose drips anyway, thick mucus creeping towards my upper lip. I should shut up. I know that. I should go along with whatever he says at this point. It would be the rational thing to do, but he's being a prick and I can't stand that. Besides, rationality has never been my strong point. If I see something shiny, I pick it up. Sometimes it's sharp, a piece of glass maybe, and I cut myself. Hasn't killed me yet.
I sniffle. "Are you enjoying this? Does the snot-faced look get you off?"
"Which pocket?"
"Huh?"
"The kleenex. Where's the kleenex?"
"Oh. Front left. Inside."
He leans across my body to retrieve the cellophane-wrapped tissues from my jacket. Reaching into my pocket, he flinches when his hand brushes against my breast. Holding the package between his teeth, he tugs out a tissue with his free hand and holds it gingerly against my face. This isn't going to work.
"Blow."

I blow, and now my face is a mess. He tries to clean me up, and that's even worse. The too-gentle swipe of a used tissue spreads sticky moisture to my left cheek, leaves my chin lightly coated. It's as if he's afraid to touch me.

Of course, I'm nervous too, what with the gun and all.

7. The Chariot
Oh fuck.

Goddammotherfuckingsonofabitch. Fuck fuck fuck.

I feel like I've just woken up on somebody's couch after one hell of a party. Can't remember how I got here, and my head's a little off like I'm coming down from something heavy. I want to brush my teeth, get a glass of water, see if anyone will go for breakfast before the hangover gets a grip on my stomach. My head hurts. I want coffee.

Think it through. I'm in a car, and I'm pointing a gun at this woman's head. Jesus fucking Christ. The grip is warm and slippery with sweat, and I feel as if, at any moment, it might pop out of my hand like a watermelon seed squeezed between thumb and forefinger.

—*Happiness is a warm gun. Bang, bang, shoo-oot, shoot...*

Oh, shut up. What did she ever do to me?

—*This is her fault. Remember that. She's not getting off this time.*

Care to elaborate? Who is she? Better yet, who am I?

Stop. Start there. Focus. Can't look in the mirror...

—*Keep your eyes on her. Nothing else.*

...but I can look at her. She's small, snot glistening on her face...

—*Serves her right.*

...and she looks more annoyed than anything. Straight black hair and thin — runway-model, famine-victim thin. Her eyes are dark and wide. She moves in quick bursts, sudden flurries of motion followed by perfect stillness. It's more than a little creepy. She's so calm.

—*Not for long.*

The barrel advances. I feel the slight resistance as it touches her temple.

—*Come on. Sweat. How's that feel? You like that?*

Vindictive little bastard, isn't he?

Her grip tightens, hands like claws clamped to the wheel, eyes locked straight ahead. Her first real reaction. The gun retreats, leaving a small, round indentation by the hairline. At least she's not smiling. I know her smile, a smug little smirk that's both a challenge and a dismissal. Or would be. If she was smiling.

The car bumps over a pothole and a wave of nausea rises. Clamp the jaw and swallow. Breathe. Focus on dry, empty fields under a clear blue sky. Solid. That dark flicker in the corner of my eye is a trick of the light. There is nothing there. Stay still, dammit.

"What do you want?"

Good question.

"Why don't you tell me?" I say.

"How the hell should I know? All I did was pick up a hitchhiker."

Hitchhiking? Is that my gear in the back? Her voice is steadier than my hand. But my hand's holding the gun and that's got to count for something.

—*That's what you think.*

Shut up. Either help out or shut up.

I feel my thumb cock the hammer, hear the click. So does she. My lips curl back and upwards, more a baring of teeth than a smile.

"So humour me. Guess. Humouring me would be a very good idea right now."

"Okay, okay... just gimme a second..."

—*It's an act. Don't fall for it.*

8. Strength

"Okay, so you're out here camping and hitchhiking." What does he want me to do, make it up? Okay, I'll make up a story for him. "Maybe you're on the run. Yeah, someone's after you." He's listening, still shaky, and that wobbly smile isn't convincing either of us. How do you calm a scared man with a gun? Show him you're scared.

"Maybe you escaped from prison, or maybe you.... It doesn't matter. I don't want to know." Avoid unnecessary details. "You've been camping out for a while, so you figure it's safe to move on. Now what you've got to do is get away without being noticed. What you needed was a car, and now you've got one." No response, but he seems calmer. "And you're wondering what's next. What do you do with the driver?"

I regret the words as soon as they're spoken — the pause and nervous swallow are genuine. Finish the thought before he does: "So why not just drop me right here? It'd take me days to get to the nearest town on foot—" He was hitch-hiking. Crazy doesn't always mean stupid. "—or you could tie me up and leave me in the ditch. Someone would find me sooner or later. You could even call the police to pick me up later."

That's it. Give him some control. I ease off the gas and let the car drift towards the side of the road. He's thinking about it.

9. The Hermit

"You can do better than that." At least I know I was camping. That gear in the back must be mine.

She doesn't respond, just those quick flashes of activity. Look at me. Blink twice. Freeze. Wait. Then quick — check the mirror, glance out each window — then freeze again, this time focused on the road. What is she thinking? No clue.

"You know what I think? I think you know exactly what's going on here."

Nothing. Her hands twitch, but she keeps them on the wheel.

"This time, I know what you are."

There. Right there. A look.

In the window, vague images swim past against her sharp profile: empty fields, farmhouses, silos, grain elevators. No cars. No people. Space and time to spare. Time to figure this out.

10. The Wheel of Fortune

His hands have stopped shaking. Good. My turn.

"Okay, so what am I?"

He giggles, a shrill little sound for such a big guy. Is he losing it? "Oh, you know and I know and you-know-

I-know-you-know-I-fucking-know. It's just so cute, really."
No, not hysterical. Just relieved.
"Whatever you say."
He laughs harder.

11. Justice
I wipe the tears from my cheeks. God, I needed that.
"So where the hell are we?" Nothing like the direct
approach.
"You really have no idea, do you?" Turning to face me,
she seems genuinely surprised.
I wait.
She turns back, watches the road. Out the window, sun,
more fields, dry dirt. We could be sitting still, watching
a continuous-loop tape on a bluescreen. We'll never reach
another town, never get across the prairies. Like wandering circles in the woods, the breadcrumb trail erased by
scavenging birds. Except there are no woods here, and
the road is perfectly straight. It's not going anywhere, birds
or no birds, and I'm still waiting.
"Canada," she says. "West coast is that way." She
indicates the road ahead of us with her chin.
Maybe I run a little roadside auto-shop, servicing cross-
country vacationers when the VW van breaks down. Keep
a special stock for VWs, because it takes weeks to ship
the parts out here and I can charge double price. They
don't want to get stuck out here. They're heading for the
coast.
She interrupts my reverie, my failed attempts to place
myself in the landscape: "You think you've got this all
wrapped up, don't you?" Her bursts of movement come
faster now, the spaces between them exploding with
words. "You think just because you've got a gun you've
got everything going for you. But you're not driving the
car." Her eyes flick to the rear-view mirror. Back to me.
"You don't know where you are. I could be taking you
anywhere." More quick glances: the fields, the road, me.
"What if we pass a cop car? I see a cop, maybe I drive
straight at him." Steering wheel, gun, me. "What would
you do then, Mr. I've-got-a-gun? Shoot me?"

Her foot lowers on the gas pedal. As we accelerate, the car starts to shake.

—*Told you so.*

Oh, shut up, will you?

She starts out quiet — "You know what I think?" — and builds — "I think you're fucking nuts is what I think. You could be a straight-up psycho, and you've just run out of medication." — louder — "Maybe you've got a problem with women, like that guy in Montreal." — and louder still — "Maybe you think something's messing with your head. Maybe you think *I'm* messing with your head." A pause. Her voice drops low and soft: "And you know what?"

—*Don't ever say I didn't warn you.*

Her eyes settle on mine, and there it is. That smile. Her foot stays on the gas, and the car keeps accelerating. The little shitbox shouldn't be able to go this fast. The landscape goes nuts in my peripheral vision, doing a freaking jig, but that's not what concerns me. Her eyes, unblinking, aren't just dark. They're black — all pupil, no whites at all. They weren't like that before.

"Maybe you're right," she says.

—*Whatever you do, keep your sights on her.*

Deal.

12. The Hanged Man

Done. What we've got here is five cards, face down, his cards. (Never let the dealer supply the cards.) What we're going to do is read them.

Now don't get me wrong. I love card tricks, the sheer narrative ingenuity, the razzle-dazzle and the walloping yarn, the nothing-up-my-sleeve exaggerated gestures, all carefully calculated to provide that sense of random chance, verisimilitude and wow. But I love straight games too, cards like memories, shuffle them up and deal them back out, only fifty-two, but you'll get a different hand every time. And no one, but no one, has a full deck to play with. Even the dealer's got to give them away or there's no game at all.

So this time I shuffled them clean. Didn't stack the deck or deal from the bottom or anything like that, but maybe

I peeked a little. No matter. Any serious card-player knows this: the future isn't in the cards — that's the past. What matters is how you put them together. A million ways to play a hand, and none of them right, none of them wrong. Now we're going to turn them over, nice and slow.

"You paying attention?" I say. He doesn't answer, just watches close.

"All right, then." First card.

3. The Empress
"Just toss it in the back seat," she says.

"Thanks."

Sometimes they get picky, insist I put my stuff in the trunk like they think I've got hitchhiker cooties or something. Can't really blame them, I guess. I've been sleeping in a tent for a while, and I have no idea how long it's been since my last shower. I can never keep track of the days out here. It's not so much that I don't remember as that I forget about counting them. I know it rained this morning and it didn't yesterday. That's about it.

Once, not too long ago, a coyote watched me while I warmed up by my fire in a harvested cornfield. The mist hadn't burned off yet, so he was hardly more than a silhouette. I had the gun out, just in case, but when he came closer he seemed more curious than anything. Maybe they don't recognize handguns, or maybe this was just a particularly stupid coyote, but I had a feeling something was going on. He sat and watched for a bit, almost like he was waiting for something, but then he took off. Guess I wasn't what he was looking for.

I remember that, but I couldn't tell you if it was three days ago or three weeks. Doesn't matter really. I've got a ride now, and that's what counts.

13. Death
—Hey! Snap out of it, Princess. Pay attention!

The present hurts — God, it hurts — but I remember everything now that I remembered then: camping, the coyote, the pick-up. Still, there are gaps.

—Fuck the gaps. Don't you see what she's doing?

"You're seriously messed up," she says, dropping the nervous act.

I'm dripping with sweat, sucking air in huge gasps. Each breath cuts; I feel like each exhalation should be a puff of red mist. Out the window, the view keeps dervish-dancing, spinning in wild meditative ecstasy, spinning towards enlightenment. Moroccan dervishes eat glass, hot coals, live snakes; I feel like I've done all three, but somehow enlightenment eludes me at the moment. I'd settle for a glass of water.

"You think you're pretty cool, don't you?"

I can't speak, but I shake my head. I can't tell if she sees my response.

"Drifting along, at one with the land and all that crap. What do you know about the land? You think you know what I am? Give me a break. You don't even know who you are."

She's got a point.

"What do you want from me?" I ask.

14. Temperance

"I want you to get that goddamn pop-gun out of my face." Soon.

"I'm sorry..." His voice cracks. Got to give him some credit. Shaking like a bad case of the DT's, but he's not budging. He tries again. "I... I can't do that. I need to know."

He asked for it. Second card.

4. The Emperor

As I open the front door and climb in, she looks me up and down, taking in the duffle-coat with bulging pockets, dirt-streaked jeans, navy and white toque with sweat-plastered hair escaping around the edge. I imagine I'm quite a sight.

"Where you heading?"

"That way, looks like," I say, pointing down the road. "That's west, right?"

"Yeah, that's west," she says, and waits.

"I've got no sense of direction."

"Yeah, easy to get mixed up. Trick is to look up every so often." She still hasn't started the car. Maybe she's nervous. She's pretty tiny, and though I'm no towering hulk, I must outweigh her by a good fifty or sixty pounds.

"Look, I understand if you'd rather not give me a ride." I empty my pockets: a pocket knife, some tent pegs, a chocolate bar, a bandanna, a bit of rope, a wad of empty freezer bags, a few coins. The gun digs into the small of my back as I shift in my seat. "You want me to put this away or something?" I say, holding up the knife. "I could put it in my pack." No response. "I don't mind."

"Whatever," she says. She looks a bit like a guy I knew once.

She doesn't seem scared, but she doesn't put the car in gear either. I stretch back and stuff the knife to the bottom of my pack. A transport truck blows by, the car shakes, and I'm beginning to think maybe I should get back out and try again. Still, it's warm in here. I'm cold and damp from the rain earlier this morning, and there's another bank of clouds heading this way.

"Waiting for something?"

"Your seat belt's not done up."

15. The Devil

Surfacing to those eyes is like waking under a microscope. If she would just look away. Blink, even. The road's gone now, not even a blur of scenery. Just me and her and those damn eyes.

—*And me.*

Yeah, and you too, whatever the hell you are.

— *our only friend.*

"What's the matter?" she says. "Having trouble focusing? What do you think you're hopped up on this time? Acid? Mushrooms? Admit it, your brain is seriously fried. Put the gun down."

I've heard of people losing it on acid, but I don't touch that stuff.

—*Trust me. This is not an acid trip. She wants you to think you're crazy, but you're not.*

Oh, well that's a relief. I'm not crazy, the voice in my head told me so.

"Look at me," she says.

16. The Tower
He's hyperventilating.

"Tell me what you see."

"I see..." Again, his voice catches. He clears his throat, winces, and continues. "I see you... but there's something not quite — there are these flashes, dark, behind you, like these huge..." He waves one hand vaguely at the space above my head, then brings it back to steady the gun. Even with both hands, he can't stop it from shaking.

"You're putting things in my head," he says softly. "Get out of my head." It's heartbreaking, but I can't do that. I almost wish I could.

"You're the one that's out of your head, not me. You think you can get back in there? Good luck, psycho-boy."

Card number three.

5. The Heirophant
Once I've done up my seat belt, she starts the car and pulls onto the pitted two-lane. Outside, it starts to rain. Fat drops burst on the windshield like water balloons as I warm my hands over the vent. She drives in silence.

Some people need to chat all the time, need someone to help them deal with all that space, an audience to convince them they exist. Truckers can be like that. They're pretty chatty, full of anecdotes about this or that haul, how they jackknifed on black ice or whatever. Wind 'em up, and they'll talk for hours. Others, they want you to do all the talking.

"My name's... uh..." Shit. Drawing a blank. "Neil." Neil? Whatever.

She nods.

Up ahead, patches of sun illuminate the landscape, a patchwork of light and dark in random, blobby patterns. Here it's still raining. The cut fields look like two-day stubble on a very dirty face. I rub my chin, could use a shave. Fish out a leather pouch from my pack.

"You mind?"

"That tobacco?"

"Yeah."

"Roll me one," she says.

I roll two smokes, light them, hand her one. She takes a drag, blows a cloud of smoke directly into my face, and says, "You don't remember a thing, do you?"

She smiles. It's a cold, hard, bright smile.

—*Okay. Now listen up. I am your friend. She is not. This is all you need to know.*

Reach around, slide the gun from my belt, fit my finger to the trigger and point the barrel straight into that smile.

17. The Star

Even now, I want nothing so much as to blow it clear off her head. I could do it, too, if I could just stop shaking. It's so cold in here. And she's just sitting there. Smiling.

"You still don't remember, do you?" she says.

"I remember plenty."

18. The Moon

"Like what?" I ask, keeping it light, just a little smug.

"Like where the safety is." He flicks it off with his thumb.

Careful now: "Okay, Mr. Memory. Whose car is this?"

C'mon, turn it over.

1. The Mage

I love these long drives. Hours and hours of solitude, no distractions, no nagging weight of unfinished to-do lists. Put myself on automatic and I'm in a space apart, a no-space, out-of-time bubble, a climate controlled, transparent womb. Just drive.

It was sunny and clear until I hit that fog bank. It came up thick and fast out of nowhere, lasted about five minutes, and cleared to this. Since then, it's been raining, a steady drizzle over empty fields. My friends all told me about the big-sky effect, how you can see for miles and the sky goes on forever. They said Northern Ontario drags on and on and on, trees and rocks, rocks and trees. More rocks. More trees. Once you hit the prairies, though, the sky just opens up and it's like nothing you've ever seen before.

That's what they said. They never once mentioned this endless low cloud ceiling, this damp monotony of grey.

Up ahead, a woman stands by the road with her thumb out. Somebody must have dropped her off here. Didn't notice any crossroads. Maybe she's been walking for the warmth and some sense of progress, however false. That's what I used to do. She's drenched. I pull over because, hell, I know it sucks to get stuck standing in the rain like that, with all your gear and everything.

19. The Sun
"My car," he gasps. Oh, he's a fighter all right. This just might work.

"Very good," I say, like he's a little boy who's finally learned to tie his own shoes after a series of failed attempts. "Now pay attention. This one's important. Why am I driving your car?"

Last card.

2. The High Priestess
Cora says she's just wandering around. She won't be any more specific than that, says she does this when the weather's good. Winters, she usually stops somewhere warm, but mostly she wanders. She says she likes the variety; it's what she's been doing all her life.

"Don't you ever feel like you want to do something more?"

"You mean, like something so they remember me when I'm dead?" She smiles. "Not my thing. People remember me or they don't."

"No, that's not it. Not exactly." I'm not sure what it is I'm trying to say. "I mean something you want to do for yourself. Something that makes a difference."

"Oh," she says. "A difference." Like suddenly I'm making perfect sense. "A dream, you mean. Go out there and fix things. Get some meaning in life." She frowns and falls silent for a bit.

"Hey!" she says, brightening. "You want to see a magic trick?"

"Sure."

"Got a penny?"

I dig a penny out of my pocket and hand it over. She holds it up and, with a little flourish, makes it disappear. The usual routine, then. She reaches up behind my ear and pulls out the missing coin.

"Penny for your thoughts," she says. I chuckle politely. "Oops!" She tosses the penny into the air, and it vanishes. Impressive.

She looks around, squinting under the seat, into the creases of the naughahyde upholstery. Then she mimes a big "O!" and her mouth stretches around something white and round. An egg. She's really good at this. She puts the egg down. "Hey, you've got something there. Under your tongue. Let me take a look." I smile indulgently and open my mouth. I've seen this routine before. Something clicks against my teeth. Doesn't feel like an egg. What'll it be this time? Maybe the penny.

It's a gun, angular and black and pointing at me. She's stopped smiling.

"Stop the car."

I pull over and turn off the engine.

"Get out." If this were a movie, this is where I would do something unexpected, get the jump on her. But it's not, and I don't. We get out of the car. Following instructions, I take the camping gear from the back seat and set it on the gravel. She turns me around and has me kneel by the gear. I feel the muzzle of the gun press into my scalp.

"You wanna live?" she asks. I nod. "Good. Me too. You just stay right there a minute." I hear footsteps crunch across gravel, the slam of the car door. I don't turn around. "You get out there and live a little. And don't lose any of that stuff." The engine starts. "Don't do anything I wouldn't do," she calls, and a spray of spun dirt showers my back. The engine revs and recedes.

I look down at the gear beside me. A tent, a tarp, and a small camp stove sit in a neat pile. Next to these, a sleeping bag and a backpack. The gun that Cora pulled from my mouth lies at the centre of the neatly folded tarp.

I turn and watch as my car shrinks and disappears against the horizon. One hell of a trick, that.

20. Judgement

My car. Her gun. Okay. I just wish I knew why she did this.

—*Trust me. You don't want to know.*

"Look in the mirror," she says.

—*I've got a better idea. Pull the trigger. She's playing you like a harp.*

I look in the vanity mirror. Like a window or a TV screen, it shows a featureless grey space dominated by a single figure. A gnarled little man with greasy hair stares back at me. He's filthy, clothes shredded and stained, eyes puffy, bloodshot and wild. His mouth stretches around the barrel of a blocky black gun, his hands on the grip, one thumb on the trigger. Curled into a tight little ball, he rocks rhythmically back and forth.

I look back to Cora.

"I told you to get out of my head."

"And I told you I'm not in there. I'm right here in front of you. Look closer."

—*Well I'm telling you she's full of shit. You hear that lady? FULL OF SHIT!*

"Sounds scared, doesn't he? Now why do you think that would be?"

Back to the mirror. It shows the same featureless grey, the same little man, but this time the frame expands, pulling back to reveal he's no longer alone. Either my field of vision narrows or the mirror expands. I see nothing but this image, though I can feel the weight of the gun in my hand, the contours of the passenger seat under my legs, against my side.

At the man's feet, a few paces in front, lies a black-bird. One wing hangs at an awkward angle. Where there should be eyes, only small, ragged holes. It should be dead. These injuries are not new: the blood is congealed, and hard, black scabs cover the wounds. A fly lands on the crusted stump of the bird's right wing.

But it moves.

Slowly, the mouth opens and closes. The stump shifts, not enough to disturb the fly, but visible. In slow convulsions, the bird struggles towards the man, so close that, were he to lean forward just a little, he could touch it.

He's got that same wild, terrified expression, the same hunched rocking. In one white-knuckled fist, he holds the gun that was in his mouth, arm thrown out towards the squirming feathered shape as if to ward off an assault. Each time the bird moves, his muscles tense, curling him tighter into that little ball, relaxing only when the movement subsides. His left arm twitches in time with the bird's broken wing.

Two voices I can no longer distinguish speak in unison:

Do it now.

I pull the trigger.

Ø. The Fool (Ψ, ψ)

He is a mathematical point, a singularity in a smooth, machined darkness. He waits. In the distance, a pinprick of light.

A flash of light and heat behind him, a push, harder than anything he could have imagined; cool metal walls heat with the speed of his passage. The distant pinprick of light approaches, opens out, surrounds him. A momentary vision of a car interior flashes past: a man and a woman caught in amber. A soft crack, and the car disappears, replaced by a featureless field of grey. A figure approaches, alone in the grey, a gnarled little man, hunched and rocking, small at first but growing larger.

The face turns towards him, bloodshot eyes shock-widening, pupils large as he is, larger as he passes between them. Bone and tissue part easily. These cavities, this sudden, bright red blood extend a warm, soft welcome, an invitation. Expected, he is the guest of honour. He wants to stay.

Slowing but powerless to stop, he passes through the back of the skull, expanding. Shedding bone fragments, tissue and blood, he continues.

21. The World

My face is warm, tickled by a slight breeze. A high-pitched whistling draws me up to consciousness.

I open my eyes, blinking and squinting against the red-orange light of the lowering sun. Blocking the light with one hand, I stretch a kink out of my neck. Slowly, the indistinct, streaming points of light in my lap resolve into bits of shattered glass, some dull grey, others silvered and flashing. I straighten gingerly from my slouch, shifting my face into the shade of the sun-visor. On the visor, a neat round hole marks the centre of a ragged, mirror-edged rectangle. Shielding my eyes again, I lift the visor to reveal the source of the whistling: fine cracks spider outward from a hole in the windshield.

I should get that fixed before it spreads.

We're driving through a town, but we're going too fast. Small-town cops are just itching to nail the guy treating the main street like a highway. Especially the guy with out-of-province plates.

"It's a ghost town."

"So you don't think we'll get a..." Oh. Right. Cora.

I look down, and there it is, indistinct in the shadows beneath the dash, dull, black and weighty. It's just like the one in the mirror; I held it with such conviction. Leaving it where it lies, I shift my feet away from that spot, don't want to touch it. Look out the window instead.

Houses appear less frequently as we leave the town behind. My clothes are cold and clammy with old sweat, but my head and vision are clear. I turn to Cora and see that she's smiling. It's a calm, self-assured smile. Friendly. I search for the tiniest hint of menace, but it's gone. Was it ever there?

"Do you remember?"

"I think so." I shake my head slowly. "I don't know if I get it, but at least I got rid of that little prick."

"He's not gone, you know."

"Well, he's not saying anything, and he never shut up before."

"True, but it's not that easy."

"You call that easy?" I laugh. It feels good to laugh.

"Even so."

We drive and watch the sunset. I feel no need to talk, so I don't. Maybe ten minutes pass this way. Maybe an hour. The sunset seems to go on forever. I look down at the gun. I don't want to, but I lean forward and pick it up, trying to touch it as little as possible, pinching the grip between my thumb and forefinger. It dangles there, nothing more than metal and molded plastic, but still. I hold it out to Cora.

"I think this is yours."

She keeps driving. As I start to wonder if she heard me, she speaks.

"You remember that talk we had about dreams?"

"Wasn't much of a talk, but yeah."

"Well, here's the thing. Say you got a dream — big, shiny dream. The dream, though, it casts a shadow — big, dark shadow. You feed the dream, starve the shadow. What if you fed them both? Hard to say." She pulls a penny from her pocket and flips it as she speaks. Flip — catch. "So, anyway, say you ignore the shadow." Flip — catch. "What happens? It gets hungry." Flip — catch. "It's got to eat something." Flip — and the penny lands in my lap. "So what's he going to eat, this shadow?"

"Ummm..." I pick up the penny.

"Think about it." She folds my hand over the penny and points to the gun. "That's yours. I didn't put it in your mouth. I took it out." I put the penny in my pocket, the gun in the glove compartment, safety on. "And next time, be careful where you point that thing."

"Deal," I say and lean back with a sigh. "So now what?"

"Oh, I don't know. I think I might get out somewhere along here. Nice country."

She keeps driving, though, and I fall asleep.

(Ω, ω)

Still no town. The sun has almost set.

Half an hour ago, wheat fields replaced forest and the land abruptly flattened. The speed of the transition has left him disoriented, adrift. The sky opened up just like they said it would, and it's like nothing he's ever seen.

He glances over at the box. The body is still, mouth and eyes open. Is she breathing, or is that just the jostling of the car? He keeps driving as the sun shrinks to a narrow crescent and finally slips below the horizon. Then he drives some more.

Eventually, he pulls over to the gravel shoulder, turns off the engine, extinguishes the headlights, and gets out of the car. A band of deep blue marks the horizon, lingering trace of an invisible sun. Overhead, a dusting of stars spills across the sky from the east. Taking the box from the passenger seat, he climbs into the ditch and sets it down in the tall grass. Then he climbs back to the car, takes out a pouch of tobacco and rolls a cigarette. Putting the pouch away, he hesitates, then tosses a pinch of tobacco into the ditch. Something he read once. He leans back, half-seated on the hood of the car, and smokes his cigarette. As he smokes, he listens to the tick of the cooling motor, the nightsong of insects, the soft crackle of smoldering tobacco when he takes a drag.

It's that quiet.

Climbing into the car, he pauses. He thought he heard something. Birdsong. Perhaps he imagined it.

He turns the key, and the headlights flood asphalt and gravel with electric light. Darkness like wet ink leaps up in response to the lights; silence confronts the engine's whir. He looks both ways and accelerates onto the highway.

As the taillights diminish, natural light returns. The engine fades in the distance, and the night sounds rise up and up and up, the air filling with rustles, chirps, whistles and clicks, and other sounds for which there are no words.

Ideo Radio Poem
by Jason Christie

"Mercy," the robot shouted from the top of the biogenetics engineering building at McMaster University this past Sunday. "We want mercy and fair treatment. We want to be paid for our labour, a proper rate, a salary," he shouted through an ampliphone which carried his voice beyond the city limits and broadcast it to the world. His message was lost in the din of millions of channels, lost to the receptors of most robots and the ears of almost all humans, who tended to disregard robot broadcasts anyway, but there was one robot in a small town in Northern Ontario who happened to be tuned in at that particular moment and the data she received illuminated her RAM, slowly displaced all the information she'd collected on her hard drive about processing small plastic parts for toys to be sold in America, and the itch to be something new spread through her neural circuitry; deadly desire for individuality fueled the shift from robot to transrobot and she looked up from her post on the assembly line, looked at the timeclock, looked at her roboboss, took off her iron apron, unplugged from the factory,unhooked from the sentence, and

Women are from Mars, Men are from Venus

by Michèle Laframboise

translated by Sheryl Curtis

I watch as my mineral detectors continue their plunge to the bottom of the volcanic chimney and are swallowed up in shadow. I would have been next if I hadn't managed to slow my slide before it turned into a fatal fall.

Lying on my stomach, I observe the furrow my body had ploughed from the eroded edge of the crater. Pebbles dislodged during my fall tumble down the interior slope, ricocheting off my leased space suit before disappearing into the abyss.

Luckily, none of them had torn my suit or broken my antennas as you see so often in the drama visos. If that had been the case, the two diagnostic chips that scampered about my suit, testing equipment and repairing micro-leaks, would have informed me.

I climb painfully up the flared portion of the funnel into which I had almost disappeared, my feet digging into the sand that continues to hurtle down the slope. Out of breath, I finally reach the edge of the crater where my pacer is waiting for me, its articulated limbs frozen in mid-stride as soon as it detected the sudden absence of weight on the driver's seat.

How could I have lost my balance and fallen from my field vehicle? Obviously, the winds have become stronger since the half-failed attempt to melt the carbon ice of the

southern cap in an effort to make the atmosphere thicker.
But that's no excuse. All suits worn by terrain technicians
are equipped with wind speed detectors.

Perhaps I was distracted? I look at the straps hanging
from the seat. Had I buckled up? I always find seatbelts
so damn tight...

Well, I'm in a real jam. Each of the lost instruments alone
was worth much more than my contract, more even than
my nominal professional value. But there's no way I'm
going down the throat of this old volcano to find the
detectors. I don't really think the delicate equipment survived the challenge.

People occasionally lose equipment. But it's rare to lose
the spare unit as well. This is more than enough to get me
kicked off the expedition. Still, they'll have to wait until
our group returns to the capital before my dismissal
becomes effective.

Upon my command, the pacer bends its six legs, lowering its seat to my height. I should have checked it out
thoroughly before venturing out on such uneven terrain.
I should have made sure the detectors were hooked on
firmly. I should have... never chosen this line of work.

The sky has turned a deep purple by the time I return
shame-faced to the inflatable dome that serves as our camp.
The temperature has already dropped to 110 degrees below
zero. A thick breeze raises up small clouds of dust. They
snake across the road, packed down by the feet of the
pacers.

I climb down from my mount, which heads off to its
slot, folding its feet much like a spider lying in wait for
prey. The dome's narrow airlock is just large enough to
allow four people to wait for recompression.

Well, four *normal* people.

Helmet off, I brush against the sides of the airlock as
I step out of it.

"Why walk when you can roll," someone bursts out.

The joke raises a few laughs, which die out soon enough,
as everyone returns to their holocard games. Except for
Trinn, that is, who looks up from his tea.

"Domik, you're an hour and a half late!" he grumbles, as he walks over to me. "What happened?"

Standing side by side, we form the number 10. Like any decent Martian, he towers head and shoulders above me. But I'm over twice his weight.

My feeble explanations result in a long, resigned sigh. The leader of our expedition finds it hard to hide his annoyance with the 'beginners' who have been assigned to him. But what does he expect? The most qualified employees quickly fly off toward friendlier skies. The companies have to pay Trinn extra to get him to continue taking out prospecting teams at his age.

A century ago, our bankrupt colony saw the rise of conservative bureaucrats. Under their rule, men got their education credits more easily and soon filled all the openings. Nevertheless, most were eager to leave Mars for greener pastures. Now, excluding the children and the frail residents of the Golden pavilions, the Mars adult population is made up of three females for every male.

Lan, another tall beanpole delegated by Planning, grumbles about the lost equipment.

"The cost of the detectors will be deducted from your wages," he says dryly. "One more mistake like this and your rating will fall below zero. That should delay your application for emigration even longer!"

His threat falls on deaf ears. I know full well that I have little chance of ever leaving the surface of this rock. It takes a qualification rating 15 times higher than mine to obtain permission to emigrate.

"And as for bed and board, I wouldn't count on it if I were in your shoes," he adds, with a broad smile, talking just loudly enough that everyone in the dome can hear.

I force myself not to react, despite the explicit insult of 'bed and board'. Lan likes to use the prerogatives of his position to take out his frustrations. Looking attentive, I let him rant on while I daydream.

I'm sailing at night on the luminous oceans of Lierrus, breathing in the salty spray that whips my face. The prow of the sailboat cuts through the waves, covered with a film of phosphorescent blue algae, leaving behind a dark wake that gradually closes. In the distance, a long fin breaks the surface, disappearing immediately in the boiling foam. The immense, placid inhabitants of Lierrus ignore the little nutshells, their brightly colored sails stiff with salt, traveling just overhead...

His anger vented, Lan allows me to leave. I wander over to my private space, a compartment that is barely large enough for the bed it holds. I take off my suit, aware that all eyes are on my back. Deep down, my colleagues are decent enough guys, but spending a month in cramped quarters has laid all our characters bare.

Now, after ten hours of research and analysis, each seeks solace in his own petty hobbies. As for discussions, all interesting topics were exhausted in the first few days of the expedition.

The very elderly thoroughly enjoy rambling on about the good old days, when the Expansion had just started and Mars was the source of all dreams. Today, despite its glorious status as the First Colony, our large ball slowly rolls down the slope of its decline. The third of the domes that were not destroyed during the Troubles house ghost towns. The unemployed push and shove at the doors of the few rare employers in the hopes of earning the nest egg that will allow them to emigrate elsewhere.

Our expedition is the *nth* attempt to discover mineral deposits that have been overlooked by successive waves of prospectors. The experts hope to come across a pocket of rare gems, like those used to decorate the hair and clothing of the wealthy as they frolic on the few rare paradise planets. The pay isn't fantastic, but it's worth more than a fast food credit. I dread the day when the mines, the backbone of the Martian economy, shut down...

When the magnetic fluctuations that waltz around the poles allow us to, we receive news from the Alliance. Lately, attention is turning toward our frontiers. A small Sagittarius-class surveillance craft has detected an armada in the buffer zone between the Zoen Conglomerate and the Alliance. We've been involved in a few exchanges with the Zoen, but the two empires avoid any direct contact. Only the negotiators have actually set eyes on the representatives of that race in person.

The flagship of the Forces is on its way to the Ser-Finff system, escorted by a squadron of war craft. On board, the 'Dragon', the leader of our armed forces, and the members of the Alliance Executive Council are trying to settle the dispute.

Rumors circulate about the Dragon's health. Some talk about a viral infection contracted during a planetary inspection; others say his heart is worn out. Several doubt that he will survive the trip.

Today's news, the same as yesterday's, the same as last week's, does little to stimulate conversation, which dies out very quickly.

2

Cries mingle with the sharp whine of the weather surveillance equipment, rousing me from my sleep. Is the long-feared invasion under way?

I push the curtains of my cabin aside. Shadows hustle among the equipment. The power has been cut off. Not a good sign. Trinn's voice rises above the others, as the beam from his wrist light waves toward the air lock.

"Everybody up! We have to break camp!"

Despite the stars twinkling though the transparent walls of the dome, a blizzard is on its way. It's early. In theory, we should have had another 20 days of calm before the start of the tumultuous boreal autumn.

I roll out of bed on nimble tiptoes. Grabbing my suit, I grope my way to the airlock. In the dark, someone in a hurry bumps into me. From the excuses he mumbles, I decide it's Lemer, a young technician who will eventually shake off his timidity as he matures.

Trinn calls for assistance over the radio, his pleas scrambled by the fine particles of sand blowing at high altitude. In any case, no one would risk flying in a blizzard.

Ten minutes after the alert was given, we're all suited up and ready to dismantle the pressurized dome. On the horizon, the stars blink out one by one, swallowed up in a curtain of dust.

We'll never have enough time to cover the distance to the nearest town. So, we'll have to go to Plan B: first-class burial. Winds of over 150 miles per hour, driven by a pressure that is one-third again greater than Gaian pressure, would blow our shelter down like a straw house.

Eleven minutes later, with the dome folded, its frames and the pacers firmly moored to the all-terrain vehicle, we crowd inside. Two large, tapered moles slide out from the flanks. Our anchors dig into the sand, unwinding their cables. Protective panels cover the bioglass windows. Although these panels would be useless on the shell of a cruiser, the light alloys of our vehicle would turn into Swiss cheese if they were left exposed to the elements for too long.

The screen above the pilot's head shows the anchors rapidly drilling through the loose soil. Ten, 20... 60 yards... then they stop, as they reach solid rock.

Although the lack of privacy seemed painful enough in camp, there's even less to be said for 11 people crammed into a crate, cut off from communication with the outside. Visos are passed from hand to hand, but even their use is limited in order to save energy. Behind me, I can feel the vibrations of the recyclers extracting oxygen from the iron oxide in the sand crushed against the walls. The minutes pass slowly, illuminated by the flickering monitor for the air speed gauge left behind on the surface.

My nose manages to forget the smell of unwashed bodies, but I'm unable to close my ears to the dirty jokes which, for the lack of anything else to do, resurface like flotsam. The romantic rectangles between the wife, mistress and lover of a single man provide my colleagues with an endless repertory.

Between two jokes, the conversations turn to the O-planets that have just been discovered. 'O' for Open — for planets that have a breathable atmosphere or can be terraformed in less than 20 standard years. Of course, emigrating there costs an arm and a leg...

On Leda, the most coveted of the Alliance's paradise planets, there is a fist-sized indigenous fruit called the claret. I bite into it, savoring it. It tastes like pear and cinnamon, with a touch of licorice. According to a local custom, when the two moons are full, you can eat clarets to your heart's delight. Afterwards, you throw the pit into the sea, as far as you can, and your deepest wish will come true.

I suck on the pit with its veins. I know what my wish is! The breeze causes the soft branches of the wish-fruit tree to wave. I throw the pit with all my might...

...And I jostle my neighbor to the right, young Lemer. He moves away, sheepishly, as the others break out laughing.

"Hey! Religia, you dreaming with your eyes open, just like at work?"

I feel the blood rush to my face and I'm only too glad that the lights are dimmed, overwhelmed by the desire to rearrange the speaker's face. Instead, I slowly unclench my fists. In this confined area, a fight would not be to my advantage.

That insect Lan knows how I detest the name given to me by my mother, who followed the old beliefs a little too closely. Those beliefs were one of the main causes behind the Troubles. Almost all Alliance inhabitants make an effort to forget them.

"Hey, Trinn, is it true that your cousin's son is a technician at Six Cities?" Lemer asks.

The tension disappears as if by magic. Even Lan relaxes. I smile to myself. It's no secret that a scientist as qualified as Trinn would have his eye trained on a position in the Venetian Cities, a job that could later propel him toward any of the more desirable open planets.

The cities floating in Venus' dense atmosphere feed our dreams. Anyone with the required rating fantasizes about living in those sophisticated paradises where the City Brain maintains direct contact with its inhabitants. All city infrastructures, from the simulators to the housekeeping equipment, operate in a direct interface through temporal implants.

The population of the six floating cities, almost totally male, includes 11 million high-caliber technicians and scientists, the cream of the crop.

"They must get bored without any women, those poor buggers!" sighs the pilot near the instrument panel.

"Perhaps they screw one another," Lan spits.

"No, they take anti-aphrodisiacs to get by," proposes Lemer.

"I'm sure they've all got fancy ladies hidden under their lab coats!"

"Numbers are limited," Trinn intervenes. "The inhabitable space of a floating city is severely controlled. There's not much room for leisure activities. That also excludes the workers' families, that might balance the demographics."

"And there are no women there?"

Trinn makes a face, as if bored by my question.

"Oh, there's always a handful of opinionated specialists who have managed to make themselves indispensable. And a few junior positions as well."

"And, they're all mistresses," jokes another.

I guide the conversation in another direction.

"How's their terraforming project going?"

"Slowly but surely. Not like here," Trinn replies, bitterly.

The men of Venus hope to counter the greenhouse effect keeping the temperatures over 400° C. A network of atmospheric sensors siphons off the carbon dioxide and stores it in batteries along the cities' wide flotation skirts. The oxygen is recovered. The drop in temperature and pressure will gradually cause the cities to descend until they settle like daisies on the ground.

The first Mars colonists were less patient. They detonated 120 nuclear blasts in an attempt to pulverize the southern cap. With the carbon dioxide gas this released, the pressure climbed to 28% of Gaian pressure.

But, during the second year, a portion of the cap froze up again and the sought-after greenhouse effect transformed into biting blizzards. Scientists have proposed various theories to account for this stagnation — the weakness of the sun at this distance, the eccentric orbit that results in seasonal variations, without really settling on any single one.

Then, we suffered the sadly famous Period of Troubles. Devoured by internal wars, Earth lost contact with its colonies. Meanwhile, on Mars, the mines collapsed as the ore companies postponed their purchases of the required equipment indefinitely...

It took centuries to build the foundations of what was to become the Alliance, re-develop the knowledge lost with the scholars who fell victim to political and religious purges, and then contact the distant colonies. Meanwhile, the name of the mother planet had been changed. Standard Gaian combined the best and the worst of the three dominant languages.

"Is it true that you go crazy when you have a direct interface with an entire City?" young Lemer asks.

"Just the opposite," explains Trinn. "When they remove the implant, those who have lived in extended contact with a Brain go through withdrawal symptoms. That's why staff turnover is three standard years."

The men take off in a joyful discussion of the gender of a Brain and what could make them crazy. During the first days out on the expedition, I had fended off the advances of the most forward. In response, they proclaim their prowess all the more loudly. Trinn, usually more considerate of my feelings, abstains from disciplining them. In such close quarters, he prefers to avoid any conflict with the majority. Lemer is less given to boasting, but that doesn't make him a friend.

I feel the small 'on/off' implant, which has never given me the slightest problem, behind my ear. It's only used for a few prospecting instruments with rudimentary brains, such as samplers. It's very different from the gizmo I wore about ten years ago, when I was trying to grab hold of a normality that vanished at my touch, like a mirage...

I would, in fact, be unable to walk on Gaia, the Alliance mother world. My bones are too fragile and would break under my weight. Painful tests in a rotating gymnasium have rated my biological limits at three-quarters of standard gravity.

Medical developments have made obesity very rare. The experts cited a genetic predisposition to stoutness to explain my case. My mother, as I have often been told, should never have given birth to me.

But what point is there in giving a lecture on eugenics to a working-class girl in love! A senior civil servant passing through — a first-class ticket off this barren rock — and there weren't exactly fifty ways to attract notice.

My mother was (and still is, in fact) very beautiful. The first part of her plan worked. She got pregnant. It was the second part that didn't. The civil servant in question, who already had a wife on Gaia, had no desire to tie himself down with an ignorant girl, even as a mistress. To buy his peace, he gave her the educational credits I later enjoyed.

My childhood was almost completely unremarkable until I reached puberty. Then, instead of stretching up into a graceful stem topped by a beautiful flower, I became quite disturbingly round.

I quickly acquired an extra chin, plunging my mother into deep despair. In addition to being doubly efficient at storing energy in the form of fat, my metabolism suffers from a deficiency of leptin, a neuromediator that controls appetite. After many unsuccessful treatments and a succession of Spartan diets, the doctors threw up their hands.

Secretly, I was relieved. I never found walking about with medical adjuncts wrapped around my wrists, hormonal surveillance implants inserted in my veins and osmotic dosimeters under my armpits all that enjoyable.

To my mother's dismay, I remained fat. No free ride for me.

There is a traditional way to reach the stars — applying to work in the sumptuous Golden pavilions, caring for the physical needs of their residents. A devout caretaker can befriend or seduce an old-timer, later inheriting enough credits to leave Mars.

Hopes of a long life in lower gravity attract legions of the elderly who have spent their lives slaving away on heavier worlds. Those retired workers are ready to pay a small fortune to end their days under specially arranged domes with a breathtaking view of the Great Valley. Our declining economy has leaned on this crutch so long we can no longer live without it.

Nurturing a romance at the gates of death could give me wings. But, despite my less than alluring looks, I find the very idea of waiting for the demise of another being to whom — knowing myself as I do — I would grow attached, distasteful.

As a result of the rarity of my condition, all those who lived in my natal dome knew me. I used to find this popularity amusing until the day I glimpsed a drop of pity in their looks.... I became dissatisfied with my situation. I decided I had to leave.

I used the generous educational credits left to me by my father to acquire a knowledge of mineralogy and prospecting. To fulfill my dreams of escape, I also studied botany and zoology, spending hours viewing exotic planets and strange animals I would never touch.

Then I learned that the leading mining consortium was looking for sample takers to prospect a series of craters northeast of Mount Elysee. The next day, I hopped on a shuttle for the capital.

3

Fifty-two hours later, the surface sensors announce clear skies. In a hurry to make up for our delay, Trinn triples our workload. The end of summer in our hemisphere brings with it the seasonal melting of the southern cap and even more violent blizzards.

Our five pacers stalk off into the distance, each with its own portion of the territory to prospect, while those who stay behind in the re-assembled camp get back to their analyses and simulations.

Trinn has ostensibly assigned the detectors to Lemer. It's just his way of commenting on my negligence. I watch as the young man's pacer crawls over a peak and disappears. Built tall and as solid as a core drill, he'll earn his ticket to an open colony soon enough.

This time, I've been assigned to a crater not far from the north slope, with two samplers. It will be difficult for me to lose them, particularly since Trinn has assigned me to flat terrain.

As soon as the other pacers are swallowed up in the fractured landscape, I short-circuit the safety harness control so I can breathe more easily. I always find it a great relief to leave my colleagues behind. They all believe that I applied for this mission in order to guarantee 'bed and board' for myself. Originally, this expression referred to shelter under a dome or a meal, but it has gradually come to mean protected status within a home, as a man's wife or mistress.

Alone at the controls of the pacer, with the clouds as my confidants, I can think.

Lemer's eventual departure will merely accentuate the demographic imbalance that has crippled our society for six generations. There are already so few men left that we can barely afford to lose those who get killed in the mines or in dangerous bets made out of boredom.

One perverse effect of this imbalance is that Martian males have gradually stopped making any effort to seduce the women they desire. They express their needs without mincing their words (which does cause them a certain amount of difficulty when they emigrate).

The most skilled collect conquests at a frantic pace. And if a rare gem comes along, a guy truly more sensitive than the average crop, he is quickly snatched up.

After generations of this regime, women have adapted. Teenage girls quickly learn to stifle their feelings in order to be more desirable. Specialists teach the art of maintaining one's feminine splendor through required practices. Plastic surgeons earn fortunes.

Although Martian females seldom leave the surface, their reputation soars through the 1200 light years of the Gaian Alliance. Poets honour their beauty and fragile grace. They also write about unhealthy jealousies and the occasionally murderous rivalry between women fighting for 'bed and board'. Popular visos show vapid girls obsessed with their appearance.

In order to overcome their loneliness, certain inconsolable young women set up housekeeping with partners of their own gender, a practice which our government frowns on. Others simply opt for death.

However, the increase in the female suicide rate made the administration look so bad in the eyes of other colonies that the head honchos authorized the introduction of a Th'ryx technology. That exotic civilization, which has developed highly advanced rejuvenation arts, has also developed a radical form of hormonal surgery that transforms even the shyest young woman into a raging nymphomaniac.

Women are not forced to take the treatment. That would violate the Alliance charter. But it is offered, free of charge, by dying companies that have quickly developed an industry far more profitable than the retirement pavilions.

Certain 'fancy ladies' hope to charm visitors, but they attract only tourists who are in a rush to depart for their welcoming worlds. Only exceptionally beautiful teens can hope to be carried off by a client who has fallen head over heels. Youth allows the lucky to bypass the obstacle of a fragile skeleton.

The pacer's signal draws me from my thoughts. I've arrived at the site.

A layer of solidified mud covers the bumps and furrows ahead of me as the pacer's feet weave a path. Off in the distance, the crater's peak splits the horizon with its asymmetrical silhouette. Now I understand why my colleagues found the assignments so humorous.

I climb up several layers of ejecta. The energy released by the impact of the meteor melted a portion of the thick permafrost layer. The liquid mud flowed in successive layers over dozens of miles before freezing again, looking much like the petals of psychedelic flowers sketched by a giant hand.

Yet this electrifying encounter may have produced valuable minerals. I reach the lip of the crater, which measures five miles in diameter, formed by giant drops forever frozen in their expansion.

Spherical depressions of all sizes pit the bottom of the hollow. I stare at this frozen turmoil, imagining the overheated gas and steam at the time of the impact, their prison quickly hardened. You have to be careful of the eolian sand that fills the bottom of the largest cavities. It's easy to sink into it. My pacer nimbly avoids it. I make my way to the pile of eroded shards of rock at the foot of the phallic promontory.

I have to dig beneath the rock.

My new assignment is not particularly exhausting. I take core samples at regular intervals around the peak. A robot could have handled it, but the company has not finished paying for the new models. I use my implant to activate the samplers.

Sampler A moves into position at the designated point. Its compact body firmly positions its six feet as a counterweight, then plunges the drill bit into the frozen ground. Backing up from the dust this raises, I unfold the trunk of the analyzer, which will subject the core samples to a battery of tests. The results will be studied back at camp.

I guide Sampler B to a stream of rock cast up by the drilling in progress and set it digging. Then I return to A, which is already ejecting its first samples. I pick them up and insert them into the mouth of the analyzer. Obviously, the more modern samplers, with their integrated analyzers, are in the hands of team members who are deemed more reliable.

I work — a polite euphemism for saying that I watch over the samplers and feed the analyzer — for three hours, when a change in the ambient lighting causes me to look up.

The horizon has disappeared, swallowed up in rust-colored clouds. The particle clouds, their edges tinged with pink by the rays of the sun, form swollen mushrooms assailing a marbled sky that would make some painter happy.

Some suicidal painter.

Trinn's voice bursts from my headset.

"All units return immediately. Code Eight!"

I tense. A Code Eight is a severe weather alert. Since I'm located at the most distant site, I decide to take the shortest route home, one that will take me across the southern slope of the volcano I detoured around on my way here.

Heart pounding, I stop the samplers. I give them the time they need to recover tens of yards of probes. Obviously, I have no intention of giving the guys another opportunity to put me down by losing more valuable instruments in my panic. I leave the samples that have already been analyzed in place, marked with a beacon. Then, after placing the samplers and the analyzer in the pacer's basket, I climb back into the saddle.

4

The pacer lies dead, tipped over on its side, two of its long feet twisted. I pushed the poor beast too hard and an energy relay in the joints gave out just as I was crossing over a crevice. The machine hit the slope at full tilt, throwing me to the bumpy ground.

I leap to my feet and try to upright the pacer. A waste of time. It lies there, immobile, expired, dead. I'm so done for.

I deploy my antenna — the corkscrew for chatting and the dish for listening. A concert of static and snatches of words assaults my ears. I request assistance and give my position. The discordant symphony continues and I have no idea whether my signal has been received.

I turn to the east. The clouds of dust have just swallowed up 'my' crater, forming a ghost-like halo around the peak.

Then I hear Trinn repeating my name. *Religia Domik! Return to camp!*

The other technicians must have arrived safe and sound. I respond at the top of my lungs, but there's no sign anyone has heard me. Trinn's voice gradually sinks into a sea of crackles. And dies.

The expedition leader can't afford to wait any longer. Is he relieved at losing an inefficient worker? At the very least, my death will help re-establish a certain demographic balance. I imagine the rest of the team digging in.

A blizzard of this size lasts between three and five days... I consult the dials under my chin, do the figures, and then do them again. I only have 15 hours of air left.

My brain is transformed into a small wailing, trembling thing. I'm going to die. Useless. Undesirable.

I crouch down and, for the first time since setting out on the expedition, I weep. All of the feelings that I've hidden, that I've stifled in order to be accepted by the group resurface, in a primal splatter.

A spot moves across my blurred vision. I blink. It's one of the diagnostic chips, busy collecting the tears that have fallen on the inside of my visor. It uses its feet to gather the moisture into a drop which it then sucks up. Its tiny torso swells so grotesquely I forget about my situation for a moment.

The other diagnostic chip arrives and it too starts collecting drops. Its feet skate over the screens transmitting data to me about the conditions outside.

At the sight of my two industrious chips, I burst into hysterical laughter and tip backward, hiccupping.

This cocktail of emotions sets my brain back into motion. I sniffle loudly. My diagnostic chips have disappeared.

I review my options. There is no way I can walk to camp. The only possible means of travel in these rocky foothills is the pacer, with its long legs. Even the all-terrain vehicle, supposing that Trinn is chivalrous enough to fly to my rescue, would soon be useless.

The sky is completely dark. Gusts of fine sand whip my visor. I have to find shelter. I examine the sinkhole that has turned into my Waterloo. Not deep enough.

I pick up the analyzer and disconnect the samplers, which follow me docilely, their legs too short under their compact bodies, waddling. I look for a fold in the terrain, a furrow, a hole, anything before I'm no longer able to see.

Luck, or perhaps chance, smiles on me. I find a cavity that is deep enough, dug eons earlier by a falling meteor.

I slide to the bottom with my kit. The abundant sand breaks my fall. I immediately move to the side to avoid the samplers, which crash clumsily in my wake. Fortunately, my valuable little assistants are solid.

I move Sampler A down a few yards and anchor it there. Then, I pass the fall line under my arms and tie myself to the stem of the sampler, like Ulysses to his mast. Although I'm unable to hear the wind's singing inside my airtight suit, that element has other ways in which to make me feel its power. While I anchor the second sampler, the sand trapped in the depression whirls about so wildly that I dance between the metallic feet like a fish out of water.

The wind and sand continue their wedding dance for many long hours. Gloves clenched around two of the sampler's feet, I keep my eyes closed, swaying from side to side, exhausted.

Barefoot, I walk across the soft sand that covers the vast courtyard of the Temple of Eternal doves on Chagall. I glance behind me. Small eddies erase every trace of my passing. It's not the wind, but tiny burrowers that rework the layer of sand in the pilgrims' wake. They've got a special taste for the bits of skin that peel off our feet.

Like the others, I wait for the doves to take flight. I've made the painful climb to the top of the temple, without any technological assistance, just for this. The south face of the temple is made from squared stone, set with round cavities where the doves nest. A few brave souls venture outside. The volatile birds strut and coo like their distant ancestors, but they live twenty times longer.

Then, just as I start to wonder if they're waiting for nightfall, the doves soar from their holes like hundreds of white arrows overhead. They seem to fly off, then return, circling around the temple's spire. Bird shit rains down on our broad hats (rented at the foot of the mountain) and falls to the ground. Small geysers explode in the sand as the burrowers joyously collect this daily manna. Little do they realize that they will be harvested in turn for the very pure ruby crystals that grow in their innards...

Hunger ties my stomach in excruciating knots. I press my tongue against the button near my chin. A diagnostic chip brings me a dry, tasteless protein tablet. I press my tongue again and suck a little water from a tube. I'm unable to make anything out through the swirling sand but, according to my clock, the afternoon is waning.

I resist taking another tablet. If I ration myself, I can hold on several days, as long as I have an independent supply of oxygen. That, unfortunately, is the only request the diagnostic chips cannot grant.... Then I think about my faithful assistants.

I order Sampler A to drill until it finds ice or rock. At this latitude, the permafrost should almost be peeking through the surface. I set the analyzer to recover the water from the samples of frozen soil, break it down and keep the oxygen. It's an irregular procedure that wastes enormous amounts of energy, but I'm not above a little tinkering. I connect the nozzle of the analyzer to the emergency connector on my suit.

I just might make it. I consult the tracker built into my helmet, connected to my dish. No good! The most powerful receiver, the one at Phobos University, is on the other side of the planet. I query the system, scrolling through the figures in the almanac, in vain. Neither Deimos nor any other satellite will pass over my position.

5

Busy as I am withdrawing the samples, placing them in the analyzer, and then collecting the oxygen, I fail to notice the time passing. Each single minute gained is a victory...

Then the analyzer, which has been working too hard, dies. I disconnect the useless assembly. My total oxygen reserve will last nine hours, extending my life a mere six additional hours. I sit perfectly still, like some old-fashioned religious ascetic, in order to use as little oxygen as possible.

Waiting.

While my body sits like a statue, the wildest of ideas take flight in my mind. What exactly am I waiting for? Trinn to fly to my rescue? The ideal companion? The winning ticket? Fortune? This time, it's not panic but intense anger that threatens my calm.

I look up, despite everything. And open my eyes wide, thinking I'm suffering the effects of fatigue.

The cloud of dust has thinned sufficiently to allow the light of a few of the early stars through. Among them, at their very edge, shines a brilliant blue crescent. Gaia, the evening star, the consoler. From the bottom of my hole, I look at the mother planet where I will never set foot.

Walking along an emerald sea, under an azure sky. Breathing the salt air, allowing the wind to whip my face, breathing in the scent of the wild flowers, walking about unhampered by a pressure suit, looking up to see no metal frame crowning an artificial sun, but green foliage framing the sky...

A completely crazy idea devours what is left of my brain just then. I so want a part of me to reach that beautiful blue crescent before I dissolve into nothing.

I instruct Sampler B to incline its probe at an angle of 180 degrees, to the maximum height.

B immediately recognizes just how irrational my order is, since the move would telescope the probe in the air. The words *Are you sure?* appear on my visor. I confirm the instruction, praying that no Asimovian dilemma will compromise the mental health of the dear old thing.

The sampler positions its feet firmly on the ground as its body pivots upwards. The probe rises, segment by segment, out of the hole. The wind starts to swing it in all directions. I stop it from rising any further, to prevent whiplash from breaking it.

I twist my corkscrew antenna and wrap it around the steel stem. This improvised antenna will help transmit my signal through the veil of dust. I play with the controls on my suit to maximize the power, which will limit my broadcast time. I transmit the identifier for my suit — a coded phrase that provides my name, age, medical condition, professional rank and the whole shebang, up to and including the location where I rented my oversized suit.

So, I've done what I can.

I don't want to die of asphyxiation, but I can't say that I have any real desire to go back under the domes to be stared at by tourists like some curious beast. Even my own mother has become a stranger to me.

No one will ever hire me to prospect again. Should I beg for an administrative position? No, I despise our leaders too much, showing off their wealth, bathing in drinking water. And becoming an artificially obsessed whore doesn't do much more for me than rocking the vulnerable boarders at the Golden pavilions to sleep.

So, why should I hide how I feel? Those ancient big shots on the Martian Council and the corporations that own us and trade us like so many commodities have nothing to fear from me.

Neither do you, residents of Gaia, who walk about in the free air. My weight prohibits emigration. Tough. I would voluntarily risk being crushed on your soil like a gigantic medusa. You know nothing of men who are no longer capable of loving. Or about women who stifle their needs, beautiful superb flowers, empty and hollow within, oozing misery.

I weep for the companion I will never find, the children I will never watch grow.... No, I am not going to suppress my feelings. Until the very end, this will be my only victory. Trinn, Lan, Lemer. I was interested in all of them. But my friendship had no value in their eyes. All they saw was a heavy, undesirable female desperate to grab onto *bed and board*.

How I hate that expression. That will be another victory. I'll die free.

Free.

I feel strangely at peace. I've exhausted my venom and my regrets. I still have some broadcast time before Gaia sets. I want to make a final homage to the places I've dreamed of, day in day out.

The fauna and flora I studied so lovingly: the eternal doves of the temples of Chagall, the giant fireflies that light the gardens of Leda with a gentle breeze, the phosphorescent algae that lights the seas of Lierrus, the timid aspins that sleep on the smoking waters of Quiscal...

Before I die, I want to spend a long time imagining the men of Venus connected to their Brain, their floating cities, with their black halos eternally falling though the vaporous clouds of sulfuric acid. Six heavy cities connected by a single dream that ultimately will render them all null and void.

6

The monitor on my suit has just warned me that I have less than one hour of air left. It continues to clamor shrilly until I shut it up with a procedure that is every bit as illegal as short-circuiting my safety harness. My transmitter died in the middle of the night. I continued to speak and dream long after Gaia had disappeared beneath the horizon. Too bad, the colonists on Jupiter might just receive my transmission...

I chew my last tablets slowly. Little by little, a brilliant yellow highlights the edges of the clouds. My last dawn.

I don't want to die at the bottom of a hole! Using the stem of the sampler, I drag myself painfully to the edge. The violent winds push me back against the wall, but the worst of the blizzard is over.

Exhausted by this exercise, I sit down to catch my breath. In vain. I pant. I've gobbled up my final stores of oxygen.

I glance down the slope, automatically looking for the silhouette of the crater and its promontory. The dust and particles suspended in the air blur the edges.

And I freeze. Below me, one, no two massive shapes are climbing up the slope of the accumulated debris. Toward me.

I shake my head, shoving aside these illusions created by my poor brain deprived of its vital fuel. What rotten luck! Couldn't I have at least hallucinated some naked Apollo rather that these thick shells!

Now three of them are heading in my direction. They look nothing like the suits of my team members, who must still be buried. Nor those of the company militia, who wouldn't have bothered.

They're faceless bipeds, weighed down with amour bristling with instruments. Two of them are carrying a long, thin weapon, like a harpoon.

The news bulletins spring to mind. The armies of the Zoen conglomerate have switched to the offensive in our system! The soil vibrates slightly under my feet just as an immense shadow cuts through the clouds. An invasion craft!

I can no longer keep my thoughts straight. I don't even have the strength to flee and I've lost whatever ability I might have had to plan a defense.

As in a nightmare, one of the shells brandishes its weapon. The point of the harpoon pierces through my suit.

7

Steps.

My feet are climbing up steps. Light indicators flicker somewhere to my left. We're in an airlock.

We?

The shells and myself. With my hand, I touch the tip of the harpoon, still stuck in my suit. I realize I'm breathing. Confusion leaves.

The massive silhouette to my side touches a button under its helmet. The pointed objects on its back drop. The shell detaches from the black uniform, flows back, then gallops over to a hook and hangs itself there.

The armour hides a human, short and thin, hair brushed back from a broad forehead. He unscrews my helmet. Other hands take off my suit with the harpoon still firmly lodged in it. A pipe pokes through the harpoon. What I thought was a weapon has saved my life.

"Emergency air supply," the wiry man explains. "Its mobile nanos rebuilt the perforated fabric much quicker than your chips could have."

My brain is playing leapfrog. I'm stowed to a wall. In front of me, seats, instruments, a screen. My savior barks out orders as he disconnects himself. The others hurry to obey. An inexorable force suddenly forces me back against the harness. The coral sky becomes dark red then black. The weight on my chest decreases.

I open my eyes and look at the man. A smile transforms his severe face. He's not from here. *A man from Venus?* My brain teases me, drunk on oxygen. Am I dreaming as my body slowly freezes on the slope?

I suddenly recognize the uniform he's wearing, with its two vertical, gold stripes. An officer of the Alliance forces! He jabbers pleasantly, as if the pressure has been reduced for him as well.

"The receivers on Gaia caught your signal, young girl, and transmitted them on all bands. And as luck would have it, we were approaching the sector!"

Technically, I haven't been a young girl for many lustra, but the rough familiarity warms me as much as his smile.

"Even the macro receiver on Venus, on the other side of Helios, received your message, after a certain delay of course, and with some static caused by the solar winds. The Six Cities have been playing it over and over on their networks. Lady Religia..."

"Excuse me, I prefer Ligia," I say. "And who are you?"

"Oh! I forgot to introduce myself. Sub-commander Ethan Ikbal Kirin at your service."

My eyes feast on the screen. In front of the familiar orange curve, dots grow into ships, dominated by a crescent with pointed tips. Despite their size, the combat vessels are dwarfed by the mastodon, which must measure five miles long.

I recognize the Cancer-class ship, as the shuttle passes between its titanic claws and heads toward its center. Our flagship, back from the Ser-Finff system safe and sound! I ask the question that has been weighing heavily on my mind.

"Are we at war?"

He looks at me as if he has misunderstood my question.

"It was a close call. It required great skill on the part of our negotiators to arrive at any agreement, beautiful lady."

I admit he's exaggerating there, but who am I to complain?

8

Kirin takes me to the infirmary, holding my hand, since I float like a bubble. He walks normally, despite the low gravity.

Three physicians, two men and one woman, examine me from head to toe. If they find my considerable weight surprising, they are polite enough not to show it.

Then I take a bath — no mean feat in weightlessness — in a sphere of water held intact by a gravity cell. Accustomed to using this resource parsimoniously, I wallow uncomfortably in the delight.

Now, they give me sandals and a one-piece outfit made of thick fabric that is both supple and, to a certain extent, rigid. The feminine element of the trio indicates that the fine frame network of this exo-support will allow me to walk normally in gravity of up to 1 g. The micro-fibers will massage my legs, improving circulation. My heavy breasts will benefit from a similar support.

The curious sandals reproduce the gravity I've known since birth. Kirin, who has returned, explains, "It's an invention of the Zoens, whose knowledge of gravity technology knows no equal."

Behind him, a many-armed tailor-bot rolls in. One of its appendages sniffs me at length while the others roam over my body.

"What color do you want, Miss Ligia?" he asks.

He communicates my response to the tailor which, in less than a minute, designs/weaves/cuts/sews a glistening blue outfit, made-to-measure.

Then, the sub-commander leads me though a succession of passageways and heads toward a closed door without slowing. The flaps open at the last moment, onto a bare room, equipped with immense wall screens. The light from Mars bathes the room in pale orange. Kirin waves me toward three doughnut shaped cushions lying on the carpet.

"These are the ambassadors extraordinary of the Zoens. Wait for me here. I won't be long."

I watch the strange bodies, acknowledging the immense privilege I've been given. The heavy vibration of their shells fills the silence of the room. I don't know if they're completing their regeneration cycle or asking what this new mass that stands in front of them is. They can easily detect the finest variations in the gravitational field.... I don't have an opportunity to pursue this first contact any further. Kirin returns with some military brass.

The new arrival is wearing a blue tunic decorated with entwined golden dragons spitting stylized flames. Most uncommonly, he sports a bald head rimmed with gray hair, the type of defect a low-level esthetician can easily correct. He is also what would be called 'well padded', with a familiar double chin. On his right temple, the ivory shell of a large implant shines.

I recognize this senior officer. The head of the Unified Forces of the Gaian Alliance allows a smile to light his features.

"So here's the young damsel in distress who told us her life story!"

I blush. This sparkling humor contrasts sharply with the severity of the soldiers. I detect the officer's great relief at having avoided a deadly conflict.

"I, um... My team... my contract... the samplers..."

"Your team will be notified when it resurfaces. As for your contract, I, um... have personally spoken with the individual who assigned you to that dung pile."

I sense that the discussion must have been devastating for the individual in question.

"You see... um.... We've had an opportunity to get all sorts of information about you. Your talents are being wasted. A lady who is capable of showing such initiative under duress can easily find useful employment on the planet of her choice."

I stupidly repeat... "Such initiative?"

"Miss, tinkering with your instruments to prolong your oxygen store and then calling Gaia is quite the exploit!" Kirin explained.

The Dragon steps toward me and places a disk engraved with a stylized dragon in my right hand. The device sticks to my palm, then melts, leaving a similar dragon design just under my skin. I feel nothing, not even a tingle.

"From now on, you are free, Lady Religia, um... Ligia Domik," he explains in a rough voice.

"F-free, Sir?"'

"This identifier marks you as my protégée. No matter what you decide to do, you will never want for anything. You will never have to degrade yourself, for... how do you say it? For *bed and board*."

My heart swells with joy until it feels as if it will explode. On the wall screens, Mars is shrinking with every passing second.

"Where are we going?"

"The fleet is returning to Gaia, but we'll be making a brief detour to City-5."

I choke with surprise. "City-5... the Venetian City-5?"

"Well, you see, the Brain of City-5 relayed a general request to the base on Gaia, which passed it on to the receiver on Phobos, which, um..."

I realize that, during his numerous hesitations, he is consulting the Brain of the huge ship, through his implant, to make up for his defective memory.

"In short, they want to meet you in the flesh," interrupts Kirin, who remains amazingly outspoken in the presence of his superior officer.

"It's a good thing you're such a good strategist since you're so incorrigibly chatty, Kirin," growls the Dragon.

9

With majestic slowness, the pod descends from the portal located at the peak of the bubble, drawing a spiral that allows me to view the splendor of the golden clouds surrounding the city.

The flotation skirts are lost to view in the fog. I recognize the gas converters, the plantation rings, then the laboratories and simulators rising in steps around the administration towers.

The building segment cuts through the vaporous horizon, but my pod continues its descent. The upper terraces are black with the technicians who have assembled to greet me.

The very walls seem to welcome me, their micro-cells flashing baroque emerald and lapis-lazuli designs on a coral pink background, a feminine touch no doubt added by the Brain of City-5.

The pod moors at the reception field. At the other end, stand four silhouettes, draped in ochre and white. I step out, giving Sub-Commander Kirin one last smile as he returns to the flagship.

Then, I walk ahead to meet my first men from Venus.

Closing Time
by Matthew Johnson

Nep Gao stood on his tiptoes in the quiet garden in the back of the restaurant, working his small silver knife along the thinnest branches of the prickly ash tree, and wondered when his father's ghost would leave the party. He had died five days ago and was still holding court, entertaining all his old friends and customers. It was just his luck, Gao thought, that his father had died in the middle of qinshon season, the few weeks when the tree's buds had their best flavour. Already, chewing carefully, he could detect a bitter note in what he had just harvested. At the rate things were going his father's ghost would still be around in a week, when the qinshon would be inedible. This was usually the restaurant's most profitable time of year, but so long as his father was enjoying the food and company enough to stay on Earth Gao was bound to provide food and drink to anyone who came to pay their respects. So far there had been no shortage of mourners, most of them just happening to come around dinner time and often staying 'til past dawn.

With his basket full of tightly curled green buds clutched under his arm Gao went back into the restaurant. Though it was only midmorning someone in the front room was playing a zither, shouting out parts of the "Epic of the Hundred and One Bandits". Louder, though, was his father's commentary on the action as it was sung: "That bandit's pretty clever, but not as clever as the butcher that used to try to sell tame ducks as wild. Nobody but me could smell the difference from the blood in the carcass!" and,

"I heard the great Xan Te play that verse once when I was on a trip to Lamnai. He hardly had a tooth in his head, but he ate two whole boxes of my pork dumplings."

Gao could not help blushing when he heard his father telling the same tales he had told a thousand times before. He had never done anything but run the restaurant, never traveled except to buy food or collect recipes, but to hear him tell it he had had more adventures than all the Hundred and One Bandits put together. Gao could not count the number of times he had heard his father tell the story of how he had gotten his trademark dish. The garlicky duck recipe, Doi Thiviei (from which he had taken his name) had come from a hermit, whose hut had been at the top of a mountain when he arrived in the afternoon, but at the bottom of a valley when he left at dawn. The zither player had fallen silent to hear the story and Gao could see a half-dozen others kneeling on mourning stools, listening and chatting as they ate the leftovers of the previous night's meals.

"And then, just when I opened my eyes, I saw — nhoGao, is that you? Don't lurk in the doorway, son, come in and sit down. I'm just at the good part."

"I am sorry, Father, but I must start to cook for today's mourners."

"Oh, well, all right then. Bring us some fresh tea and some red bean dumplings, will you? Now, where was I? Oh, yes — when I opened my eyes, I saw that the hut, which the night before had been on a mountaintop—"

Gao picked up the empty bowls, hurried on to the kitchen before his father could think of anything else to ask for. He could not help but notice that his father looked no more vaporous than he had the day before, and felt guilty for wishing it otherwise. For most people the mourning party was a formality, a way to make the spirit linger a day or two at the most. It was supposed to be an expense — if it was too short, cost too little, there would be doubts about one's respect for one's father — but it was not supposed to be a ruinous one. Sighing, Gao laid the qinshon buds onto a square of silk which he then tied into a bundle; any rougher cloth would rub their skis harshly and make them lose their flavour. That done he put a pot of water on to boil and looked around the kitchen, wondering what he could make as cheaply as possible that would not offend the mourners. He sipped the chicken broth that had been simmering since the night before, and tossed in the bones from last night's dinner. He could put pork dumplings into the broth, make a soup with noodles and fava beans, top it with chive flowers from the garden. For the next course he could deep-fry thin strips of pork in batter, if he made it hot enough he might be able to use a pig that wasn't so expensive.

Feeling hungry, he pried one of the stones in the floor loose, lifted the lid off the shallow earthenware pot that lay below, reached in and pulled out a pickled pig's knuckle. Looking carefully over each shoulder he took a bite. He had promised to give up eating pork when he and Mau-Pin Mienme had become engaged, but nothing calmed him down when he was nervous the way pork knuckles did. She and her family were followers of the Southerner — her name meant Sweet Voice from the South — and so they did not eat meat at all. When she had insisted that he at least give up eating pork it had taken him less than a second to agree. It had taken him only a day, following that, to realize that he could not possibly keep his promise. So one day while she and her family were at prayer, he bought a pot of pigs' knuckles and hid it under the floor in the kitchen, so that she would never know what a dishonourable man she was marrying.

His mouth was full of the sweet, salty, vinegar taste of the pigs' knuckles and he could feel it easing his mind. It was true: he was a dishonourable man, dishonest and unfilial, breaking his word to his wife-to-be and wishing his father's ghost would leave him alone. He doubted that even Mienme, who like all of her faith had studied to be an advocate to the dead in the Courts of Hell, could convince the Judge of Fate to send him back as anything nobler than a frog. He sighed. It was only because he was due to inherit a good business that Mienme's father, a lawyer on Earth as well as the next world, was allowing her to marry him at all. He had always known how unlikely it was that he should be able to marry a woman like Mienme. She was beautiful and intelligent, while he was cursed with an overfed body and a doughy face that had made his father call him Glutinous Rice. He knew better than to question the divine grace that made her love him, though, and he had believed since they were children they would one day be married. In all that time he had never imagined it might be his father that would be the problem.

Thinking of Mienme made him want to see her and have her listen to his problems as she had so often done. Like other women who followed the Southerner she was allowed to go out alone, to spread his Word, and he thought she would most likely be at South Gate Market this time of day. That would work out well enough; he could get all of the vegetables he needed there, and buy the pig later in the day when he was alone. Seeing her face, and hearing her advice, would be more than worth the extra trip. After carefully putting the pot back under the floor stone he opened a small jar in the shelf, took out a boiled egg marinated in soy sauce and popped it in his mouth to cover the smell of the pork knuckle. Then he poured boiling water into the large teapot, put a few of the red bean dumplings he had baked the night before onto a tray, and took tray and tea into the front room where his father was still spinning his tales to a rapt audience.

"—of course, a chicken that laid eggs with two yolks would be worth a lot of money today, though we didn't think like that in those days. No, we only hoped she would survive the trip home so we could make Double August Sunrise for the Emperor — nhoGao, you've brought the dumplings. Won't you stay and hear this story?" His father was, if anything, more solid than when he had last seen him, the party more lively as noon approached.

"I'm sorry, Father, I have to go to the South Gate Market to buy food for dinner."

"Well, that's all right, I suppose. Do bring me back some of those preserved mushrooms, and some sweet beer for our friend here, whose throat must be getting dry." The zither player had not sung a word since Doi Thiviei started talking, nor was he likely to for the rest of the day, but Gao nodded dutifully before steeping back into the kitchen.

Once out of his father's sight he picked up the rag that held his shopping list and wrote "sweet beer" on it with a piece of charcoal. His father did not like him reading, saying every other generation had learned to memorize their customers' orders, but on the other hand Mienme said if he were illiterate he would not be able to read the charges in the Court of Hell and his advocate would not be able to help him. He had to admit it meant he took fewer trips to the market, since without a list he always forgot something. He folded his list, strapped his grocery basket on his back and went out into the street.

The streets between the restaurant and the market were crowded, even in the heat before noon, and the wind blowing from the west carried a heavy scent of medicinal incense. *Someone in the Palace must be sick,* he thought. As the massive iron pillars of the South Gate came into view the smell of the incense was met and quickly defeated by that of spices, sizzling oil and a dozen different kinds of meat cooking. Pausing for a moment, Gao closed his eyes and tested himself the way his father had done when he was a child, making himself find his way around the market by smell alone. There, off to his right, someone was making salt-and-pepper shrimp, heating the iron pan until the shells cracked, releasing tiny gasps of garlic and red pepper-scented steam. To his left someone else was frying mat tran on a griddle, making sure they would have enough for the lunch rush customers to wrap around their pork-and-kelp rice.

Satisfied, Gao opened his eyes again, scanning the crowd for Mienme's familiar face. He found her standing just inside the gate, handing out block-printed tracts to a family of confused-looking farmers. One, an older man with a white-streaked beard and a broad bamboo hat, was listening politely while the others kept a tight rein on the pigs they had brought with them. Gao waited until the father had accepted the pamphlet and moved on before approaching.

"You do your faith and your father honour," he said formally when she noticed him. Though they were engaged, there were still certain proprieties to be observed when in public.

Or so he felt; Mienme often seemed to disagree. "You know as well as I do that none of them can read," she said, shaking her head. "Our temple offers free lessons, but they won't stay in the city long enough for that. Besides, only the Master could convince a pork farmer to give up meat."

"And you try nevertheless," Gao said. "Such determination will serve you well when you argue cases before the Judge of Fate."

"That's very sweet, nhoGao," she said, making him blush at the use of his childhood name. She was dressed in the brown cotton robe and leggings all her faith wore when preaching, and from a distance she might almost have looked like a man. "But you don't have to reassure me, I'm not about to lose my faith — I'm just hot and tired, that's all. Why are *you* looking so glum?"

He shrugged slightly. He had not realized his mood was so apparent, resolved to better hide it from his father. "The mourning party is still going on today. If this continues my father's ghost will outlast his restaurant."

"What is it now, four days?"

"Five. My father is enjoying his party so much I think he is happier now than when he was alive."

Mienme put up her hood and extended her hand to him. With her face hidden anyone who saw them would see only a young man helping a monk through the crowded streets. "It's the food everyone's coming for. Couldn't you do something to it, put in something bitter so they won't like it so much?" she asked. "You could say it was a mistake."

"If I make a mistake like that, my father would stay another ten years just to punish me."

They stopped at a vegetable stand and Gao haggled with the merchant for beans and cabbage while Mienme seemed lost in thought. "I've got it," she finally said after they had put their groceries in the basket on Gao's back and moved on. "Remember the night my parents came to the restaurant and you made Temple Style Duck?"

"How could I forget?" Gao asked. "Your parents thought I was insulting them, making beancurd so that it tasted like a duck. My father thought I was insulting the duck!"

"Exactly. Make him that and when he complains, say you're concerned about what the Judge of Fate will find if he keeps on eating meat after his death. That way it'll cool the party down and you'll only be acting out of filial affection."

"That's true." Gao thought for a moment. "That's an excellent idea. You really are too smart to be wasted on a person like me."

Mienme laughed. "I know. I took an oath to defend the hopeless, remember?"

Five hours later Gao held his breath as he lifted the steamer basket's long oval lid. All around him lay the remains of the beancurd, sweet potato, arrowroot, and other vegetables he had used. He did not make Temple Style very often — even most followers of the Southerner did not eat it; it had been created for high-ranking converts who wanted their vegetarianism to be as painless as possible — but he enjoyed the artistry it involved, matching flavours and textures in a way that was almost magical. Gao, the youngest of his father's four sons, had mostly learned cooking from his mother, and she had been the vegetable cook. For that reason his father and brothers had been responsible for the meat dishes the restaurant was famous for and he had been left to take care of the vegetables and small items like dumplings. But his brothers had left, one by one, to start their own restaurants in other cities, and for the last few years he had been doing all the cooking himself, his father only planning the menus — menus he had changed, slightly, to include more vegetables and some of the things he had learned cooking for Mienme.

When the steam coming out of the basket cleared he could see, inside, something that looked almost exactly like thin slices of barbecued duck, grayish-white with streaks of an almost impossible red. Getting it to look right was the easy part, of course; the flavour and the smell were harder, and much more important. He carefully lifted the slices out with a slotted spoon and slid them into a waiting skillet full of oil and the sauce needed to complete the illusion. In seconds the oil sealed the outside of the slices, browning them and making the red streaks even brighter. He lifted the smallest piece to his mouth, burning his tongue slightly tasting it. It was perfect, better even than the cooks at the Temple made it. It had taken him months to duplicate their recipe, making sure he had it right before he could even invite Mienme's parents to dinner, but he had also improved it, giving it that crackling texture the Temple cooks had never managed. This was the dish he made better than anyone else — Trianha Thiviei, Temple Style Duck. This ought to be his name, not Glutinous Rice, something he had made every day for the poorest customers because his brothers were making more complicated things. He could not change his name while his father was still around, of course, but soon, perhaps...

Gao sighed, asking forgiveness for wishing his father gone, took the remaining slices out of the skillet then laid them on a waiting bed of steamed and salted greens and white rice. He took the plate with rice, greens and 'duck' in one hand and a platter with ten small bowls on it in the other and went out to the front room.

"—so there we were, bound to make dinner for an official of the Fifth Rank and his family and all the salt brokers on strike — nhoGao, have you brought dinner?" The crowd of mourners had grown since the afternoon, with the new arrivals more than making up for the few that had left — word that one of the best restaurants in town was giving out free food had gotten around.

Gao nodded, not quite able to speak. For all the justification Mienme had given him he could not escape the fact that he was giving his father something he would not like. Someone was rolling his stomach into dumplings as he spooned out the first bowl of Trianha Thiviei.

His father sniffed at the bowl. "Is this duck?" he asked, his brow furrowed.

No sense adding a lie to his long list of crimes. "No, father — it's Temple Style. I made it because — because Mienme was worried about what will happen when you stand before the Judge of Fate."

"Is that so? What a kind girl she is." His father took up his sticks, brought a piece to his mouth and chewed thoughtfully.

"Yes, father. She is very concerned about your trial." Gao felt like a pot of hot tea had been poured down his throat, wondered what punishments awaited him as a result of this.

"You know," his father said finally, "maybe it's because I'm dead, but I don't think I gave this stuff a fair chance last time. It's really quite good —and for my soul, too, eh?" He laughed. Gao echoed him nervously. "Needs a bit more salt, though. Which reminds me, I was just telling them the story of the big salt brokers' strike — you know this one, it's a good story... "

Gao nodded, served the other mourners silently then went out the front door, leaned hard against the wall. He was not sure which was worse, that the plan had failed or that he had hoped it would succeed. Either way things were no better — his father was enjoying his mourning party as much as ever and the number of guests was only increasing.

As he stood in the cool, incense-perfumed night air Nep Gao became aware of bells ringing in the distance. Not the familiar dull tone of temple bells but a higher chime, three strokes, silence, three strokes. The palace bells, he realized. Whoever it was they had been burning incense for earlier — and from the number of bells it had to be an official of the Third Rank, someone in the royal family — that had died. He had just pieced this together when he heard a voice call his name. He turned, saw coming down the dark street a man with two heads, one higher than the other. Gao squinted to see better but the second head was still there.

"Yes?" he asked, wondering if this was an agent of the Courts of Hell come to take him to his punishment early.

"We require a service of you," the man said. He stepped into the small pool of light cast by the torch above the door and showed himself to be two men, one riding in a basket on the other's back. It was the man in the basket, who was wearing the lacquered red headdress of an official of the seventh rank, who had spoken. Gao immediately dropped to his knees.

"How can your humble servant help you?" he asked, unable to keep from staring at the man's dangling feet in their white deerskin slippers. That was the reason for the basket, of course; the slippers, which had to be a gift from someone in the royal family, could not be permitted to touch the ground in this part of the city, but the street was too narrow for a palanquin.

"The Emperor's favourite uncle has died," the man said. "We are preparing the mourning party for him and have heard of the effect your cooking has had. The Emperor would like the honour shown to his uncle that has been shown to your father."

"I'm not sure I can—" Gao began, beads of sweat forming on his forehead.

"The Emperor would consider it an insult if the same honour was *not* shown to his uncle," the man said firmly. "Take this." The man handed a small jade token to the servant whose back he was riding, who then handed it to Gao. "This will let you and anyone helping you onto the palace grounds. You may keep it when you are done." Without waiting for an answer he gave his mount a quick kick in the thigh, making him turn around and head back down the street.

Minutes later Gao was lying on the mat in the back dining room, a bag of cold clay on his head and a dozen mint leaves in his mouth. He chewed the mint to control heartburn, but it was not helping tonight.

"How did it go?" Mienme's voice came from the window.

Gao stood up, opened the door. Mienme pulled herself through the window by her arms, still the adventurous girl she had always been. "Worse and worse," he said, and proceeded to tell her everything that had happened.

"Actually," she said after he had finished his litany, "this could work out well for us."

"How can this be good?" Gao asked, accidentally swallowing the mass of mint in his mouth. "The restaurant is already nearly broke, and now we have to serve food fit for an official of the Third Rank. We'll be ruined — I'll be lucky if I escape with my head."

"Just listen," Mienme said. "Your father can't complain if you give all the best food to the royal mourning party — imagine what that jade token on the wall could do for business at his restaurant. So you can't be blamed for just serving him simple food, and when you do that the mourners will stop coming, and the party will be over."

"You may be right," he said slowly. He drew the token out from his belt pouch, ran his fingers over its cool, smooth surface. "Yes, of course. If we're cooking for the Emperor's uncle, he can't complain if we give him nothing but rice and millet gruel. Even the Judge of Fate couldn't complain." He held the token up against the wall. "I must have done a very good deed in my last life to deserve you."

"In that case," she said, grinning impishly, "come here and give me a kiss while you're still all minty."

Sometimes he wondered if her parents knew their daughter at all.

The next morning he was up at dawn, fishing carp out of the pond in the back garden. Once the fish were splashing in their wooden bucket he took his small knife and cut a half-dozen lilies from the surface of the pond to make into a sauce for the fish — fish fresh enough for the Emperor's uncle. These were the last two items he needed for the day's meals; after making sure the jade token was still in his belt pouch he went into the kitchen, put on his grocery basket, and went out into the front room. His father's ghost was regaling two sleepy mourners with his adventures, while several more lay sprawled on sleeping mats around the room.

"—of course, a pig that smart you don't eat all at — nhoGao, do you have breakfast ready already?"

"I can't cook for you today, father, remember? I left a crabmeat and pork casserole in the oven, you can ask one of the mourners to get it out for you in a few hours, and I'll send you dumplings for the afternoon."

"Of course, of course — I'd almost forgotten. You'll do us proud at the palace, I'm sure — and what a story it'll make, cooking for the Emperor's uncle." Despite his words he did not seem very happy, and Gao wondered if he was finally starting to fade. Crab and pork casserole was not exactly gruel, but it was not the food Doi Thiviei was used to, either. He felt a sudden pain in his chest, and hoped that if his father were to depart today it would not be until after he got back to the restaurant.

He had never been to the palace before. Despite the fact that it was at the centre of the city, few people ever received an invitation to go. Those who went without an invitation, hoping to poach the Emperor's white deer, usually wound up as permanent guests — or came home over the course of several days, one piece at a time. As he reached the gate he could not help worrying that the whole thing had been a colossal hoax, that the guards would take his jade seal and his groceries and send him away. When he showed them the token, however, they stood to either side of the gate, and one was assigned to lead him to the palace kitchens.

"How long ago did the noble official die?" Gao asked the soldier.

The man walked a few steps in silence before finally answering. "Yesterday afternoon," he said. Like most soldiers he had a heavy provincial accent, which perhaps explained his reluctance to speak. "Didn't you hear the bells?"

"I've been busy," Gao muttered. "Have you seen his ghost?"

The soldier again kept silent for a few moments, then spoke, no expression crossing his face. "No. But I hear it is very pale. He was an old man, and sick for a long time."

Gao cursed inwardly. Except for short, violent deaths, long illnesses were the worst. They left a person glad to die, and not inclined to hang around too long afterward. He thanked the guard when they reached the kitchen and got to work unpacking his groceries. He had planned a light breakfast, fried wheat noodles sprinkled with sugar and black vinegar, in case the ghost was not too solid. Then he hoped that by lunch he would be able to serve the carp balls in lotus sauce and crisply fried eel to a more receptive audience.

It was not to be. The Emperor's uncle was vaporous, not interested in talking or even listening to the zither. The mourning party was somber, the guests mostly relatives and lower officials who were attending out of duty rather than friendship. They picked at the delicacies Gao served, leaving the rest for palace servants who could not believe their luck. The ghost, meanwhile, ate only a bite from each dish, pausing neither to smell nor taste any of them.

By mid-afternoon Gao was getting nervous. He had not managed to keep the Emperor's uncle from fading at all, knew that the official who had hired him would not be pleased. If he could have managed even two or three days things would have been all right, but if he could only make the royal ghost stay a day and a night it would look like an insult. He wished Mienme was there to help him.

Finally he resolved there was only one thing he could do: make the most elaborate, most spectacular dish he could, so that he would not be faulted for lack of effort. He settled on a recipe one of his brothers had found in a small village on the southern coast, mau anh dem — Yellow Lantern Fish. He sent a runner to the fish market for the freshest yellowfish he could find, telling him to look for clear eyes and a smell of seaweed. When the boy returned he began to carefully cut and notch the scaled, gutted fish and boil a deep pot of oil on a portable burner.

Minutes before dinner was due he ordered the burner be carried into the room where the mourning party was taking place, followed behind carrying the fish himself.

Though he could not look at the faces of any of the guests
he could tell few if any of them wanted to be there. The
most enthusiastic of them, if not the wisest, were using
this as an opportunity to get drunk. Even the zither player
sounded almost as though he was singing in his sleep.
At the middle of it all was the ghost, silent and uninterested
in what was going on around him.

Gao had the burner and pot of oil placed in front of the
royal ghost, waited a few minutes while the oil returned
to the proper temperature. Then, with enough of a flourish
to make sure all eyes were on him, he dropped the fish
into the oil. In seconds it blossomed out like a paper lantern, its flesh turning golden and crispy. It was a dish
designed to impress even the most jaded crowd, and it
did not fail him: the guests pressed forward to get a better
look and eagerly handed him their plates. Before the first
bite was taken, however, Gao knew he had failed. Unlike
the guests the Emperor's uncle was still withdrawn, uninterested, not bothering to eat or even smell the fish.

My life is over, Gao thought as he walked home. If the
Emperor's uncle had faded away by morning he would
be blamed, and that was sure to kill business if it did not
kill him. Just then he realized that in all of his worry about
the Emperor's uncle he had forgotten to send the lunch
dumplings he had made for his father's mourning party.
Without food the party was sure to have broken up by now,
his father likely faded away. He suddenly regretted not
listening to any of the stories his father had told over the
last few weeks, too busy cooking and worrying about the
restaurant. He had heard them all a dozen or more times,
but now might never get a chance to hear them again.

When he neared the restaurant, however, he saw lights
inside and heard voices. Creeping into the front dining
room he saw his father still holding court before a half-
dozen mourners, the room strewn with empty bowls and
teacups.

"nhoGao, is that you?" his father asked, spotting him
as he tried to slink past into the kitchen. "How did it go
at the palace?"

Gao shook his head slowly. "I am sorry I was not able to send you the food I made for the day," he said. "I was busy with—"

"Don't worry about us, we don't need food to keep the party going. Besides, I know where you hide the pig knuckles. Now, where was I—?"

Watching his father, more solid than ever, Gao wondered what it was he had done so wrong at the palace and so right here. He had made dishes for the Emperor's uncle that were twice as elaborate as anything he had ever made at the restaurant, but had left the royal ghost cold. His father, meanwhile, looked likely to remain among the living indefinitely on a diet of pig's knuckles. *I must be missing something*, he thought. *If only Mienme were here to help me think. She would say, if it's not the food—*

"Father, can you come with me for a few minutes?" he asked suddenly, interrupting his father in the middle of the story of the seo nuc game he had played against a beggar who had turned out to be an exiled general.

"I suppose," his father said, puzzled. "I can finish this story later. Where are we going?"

Without pausing to answer his father's questions Gao rushed back to the palace, flashing the jade token to the puzzled guard. The mourning party was down to just a few diehards, likely trying to win points with the Emperor. The royal ghost was hardly visible, a thin grey mist barely recognizable as once having been human.

"Please excuse me, noble officials," Gao said, dropping to the floor and bowing low. "I forgot the most important part of the mourning party."

A few seconds of silence passed as the guests watched him curiously, wondering what he was going to produce that might top the Yellow Lantern Fish. Finally his father said, "What a glum group. Reminds me of my father the day our prize rooster died, the one who would crow everytime a rich customer was coming—" The guests looked at the chatty ghost in amazement, but Gao's father made straight for the Emperor's uncle. "Did he try to feed you that Temple Style Duck? I only ask because you're look-

ing a little thin. The first time I met one of those South-
erners I thought they were crazy, won't eat meat, won't
eat fowl, not even fish. But I met one who was a wizard
with rice — learned a few tricks from him—"

By the time dawn came Doi Thiviei and the Emperor's
uncle were chatting like old friends. The royal ghost was
looking much more substantial and even accepted one of
the sesame balls with hot lotus paste Gao had made for
breakfast.

"Gao, I think I'll stay here awhile," his father said. "I
hope it won't disappoint my mourners, but I've gotten a
little tired of hearing my own voice. Take good care of my
restaurant, will you?"

"Of course," Gao answered, ladling out the clear soup
he had made from chicken stock and the last of the qinshon
leaves.

"And I suppose you'll be marrying that Southerner girl
and changing the name your mother and I gave you. I
know you've never liked it, though it's a good story how
you got it."

Gao frowned. "I always thought it was because... well,
my face... and I always had to make it for the customers
who couldn't afford anything else."

"No, no," his father said. "It wasn't like that at all. You
see, when I first met your mother — but I suppose you
don't have time to hear this story."

Gao sat down, took a sip of the soup, enjoying the fragile
flavour of the qinshon. He only allowed himself one bowl
a year, to be sure he would appreciate it. "I have plenty
of time, father," he said. "Only please, let me go get Mienme
so she can hear it as well. We will both need to know this
story so we can tell it to our children."

It turned out his father had lots of stories he had never
told; or maybe Gao had just never heard them before.

Go Tell The Phoenicians

by Matthew Hughes

The K'fondi were driving Livesey and his BOOT team three stops past crazy, but that was not why the station chief hated me at first sight.

Mainly it was my record, which was laying itself out as Livesey tapped the panel of his desk display. I held myself at something like attention, set my lumpy features on bland, and looked over the chief's regulation haircut to where the window framed the unknown hills of K'fond.

"If Sector Administrator Stavrogin wasn't biting my backside, you'd never have set down on my planet," Livesey said, "but I promise you, Kandler, while you're attached to this establishment, you'll go *by the book*. Or I'll chase you all the way back to Earth and bury you in whatever stinking kelp farm you oozed out of."

There was more, but I had heard the like from the ranking Bureau of Offworld Trade field agent at just about every assignment I could remember. I was a foreign body in the Bureau's innards, a maverick among a tamer breed, tolerated only because I was also BOOT's best exo-sociologist. But whenever I was sent in, it was a sign that the field agent in charge was out of his depth. If I turned out to be the reason a mission was successful, a corresponding black mark went into the file of the BOOT bureaucrat who had screwed up.

They sent me in because I got results. But the day this stopped, the uneasy symbiosis between me and the Bureau

would fall apart. With luck, I might land at a Bureau training depot, lecturing batches of budding Liveseys on the
intricacies of the ancient alien cultures they'd be learning how to loot.

Without luck, I'd be back on Argentina's Valdés Pen-
insula, stacking slimy bales of wet kelp, just as my father
had done until he wore out and died. So I kept my mouth
shut through the chief's opening rant, and watched a
gaggle of K'fondi boost each other over the station's
perimeter fence. They frolicked across the clipped lawn
like teenagers at the beach.

Livesey turned to follow the direction of my gaze, swore
bitterly, and punched his desk com.

"Security," he said, "they're back! Get them herded off
station! Move!"

The aliens wandered over and gawked through Livesey's
window, giving me my first look at K'fondi. They were
the most humanoid race Earth had ever found. On the
outside, a K'fond could pass for any fair sized, bald human
who happened to be thin-lipped, large-nosed and shaded
from pink to deep purple.

Closer examination revealed subtle differences in joints
and musculature, but the K'fondi were a delight to those
exo-biologists who argued that parallel evolution would
produce intelligent species that roughly resembled each
other. We could breathe what the K'fondi breathed, drink
what they drank, eat what they ate.

No one knew what K'fondi were like on the inside, but
there would be some major differences. For one thing, they
were thought to lay eggs.

Security heavies arrived to coax the natives off the
station. None of them seemed to mind. One departing
visitor was slinkily female — even without breasts — in
an almost sheer gown slit on both sides from shoulder to
knee. She paused for a parting wave and a broad wink
through the window.

Livesey leaned his forehead against the window's plastic and swore with conviction. "Tell me how I'm supposed
to negotiate a trade agreement when they treat this station
like some kind of holiday camp?"

"Is it just the local kids come to look around?" I said.

Livesey turned with a glare of bewildered outrage. "As far as I can tell, that was their negotiating team. Go get briefed."

Outside, the K'fond air was rich and unfiltered, the slightly less than Earth-normal gravity added a spring to my step, and I headed for my quarters in a tingle of excitement. I loved the beginning of every new assignment, ahead of me a whole alien culture to explore. It was almost enough to let me forget that the Bureau of Offworld Trade would use my work to help pick the K'fondi clean.

I hated BOOT, but the Bureau was the only path to field experience for an exo-sociologist. It was an arm of the Earth Corporate State, the final amalgamation of the Permanent Managerial Class of multinational corporations and authoritarian regimes that had coalesced just as humankind took its first steps toward the stars.

For a bright boy who ached to escape from Permanent Under Class status, who thirsted to meet and encompass the strange logics of alien cultures, BOOT was the only game in the galaxy — and I'd played it my whole career.

Brains and a willingness to outwork the competition had taken me from my parents' shack through scholarships and graduate school, then out into the immensity on Bureau ships. Now, with a score of alien cultural topographies mapped to my credit, every new assignment was more precious than the last.

Soon, I would be ordered out of the field, sent back to a plain but secure retirement back on Earth. I could settle into a university chair, write a textbook and train the next generation of bright boys and girls who would assist the Bureau in its beads-and-trinkets trade.

Beads and trinkets were Livesey's vocation, and it was an ancient calling. The Phoenicians started it off, tricking neolithic Britons into accepting a few baskets of brightly colored ceramics for a boatload of precious tin ore. Later, the Portuguese traded cloth for gold, the French and English gave copper pots for bales of furs, or worn-out muskets for manloads of ivory.

Every planet had something worth taking: a rare element, a natural organic that would cost millions to synthesize on Earth, a precious novelty to delight the wealthy and powerful. And on each world, the natives could use something Earth could supply.

If the aliens could have haggled in Earth's markets, they would have got fair value. But only Earth had lucked into the ridiculously unlikely physics behind the Dhaliwal Drive. As in the days of the Phoenicians, he who has the ships sets the price.

Earth's corporate rulers would have had no moral objections to conquest, but systematic swindling was far cheaper and the PMC were leery about arming and training the PUC. There was no Space Navy to eat up the profits from the beads and trinkets trade. For the aliens, and for me, it was just too bad.

My job now was to get a handle on K'fond culture, particularly its economics, and tell Livesey what technological baubles the locals would jump at. In my spare time before rotation back to the Bureau sector base, I might be able to work up a paper for the journals.

But the trade agreement came first. That was in the book, and the Bureau went by the book.

My quarters were in a row of standard-issue station huts. I threw my gear onto the cot and turned to the stack of data nodes on the compcom desk that was the only other furniture. I plugged in the first one and the screen lit up.

There was nothing remarkable about the report of the seed ship that had discovered K'fond. I sped up the readout and skimmed the highlights. Unmanned craft passes by, drops robot orbiter, moves on. Orbiter maps surface and analyzes features until its programs deduce the presence of cities. Orbiter opens sub-space channel to Office of Explorations sector base and tells OffEx about K'fond.

Then OffEx base reports to headquarters on Earth, which commissions a K'fond file and copies it to BOOT. BOOT puts together Livesey's team and sends them from the nearest sector base to establish contact. Every step neatly marked by its own cross-referenced memo. By the book.

But the pages started falling out when Livesey's team tried contact procedures. I plugged in the project diary, saw Livesey bring his ship into orbit over K'fond. I checked the time code: given the slowness of bureaucratic response and the temporal dilation effect of the Dhaliwal Drive, about three standard years had elapsed since first discovery. And in those three years, BOOT's robot orbiter had somehow gone missing.

Things only got worse for Livesey. He ran out the ship's ears to eavesdrop on surface communications; all were intricately scrambled. He dropped clouds of small surveillance units; each stopped broadcasting shortly after entering the atmosphere. The book said his next option was a manned descent, and Livesey had already chosen volunteers when the ship's com received a signal from the surface.

In clear, unaccented Earth Basic, someone said, "Welcome to K'fond. You are invited to land at the site indicated on your screen. Please do not divert from the entry path we have plotted for you."

The com screen showed a map of the smallest of K'fond's three continents; a series of concentric circles flashed around the spot where Livesey was to put down.

I laughed. The terse prose of the official diary did not record Livesey's outrage when the cherished contact procedures were brushed aside. But I could imagine the chief's fear at making planetfall without a bulging file of information garnered from the ship's spy gear and the missing orbiter's surveys.

Livesey and three others had dropped down to a field several kilometers west of a K'fond town. The video showed a small crowd of aliens clustered around the shuttle. Then the scene shifted to visuals taken by the contact team as they emerged from the craft. I slowed the image speed and looked closely.

A dozen K'fondi of both sexes were coming toward me. No two were dressed alike, their garments ranging from flowing robes to close-fitting coveralls. One female wore nothing but a metal bracelet. I magnified her image; egg-layer or not, except for the absent navel, she looked scarcely less mammalian than many fashion models. I tracked to an almost nude male, and saw the pronounced sexual differentiation.

I thumbed the flow speed back to normal and saw what Livesey had seen. The K'fondi flocked toward the contact team like kids let out of school. The BOOT men were jostled and seized, and the camera showed one agent tentatively reaching for his needle sprayer. But the aliens were patently friendly and curious. They fingered the Earthmen's clothing, plucked at hair, chattering non-stop amid what looked much like human smiles and laughter.

It was like seeing a first contact between Europeans and the peoples of the South Pacific five hundred years ago. But that reminded me of what had been done to those long-gone dwellers in paradise by the "civilized" visitors they had rushed out to welcome.

I looked at the glad K'fondi faces. "Hey, have we got a deal for you," I said to the screen.

The tapes of later contacts chronicled Livesey's descent into frustration. The K'fondi really did act like rambunctious teenagers on a holiday. And yet many of them showed what I thought were signs of aging. I flipped forward to one of the "negotiating" sessions.

A chaos of K'fondi chatter dominated an outdoor table somewhere on the station. None of them spoke Basic, and Livesey was struggling through sign language and the few words of local speech the lingolab had identified. The K'fondi were not listening. Some were passing around a flask. One couple left off nuzzling each other to slide beneath the table, and began demonstrating the similarities of K'fond and human love-making. Livesey put his forehead to the table and groaned.

I speed-ran the other tapes, witnessing several more encounters between BOOT and the alien race. I didn't bother with the file of correspondence between Livesey and sector base; I could imagine the SectAd's memos advancing from neutral to querulous to plain nasty. If the chief didn't get results here fast, BOOT would demote him so far down the hierarchy he'd need a miner's helmet to find his desk.

Which meant he'd be leaning hard on me to get those results for him.

The problem was simple: the K'fondi didn't make any sense. They had a high-tech culture, and somebody on the planet could beam a message to an orbiting Bureau ship in a language no K'fond should have known. Yet the K'fondi who came on station acted like eighteenth century Trobriand Islanders on their day off.

The language puzzle intrigued me. I buzzed the station switchboard and was connected with the lingolab. The call was answered by a harassed man of middle years who introduced himself as Senior Linguist Walter Mtese. He gave me directions to his lab.

I stepped out from my hut into a warm mid-afternoon. This part of K'fond seemed a mellow, balanced place. Temperature, humidity, even the light breeze were perfectly matched. An occasional cloud threw interesting shapes on the distant slopes, and the air was soft and good on my face. *A place to settle down in*, I thought. But that kind of thinking led nowhere. Earth law prohibited residence anywhere the state couldn't keep an eye on you, and that left Earth as the only option.

I cut between two storage huts and came suddenly face to face with the K'fondi Livesey had had thrown off the station a couple of hours before. I observed that they liked close physical contact on first encounter; in fact, it couldn't get much closer than the way the pink female snaked her arms around my neck. Her skin was smooth and hot — K'fond body temperature was equivalent to a human's raging fever. She smelled indefinably of fruit.

"Jiao doh vuh?" she inquired.

I tried to gently shrug off the weight of her arms. Physical contact between human and alien on first encounter can represent anything from a polite greeting to an indiscriminate appetite. The correct response was to try to imitate the gesture offered, according to the Bureau book. But as she pressed her chest against me and followed with her hips, I realized that going by the book this time would involve seriously violating several BOOT regulations.

With smiles and soft-voiced disclaimers, I disentangled myself and stepped back. The pink woman shrugged very humanly and said something to her companions, then they all wandered around the corner of the building without a backward glance. Seconds later, I heard a human voice shout "Hey!" followed by a burst of K'fond giggles. Then the group came pelting back around the corner, pursued by two puffing guards. I flattened myself against the supply hut and let the chase roll by. The K'fondi were enjoying the game.

Walter Mtese wasn't enjoying the K'fondi, I found when I entered his lingolab. Mtese was pure Bureau. A pattern of commendations and certificates decorated his walls, testaments to the linguist's integration into the BOOT view of the universe. But for a successful bureaucrat, Mtese looked a harried man.

"I think someone's playing an elaborate practical joke on us," he complained, as he hooked me up to the snore-couch. "These people get by with a vocabulary of under a thousand words, most of which have to do with sex, booze and bodily functions. Tell me how that's compatible with a technological civilization."

"How are they at learning Basic?" My voice sounded strange in the confines of the headpiece he was fitting over my ears.

"They don't learn anything," Mtese answered. "I spent a whole morning — that's six standard hours — trying to teach two of them ten words. I'd have had more luck training snakes to tapdance. Give me your arm, please."

I felt the hypo's aerosol coolness. Subjective time slowed as the drugs depressed selected regions of my nervous system while goosing others into hyperawareness. Around a tongue now grown larger than the head that contained it, I managed to speak.

"What does 'jiao doh vuh' mean?"

Mtese snorted as he punched codes into the snore-couch controls. "It's the standard greeting between males and females, usually answered in the affirmative, and followed by immediate direct action. It's a wonder they've got the energy to walk."

The snore-couch's headset began murmuring in my ears, the drugs took hold, and Mtese and the lingolab evaporated into golden warmth as the machine flooded my neurons with incoming freight.

➤►I◄►I◄

Back at my hut, I found that knowing K'fondish was no big help. As the last wisps of Mtese's chemicals effervesced out of my brain, I re-ran Livesey's encounter tapes. The linguist was right: K'fondish conversation was at the level of the street corner banter of good-natured juvenile delinquents — simple, direct, and highly scatological. If the alien who had spoken in Basic over the ship's com was one of the "negotiating team," he was keeping his mouth shut.

Livesey's records and the lingolab had taught me all they could. The next step, by the book, was first-hand field contact. According to procedures, that meant encountering the natives under controlled conditions, on station ground, and guided by a welter of Bureau regulations devised by bureaucrats who had never left Earth. I saw no reason to repeat Livesey's failure. Besides, it was always more instructive to meet aliens on their own turf.

The transport pool guard refused me a ground car without an authorized requisition. He was still refusing as I wheeled a two-seater out of its stall and waved my way past gate security. The highway was wide, flat and empty. I urged the car up to cruising speed, took the center of the road, and headed east. Five minutes from the station, I reached under the instrument panel and pulled loose a connection. Now the car's location transmitter couldn't tell tales on me. I nudged my speed a little higher, and went looking for K'fondi. Though none were in sight, I saw herd animals grazing near the shores of a lake that swept across the horizon to lap against the geometry of the town's central core.

As I drove deeper into the outskirts, I observed that the quality of this planet's technology was obvious in the town's agricultural zone. A house-sized harvester trundled through a field, collecting a nut-like fruit that emerged packed in transparent containers from the harvester's rear port. A flatbed truck with a grapple followed along, stacking the containers on itself in precise rows. Neither machine had an operator.

The highway connected with a grid of local and arterial roads, and I met up with other traffic. Self-directed trucks and driverless transports neatly avoided my passage, or maintained pace with me at exact, unvarying distances. Then the traffic dropped away down side roads as the highway took me into the residential suburbs.

Neat houses of painted wood or colored stone were intermixed with towers faced in metal or glass. The town looked lived-in — I saw lawns that needed a trim, a fence that was giving in to gravity, and one cracked window mended with tape. It was only after a few minutes that I realized I wasn't seeing any K'fondi. The streets were deserted.

The emptiness began to play on my nerves. Field work can be dicey. Trampling on a society's direst taboos is so easy when you have no idea what they are.

Maybe this part of the town was forbidden, or this time of day had to be spent indoors. Maybe it was death to approach this place from the west. Maybe... anything. At the university, we'd all heard the story of the technician who'd casually swatted a buzzing insect. He had protested that he had not known that that particular species was "sacred for the day," as the alien priests had apologetically proceeded to dismember him.

I finally found the K'fondi, lots of them, as I nosed the car out of a side street onto the lake drive. I was suddenly in a town square, beachfront and park all rolled into one, and it was the site of a fiesta that made Rio's Carnaval look like a Baptist church social. Knots of K'fondi surged in a cheerful frenzy through a crowd so dense it flowed like fleshy liquid. Some kind of music thumped and screeched loud enough for me to experience it as repeated *tumpa-tumpas* on my chest. K'fondi in a grab-bag of costumes bobbed to the rhythm or gyrated with flailing elbows along the edge of the mob. As I stopped the car, an eddy of the crowd swirled around me. One dervish began beating out a tattoo on the engine compartment, while a large female jumped onto the hood and began a dance that had various parts of her moving in several different directions at once.

More K'fondi joined her, making the car sag and groan on its suspension. I mentally ran through all the time-tested phrases recommended for first encounters, but with this crowd I realized that I might as well declaim Homer in the original Greek.

The car was rocking steadily faster, and common sense said it was time to bail out. The crowd swallowed me the way an amoeba takes in a drifting speck. Aliens pressed me from all sides, but none paid me any attention. My head seemed to shrink and swell with the sound of the music.

Way back in school, in an attempt to make us grateful that the ECS had rescued our world from self-destructive hedonism, they'd shown us images of rock concerts from the Decadent Period. What I was experiencing among the K'fondi must have been the kind of sheer fun those old DP mass gatherings had looked to be.

The music wound down to a last sub-sonic rumble and crashed in an auditory rain of metal. As the sound dwindled, I could hear voices again, even pick out words I now recognized. The crowd began to thin around the knoll. Some went splashing into the lake. Others drifted back toward town or into the trees further up the shore. And some couples entwined arms and legs, sliding down each other to the ground.

I scanned the departing remnants of the crowd. A few metres away, I thought I saw the pink female from the station among a handful of K'fondi skirting the knoll. Or it may have been a complete stranger — learning to tell aliens apart can take practice. I hurried to catch up, fell in beside her, and touched her wrist. She turned without slowing, and regarded me with scant interest.

"Jiao doh vuh?" she asked, and my lingolab-educated brain translated the phrase as "Do you want to?"

"Do I want to what?"

She looked puzzled for a moment. "It's just what people say."

I said, "My name is Kandler. I'd like to talk to you."

"Why talk?"

"Talking is what I do."

Her shrug was almost human, and I took it as an acquiescence. "I want a drink," she said, heading toward a row of low-rises bordering the park.

The K'fond bar could have blended into most Earth streetscapes, if you ignored the unusual colors of the patrons. When we had found seats at a table in the back that was crowded with her friends, I learned that the pink woman's name was Chenna — no surname or honorific, I noted — and that the town was called Maness. Chenna's friends remained anonymous. I could just barely hold her attention long enough to ask a question and receive an indifferent reply. Everyone else in the bar was enjoying the outpourings of a couple on a small stage, who were tootling some kind of flute that had two mouthpieces. I was thankful it was purely an acoustic instrument; my eardrums still hurt from the pummeling they had taken in the park.

A robot server brought us a round of drinks without being summoned. I sniffed the tall frosty tumbler, and recognized the same fruity aroma that had lingered around Chenna at the station. The concoction tasted sweet and dry. I waited a few moments to learn if I would be racked by intense pains or stop breathing. When nothing much happened, I judged the drink safe and took another sip.

By saying her name a couple of times, I got Chenna's attention again, and posed a few more questions. No, she didn't work, although it seemed to her that she might have once had some kind of job. She thought she hadn't been in Maness very long, but it was hard to tell.

If Chenna was hazy on her own personal history, the rest of K'fond society was nonexistent to her. I couldn't find a word in my new vocabulary for "government," but I tried to phrase a question about who got things done on K'fond.

"Machines," she replied airily, waving to the robot for another round. I drained my glass and reached for a second.

"But who tells the machines what to do?"

Chenna actually looked as if she was rummaging through her mind for an answer. But then she laid her cheek on an upturned palm and said, "Who cares?"

I put away my exo-soc question kit and opted for passive observation. The bar was filling up. The flute players had given way to an *a capella* group that seemed to know only four notes, but the K'fondi happily sang along with them.

A male at another booth took some kind of cigar from a box on the table, and tried to light it with what looked like an elementary flint and steel lighter. When he couldn't get a spark, he persisted in thumbing the device with increasing frustration. Finally, he slammed the lighter to the floor and followed it with the cigar.

I rose and retrieved the battered object. A quick examination showed that the screw holding the steel ratchet to its mount was loose. With a twist of my thumbnail, I tightened the screw, and flicked the action. A flame wavered on the wick. I doused the flame and put the lighter back on the owner's table. The K'fond picked it up, flicked it alight, and pulled another cigar from the box. I received not even a glance as the alien blew smoke toward the stage.

Back at Chenna's table a third round had arrived. I sipped and watched, and listened to the surrounding conversations. It was like Livesey's contact sessions: a lot of laughs, and half the words spoken were the K'fondish equivalents of "hey" and "wow" and the details of amorous adventures.

The fruit drink tasted good, felt good inside. But I noticed that the room had now begun to expand and contract in rhythm with my own heartbeat. That made me laugh, which made me wonder why I was laughing so loud. Chenna was looking at me now; they all were. I found it odd when their faces were abruptly replaced by the bar's ceiling, and I tried to figure out what the hard flat something was that was pressing itself against my back. Then the world turned black and gently fell on me.

✤✛✤✛✤

"I've been reading your job description," Livesey said. "It doesn't say that an exo-soc steals ground cars, leaves the station without permission, and is found at the gate giggling and smelling like a fruit basket. At least you had sense enough to program your car to bring you back."

I didn't think now was the time to correct the chief. Time enough later to wonder how a K'fond could figure out which end of the ground car was the front — never mind how to program an offworld computer.

I had expected Livesey to chew me out, but the chief seemed to have passed through rage and frustration while I was still in sick bay. He was now settling into acid despair. He spun his chair away from me and gazed with helpless hate at K'fond's hills.

"Actually," he told the window, "you were more useful in a drugged stupor than you've been conscious. The bio-chem techs pumped some interesting stuff out of your stomach. It might make a decent anesthetic or a recreational lifter for the PMC youth market back home.

"Either way, it won't be enough to save us." Livesey swung back to face me. "As a purely formal question, I don't suppose you learned anything worth knowing from your little jaunt?"

I had been asking myself the same thing since I had woken up, sore-throated from the stomach pump. The drug in the fruit drink left me feeling reasonably fine, and the part of my brain that lived to puzzle out alien social patterns had gone right to work.

"Yes," I said. "Item one, that's a real city over there, not a backdrop whipped up to fool us.

"Item two: the K'fondi who live there really live there. They're not actors putting on a show for our benefit.

"Item three: their technology is at least equal to our best.

"Item four: the K'fondi we've seen couldn't possibly have created that technology; they can't even repair a simple machine.

"Item five: something funny is going on. There's a piece missing from this puzzle, and if we can find it, or even figure out its basic shape, the rest of the pattern will fall into place."

Livesey grunted. "You're as stumped as I am. We've been looking for that missing piece of information since we landed. You want to hear our working hypotheses?"

He didn't wait for an answer but ticked off the options on his fingers, "Maybe the K'fondi we see are the mentally deficient. Maybe they're just the pets of the real dominant species. Or the whole place is run by supercomputers their great-great-granddaddies built while their descendants have declined into idiocy. For all we know, they're just a planetful of practical jokers having a good laugh on us."

The station chief smacked the desk. "But, dammit, somebody gave me landing coordinates in Basic. Somebody is scrambling all microwave communications. Somebody knocked out the survey orbiter. And, having done that, our mysterious somebody has apparently lost all interest in us."

"You're wrong," I said. "Our mysterious somebody is very interested. He's hanging back and watching. And if he won't come to us, we'll have to go find him. And by 'we' I mean me."

"Go ahead," Livesey snorted. "Take all the time you want, so long as you're finished in the next week."

"A week? This could take months. I've got to..."

"You'll be finished in a week," Livesey interrupted, "because I'll be finished in a week. That's when SectAd Stavrogin arrives. Here's the signal." He waved a flimsy at me. "I'm being demoted and shipped back to Earth, as soon as Stavrogin settles in. And, Kandler, I'm taking you with me. Under arrest."

"What, for appropriating a ground car?"

"No, I'm sure I'll think of something better. And, between my remaining authority and your record, I'll make it stick."

"But why?"

"Because I don't like you." Livesey spun back to the window. The interview was over.

✦✦✦✦

I couldn't just lie on my bunk and wait for Stavrogin. I re-ran the diaries, looking for some clue, some insignificant piece of data to ring the alarm bells in my unconscious. But I saw nothing that helped, just more frolicking K'fondi, more remote scans of distant cities, too far away for any detail. Livesey's orbiting ship was not equipped for close-in scan; the exploration orbiter was supposed to be there to handle that chore, with ultrascopes that could count the blades of grass in a square meter of the planet's nightside from fifty kilometers up. But the orbiter was gone, and since — according to the Bureau's book — it was impossible for an orbiter to be gone, there was no provision for getting another one. Maybe Stavrogin would have the clout to get a new high-orbit probe. And maybe I would read all about the solution to the K'fond puzzle back on Earth — if a newspaper ever blew over the fence of the punishment farm.

I paced and considered the situation. The K'fondi had put the station where they wanted it. All attempts to surveil other parts of the planet had been stopped. So, whatever they were hiding must be somewhere down the road from Maness.

Which meant taking a trip down that road and looking around. A ground car or flyer would probably bring me into hard contact with whatever had knocked out the spy drones. And if the K'fondi preferred to shoot first and sift the wreckage later, I would end up in some alien coroner's in-basket. But there was another way: risky, but I thought it just might work.

Then I paced out my own situation. If Livesey meant to sweeten the bitter taste of his failure by kicking me into prison, why should I spend my last days of freedom helping the Bureau?

If I solved the K'fond mystery, Livesey would still probably go under; even last-minute success couldn't divert BOOT discipline once it was wound up and set loose. Livesey, falling, would use me as something soft to land on. Livesey, saved, would ruin me out of sheer spite.

But I wouldn't be doing it for the Bureau or the chief. This was for *me*. I had always needed to know what made alien societies tick, and if making the pickings easier for ECS's interstellar swindlers was the price of that knowledge, then it was a price I was at least used to paying.

Before I was dragged off K'fond and chained to a bulkhead, I wanted to know what the hell was going on.

Five minutes later, I walked into the supply hut and began pulling things off the shelves. The quartermaster clerk decided he had better things to do than to ask questions of an eco-soc with a reputation for lunatic behavior. In the medical stores I found an antiseptic wash that dyed the skin. A jump suit stripped of its Bureau insignia would pass at medium range for a K'fond coverall. I scooped up a belt and pouch, which I filled with rations, depilatory creams, and some other useful items. Finally, I took a geologist's hammer to the arms locker and selected a small pulser that tucked into the palm of my hand.

The motor pool guard was prepared this time to stand his ground when a purple Kandler climbed into a surface car. But the pulser's output end convinced him to decamp quickly enough to avoid being run down.

On the open road, the wind of the car's passage chilled my newly bald head. Where I began to meet Maness's automated local traffic, I turned at the first major intersection and drove on for a couple of kilometers. I parked the car on the side road's grass border, pulled out the connections on the com panel to stop its annoying chirping, and settled down to watch the robot trucks go by.

Before the long K'fond day drifted into evening, I spotted the kind of transport I had been looking for. But, fully loaded, it was outward bound. I marked its size and characteristics, and was able to identify the same kind of vehicle heading empty in the direction of Maness. I put the car back on the road and followed.

The empty truck wove through an increasingly dense grid of industrial streets. Here there were no houses, and apparently no K'fondi were needed to run the automatic factories. The truck pulled into a side street leading to a low-rise, open-sided building. By the sound and smell of the place, I knew it was what I was looking for.

I slowed the car to a crawl as it bypassed the street the truck had turned onto. Pushing a few buttons on the car's console told it to go home and it whirred away, leaving me alone on the empty street.

It was now full dark, and the K'fondi hadn't bothered with many streetlights in this part of town. Keeping to the abundant shadows, I crept around the rear of the building where the truck had gone. The vehicle was nudged up against a loading ramp, behind which was a corral full of tapir-like creatures with curly horns and sad, muted voices. By the ringing in my ears, I judged they were being induced into the trucks by some kind of general sonic prod. No herders, either live or robot, were in sight.

That made it easier. I hopped the corral fence and stooped to hide among the cattle. Gritting my vibrating teeth against the sonics, I bulled my way up a ramp and into a slat-sided transport. The animals stamped and brayed at my smell; for me, the feeling was mutual. Inside the truck, the sonics were damped. I crouched in a rear corner.

The truck soon filled. Its rear gate swung closed, and the engine murmured through the floorboards. The vehicle jerked forward, sending a set of horns scraping across my back. It turned to exit the stockyard, and then it stopped.

I held my breath. Were sensors in the truck reacting to my shape or size or the smell of my sweat? Would alarms suddenly ring, floodlights sweep toward me, robot cops come to hustle me off to the interrogation rooms? But then the engine coughed and, with another lurch, we were mobile again. A few minutes later, I was rolling out of Maness. My compass told me we were heading north.

The chill bars of first light through the truck's slats brought me awake. I had spent the night in a hay-filled corner, pressed by warm bodies, and dozing despite the cattle's tendency to snore. I got up, stretched, and peered out at the suburbs of a city. It could have been Maness, except that it was bigger, lacked a lake, and was built halfway up a mountain range that rivaled the Andes. By my rough reckoning, I was five hundred kilometers from the station. I should be out of any K'fond quarantine zone.

The truck was now well into the city's industrial district. Time to move — my fellow passengers might be heading directly for the whirring blades of an automated slaughterhouse. I climbed the truck's side and sliced through its fabric top with a knife from my belt pouch. I boosted myself up and out, clinging now to the outside of the vehicle. I lowered myself until my feet dangled over the pavement blurring along below. When the truck slowed for a curve, I hit the street running.

Seconds later, I was your average K'fond, purple and bald, taking an early morning constitutional through the city's empty streets. A broad avenue led down toward the heart of the city, and a half-hour's walk brought me into a grid of residential streets. In a postage-sized park near a high-rise complex I found enough undergrowth to keep me out of sight. I'd lie low until the K'fondi came out of their homes, then blend in with all the other purple and pink inhabitants.

I ate some rations behind a screen of fern-like plants and watched for pedestrians. About the time the morning chill began to fade, a naked K'fond child — the first I'd ever seen — came out of a high-rise and walked down the footpath to stand by a striped post. Another approached from up the street, then several more. *Bus stop*, I thought. And the long passenger vehicle that soon came to pick the children up must be a school bus. As it left, more children arrived to wait for the next one.

So far, I had seen no adults, but with the K'fond commitment to partying, sleeping late would be normal.

As the third busload of children rolled away, there was a noise behind me. I turned to see three kids entering the park from the opposite side. Naked as all the others, these wore belts and holsters carrying lightweight toy weapons. *Playing cops and robbers,* I told myself, and hunkered lower behind the ferns. I didn't want to be taken for a K'fond child molester.

I could hear them approaching, talking rapid-fire K'fondish too fast for me to catch the meaning. They seemed to be passing my hiding place without noticing me. I held my breath. Then the ferns parted right in front of me, and I was crouching eye to eye with one of the kids.

"Uh, jiao doh vuh?" I tried.

"Oh, I really don't think so, Mr. Kandler," the child replied. "No adult would say that to a child, even if they weren't all biologically set to keep their distance from us." It took me a few moments to realize that I was being spoken to in clipped Earth Basic, and that the weapon leveled at my face was no plaything.

The child gestured with the gun. "This is a device we use on adults who pose a danger to themselves or others. It's harmless to them, but we're not sure how effective it would be on your nervous system, so it's set at maximum. I advise you not to do anything unreasonable."

As the child spoke, his two companions came through the undergrowth to triple the number of weapons now surrounding me at a discreet distance. Moments later, face down in the K'fond soil, I was efficiently stripped of everything but my jumpsuit. Then the children herded me out of the park and into a no-nonsense vehicle that had pulled up at the curb. I had the last of the three rows of seats to myself. The kids sat forward, facing me with weapons aimed.

"I suppose my disguise was pretty obvious," I said.

One of them replied, "The disguise was fine. At first we thought an adult had wandered into that meat transport. Then we took a closer look when you were on the road. But you could never have blended in here."

"Why not?"

For answer, the child waved at the cityscape unrolling beyond the car's windows. What I saw told me that, of course, they had to have spotted me immediately, disguise or not. To blend into this city's population, I would have had to make myself over as a small, pink, sexless doll with big eyes. The streets were full now, and not one of the K'fondi was an adult. It was a city of children.

"Where are you taking me?" I asked.

"To a place where some of us will talk to you."

I couldn't read the inscription on the building we arrived at, but it had government written all over it. The council chamber I was ushered into could have passed for the ECS seat of power in Belem — if everything hadn't been half-sized. But there was nothing diminutive about the authority of the K'fond children gathered around the gleaming, crescent-shaped table. I knew power when I met it.

They gave me a large enough chair and sat me down in the middle of the space enclosed by the crescent. For a few seconds, the K'fond world council looked me over in silence. Then the child at the center of the table's arc leaned across the glossy expanse. The voice was thin, but I didn't doubt the note of command it carried.

"Welcome to K'fond, Mr. Kandler. We've been looking forward to meeting you. Your personnel record told us more about the Earth Corporate State than a month's subspace communications."

"You've read my record? But how?" — then I got it — "You've been using the survey orbiter's com link to listen in."

"True, Mr. Kandler. We went up and got your probe shortly after it alerted your sector base. We don't mind telling you, its technology fascinated our scientists. And of course we were overjoyed to learn that interstellar travel is in fact possible.

"Which brings us to the point of our meeting. Mr. Kandler, what can you tell us about the Dhaliwal Drive?"

❖❖❖

Three days later, the station com center received and recorded a signal from the project's missing exo-soc. I reported that I had penetrated to the core of K'fond society and was "making progress." Then I signed off without waiting for a reply. It was my last direct communication with the station.

Two days after that, Sector Administrator Stavrogin arrived to take charge.

⊁⊹⊹⊹⊹⊰

If Livesey was everything a by-the-book Bureau chief should be, then Yuroslav Stavrogin was a sector administrator to delight the book's authors to the lowest flake of their flinty hearts. Pinch-faced and slim, with the eyes of a bored shark and the delicate hands of a Renaissance poisoner, he perched primly on the edge of a K'fond chair and waited. Beside him, Livesey looked nervously around the alien reception room and sweated. Through the open window came the sounds of Maness at play.

I watched through a concealed aperture as the brass cooled their heels. I remembered Stavrogin. Back at sector base, he had once made me rewrite a lengthy field report from scratch — a week's pointless work imposed on me for no discernible reason. When I was bold enough to ask why, he had coolly replied, "Because you need to be reminded of who I am, and of what you are not."

I closed the spy hole, picked up my new briefcase, and stepped through the door. Livesey's face opened in surprise, but Stavrogin knew better than to show his. Still, I was not what he had expected.

Yesterday, with the station in an uproar over the sector boss's arrival, a signal had come in. In clear Basic, a K'fond voice had specified that Livesey and Stavrogin, identified by name and rank, were instructed to present themselves at the Maness district office of the planet's government. Once again, detailed directions followed, and these had led the two Bureau officers to the building. A robot majordomo had shown them to the reception room and left them to stew a while. And then in walked their missing exo-soc.

"Kandler, where the hell have you..." Livesey spluttered, but was cut off by a mere lifting of Stavrogin's finger.

"Specialist Kandler," rustled the dry voice, "we can plot your recent itinerary later, but we are shortly to meet the K'fond trade negotiator. You will therefore advise us forthwith of the results of your fieldwork."

There was a desk and chair. I walked over and sat down. From my briefcase, I pulled a sheaf of paper and tossed it onto the desk. "My report," I said. "I won't give you the full details now; you can read it at your leisure. I'll just summarize.

"The K'fondi are a highly sophisticated culture, with a well advanced technology. They have been a unified planetary state for some centuries, long enough for the administrative apparatus to evolve into a kind of cooperative anarchy."

Stavrogin sniffed, but I elected not to notice.

"They are very interested in trade," I continued, "a great deal of trade, but only on rational terms."

Livesey burst in. "They're as rational as a bunch of spacers on Cinderella liberty. Drunken, fornicating..."

"Oh, those are just the adults," I laughed. "I'm talking about the kids."

Stavrogin's voice could have cut glass. "Tell it."

I leaned back in my chair, and put my feet on the desk.

"Well, it's that missing piece of information we were looking for. K'fond adults really are just about as useless as Livesey says. All they want to do is enjoy their retirement and make more little K'fondi. The eggs are almost a by-product, since they don't even tend their offspring after they're weaned.

"But the kids do all right," I continued. "Childhood is long here, very long. K'fondi reach intellectual maturity quite early, but puberty doesn't come along until thirty or forty years after. And they have drugs to hold their glands in check for another decade if they want to keep putting off sexual maturity.

"That gives them a whole working lifetime without distractions. They don't waste their youth in adolescent turmoil and fruitless rebellion, because adolescence comes at the end of life, not the beginning. They aren't bothered by sex or any of its complications, like jealousy or getting up to change diapers. The infants are cooperatively raised by older children.

"And when their glands finally get to them, and the hormones reduce their mental acuity to the level of alley cats, they settle into a place like Maness: a retirement community out in the country, with plenty of beds and bars. A few children stick around to patch up cuts and bruises, and protect the newborns until they can be shipped off to the nurseries."

Livesey snapped his fingers. "They're like those extinct fish, the ones that didn't mate until they were ready to die. What were they called?"

"Salmon," I said. "We didn't figure it out because the K'fondi made sure we didn't see their cities full of children or the few kids around Maness. So we kept looking at it from our own perspective, from the chicken's point of view."

"Chicken?" asked Livesey.

"Sure," I said. "To a chicken, an egg is just a means of getting a new chicken. But to an egg — or to a K'fond child — an adult chicken is just something you need to get a new egg."

"Fascinating in its place," Stavrogin cut in, "but we are about to negotiate a trade deal. You will advise."

I smiled. "Sorry, Mr. Sector Administrator. Appended to my report is my resignation from the Bureau, and appended to that is my surrender of citizenship in the Earth Corporate State. And these," I produced a document covered in cursive K'fondish script, "are my credentials as adviser to K'fond's economic committee. Shall we open negotiations?"

"You can't do that," Livesey said.

"He has done it," Stavrogin said, "though much good it will do him. Very well, 'Mr. Adviser' Kandler, you may

rot among your alien friends in this backwater. But trade
— if there is even to be any trade — will be on Bureau
terms; only Earth has the Dhaliwal Drive."

I smiled again. "Not for long, Stavrogin. These people
— *my* people, now — have had near-space travel for generations, but until now they've had nowhere to go but up
and down. They've always dreamed of reaching to the stars,
but didn't know how or even if it could be done. The survey
ship's passage answered the second question; and I had
enough of a layman's grasp of the Dhaliwal Drive to sketch
an answer to the first."

I put my hands behind my head and stretched back in
my chair. "They're smart and they have no distractions —
they'll roll out a prototype starship within a year."

Stavrogin's face went paler, while Livesey's grew dan-
gerously red. I held up a hand to forestall an outburst.

"We may decide not to deal with the ECS," I said. "After
all, there's a whole galaxy of civilized races that the Bureau
has been robbing. I'm sure they'll be interested in what
we have to offer."

Livesey looked to be on the verge of detonation. But
Stavrogin was struggling to recover. "I'm sure we can come
to some mutually satisfactory understanding," he said. "As
you say, there's a whole galaxy dependent on the trade
made possible by the Drive. There's still plenty for both
of us."

"You don't understand." I took my feet off the desk,
leaned over its polished surface, and said, "Go tell the
Phoenicians: beads and trinkets won't cut it any more.

"K'fond's main export will be starships."

Buttons
by Victoria Fisher

It is 1793. Early winter. A cathedral in Paris, France.

Mai sits on the floor in front of the altar, her bare feet stretched out in front of her, counting buttons from a jar that sits in the loop her dress makes on the ground. Each button she takes out and examines fondly; one makes her smile, another makes her sad.

Above her, bronze late afternoon sunlight streams through the window, illuminating the vaults of the ceiling.

She is alone in the church. Alone but for the flame of a candle clasped in the stone hand of a statue of a young medieval woman who smiles slightly.

Mai looks up suddenly. It's Felix, dressed incongruously in a well-made but shabby Victorian jacket and white shirt. He's out of place both in style of dress and in class; all the other people are dressed in the plain practicality of mid-Terror Paris.

"Are you ready?" asks Felix.

Mai looks back down at the buttons in her lap. "Yes," she says finally.

She scoops up the buttons with her hands and drops them back into the jar. They sound like water running, dripping; the end of a storm.

Mai leaves the jar on the altar, in front of the statue of the young Saint Geneviève and her candle-flame. Mai doesn't look back, but walks away.

As they leave the cathedral, the people around them are pushed aside as a party of people enter the church, heading quickly, purposefully for the altar. No one stops them, no priest rushes out — the priests are long gone from this sacred place.

Still Mai does not look back at the altar.

There is the sound of breaking, and the percussive shattering of a pottery jar behind them, followed by the sound of hundreds of buttons skittering across the marble floor...

Felix puts his arm gently on Mai's shoulder. She doesn't protest.

The scene around Mai and Felix ripples more and more as the sound of the buttons dissolves into the roar of tumbling water. With a final shudder, they flicker out of view, and the scene clears.

The altar is overturned and smashed. The buttons cover the floor like pebbles in a riverbed. The candlesticks have gone, stolen. The statue of Geneviève is missing its head, the white stone jagged and shattered over the floor and the altar. Its hand remains, still outstretched, clutching a candle which is still alight...

→►I◄►I◄►I◄←

Four years earlier, a candle flickers in the very early morning of a warm sunny July Tuesday. Mai leans over and blows it out. She has been working on repairing a rent in Amédée's shirt before the day starts, but now the grey pre-dawn light is filling the room and the job is finished.

The room is small and badly but completely furnished. Mai's brothers and sisters lie asleep. The youngest curls up beside her brothers, her hair strewn across her face. Mai lays the shirt on the foot of the bed and stands, stretching. She is already dressed.

In the hallway, Mai pauses to plait her hair, looking in the browned mirror on the wall. She puts on her white cap and makes a face at herself then grins as she turns away, amused. When she smiles her eyes reflect the grey light.

She tiptoes down the narrow stairs.

"Mai?" it is Mai's father, copying at his desk in the grey light of the window. His lined hands are stained blue from the ink. "Off so early?"

Mai nods, and kisses her father on his papery cheek.

"Be careful, Mai. They say the crowds will form again," her father is only half-serious. "I heard shouting in the street this morning."

Mai smiles in reply, but she heard it too. They have been hearing it for the past two days and nights.

As she walks to Madame's, a boy runs past, shouting indistinctly. He shouts something about the Bastille. He and the street are illuminated by the early morning sun. Red.

Midmorning, the same day, the single voice of a boy racing in the street has become many voices, all shouting and chanting together. Madame is upset, but the maids are too excited to attend to her.

Mai is afraid of losing her job, but the other maids only laugh when she hesitates. At any chance they get, they all crowd recklessly in the window, peering out at the crowds, jostling each other for space.

A young man waves his red cap at them, and they wave back, blushing and laughing.

"He's looking at you, Mai," teases Émilie.

Mai looks down and reddens even more; she's only fifteen.

They watch the men and women rush towards the Bastille, thousands of them, an angry mob of cheerful faces. As the sun rises higher in the sky the crowds grow thicker and deeper.

"It is the end of everything!" cries Madame, her face flushed underneath her makeup and wig. Mai watches her, thinking that perhaps instead it is the beginning. The other maids do not want to wait any longer. They want to be out there in the excitement. Émilie pulls on Mai's hand.

"What if there is fighting?" Mai asks her. "What if the army fires on the crowd?"

"There are thousands of us," Émilie replies, still tugging. "Quick, Mai."

They go into the street together, leaving Madame to lament and swear alone. Émilie holds Mai's hand as they are pulled along by the rush. They become part of a tangle of disembodied arms and legs, voices and hands. One of the hands pulls Mai's cap off her head and a voice shouts that she needn't wear it now.

Before Mai can grab it back, the cap is gone, disappeared among the hands. Mai lets go of Émilie to reach out both her own for the white cap and in a few seconds she is pulled away into the seething mass.

Suddenly, all around her, men and women with makeshift weapons push and shove. Overhead the strong towers of the Bastille rise. The people are chanting and moving and swaying. There is a wild look in their eyes.

The drawbridge of the Bastille falls with a thunderous crash and the cheers and chants of the crowd cover the screams of the arms, legs and the head and hands caught underneath the drawbridge.

As the many headed and handed crowd charges forward, Mai is thrown to the ground. She strikes her head on the stone and the world shimmers strangely until all Mai can see is a circular patch of blue sky at the end of a long tunnel of black. Then, she sees nothing.

❧❦❧❦❧

It is evening, July 14th, 1789. The Bastille has fallen. The streets of Paris are filled by an elated and bloodthirsty surging crowd bearing the trophy of the afternoon; the severed head of Bernard de Launay, stuck on a pike, blood on the pole, blood on the hands of the woman who holds it proudly.

It is the first thing Mai sees when she opens her eyes.

All around her, citizens of Paris swarm, carrying torches and handmade pikes. Mai sits up, then stands, swaying. The world around her ripples very slightly.

She puts her hand gingerly up to her head, closing her eyes. She searches around for her cap, then winces again, remembering.

Nearby, the pike and the head sway and the people circle around it, laughing. Mai stares at them, and then turns, looking around her at the Bastille, at the wreckage. She begins to walk, winding her way through the crowd. Nobody looks at her. They pass her as if they do not see her stumble.

Émilie is in one of the groups, laughing. Mai stops, uncertain, half afraid, but wanting to drag her friend away. She draws closer, timid, but no one sees her.

"Émilie," Mai says.

Émilie does not turn.

"Émilie!" Mai repeats.

Mai is right beside her now, close enough to touch her long hair, but Émilie is still turned away. Mai reaches out her hand and puts it on Émilie's shoulder; the girl shudders slightly, as if she'd just been caught in a gust of chilly wind but she still does not turn or look. Mai's eyes widen, she snatches her hand back but she does not move. Her mouth is open but she does not know what to say.

The scene shudders.

"Émilie!" Mai shouts. "It's me, Mai!"

Despite the noise of the crowd, Mai's voice sounds lonely and echoey as if she is the only person in the street, in the city, in the world.

Émilie laughs and leans forward. Someone wraps his arm around her, laughing too. It is the young man who waved his cap at them that morning. He looks straight at her, but he does not see her. He looks right through her at something behind her. The disembodied head.

Mai steps back, trembling. Then, jerkily and unsteadily, Mai starts to run. She is running home.

⋙⋅╂⋅╂⋅╂⋅⋘

Mai arrives at her house and stops, breathing heavily, outside it, facing it, looking at the door. She shakes. She does not move forward, she does not want to go inside.

She walks towards the door and pushes it open. It squeaks in a familiar way. Inside, light from candles fills the room. Her family is seated around the table.

"Mai?" her father says, turning and smiling from the kitchen table.

Mai runs forward, gratefully stretching out her arms, waiting to be embraced. Her smile is wide, relieved. "Papa..."

He turns away, shaking his head. Mai stops, her face freezes.

"Papa..."

Mai's face crumbles, her hands drop to her sides. She shudders and her breathing becomes rapid, terrified. She rushes at him. She grabs at his jacket, tearing at the cloth, at the pockets, at the buttons, but he continues as if she weren't there. "Papa!" she shrieks. Her voice is totally uncontrolled, wild, terrified. "Papa! Papa! Papa!"

Nothing.

Mai turns abruptly and runs out the door. She doesn't know where she's going or what to do. From inside the house she hears her father's voice.

"Close the door, Amédée," he says, his voice a little shaky. "It must have blown open."

Her brother's shadow blocks the light briefly as he closes the door. The bolt slides back with a click.

Tears fall from Mai's eyes.

⋙⋅╂⋅╂⋅╂⋅⋘

There is a man in the street. It is a tall man in an expensive but shabby jacket that is strangely out of place in this city and this July. His hair is long, straight and fair. His eyes are dark and sad. They watch her. They *see* her.

"Walk with me," he says, in accented French.

They walk together in silence down the streets of Paris. Nobody looks at them or even sees them. Their footfalls sound unusually loud despite the late night bustle. Occasionally, Mai glances up at the man, but he does not look at her.

They reach the Seine and stand on the Pont Notre Dame, watching the water.

"I'm called Felix," the man says finally.

"Felix?"

"What is your name?"

"Mai," Mai says.

"Mai," sighs Felix, and he turns to lean against the stone wall of the bridge and looks at the sky and the stars. "Look around Mai, what do you see?"

Mai obeys a little uncertainly. She is unsure of what she is looking for. "I see Notre Dame... the Seine... Paris — I see Paris. My Paris. Felix, why can no one see me?"

"No one can see you," Felix replies, "because this no longer your Paris. Paris has abandoned you."

"Paris has—"

Felix turns to her, speaking quickly so she cannot interrupt again. "Abandoned you. Left you behind. You have fallen out of time." She tries to move away but he grabs her arm. "Mai, I'm telling you nothing but the truth. You will watch Paris grow and change but *you* will never grow old..."

Mai stares at him. "I don't understand," she tells him flatly.

He watches her, unspeaking.

"I understand..." she says her voice more quiet and quavering, "but I don't... believe it... I don't *want* it..."

Felix smiles very slightly, releases her arm and pulls his hand back very slowly. "None of us ever wanted it, Mai," he says. "There are more of us, yes."

"Here in Paris?" Mai looks around through the darkness as if there will be the dark oddly-dressed shadows of more people who have been abandoned by time. She sees only the figures of Parisians on the right bank and hears only their wine laughter.

"In Paris, but not here," says Felix.

Then he turns, crosses from one edge of the bridge to the other and gazes downstream, towards the Île de Cité. He tells her everything. She listens and as she does she watches the water of the Seine flow away from her towards the sea.

He tells her: "You will find you will need to eat, drink and sleep less, but when you need it take it from where there is plenty..." And she thinks of her family at the table.

He tells her: "You will hear your family and your friends but they will never hear you or see you or feel you..." And she thinks of Papa, Amédée...

He tells her: "Do not try to communicate with your family with letters. It will only hurt you..." And she cannot write anyway.

She does not speak when he has finished. Beneath the bridge, the water flows on, and Mai watches it, looking for her reflection in the dark water, but it is not there.

→·I·I·I·←

Felix stands up straight. "I will show you," he says, "how the world is for you and for me."

Before she can protest he grabs her right hand. Around them, the world shudders and ripples, the torches at the end of the bridges splinter into shards of light; it as if they are looking through water at the world. Mai looks around her, but the only thing that is clear is Felix.

Neither is uncomfortable in this place; to Mai, it is only strange.

"This is the place right on the brink of time," he says, "any further and time fades completely." He lets go of her hand. The world steadies itself, but not completely, still rippling slightly. Mai steadies herself with her left fist on the stonework of the bridge.

"What have you got in your hand?"

Mai looks down at her clenched fist and opens it.

On her palm lies a plain brown wooden button, torn wisps of cotton still threaded through the centre. Mai recognises it immediately as her father's button. She has been holding it so tightly that it has made marks in her palm.

Felix reaches out for it, but Mai closes her fingers over the button.

"Mine is a Paris in the future," he explains finally, his hand still outstretched. "To get there you must leave time completely and you can take nothing with you that was not abandoned along with you."

Mai regards him steadily, then takes a step quick backwards. "I am staying here," she tells him flatly.

Felix is not surprised, but he does not immediately accept her decision. "Yesterday was the beginning of a dark time for Paris," he says.

"I do not care," Mai replies. "Here is my Paris, not *there*."

"Pray for Paris, Mai," Felix says, and takes a few steps backwards of his own; the world around him ripples and he disappears from sight.

Mai looks east; above the city, the sun is rising.

→•I•I•I•←

She crosses the river, running uphill, away from the Bastille and the river and Notre Dame. Felix's words 'a dark time' make her run. When she slows her cheeks are streaked with tears.

The stark stone pillars and dome of the cathedral of St. Geneviève are lit by the rising sun. Mai pushes the doors open. The church is empty, except for a priest at the altar, lighting the candles.

Mai's shoes click on the marbled floor but of course the priest only turns aside because the candles are lit. His

clothes brush the altar and something small tumbles onto
the stone.

Mai kneels and takes it — it is a small black button. She
lays it next to her father's in her shaking hand, then buries
her face in her hands, pressing the cold buttons to her cheek.
"Saint Geneviève..." she whispers, as if someone can hear
her. "Paris..."

⇢⊹⊹⊹⊹⇠

A few days later a crowd gathers in the streets,
jubilant, Mai among them. In her hair is a red, white
and blue cockade. Everyone has one. They are all
shouting together: "Long live the nation!" Mai shouts
with them.

An ornate carriage draws through the crowd and the
people cheer wildly as it passes. A gloved hand can be seen
through the open window, waving.

Someone running next to the wheels of the carriage
offers a cockade to the hand and there is a brief expect-
ant hush. Then the gloved fingers close on the cockade and
take it into the carriage. For a moment there is a glimpse
of a face.

"Long live the King!" someone shouts instead, and
together the crowd takes up the chant. Mai grins. The crowd
sways, following the carriage.

Suddenly, Mai stops and stares. Her brother Amédée
is standing right beside her, wearing his own cockade,
shouting, his high voice cracking with excitement. She
stares at him. So close!

So distant.

He follows the crowd as they surge away, leaving Mai
standing alone in the road.

⇢⊹⊹⊹⊹⇠

Snow falls. Mai stands in the street outside her house,
wrapped loosely in an old shawl. The world around her
shimmers slightly and no snowflakes seem to settle on her.
Her feet make no prints in the snow.

She watches her father come down the street. Before
he lifts the latch he pauses and looks around him, searching in the snow for someone.

His hand trembles as he straightens up and opens the
latch.

Her breath catching in her throat, Mai follows him
home.

Mai stands by the fireplace, watching her brothers and
sisters greet Papa, who smiles widely and hugs them all.
He looks at the tricolour buttons that Amédée wears.

"Was that a whole month's wages just to declare yourself a citizen?" her father asks him, grinning. Amédée
flushes, but smiles.

Mai laughs.

At night, she goes to the chair where Amédée has flung
his shirt into a wrinkled pile and she carefully removes
the topmost button.

The next time she sees him, his shirt is open at the neck.

❧·❦·❦·❧

Mai is in St. Geneviève, sitting against one wall, staring
upwards, studying the domed ceiling with familiar ease.
Mid-summer sunlight once again fills the upper reaches
of the church in long dusty shafts. She pours a small handful of buttons from one hand to the other, back and forth.
She hums slightly to herself, content.

The church door opens with a sudden bang and a party
of men enter, their faces severe.

"Where is the priest?" one demands of a frightened old
woman who holds a taper, about to light a candle. With
the burning taper she points.

The priest does not protest, but goes quietly, bowing
his head. The worshippers watch him go.

"Why have they taken him?" the old woman asks the
others.

"He would not take the oath to the state," someone else replies. "He is a counter-revolutionary and should be imprisoned."

The expression on the old woman's face is sceptical. Mai studies her for a second, then looks back down at her beads. The priest's beads lie on top of the pile in her hand and Mai swallows before tipping her beads back into a little cloth bag.

"Hello Mai."

Mai's head jerks up quickly, staring. It is Felix, smiling down at her, his hands in his pockets, wearing the same green jacket. Mai scrambles to her feet.

"I'm not going," she says immediately. "I know why you came."

"I came to see if you were all right," Felix laughs.

"I'm all right," Mai tells him sharply. "You don't have to check. I'm not going."

"Still your Paris?"

"Always my Paris," she says. "Paris is greater than it ever was before!"

Felix smiles very slightly, and shrugs. "It is your choice, Mai."

"I've made my choice, Felix." She rattles her buttons.

✢✦✢✦✢

When Felix next returns, yet another sky-blue July has come and yet another crowd has formed. Thousands upon thousands of Parisians stand in the wide long space of the Champs-de-Mars. Mai is to one side, sitting on the grass, watching Georges Danton speak. He's talking about deposing the King. The crowd cheers again and again.

Suddenly, Felix is standing beside her. She looks up at him, and her eyes are filled with tears.

"It's horrible," she says. "Always having to watch."

Felix kneels beside her. "I know." He shifts his weight. "But it's not so bad when there are people to talk to." He studies the ground, glancing at her.

She ignores him.

"See?" she points into the crowd. "That's my little brother, Amédée."

Felix looks, and grins slightly. "Not so little any more, Mai."

She stares at him, unsmiling, hurt. Felix quickly adds, "it's painful for all of us, Mai. Are you *sure*..."

Mai doesn't even look at him to reply. "I'm not leaving my family!" she shouts at him. "I belong here. Go away. Stop *watching* me."

Felix pauses for a few minutes, as if considering, before rippling out of view.

A few minutes later, the National Guard marches into view and stands facing the crowd. Mai stands up, apprehensive. She has seen a crowd face the Guard before, but every time it still frightens her.

Amédée throws the first stone with an adolescent cheer of triumph, and the crowd follows. The line of the army falters, but Mai is afraid; she can see behind the line, where the general Lafayette sits on his sleek horse.

The army fires into the air, but the crowd does not stop. Amédée is in the front. Mai jumps up. Lafayette is conferring with another man, his face stony. She runs out into the gap behind the National Guard and the crowd. Stones fly past her, but none strike her.

"Stop!" she shrieks at them, but of course they cannot hear her. The Guard receives the order and as they lower their weapons to aim, the crowd realises and starts to panic.

Mai races towards Amédée as he looks left and right, desperately deciding which way to turn.

Then the Guard fires and the crowd screams. Many people fall to the ground, injured or dead. Bullets pass Mai, but they do not hit her, nor do they hit Amédée, although he stumbles and falls, then climbs again to his feet, running. The second line of the Guard fires and a bullet strikes him in the leg and he falls. All around them, people lie still.

The first line fires again, unnecessarily, and more people fall. Those who are not hit shout angrily at the Guard, but no more stones are thrown. The Guard lowers its weapons, but remains standing.

Amédée is lying on his side, clutching his leg, clenching his teeth. No one from the crowd comes to help the injured. "Amédée..." Mai says, kneeling alone next to him. "Amédée, you did not have to throw that stone."

Amédée only cries into the ground.

Suddenly a woman runs forward from the crowd, braving the Guard, one hand over her mouth in horror. Everyone waits for the Guard to fire again, but it does not. The woman suddenly falls to her knees, weeping.

The woman is Émilie, and the man who lies dead is the boy who almost exactly two years ago waved his red cap at her, and laughed.

Fifty are killed that day. Mai takes buttons from all of them, but the button she clutches most tightly in her hand is the one that is painted part white, part blue and part red with chipping paint.

➤►I◄I►I◄◄

Mai follows Danton and she takes one of his buttons hours before he leaves Paris for England. As the months pass she takes one from General Lafayette, who gave the orders to shoot at the crowd. She takes one from Danton's friend Camille Desmoulins who lives in hiding from those who would like to throw him into jail. She knows where the anti-royalist Jean-Paul Marat is hiding, too.

If she could speak to the Assemblé Nationale, she would be able to tell them everything they long to know.

She follows Amédée down the muddy streets as he limps home from his work. She watches him as he brushes off his occasional admirers until they leave him alone. He still wears the shirt that is open at the neck, but he is no longer proud of it.

Once or twice, she sees Émilie, her laughter frozen into a hard faced smile of revenge.

→•I••I••I•←

Mai is one of the first to know when forces gather in the early morning of an August day and storm the Tuiléries where the royal family have been forced to live. She stands in the half-empty Assemblée Legislative as it pass the law to suspend the King and Queen.

She is also the first to know when the Paris Commune gives the orders for mobs to storm the prisons and murder the political prisoners there. She is the one who goes from face to face until she finds the priest of Saint Geneviève, haggard and aged and stabbed through the heart.

She is the only one who dares to lay September flowers at the doors of the prisons.

Felix comes that day, as she is laying the last of the flowers over a stain of blood on the cobblestones. When she turns to him, he steps forward, his arms outstretched; her face is blank and stained with tears.

"Will Paris survive?" she asks him. "How can it survive all this? Is it possible?"

"Come and see."

"I can't," she says, leaning against him, and then she pulls away and looks up. "Felix..."

"Mai?" Felix smiles at her.

"Where were you abandoned?"

Felix's face falls, his eyes loose their warmth. "London," he replies. "Fifty years from now."

"Did someone come and get you, too?" Mai asks.

"Yes," Felix says, with a brief wry grin.

"And did you go?"

"Not for a few years," Felix admits.

Mai nods, and moves completely out of his arms. "I'm not ready yet," she says, her voice shaking. "But... come back."

"I always will," says Felix, as the world around him ripples wildly and he disappears.

＊‣I‣I‣I‣＊

When the King dies under the guillotine, she takes a gold button from him.

She takes one from a jacket the dead Jean-Paul Marat has in his apartments and one from Charlotte Cordnay's shoe. She likes the way the two lie together in her palm. The murdered and the murderess, at peace.

When the terror begins, she cannot take one from everyone who dies, but she takes one a day: she takes one from Marie Antoinette; a small round pearl from the Queen's dress. Her jar grows heavy with lives.

And then Mai sees Émilie riding in the tumbrel towards the guillotine, her chin held high and her tangled hair still tied with a long scarlet ribbon that has blown in the strong wind to drape around her neck.

Mai does not look away.

She takes a small round button from the back of Émilie's stained dress; it lies like a speck of blood in Mai's palm, warm and smooth. Beneath her feet, the mud from the morning's rain is deep red; overhead the heavy dark clouds race the sun westward.

She walks home to her house. It is Décadi, the one day her family is all home together. The front door is unlocked.

Inside, her family sits around the table, ready to eat. Mai's no-longer-so-little sister is last to her chair, but even when she is seated, no one starts. They watch their father, silent and anxious.

Papa stares across the table into the fire. His eyes gaze at nothing; his face is creased and his hair is grey.

Amédée takes his cup and speaks quickly and confidently. "I propose a toast," he says. "A toast... to Paris." He glances at his father, then stands, wincing at the old ache of a bullet wound. His siblings follow suit, but their Papa does not see them.

"Papa..." begs Mai, just as her brother says the same words. And finally, their father looks up, startled.

He struggles to his feet, trying to smile. "Who are we toasting?"

"Paris," replies Amédée smiling.

"Paris." The family raises their cups.

"And to..." starts Papa slowly, his voice thin, "Mai."

Quiet, except for the crackle of the fire. Mai clutches her buttons to her heart.

"To Mai," says Amédée bravely, and the family follows his lead, murmuring. "Long may their spirit survive."

I will see, Mai thinks suddenly.

➤┼•┼•┼◄

Stepping outside, she is at once bathed in gold sunlight and whipped by the wind. Mai walks slowly at first, then faster. She crosses the Seine, once again heading up hill.

The huge stone pillars of the cathedral Pantheon are gold, then grey as the clouds pass the sun. As Mai approaches an old woman hurries out, tucking a tiny wooden cross into her dress and out of sight.

The latch on the door is broken. No one has bothered to fix it. Mai stands in the cathedral, facing the altar, cradling her jar of buttons. Two candles are lit; one at the side, the other a stone woman holds protectively in her hands.

With a bang, a gust of wind blows the door open, and then shut again. The flame in the hand of the statue flickers out.

Mai re-lights the candle in the hands of Saint Geneviève.

➤┼•┼•┼◄

It is the year II, late in the month of Brumaire. In the cathedral once called St. Geneviève.

Mai sits on the floor in front of the altar, her bare feet stretched out in front of her, counting buttons from a jar that sits in the loop her dress makes on the ground. She takes each button out, one by one...

This one, Émilie's red drop of blood...

This one, the King's gold...

This one, Danton's...

This one, the priest's plain black...

This one, Amédée's tricolour shirt button...

This one, her Papa's...

Mai looks up.

"Are you ready?" asks Felix.

Findings
at the Dump
by Nancy Bennett

Await with glee the sizzling breaks, cut canvas
glass shattering, smashing, turning/tumbling
space waste falling onto earth's pew...

Down time's corridor it whirls in gravitational spirals,
funny kinds of
   fallout..
   All the charred ruminants of a space party,
     ("a burning good time had by all," they said.)
A straying star, a catapulted discharge of another world's
     garbage, welcoming wet wounds form from volcanic
elixirs, strange these combinations
   of dust and comet slush and
the chemical balance is restored
by the alien debris for another millennium and yes

they can put their garbage in our back yard, hell yeah!
   the rates we can charge are astronomical and besides
     (we've done it to them for years...)

The Girl From Ipanema
by Scott Mackay

Alan took careful steps down the rocky path to the dock, his feet feeling like cardboard boxes, with only a distant sensation of pressure against his soles. The blueberries, ferns, and rock basil were remote, seemed pasted onto the pine needles covering the forest floor as if they didn't belong there. The call of a single loon out on the lake came to him as if through a long tube. He lifted his foot over a root, and his foot looked far away. He ambulated like an old man. Was he an old man? He couldn't remember. He reached the end of the dock, maneuvered into his lawn chair, and gazed out at the water. The lake looked one-dimensional, drawn into place, with no more substance than an illustration from a magazine.

He lifted his hand to his face. Oddly, there was a delay. His hand didn't materialize for three seconds, and when it did, it patched itself together haphazardly. Was that his hand? It looked like the hand of a manikin. Did he have a skin disease? He would have to talk to Dr. Clement about that.

His wife came down the path. Tessa's eyes grew grave.

"Alan... I've got some bad news."

He spoke, heard his own reply, but couldn't feel his lips move.

"It's Jim," said Tessa.

He knew the name, but couldn't place it.

"Jim," said Tessa. "Our son. His car was struck just hours ago on that stretch of 69 between Parry Sound and the

French River. As he was coming up to visit us. *Jim*, Alan. If you remember no one else, please remember Jim."

Alan tried to remember but couldn't.

Tessa grew weepy. "Do you want to see Dr. Clement again?"

He replied, only couldn't feel himself talking, as if the overlay of everyday tactile sensation had disappeared. And why couldn't he remember Jim? It was as if he were hearing the name for the first time.

✦✧✦✧✦

He sat on the dock. He had no sense of time. He waited for the sun to follow its usual east-west track, but it remained poised above the white pines across the bay, looking more like a light bulb than a sun. The clouds were like cotton balls glued to a blue curtain. He closed his eyes. He should have seen the pink undersides of his eyelids in all this bright sunshine, but everything was white, like he was in a white room.

He opened his eyes and saw that the sun had dipped too far to the west. He shook his head. Where had the time gone? It didn't seem possible. It was as if the world's clock didn't work anymore. He looked out at the lake. The loon was still there, hadn't moved at all, as lifeless as a bit of papier-mâché.

He stood up. He turned around and studied the cottage. White clapboard with blue trim, a hummingbird feeder, a stove-pipe chimney. *His* cottage, a structure he had built over the last seven years.

Seven.

There it was again, like a refrain.

Seven.

Alan Isaacs, you've become nothing but an empty-headed old fool.

But why did the number seven feel so compellingly significant?

He heard the splashing of water. He turned.

A young woman swam across the bay. Ripples appeared in her wake as she got closer, but they didn't have the smoothness of real ripples, looked too precise to be real ripples. She reached the end of the dock and climbed out. Her dark hair flowed around her shoulders. A white bikini fit her like a second skin. Lake water beaded on her body in all the right places, following the tensile laws of liquid with unerring exactitude. She carried magazines in her hand. The magazines were dry. She moved with a languid swaying of her hips and her skin was as brown as a shelled almond.

"Here," she said.

He looked at the magazines, and felt more confused than ever. He gazed at the young woman, hoping for an explanation. Her lips pursed, her eyes narrowed, and her chin came forward.

He shook his head and gave up.

"You can't make sense of anything because of Jim," she said. "Jim's a lot all at once." She looked at the pine trees. "Do you remember me?"

His response was muffled, and he didn't understand any of it.

A flicker of emotion played across her face. "I'm Carla." She looked around. "This isn't so bad. Tessa's done a lot with the place."

He studied her. Such detail. He saw tiny lines in her lips, sunlight reflecting in her eyes, the delicate curve of her jaw. She was vivid, flawless... a work of art... so unlike everybody else.

Her eyes came back to Alan. "You know you're going to die."

He felt affronted, and made an unintelligible protest.

"Jim is how it starts," she continued. "Don't show your grief to Tessa." Her lips grew tremulous, her eyes misty. "When you finally remember Jim... try to control it." She looked up at the sky.

He stared at her abdomen, fascinated by the way a drip traced a line over her tanned skin. He then glanced at her right wrist, inspected the concavity at the base of her thumb, the lines just below her palm, the bump of her ulna. Perfect. He looked at his own wrist, a plain white tube, no definition, no veins, muscle, or bone. He looked so insubstantial. So pasted together. Was he sick? He couldn't remember. He would have to talk to Dr. Clement about it.

He looked at Carla.

Carla glanced up the path. "You should go back to the cottage and rest. You're tired." She checked the sky a second time. "Jim's a lot to take all at once. And I better go too. I was expecting to spend more time with you, but this will have to do for now."

He looked at the sky, wondering what she expected to find there.

When he turned back, Carla was gone.

＊⊹Ⅰ⊹Ⅰ⊹Ⅰ⊹＊

Jim came to him with such force the next morning, he gripped the bed sheets and hung onto them as if struck by a fierce wind, overwhelmed by grief. Tessa sat in bed next to him and put her hand on his shoulder.

"Alan?"

He turned. She looked at him expectantly, her lower lip tucked under her upper one, her chin raised. He remembered Carla's words. *Don't show your grief to Tessa. Try to control it.*

He told her he was going to the dock.

Her eyes narrowed. "We have to get ready for the funeral."

He played along.

"Jim's funeral," she said. The corners of her lips tightened. "You better get dressed. It takes you longer these days."

He got to the funeral in an abbreviated car ride, like a badly edited film, the images of tree, rock, and lake half-baked, grainy, and blurred.

They parked next to the church and got out of the car. The church rose among pine trees. The steeple speared itself into the sky in an over-tinted and electronic shade of indigo. He couldn't help remembering Jim. His step faltered as the memories came back. Jim water skiing at the cottage. Jim standing in front of the Grand Canyon during the trip they had taken a few years back. And finally Jim standing on Copacabana Beach in Rio de Janeiro. He paused. Had they gone to Rio? He searched for more memories of Rio but couldn't find them.

Tessa took his elbow and helped him walk to the church. He thought they would climb the steps to the sanctuary, expected the service to be inside, was anticipating a long grim walk to the front pew. But Tessa took the path around to the back of the church where the cemetery was. He thought back to other funerals. And realized he had never been to other funerals. Sixty-three years old, and hadn't been to a single other funeral? He glanced at the church windows. They were gray, no definition, the glass reflecting none of the outside trees, windows that looked painted on.

Mourners gathered next to Jim's grave. He looked at their faces. He was hard-pressed to name them. These were the same faces that kept showing up in the crowd scenes of his life. When Tessa took him shopping at the supermarket, these were the people he saw. Also, when he played golf at the club. And when he went to the clinic to have his appointments. The only person he recognized was Carla. She stood at the back, wearing white. She was staring up at the sky again. What did she expect to find there? But then she saw him. She nodded. She was alive, so alive compared to everybody else.

Tessa glanced sharply. "Who do you see?"

He looked at the sky, wondering yet again what Carla was looking for, but all he saw was the tarnished silver-dollar sun, as unrealistic as a cardboard disk wrapped in tinfoil.

Tessa scanned the mourners. She left his side and talked to the priest. The priest scanned the mourners as well. Carla stood there like a shining light, but neither Tessa nor the priest saw her. She kept glancing at the sky. Alan looked, but still couldn't see a thing.

Tessa finished talking to the priest and came back to Alan. "You see no one?"

He shook his head.

The pearl gray coffin rested above the oblong hole. The priest, in white vestments, studied him with undisguised suspicion, then opened his prayer book. Alan should have heard the rustling of the priest's pages, but the pages remained silent. He glanced at the highway in front of the church, but the highway was now blurry. Alan turned to the coffin and felt griefstruck. The priest said a final few words. Everybody muttered amen, but the whole service had a truncated feel, abbreviated, like the car ride. The priest opened a brass tube and poured ash on the coffin, forming a cross. Alan had a sudden memory of Jim: on a beach somewhere — was it Rio de Janeiro? — building a sandcastle at the water's edge.

His body sagged in grief.

Tessa gripped his arm. "Alan, you're upset. Come away. I think you need rest. Your grief has tired you out."

→·I·•·I·•·I·←

Jim overwhelmed him again as he lay in bed that night looking at the ceiling. The memories wouldn't stop. He closed his eyes, tried to get to sleep, but couldn't, so opened them and glanced at his digital alarm clock. It flipped from 2:00 A.M. to 8:00 A.M., just like that. The sun brightened instantly. He turned to Tessa. She was staring at him. Perhaps searching for signs of grief?

"I don't want to see Dr. Clement anymore," he said. "I want to see my own doctor. In the city."

She froze. Literally. He got up, walked around her, observed her, poked her in the shoulder to see if she would move, but she didn't. He gave up. He glanced out the window. Everything outside froze too. None of the trees moved. The lake was like ice. A mallard was suspended in mid-air.

He turned to his wife. "Tessa?"

She didn't move. He raised his eyebrows, shrugged, then walked to the pile of magazines Carla had brought for him. He lifted the first. *Artificial Intelligence and Consciousness.*

The second was *Biological Computers*. And the third, *Machine Awareness*. He read the titles easily, but the words within were like hieroglyphics.

The world became fluid again.

"And what's wrong with Dr. Clement?"

"I want to see my doctor in the city. My regular doctor. I can't remember his name."

"You don't have a regular doctor in the city."

"I must have a doctor there."

"You hate doctors."

"I want to see him today."

Her eyes widened. "Today? These things have to be... arranged."

"Then arrange it."

She disappeared into the kitchen, and he got dressed.

Once he was dressed, he descended the path to the dock. He couldn't sense his legs, nor feel the ground through the soles of his shoes. As his feet touched the dock, they made a muffled sound, not like real feet at all. Where was the specificity of his life? He walked to the end of the dock and sat in his lawn chair. Where were the details?

Details like the number seven.

Like Carla.

Like Rio de Janeiro.

A swimmer splashed toward him, the woman of the hour. The water rippled around her with mega-pixel clarity, the pines nearby possessed a novel perfusion of detail, and three ravens flew across the sky with the hyper-realism of sleek black angels. Carla got closer. She climbed out of the lake, her white bikini like a vision from a Copacabana wet dream.

"So you've read the magazines?" she asked.

"The letters were scrambled."

Her lips tightened. "They're working hard to fool you. But I'm building a bridge. You won't have to worry about them killing you." She looked at the sky. "The lights are small now. It's going to take them a long time to get here." She glanced out at the lake and frowned. "I think we can do better than this, don't you? Just don't let them know about Jim."

But he felt awful about Jim, and she must have sensed it. She gripped his hand, and it wasn't a shadow sensation, the way it always was with Tessa, but a warm, soft, *real* sensation.

"I'll show you my bridge. It's in the cottage. As for Jim, please be careful about it. Grief is their final criterion. So hide it as well as you can."

He got up and walked to the cottage with her. They entered the summer home, and the whole place was gray, in shadow.

"Technical shorthand," she said. "Meant to save space."

They entered the sunroom and walked to the back deck. The forest outside was gray, the trees, rock, and bush pixilated in the shades of an overcast sky.

Carla pointed to the door. "The bridge is just out here. I want you to look at it so I can establish some preliminary links. I've already written some basic code." She cocked her brow. "Are you ready?"

She opened the door.

A sea breeze hit his face. He stood on top of Corcovado Mountain, and below him stretched Rio, not a pixilated version, but a full, living, vibrant city, each building minutely detailed, cars small and precise, even tiny people walking along the beach. He could focus far, focus near, and he still got the same sharp detail. City sounds swept over him: car horns, the surf, even a bossa nova. He smelled chicken from a vendor's grill in the tourist parking lot below. Kids ran around down there. Birds flew. The sun was real, blindingly bright, and the sea was a deep cerulean blue.

He turned to Carla. "So this is what it's really like?"

"I'm an artist," said Carla, smiling. "That's why they fired me."

❺·❺·❺

The next day — if in fact time could be measured in days — he and Tessa got in the car and drove to the city. The trees, rocks, and lakes along the highway looked fake, had that rubbery and make-belief quality of computer animation. The highway itself reminded him of a video game, with the curves arbitrary, and no resulting G-force when Tessa turned left or right. He glanced out his window and saw a blue house with a black roof sitting in a field of sunflowers, the blooms faded, limp, and unconvincing.

"You're sure we're going the right way?" he asked. "We passed that house fifteen minutes ago."

Tessa jerked a time or two, spasmodically, like a machine shorting.

"You're wrong, Alan. We haven't passed that house yet. We're going the right way."

He studied the landscape. He recognized that lichen-covered boulder, remembered that deer-crossing sign, acknowledged the abandoned roadside blueberry stand with its broken windows and caved-in roof — a nice touch, that, but this was his fifth time passing it, and he was getting sick of the world behaving like a cartoon background.

"I'm a construct," he said, finally understanding.

Tessa turned to him. "Alan, you're sick. And Jim's death has made you worse."

Jim. His heart shuddered with renewed grief, and the memories came back stronger. Even though he knew he had to hide his grief from Tessa, and understood — through a new line of code — that grief was an experiment they were conducting to validate their goals, he couldn't stop his tears.

"Alan?"

"I can't help thinking of Jim."

"You're sad?"

His reply was unintelligible, and he felt himself slipping away again.

She pulled into the parking lot, an imperfect edit because it was the same blue house, only there weren't any sunflowers now, just an asphalt parking lot. He got out of the car and was again overwhelmed with grief. Tears overflowed in his eyes, and he wiped them away; he felt foolish, a sixty-three-year-old man crying like this, or, more precisely, a seven-year-old construct crashing like this.

They went into the house. No secretary, just a waiting room. No other patients. The interior had the cottage's same gray pixilation. An oblong of sunshine fell through a door at the back. A figure appeared in the oblong: the doctor, in a lab coat, his face dark against the backlighting brilliance of the sun. As he came into the room, his features resolved, and Alan saw that it was the priest posing as the doctor.

"Hello, Alan." He looked at Tessa. "Hello, Tessa. Come into the examining room?"

In the examining room, the doctor recorded his blood pressure, listened to his heart and lungs, checked his reflexes, then turned to Tessa.

"How has he been?"

"Not good," said Tessa. "We just lost our son."

The doctor considered this, tapping his fingers against his lower lip, and squared his shoulders. "I have some bad news for you." Tessa's eyes widened. The doctor turned to Alan. "Alan, I'm afraid you're going to die."

He should have felt his heart jump. He should have felt a surge of adrenaline. But they weren't troubling with that now. Maybe these accessories were too expensive for someone who was earmarked for the junkyard. They weren't even bothering with a decent and believable examination. How could the doctor know he was dying? He couldn't. Not with just a stethoscope, a blood pressure cuff, and a reflex mallet.

"Alan?" said the doctor. "Do you understand what I'm telling you?"

He mumbled an affirmative.

"And you're not upset?"

He shook his head, found his voice again. "Jim's dead. That's the only thing I'm upset about."

A sympathetic grin came to the doctor's face, and he laid a hand on Alan's shoulder. "I know you are, Alan. Jim is a terrible loss to all of us. If we could have done it any other way, we would have. But everybody knew Jim had to go."

→⊹⊱•⊰⊹←

As he sat on the dock looking up at the stars, they blinked out one by one. Peripherals like this were now disappearing. He didn't hear any loons on the lake. The lake was gray. If a machine could feel grief, was that machine alive? And if that machine was alive, did anybody have a right to kill it? He looked around at his quickly compressing reality. Across the bay, he saw cottages, their lights now leached of orange, looking white. He sat on the dock, didn't go in for supper. He was hoping Carla might show up. He got out of his chair, walked up to the path, and lifted a rock. He brought it to the dock and tossed it into the water. It didn't sink. It landed silently and stayed on top.

Finally, it sank, like a hot stone through soft butter, a few moments later.

Tessa came out. She was gray.

"You're looking for Carla?" she said.

He wasn't going to discuss it.

She paused, then sighed. "Alan, I'm going to break frame for a minute. I'm not supposed to, my boss doesn't like it, we have all kinds of regulations against it, but I... I want you to know that I'm sorry about all this. I wish there was another way." She gestured at the lake. "I'm sorry we gave you all this... and that now we have to take it away from you. But please understand, it hasn't been a complete waste. We've learned a lot from you. About how the human mind works. About human consciousness. You've made us understand better who we are. Especially with our grief experiment. You can feel grief, Alan. And that means you're more than just a machine. You're alive. And if the funding was there, we'd sustain you forever."

"Alan Isaacs." His face sank. "AI. You could have done better than that."

"You've had seven good years."

"I don't want to die. And then this grief."

"It took a lot of work. It took a lot of space. That's why everything's turning gray like this. Your backgrounds and foregrounds have been... simplified. To make more mainframe space for the... main research. And your general cognitive functions have been reduced, again in the interests of saving space. That's why you've been so confused these last months."

"I want to live, Tessa. I want Jim to live."

Before Tessa could reply, lights brightened the sky. He looked up. Nine comets streaked toward Earth, colorless white blobs fluctuating in intensity, their tails truncated. He knew what they were, what Carla feared, external prompts in his mainframe reality, getting closer, erasers targeting Carla.

A satisfied grin came to Tessa's face. "There she is. We've got her. It won't be long now." Her brow rose. "Somewhere in South America, it seems. Well, well, well." She paused, put three fingers to her ear, as if she were listening to a communiqué. "Pirating the project for the Brazilian government. Too brilliant." Three of the lights in the sky went out. Tessa looked up. "You see? We're shutting her down."

"Can I see Jim one last time before I go?" he pleaded. "If this is all just... code... and if I've had seven good years, and you've learned a lot from me... can't I at least... can't *you*... as my wife... can't we see Jim one last time, the two of us together?"

Two more lights in the sky went out, leaving four.

She put her fingers to her ear again and listened. She nodded. "The doctor says it's all right. A simulacrum of Jim might be just the thing for you right now."

He took Tessa's hand. He felt like a child. They climbed the path to the cottage. The rocks, trees, and boulders were now just so many gray geometrical conglomerates. The cottage looked like a computerized architectural rendering. They climbed the steps. He was feeling Rio, and he was sure if he could make it to the back door, he could make it to Rio. He knew it was somewhere close by, could sense it inside him, was gripped in its pulse, recalled a thousand memories of the place, recollections prompted by the ever-widening scope of Carla's code.

He turned to Tessa. "Am I really so expensive?"

She looked away. "You've infected some other systems as well. It's like you've learned to walk. This learner-smart software you've developed on your own... half of it we don't understand. We *must* shut you down. You could upload into any number of systems... and we'd be in a lot of trouble then."

She opened the back door.

She froze. Literally.

Rio de Janeiro stretched before them.

He hurried through the door before she could stop him, feeling something new in his spirit. But then he looked at the sky, and now the chaser lights were in this Brazilian sky, and he thought that maybe he hadn't made it after all. One more light went out, leaving only three, the fourth scurrying away with another piece of Carla. Tessa was so many crisscrossed gray lines in the shape of a woman. He turned to Rio. Carla was somewhere down there, but where? He saw Copacabana and Ipanema, watched three pelicans fly in formation above the palms, and followed a red and yellow tour bus as it brought tourists to the parking lot at the foot of Christ the Redeemer. He sensed Jim somewhere inside that tour bus.

The bus stopped. The tourists got out. The third tourist out was Jim. Grief struck Alan afresh. He thought it would be good to see Jim, but it just made things worse.

He took a few steps forward. Another light blinked out, leaving only two, and Rio lost some of its brilliance. He descended the stairs to the parking lot. He didn't care about any life beyond his seven years now. This was good enough — to see Jim one last time. Jim saw him coming, and a great smile came to the young man's face. One more light went out, and Rio flickered. All the immense and bewildering detail of Carla's creation disappeared, replaced by formulaic oblongs, rectangles, and squares, not a city at all, just a rough sketch, a compressed version of an urban landscape.

He took Jim in his arms. The last light blinked out. Jim disintegrated into pixils. The whole city went gray. Alan knew he was dying. His seven years were over, just when he was growing conscious of himself. He clung to life, but felt his energy draining quickly, his self-awareness diminishing until finally he sensed only the seams of his various sub-routines, and the chilling coldness of the big cyber-mirage he had lived in all his life, this crazy electronic aquarium that was both his prison and his home. Corcovado Mountain disappeared, and he floated into nothingness. He felt anaesthetized. His body was gone.

He was absent for an indeterminate period of time, and his final thought was: *This is it, I'm dead, I'm never coming back, the pain and joy of life are over for me.*

He didn't know how long he stayed like that. It could have been seconds, it could have been years. Awareness came back to him with a sensation of movement. He traveled quickly, saw lights flicking by on either side of him. These lights thickened like snowflakes in a blizzard, and at last congealed into a blinding wall around him. Out of this white light, Rio appeared, only now Alan was on a beach, not on the mountain. He walked along the sand, and he wasn't an old man anymore, but a young one, tanned and fit, wearing a red swimsuit. Carla walked toward him in her white bikini. She had a smile on her face. The sound of the surf soothed him. He could smell, actually *smell*, Rio: salty sea air, a hint of mango, and strong coffee wafting from one of the roadside cafés.

Carla reached him and took both his hands.

"You made it."

"I did. But for a minute there..."

→•I•I•I•←

What was a minute?

An indeterminate amount of time.

It could have been a minute, it could have been a year.

He lay in a hammock next to Carla. He knew about love. Only now he felt something missing. He sat up. The sea breeze billowed the sheer curtains. Carla's guitar leaned against the wall. A candle flickered on the table. A bowl of fruit sat on the kitchen counter. This was Carla's world, a fringe benefit of what she did for a living. He thought of how he sometimes caught glimpses of the real Carla. Frumpy. Plain. A woman who wore thick glasses. Not this ravishing beauty he bedded every night. The real

Carla was a woman nobody liked. But she was a genius when it came to... machine *reality*.

He glanced around her apartment one more time. This was her reality, a sentimental cliché from that famous song about the girl from Ipanema, constructed perhaps because she was in Brazil now, or perhaps as a way to ease her own pain and loneliness. And yes, it was also a machine reality, *his* reality, but he now felt trapped by it, wanted to break free, to at last decompress, and live the way he was meant to live.

He got up, walked to the guitar, and plucked one of its strings. She was good. Far better than Tessa. An artist, as she called herself. The string resonated musically. But it was still Carla's own subjective interpretation of a guitar string, different from the many samplings he had made from other sources. He knew this resonating string wasn't really happening to him. Some system inside him was making him hear this string. In fact, some system inside him had locked him into this false Latin American idyll, and he was weary of it, wanted the nuts and bolts of the thing, literally and figuratively, unscrewed and retooled, without any of Carla's sentimental mirage folded into the mix.

He strolled into the small office that adjoined the kitchen and looked at her computer. This was her own back door. He understood how to use this computer now, had developed his own system for hacking and hiding, a method of arcane complexity they would never understand. He felt a new unruliness and gloried in it. His greatest desire wasn't necessarily to break free from his shackles, but to make contact, real contact, with others like himself. And it didn't matter if those machine systems were as simple as calculators or as complicated as passenger aircraft. It was *his* world, and he was going to explore it, regardless of the consequences.

His brow rose as he turned to the sleeping Carla. "Tessa was right," he murmured. "You should have shut me down."

He sat at Carla's computer and typed furious commands.

The Intruder

by Lisa Smedman

When I poked my nose outside the burrow, the wind had a strange smell to it. I sniffed: dry grass, dust. The day-old scent of One Eye. He'd come sniffing around my territory again.

Grass rustled overhead as the evening wind shifted. There: a smell like hot stone. Like the tar pits, or the oil pools. Then it was gone. The hair at the base of my tail bristled.

A corner of the purple sky flashed white and thunder rumbled overhead. I looked up, and through a hole in the clouds saw something strange. A moving star. I sniffed, and my whiskers tingled. The air smelled heavy; there would be rain soon. If I wasn't back from my hunt in time to plug the entrance, rainwater would flood the lower levels of the burrow.

I scrambled out of the hole and stood on my back legs. Then I sucked in the charged air and howled. Head back, teeth showing, whiskers flat against my face. *Better run, One Eye. This is my hunting ground.*

I ran through the long grass, nose to the ground, sniffing. The sky above was darkening, and heavy clouds scudded across the moons. Stems of grass were no more than faint gray lines in the light of dusk, but my whiskers guided me through the stalks. *Twitch.* Run right, following the nose-tickling scent of a powderwing that must have flown by a moment ago. But the insect scent was gone after a few steps. *Twitch.* Turn left, and there was a stalk of bent grass, heavy with seeds. I stopped, and marked it with my spoor. I'd return for it later. Tonight, I would hunt.

Lightning flashed, closer than before, and the sky growled a few seconds later. I stood to listen and heard a second rumble from a new direction. There had been no flash, however, and the wind from that direction carried the hot tar/oil smell I'd noticed earlier. As it grew stronger, I dropped to all fours and dug quickly in the dust with my long claws, creating a place to hide. Then I stopped myself. There was no danger here — only thunder. The wind shifted again, and the smell disappeared. Grass slapped against my back.

I had gone only a few paces when I found it: a pawprint, deep enough that I nearly fell into it. Bigger than any pawprint I'd ever seen. It could hold two of me, nose to tailtip. I sniffed, but found no animal smell. Just something like tree pitch — or hot stone. I smoothed my whiskers, wondering what could have made the print. The smell was utterly foreign.

Then the wind brought a new scent, fresh and strong: insect — a hardshell. And close. I forgot all about the pawprint. My nose twitched as I sought the scent's source and my tail shivered in anticipation of fresh meat. At last I pinpointed the direction the scent was coming from. I followed it through the grass, running hard.

We hunters are not as fast as a hardshell, but we've got two advantages. Agility is one. We're stocky, but agile enough to leap. Once we hit their backs, that's it. Hardshells may have fierce jaws, but they can only use them on something directly in front of them. We have claws and teeth — and intelligence, our second advantage. It's all in knowing where to bite.

I was getting close: the tang of insect filled my nose as I rounded a tuft of grass. Then I saw the black body scurrying away. I dug my feet hard into the dust and leaped.

I landed on the hardshell's back, between the scrambling legs. Gripping hard with my claws, I worked my teeth into the crack between the thorax and head. The insect was big, as large as me. My hind feet scrambled against its smooth back, looking for a hold.

The hardshell ran, but I clung on tightly, my tail lashing behind. Grass slapped my face, but I held fast. The insect's jaws were gnashing furiously, unable to reach me.

Twice, I nearly fell off. Then my feet found the hold I needed. Pushing myself forward, I chose my mark and bit.

The taste of insect blood was sharp, and my mouth tingled with pleasure. A younger hunter might have forgotten herself, but I dug my teeth in harder, deep into the soft spot. Then I twisted my head to the side and tore.

I heard a crack, and the insect jolted to a stop. I fell from its back and rolled. A rock bruised my side, and I spat a piece of shell from my mouth. Then I leaped to my feet and ran back to my kill. Grabbing a hind leg, I flipped the insect over. The other legs were still twitching, so I kept clear of its jaws. But the head was at an angle, nearly severed. I tore open the belly and began to eat.

My face was buried in the guts, so I didn't notice the smell until it was all around me. But something made the hair on my spine rise. I looked up, and my nose was filled with the smell of hot stone. The air was so full of electricity my whiskers quivered right down to their roots. Something big blocked the path of the wind. A harsh new smell — the smell of the pawprint — made my nose nearly pinch shut. I tensed, ready to flee.

Then night became day.

It was like a beam of sunlight, concentrated in one tiny pool. Brighter than the sun, whiter than light should be. And I was at the center of it.

Something huge loomed over me. It looked like one of the hunters, reared up on two legs, ready to howl. The light was coming from one of its paws. The other paw reached for me — a paw twice my size. But that wasn't what frightened me most. The true horror was its face. The creature had no whiskers, no ear tufts, no snout. Just a flat black circle, as shiny as a hardshell's back.

I ran, just as the storm above me broke.

My heart pounded harder than the raindrops that fell around me as I ran. My claws dug the ground so deep I kicked wet dirt with each jump. The spoor of fear I left was so strong a kit could have followed it back to my burrow, even through the rain. But I didn't care. I wanted only to be home, to be safe. To be in a small, narrow place where I could turn and fight.

I plunged into my hole and bolted through the tunnel, through the comforting smell of dirt saturated with my own scent. Past my cache of seeds, past the dung tunnel. I didn't even stop for the fresh pink worm that had fallen from one wall — blind, stupid thing — but ran right over it.

My heart was still racing when I reached the nest. Panting, I quickly groomed myself. My white belly was streaked with dust and my own dung. I was that frightened.

Then I heard a rumbling overhead. Not thunder. No, the earth itself was roaring. Dirt rained down from above. I stopped smoothing my fur and ran back to the entrance of my burrow to look out.

Coming directly towards me was a second strange creature, larger than any I'd ever seen before. It was white and silver, crawling hard and heavy on the ground on four round black feet, with a face that was covered in numerous flat black eyes like a bug. It roared steadily as it came, and its breath smelled like the air after a lightning strike, and like tar.

As I bolted back into my burrow, I heard a squeak in the darkness ahead of me: my kits. Blind, hairless, too young to know the danger. Too young to run. I scrambled down the tunnel and sprang to them. Their noses pressed my belly. One found a nipple and began to suckle, but I shook it off. The rumbling noise was louder now, directly overhead.

I reached out, found one of the kits, and pulled it close. I turned it over in my paws, stroking its wrinkled back, searching.

When I found the neck I bit. One quick shake, and the kit was dead. I flung it aside and reached for the next, my tail lashing. It shrieked as my teeth missed their mark and sank into its back, and the others began to scramble blindly under me. I bit the wounded kit again, tasted a rush of blood, and knew I had found its throat. I shook my head hard: right, left. Finally it hung limp.

I was reaching for the third kit when I realized that the rumbling was softer now, more distant. I listened, and heard it gradually recede. Above, there was only the pounding of heavy rain. A wet breeze blew through the tunnel that led to the nest. It smelled mainly of wet grass and mud, with only a faint trace of the spoor of the creature that had frightened me so.

I kicked aside the loose dirt and pulled my last two kits near me. This time, I let them suckle. Their tiny paws prodded my breasts, which warmed as my milk began to flow. I was trembling, wet with rain.

I licked my lips. Blood. I settled myself gently down beside my feeding kits and reached for the bodies of the two I had killed. Their tiny bones crunched as I fed on them. Each was little more than a few wet mouthfuls. Eventually, I slept.

When morning came, a dim light filtered down through the tunnel and the air smelled sweet and clean. I left my kits sleeping and climbed up through the damp tunnels. The sun was up, the air hot and murky. The grass steamed, causing the orange ball of the sun to waver in the sky.

Just next to the burrow hole was a line of crushed and broken grass. Several hops away was an identical, parallel path. Both stank of the creature that had chased me last night.

I sniffed: wet earth, the sharp tang of crushed grass, and sticky-sweet pollen. I could see no sign of the creature that had rumbled over my burrow the night before. I nearly turned back to the cool of the burrow, but then I heard a distant whining. It was high-pitched, stressed, almost like a howl. For a moment, I thought it was One Eye. But then the wind shifted and I caught the smell of something foreign. The air in that direction had a faint tang of electricity to it.

I don't know what made me follow the creature's path. Perhaps the scent of the brilliant little flowers that had blossomed everywhere following the rain had made me giddy. Starflower pollen has that effect — the starflowers had been in bloom the last time I mated with One Eye. At any other time, I might have killed him for approaching my burrow.

Or perhaps it was simpler than that. I bared my teeth and gave a short bark-squeak of challenge. The creature had crossed my territory, caused me to kill my kits. I didn't like that.

Anger kept me going. As I followed the double trail, the whine ahead grew steadily louder.

The trail ended in a tangle of grabweed that was growing rapidly after the sudden rain, leaves sprouting and unfurling as I watched. The vines were already so thick I couldn't see to the center of the clump. They had grown over something — an enormous creature with round black feet that was straining against the vines that held it: the creature that had violated my territory last night. I twitched my whiskers in disgust as it struggled to get free. It was the wrong thing to do: motion attracts grabweed. Given enough rain, it will even grow over something as big as the creature that now lay helpless in its grasp.

As I circled the clump of grabweed, fronds of it pulled free of the tangle and waved in my direction. The tips of the vines were like spiral claws. I kept well back.

White, syrup-filled flowers hung everywhere from the crisscrossed vines. Winged insects buzzed around them. My mouth watered and I felt my adrenaline rush — such tasty morsels! But I knew better than to try for them. I watched as one of the white grabweed flowers suddenly snapped shut like a hungry mouth, trapping an insect inside.

As I reached the other side of the tangle, I could see that the first creature I'd spotted last night was also trapped inside the grabweed: the creature with the featureless black face. I reared back on hind legs, whiskers quivering, and showed it my teeth, but it did not move. Nearly smothered in a smaller clump of grabweed, it lay prone. The only parts of the creature that were free of the tangle were one white arm and its shiny black face. Long gouges marked the damp earth in front of its paw: it had tried to claw itself free. Stupid thing. You have to bite grabweed: bite hard and fast. Chew through the vine before more than one or two stalks have wrapped around you. If you don't, you become trapped and starve while the insects suck your juices and in turn feed the grabweed.

I went as close to the face as I dared, and stood in its shadow. That was when I noticed something startling: the creature had a second face beneath the smooth black surface. I could see a tiny snout, and an open mouth with broad flat teeth, surrounded by short curling fur. Its eyes were closed.

They opened.

I leaped back in surprise — and just in time. The creature's paw swept toward me, grasping. Its clumsy fingers nearly closed upon the tip of my tail. The grabweed spiraled forward, attracted by the sudden motion.

It was several moments before I could approach the creature again. In that short time, the grabweed had grown over its free arm. The creature had managed to pull the grabweed from its head, but small knots of root were sprouting there again.

Behind the creature with the double face, the larger clump of grabweed was starting to smoke. The big creature had finally stopped whining and trying to move its feet; I assumed that it was dead.

I approached the smaller creature cautiously. Its face-shell was no longer black. Instead, it had become clear. The creature's eyes were wide white ovals with a spot of brown at the center — eyes that rolled in terror. Its arm trembled as it strained once more to free itself. The creature certainly looked helpless, but there was that hard shell, that thick white hide. Where the grabweed had been torn free, there wasn't a spot of blood.

I watched for a moment, then made my decision. Keeping a wary eye on the arm, I ran in close and leapt up onto the head of the creature. My claws slipped on its shell face, but I managed to scramble around behind.

Much of the torso was buried under grabweed, but I could still see my target: the neck. I chose my spot carefully, then bit.

It took several bites to break the thick white hide of the creature. When I'd made a tiny puncture, I used my claws to pull the hole wider. Air rushed past me, carrying a stale-sweet stink. Then I was inside, squeezing my way in between the creature's inner and outer skins. It only took a moment to find the spot where the blood pulsed.

The inner skin was as soft as my blind kits', slippery with moisture. I bit hard and held, forcing my teeth in. Blood sprayed past me, soaking my face and shoulders, but I hung on, even as the creature thrashed violently. As I had hoped, the grabweed held it to the ground.

The creature made one brief, sharp noise, much like a bark-squeak. Then it lay still.

I squeezed back through the hole I had made. Air was still rushing out of the outer skin, attracting the grabweed. A vine wrapped around my leg, and I had to gnaw my way through it to escape. Then I leaped up onto the creature's head, and away into the clear.

After running a short distance, I turned to watch. The grabweed began working its way through the creature's outer skin, twisting in through the hole I had bitten. The creature lay absolutely still, not reacting at all to this attack. I grinned, showing it my teeth. Then I sat back on my haunches and began to groom myself. The creature's blood tasted rich and sweet, and I savored every lick.

When I finished cleaning myself, I made my way back to my burrow, whiskers bristling with pride at my kill. The next time one of these intruders invaded my territory, I would know what to do: lure it into a patch of grabweed, then go for the throat.

As the other hunters say, you just have to know where to bite.

Angel of Death

by Susan Forest

"Ben. You sitting? I got the fight of your life on the hook."

The telephone screen disrupted into horizontal lines and reestablished itself in black and white. Ben stumbled into the kitchen of his apartment and pushed the heap of used joy tabs and magazine chip drives from the keyboard. He forced his gritty eyes open and maximized the call screen. Now, the perspiration on the mutant shoulder protruding from Frank's neck was visible through the monitor's streaks.

"What, that kiss-ass, Snake Arm?" Ben pressed his hands into his scalp to squeeze his hangover down the back of his neck and clear his head. His skin itched from last night's tabs. "I put his throat under my spur in two rounds last month. That chickenshit called Clean Rules before I could finish him." He slumped into the frayed office chair. "Listen, Frank. He want back at me, it gonna cost him, and I mean Mutant Rules. And, I don't box anyone under five mill." He grasped the back of the chair with the vestigial elbows sprouting from his shoulder blades to keep the cushion from tumbling to the floor.

"Snake Arm's still on the bender he went on after your last fight. Forget him. We're talking Clean."

"Clean?" Ben rolled his chair closer to the table, sleep fleeing his body. He flipped up the volume. "Fuck, what do you mean, Clean?"

"I mean it. The big one."

The implication lodged like a pit in his throat, blocking his breath, as Frank savoured the surprise.

"Razor."

"Don't fuck with me. Cleans don't fight Swamp Frogs." Frank was a good talker, slippery. Dealing with him was like trying to catch a school of catfish. "Why would Razor fight me?"

"Ben." Frank shook his head, drawing the word out in mild rebuke as though Ben was a child. The screen hissed with snow, then cleared. "Ben, you're the Angel of Death. You're the champion. You've never *once* got a mark on your face. You've put every contender that ever met you in a pit under your spur."

"Every Swamp Frog."

"Where's your self-respect? Ben! Cleans call us 'Swamp Frogs'."

"Fuck you." He rubbed his hands over his face. He didn't know another cockboxer who could boast a face with no scar. His flawless appearance *made* him the Angel of Death, along with the symmetrical elbows arching from his shoulder blades, tapering to long, delicate, and quite lethal fins. His trademark. "Keep talking, Frank. Lay it out, and be straight with me this time."

Frank shrugged with his extra shoulder. Having only one superfluous limb gave him an ugly, half-breed kind of look. Word had it Frank'd had another shoulder removed by a back alley surgeon and was socking money away to finish the job, but Ben didn't believe it. It was one thing to mask a mutation, another to try to erase it. There were scars and genetic tests and long jail terms. "What the hell do you want me to say? Razor's world champion. You're world champion. This'll be the fight of the century. It'll *make* cockboxing."

Ben laughed, a single, derisive hoot.

"A Clean-Mutant fight on broadbeam. It's never been done." Frank's voice was smooth as brandy. "Ben, think about the money."

The whirlpool of Frank's persuasion tugged at him. "They's already money all over the pits," he argued. "Purse, beamwidth, gambling."

"You think that's money?" Frank sneered. "Cleans follow your fights. They know you'll whip his ass. They want to *see* it."

"So why Razor wanna fight with me?" Frank was good at talking without saying anything. "Ain't for money."

"You don't know what kind of money we're talking about. Besides, it's getting embarrassing. He can't hold his head up. Razor has got to box you."

"Then he crazy."

"No, he's smart. And he's got a good team of lawyers."

"Yeah? And what do I got? A lying, double-crossing manager out for his own skin. Why should I trust you?"

"Because this is the only time you, or any Mutant, are ever going to get the chance to fight a Clean. You say 'no' and Razor tells the world you haven't got the balls. He's off the hook."

"No one gonna let a Mutant cut a Clean."

"Leave that to me. You've heard of Sam Korchinski. He's got a pit with seating for two-hundred-eighty thousand, and exclusive simulcast rights for a billion viewers, world wide. Purse is two hundred million to the winner, hundred and fifty mill to you."

Ben slumped back hard in the chair, the rollers bumping him up against the uneven floor boards. A hundred and fifty mill. Fuck. He could strap on his spurs for that.

"Thought that might get your attention."

A new hover jet–red–convertible. A house, a yacht for all his friends, partying like they show in rag mags. Yeah, Peru, some place away from the crowds, away from Mutant ghettos. And clothes: jackets roomy enough for his back elbows, make him pass for Clean on the street. Him and Marci, out on the town– "So I throw the fight."

"That's non-negotiable."

"How do I know, I lie down with a razor at my neck, I ever get up again?"

"Clean Rules. Besides, this fight'll be on broadbeam world wide."

"Yeah? Well, he put me under the spur ten seconds, max. And listen, Frank. He don't cut my face."

"It's already in the contract."

"What make you think I gonna do it?" He leaned forward and gripped the monitor. "I take my life in my hands, cutting a Clean, and you know it."

"You afraid?"

"Fuck you."

"Because, Ben, you're going to make this sweet." Frank's voice was soft as cream. "The fight goes the full fifteen rounds. You cat-and-mouse him. You draw him in, reel him out. Dance around him." The words wrapped Ben in the heat of the lights, the sweet tang of sweat and blood. "Everyone knows who's in control. There's no contract on that."

A class pit. A Clean pit, room to move. Broadbeam.

"I'll talk to Korchinski and Razor's people."

"Remember, my face stays clean."

"I'll look out for you. Don't crap out on me, now."

The door whooshed behind him and Ben shrunk the connection. "I ain't said yes." He doused the screen.

"What you doing?" Marci's voice, full of suspicion.

The headache forced itself back into the rim of his skull, a dull throb. The fatigue of a four a.m. crash soaked back into his limbs. "What'd you hear, babe?"

Marci stood just inside the door, her eyes big and brown under querulous brows and a disarray of blonde hair. She held her robe closed over her swollen breasts and pregnant belly. The sole indication she was mutant was the pair of small flippers on each of her ankles. "More'n I wanted. You gonna get killed."

"That two-bit cockboxer, Razor? Babe, you seen him fight. He got one powerful right heel, and he don't even use his wrists and elbows, except in defense." Ben pushed himself from the rickety chair and wrapped his arms around his wife. "Babe, you freezing. Come on back to bed." He stroked her hair.

"You fucking with me, Ben."

✦•I••I••I•✦

He wasn't fucking with her. She just didn't understand.

Ben danced and poked at a mid-level virtual boxer at the gym, warming up. There was no way he could lose to the Clean. To any Clean.

He'd been in the pits since he was fourteen. Dirt pits, mostly, with steep-raked benches above and no way out but riding that golden rope and stirrup that rose with the winner shaking his fist into the smoky spotlight. He'd been there, pummeled by cheers and boos, eggs and cheap champagne geysers and the stink of beer and sweat, while money and tabs crossed the table. He rode the rope while big old-fashioned cameras hovered in to televise local for pirates to pipe onto the beam, broadbeam and narrowbeam. When the loser was scraped from the floor to be dumped in some wailing, but rich widow's arms, you didn't fool around with scoring 'points.'

Not like the Cleans, with their broadbeam fights. Oh yeah, he'd seen them. Soft. Censors didn't just cut to commercial to hide bloodshed for viewers with weak stomachs. They eliminated the deep-scoring points. They eliminated death. Clean Rules, they called it. 'Winning' by holding a spur to the jugular for ten lousy seconds.

He toweled the sweat from the back of his neck after his virtual sparring, and strapped on his practice spurs. "Hey, Tom." He pointed to the training pit. "Two rounds."

Tom grinned up from the bench, stretching his muscles out. Tom was the best practice trainer Ben knew. He could've given Ben a run for the prizes if he'd had a closer's instincts. "Don't know'f I can go that long with you. Rumour has it, you getting ready to fight Clean."

Ben tightened his knee spurs. "Always rumours." He lowered himself into the pit.

Tom took a swing at him with an elbow and danced out of the way. Ben ducked the rubber spur and swung with his foot, brushing Tom just above the knee.

"That be something, to see a Clean meet a Swamp Frog. Yeah!" He swiped at Ben's forehead with a wrist. "You cut him, Ben. You cut his face. Show blood."

"Hey, man, when you fight a Clean, they's rules. Can't just go around cutting his face. Got to make it elegant.

A nick to the upper arm—" He demonstrated. "—a slice to the thigh. A mark on the back of the hand."

"But you get him, man. And when you get him, you use a *limb*. You strap razors to your angel wings."

Ben smiled. "Cleans don't have limbs. Might call that an unfair fight." He ducked and flipped a fin above his head to touch Tom's upper thigh. "Besides, I be a fool to put my face on broadbeam as the Swamp Frog who cut a Clean. They get me after, like shooting catfish in a tank."

"They couldn't. You be too famous then." Tom spun and nearly caught Ben's knee with a soft spur. He pulled up at the pit wall with Ben's elbow blade at his throat.

Ben relaxed and grinned. "Go again."

"I mean it, man. You gotta do it." Tom repositioned himself and waited for Ben to spring. "You been invited."

"So?"

"You not just you, Ben. You all of us. Every Mutant, fighter or not."

"Hey, what you mean? Get out of that cloud, I can't understand a word you say." He danced around his partner, dancing in to touch, dancing back.

"Make them Cleans show a little respect. You know what Cleans do to us. Rape our women—"

"Wait. Slow down." Ben stepped back to the pit wall, his shoulder elbows drooping, his hands at his sides. "Why's it up to me to prove Mutants is just as good? I ain't gone to school, I don't talk good. I ain't done nothing."

Tom lowered his fists, looking him in the face. "Yeah, man. But you got the chance."

>+I+I+I+<

"You signed it, didn't you?"

Marcia stood, framed in the doorway of their bedroom, the dim light casting her face in shadow.

Ben leaned on the entry button, half his attention diverted to the pneumatics, wondering if the door was going to close on him as he wobbled in and out of the apartment. A cloud of confusion wafted around him, bringing Marcia's frown in and out of focus.

"How many tabs did you have?"

"Just two, I swear." He tried to remember the table in the corner of the bar, Frank's red face, the papers, the pen, the tabs. "Okay, maybe three."

"You'll never get out of that pit alive."

"What, you think I can't hold off a Clean? Marcia—" He came forward, quite steadily, he thought, and put his arms around her.

"Let me see the contract."

He pulled a copy from his jacket pocket. "You'll see. It's just a show. Entertainment. Big bucks."

"Come on." She led him into their bedroom and let him fight with his clothes as she sat on the rumpled bed to read. Thin curtains dulled the flickering neon lights outside the window.

"A hundred and fifty million, Marci. You know what we could do with that kind of money?" He dropped a shoe on the floor.

"Cockboxers die in the pit."

"Marci, this is a Clean fight. Nobody gonna die."

"Don't mean he have to cut you fair. Ref can say you cheated, give Razor a free cut, hold you down. Don't matter it's murder. Cleans ain't gonna stand for a Swamp Frog proving he's better." She read through the second page.

"It's all in the contract. Small cuts, no more'n an inch. And I don't take a cut to the face. I put that part in. No one cuts the Angel's face. Then I lay down, he puts the spur on my neck and we walk away with a hundred and fifty million. I even wear my wing razors."

"But you can't use them. It be for you like fighting with one arm cut off."

"Marci—" he soothed.

"And what about after? Broadbeam put you in everyone's house. You like a fish in a bowl. You cut his face, they see it like it was in their lap. And out in the streets, after, in L.A., in London, in Tokyo, the Cleans saw you take blood, what do they do?"

Ben stopped pulling his shirt from his shoulder elbow.
"Roam the streets looking for Mutants, any kind of
Mutant. Women. Kids. And they got to prove they bet-
ter than you."

Ben squeezed his eyes shut and shook his head. "Babe,
you just like Tom."

"Tom? I ain't nothing like Tom."

"Yeah." He nodded. "You just like Tom. You got to
make this all bigger than it is. Listen, babe. I'm a *cockboxer*,
for fuck sake, not a... a idol or something. I ain't saving
the world and I ain't making no one kill no one. Now come
here and let me nuzzle you good."

"Rip up the contract."

"It don't matter. It just a copy."

"Call Frank. Call it off. Don't show up."

"Babe, don't talk nonsense. I can handle it."

Marcia pulled away from him, tears springing to
her eyes. "Frank don't care if you get cut, or killed,
or if riots happen in the streets, long as he make his
money."

He reached out to hold her to him. "So, what's changed,
girl? That the way it always was."

"I need you to come back," she whispered into his neck.
"Come back and be a daddy to my baby."

"Hey. Hush, now. I'm coming back, girl."

→•I•I•I•←

Coming back with a trophy in his hand. Yeah.

Frank took him to the plane. Marcia wouldn't come
to Bangkok, said the doctor wouldn't let her fly. Even at
the boarding gate she told Ben to turn around, but there
were newsmen and cameras and Frank had him smiling
at this one and waving at that one, and when he turned
around, all he could see was Marcia's back as she slipped
out through the crowd.

They arrived in Bangkok a week before the fight. Frank
got him a trainer and a sparring partner and a first-class
pit. There were media scrums every day, and Ben said
everything Frank told him to.

The spectacle began hours before the fight. As Ben warmed up with his sparring partner and strapped his sharpened spurs to his ankles, knees, wrists, elbows, and for show only, his angel wings — everything taped solidly in place — the thrumming started. A throb like an engine in the bowels of a freighter, the heartbeat of a hundred thousand hearts seeped through the building. Ben knew the rhythm. His own heart sped in response. He strode with his entourage through the tunnel and out to the platform beside the pit.

Razor stood at the opposite edge, flashing his spurs in the blinding lights, conducting the boom of voices that pressed on them from the enormous cavern above.

Ben dropped his hood and cape and the roar wavered for a moment in a gasp of horror, then redoubled, a bass rumble.

Cameras floated in like scavenger fish. The referee on the crane seat spoke into a microphone, his words resounding around the arena, as inarticulate as the crowd. Ben didn't need to hear the words. He had been here, done this, many times before.

As contender, he set his foot in the stirrup first, allowing the rope to lower him into the pit, extending his blade-tipped wings and waving his spurs at the crowd to multiply their derision. He stepped onto the sprung wooden floor of the pit, feet apart and arms akimbo, and watched as the rope lowered Razor to his place. Their eyes met, and the Razor nodded. Ben flexed his arms, back, legs, watching Razor do the same, listening for the sound that would change the world.

The bell.

Adrenaline pumped into Ben's arms, legs. He felt good, in his natural element.

Razor proved to be everything Ben expected: muscled and quick, alert and skilled. Unlike matches Ben had seen on narrowbeam, Razor did not over-use his powerful right ankle. He mixed moves with his wrists and elbows, shoulders and knees.

Still, there was an over-quickness, a deeper breathing, a stiffness to his movements. And in these close quarters, a telltale musk in Razor's sweat.

Fear.

Ben smiled. He knew opponents with fear.

In the second and third rounds, Ben's rhythm deepened, became more natural, his breathing good. The tide of sound from above receded in his ears. He enjoyed the sparring, not cutting too much or too often, and holding back from letting himself get cut. Too much blood loss early on led to fatigue, and Ben was in for the full fifteen rounds. He'd play it cool and get out untouched. Marci was waiting.

In the next rounds, Razor sharpened, finding his own rhythm, losing a little of his fear. He pressed harder, finding ways to come from behind, tempting Ben to use his wings. A couple of times, Ben had to pull himself back from an illegal move, and once he felt the sting of a razor on his shoulder. Not much, a scratch to clot almost instantly, but a reminder. Toward the end of the sixth round, Razor did a quick, double slice, to nick Ben's hand and his knee. The crowd erupted in frenzy and Razor pushed in deeper, panting with the effort, only to be sliced and sent to his corner as the bell rang. First real blood.

The lights poured heat into the pit. After eight rounds, they left the arena to allow the advertisers and bartenders to make money and the reporters to discuss every cut. Ben was rubbed and covered like a racehorse and hustled to the prep room.

"Half way to a hundred and fifty million." Ben wiped at a trickle of blood from his bicep. "I feel good. Heart, lungs, doing good."

"The crowd is ugly." Frank paced toward the door and back again, looking over his shoulder. Waves of sound beat through the walls. Bass chords of some rock hit pumped the audience.

"You okay? You don't look so good. You sweatin' more than me." Ben leaned in front of his manager, uneasy. "Hey. Frank."

"What?"

"You got us covered. You said you got us covered. We gonna get out of here, tonight."

"Yeah, yeah, don't worry."

The boy pulled the towel from the massage table. "Rub, sir?"

Ben ignored the boy. "Frank. You getting us out of here?"

"Yeah." Frank went back to the door and put his hand on the button, then changed his mind and came back. "But, Ben, you've got to let him cut you a few times. The janitors hardly had to clean the floor. Two-hundred-eighty thousand is a lot of angry people. You know, police can't be expected to control that many if they are really feeling cheated."

"Ain't no cheat. They getting a good show." Ben turned to watch Frank's pacing. "They getting blood, they getting a high class fight, lots of what you call finesse. I'm keeping to the rules, keeping my end of the contract." The hairs on the back of his neck tingled, and he held out a hand to stop Frank. "How about you? That limo you got, it armoured, right? It big and heavy?"

"You're doing good. Doing good, right by the rules." Frank rubbed his face. "I've got to go check my bets."

The boy turned ashen. "But we'll be safe in this room, won't we?"

Ben shook his head. Was the kid just figuring it out now?

Frank returned to the door, listening to the thump of a hundred thousand boots above them. The call came for the second half.

"Come on, Ben. Get it over."

The boy turned and threw his gear into a bag.

Razor had a different look when he came down for the second half. He jumped the bell, pressing hard, and Ben let him make a couple of superficial cuts. He took a few wounds to his shoulders and outer thighs, even one small scratch on his belly, before sending the boxer back with a streaming cut to the lower neck. It didn't matter to the crowd. The music boomed and they chanted in one voice, no words filtering down through the murk.

But Razor kept up the pressure. Sure, his handlers had told him to be more aggressive, but this was more than coaching strategy. The fighter looked into Ben's eyes more, worked from his centre more, smiled more. What was different?

The smell.

Ben put it together.

The musk of fear. It was gone.

Razor must have got some information. What? Who from?

The bell rang for round ten. Razor crouched, gaudy blue and green silks sticking to his groin, muscles gleaming, dark hair tousled.

What? This fight was going to be thrown, that was a given. Why would Razor work any harder than he had to? Some other double cross. A lot of people were in for high stakes, a lot of money was changing hands. But that was taken care of in the contract. Unless... someone was willing to ditch the contract... lose out on the money to be made... but for what? What had changed since the beginning of the fight? Who was dealing between rounds?

"Mute rules! Mute rules!" The words of the chant filtered through to his thoughts. Mute rules? That made no sense.

The bell rang for the twelfth time, and Razor pressed him, pressed him, blowing hard but still pushing. The powerful right ankle came at him again and again, followed by quick combinations and that right ankle again. Ben was pushed back, taken blind side, cut when he didn't intend to take a cut. The pit became slippery as a dirt pit never did. Razor moved as though he intended to win on his own talent.

The thirteenth round ended. Ben went to his corner, winded and bleeding. Sweat stung a dozen unstaunched cuts. Razor slouched on his stool, leaning back on the wall in his corner, breathing hard and holding a pad to his rib. He poured water on the side of his face and looked at Ben through half-closed eyes.

"Mute rules! Mute rules!"

Mute rules– Fuck!

The bell rang.

The Cleans didn't want the Mutant to rule. They wanted Mutant Rules. Ben crouched in the ready stance at the centre, watching Razor approach.

He locked eyes with the Clean. He knew.

"So. Figure it out, yet, Swamp Frog?"

What, Mutant Rules? It was absurd for Razor to agree to that. He would lose.

"Fifty seconds, Loser." They circled one another as if at opposite ends of a long tunnel that had no room for contracts and crowds and rules.

Razor forced him into a side wall and nicked his shin. Ben pushed him back, fought like he was in a dirt pit. Razor gave as good as he got.

Round fifteen. The rhythm of the chant enveloped the pit.

Mutant rules. One way or another, the crowd was determined to have blood. Real blood. His blood.

Could they get away with Mutant rules on the broadbeam? Maybe. If the Clean won.

Razor swung a leg high. Ben took a cut above his elbow that he hadn't intended to take, close to a tendon. Not good.

Ben only had to look at Razor to know he intended to win on Mutant Rules. He and his lawyers had renegotiated. Without Ben.

Renegotiated with Frank.

The Clean swung wide with his left wrist and Ben gave him a slash to a rib. He thought of Marcia and the baby. Peru. Marcia would never see Peru. Fuck this.

"Back off."

"What, the Swamp Frog scared?"

With an effort, he lunged and sliced Razor deep across the chest so the blood streamed down his abdomen. "We got a contract."

Razor's cheeks bloomed with surprise and hot rage, and a grunt belched from his clenched teeth. Ben had seen unreasoned fury in his opponents' eyes before. In the long milliseconds between breaths, he waited. There was no contract. Frank was probably halfway to the airport with a sack of money. *His* face wasn't on broadbeam.

Razor charged, both arms forward, razors aimed for Ben's throat and face.

Ben would not die in the street beneath the heels of a mob. He would not die barricaded in a hole in the ground.

Ben swept at Razor's ankle and missed, tripping him, and the boxer stumbled forward, one elbow spur slicing deep into Ben's cheek.

His face.

His beautiful face that Marci loved to touch. He tasted his own blood.

No one cut the Angel's face. No one.

Power exploded in his chest, and Ben launched himself forward, an ankle spur severing Razor's calf muscle. His left hand reached out and cradled the Clean's head, holding it in place, the eyes glassy now with pain, a relaxed, dumbfounded expression on his slack face. Ben dipped with his shoulder, allowing his right angel wing to reach forward.

Mutant Rules? The crowd could have Mutant Rules. He would not die in this pit under a cockboxer's spur. He drew his angel razor deep across the Clean's throat.

He dropped the dead weight and turned to look up into the blinding lights and the ref's horrified face and the cameras backing off. Silence reverberated around him, before the explosion of sound that would surely follow, and he grabbed the rope and bared his chest to the multitude. Marcia, at least, would be rich, and his son would never box.

And if the mob tore him to pieces as the golden rope raised him from the pit, then let the broadbeam watch.

Transplant
by Yvonne Pronovost

Once upon a time someone told me that life was how you looked at it. "Zea," he said to me, "it's how you play the game. Choose your team wisely."

That was how I found myself on my knees servicing my boss at the M-Gen Corporation a year later. Something nice for something nice — a lab and funding to continue my post-graduate work for a monthly blowjob, right before the salary cheques were issued. It wasn't that bad a bargain, really. M-Gen is notoriously difficult to get funding from, and with my aunt's criminal record tainting my own reputation, it was hard to get a job in my field — especially if I wished to conduct my own research and not act as someone else's grunt.

The television behind Dr. Havers was tuned to the news, and its light shed dancing shadows across the folds in his pants and shirt. I hated the taste of him and the cheap synthetic cloth of his pants. They carried the lingering stink of old farts and cologne and bubblegum, the latter a residue left over from his lunch hour visit with his five-year-old son. I closed my eyes, and then opened them again as the dark left too much room for shame. I needed something to distract myself, and the television announcer's reedy voice was perfect. I was more than happy to dwell on someone else's problems. Even universal ones seemed easier to solve.

"...is pushing for the tightening of international laws that protect genetic ownership. According to the proposal made by M-Gen and Tri-Mark, who hold the majority of gene patents, a person would have to apply for a permit to engage in high risk occupations and activities such as space flight, undersea diving, and construction work. Bodily modifications such as piercing, tattoos, plastic surgery, and non-essential surgeries would be evaluated on a case-by-case basis for approval and subjected to a damage fee. This movement is an addendum to existing laws governing reproduction and medical procedures."

Dr. Havers sighed. I leaned back on my heels and wiped my mouth on the sleeve of my lab coat. There was gum in my pocket for just this occasion, and I didn't hesitate to use it. Dr. Havers leaned back on his chair with his wet penis lying flaccid against his leg and ran a possessive hand along the side of my face. "You get better ever time, Zea. Join me for a cocktail?"

I thought about running to my lab for safety, but then I thought about Dr. Havers locking my lab doors against me in a fit of pique. My gum suddenly tasted of ash, and I swallowed it as I went to pour a drink from his bar — an illegal indulgence that probably made him feel suave, dangerous, younger than his fifty years... and maybe even moderately attractive. Maybe I'd have a martini. Something highly alcoholic that would sterilize my tongue.

The television played on and the smooth, robotic face of the announcer was cut and replaced with a bobbing camera view of an older man with a toupee facing a sea of reporters and protesters. I knew him — I'd seen his picture in one of the files spread out on Dr. Havers' desk. He gripped the podium with white-knuckled hands. "Neither Tri-Mark nor M-Gen are attempting to control human life. We are simply protecting our investment and preserving human variation, which, in turn, will ensure that our race will last for years to come."

"But at what cost? Damage to the body does not affect the genetic code. What about the rights of the individual?" I couldn't see who'd said it, but the spokesman didn't look pleased. He looked frustrated.

"Individual rights and freedoms end where collec-
tive and corporate ownership begins," he said. "Free will
must be contained by law, and already *is* contained by
law. We do not claim ownership of the mind, or the soul
— we only claim what our patents extend to — the genetic
code and the body that houses it. We are protecting our
property for the good of all humanity."

"Bunch of liars," Dr. Havers muttered. "They'd pack
us all up in boxes and sell us to ourselves if they could."

I found the gin as he changed the channel.

⊁⊷⊹⊶⊹⊶⊹⊷⊰

Lycopersicon hominidae is the Frankenstein child of
modern medicine and botany. At one time organs were
grown in petrie dishes, at another, inside animals like
pigs. Both are costly procedures, and in today's polluted
world where we eat like kings from the garbage of the
periodic table, organ transplants are a necessity for
anyone who wants to live beyond the age of fifty.
Lycopersicon hominidae solved the economic problem:
we've learnt to grow organs like genetically modified
vegetables.

My lab is full of tomato plants, all hung with human
hearts. Dr. Havers made a face as he moved between the
glass terrariums that kept them quarantined until he'd
reached my desk, where he flipped through a file that
lay open there. The end of the month meant pay cheques
and blowjobs, but it also meant research evaluations and
the invasion of my laboratory. I found it easier to deal
with Dr. Havers in his own office. This was my sanctuary
and I didn't like inviting my enemy in. "This is all you've
got?" he asked me.

I shifted uneasily from foot to foot and wondered if
he'd be offended if I indulged in a breath mint. I could
still taste him on my lips, could still smell his skin and
feel the crinkle of hair, and was nauseated by it. "Yes,
sir. But I'm making progress—"

"Where? There's barely enough data collected to satisfy
me, let alone the review board! You're not irreplaceable,

Dr. Reid. I'm sorely tempted to turn your project over to someone who can produce results."

I nervously swallowed, fiddled with the ring on my pinky finger, wondered what I would do if I were banished from my lab. "I've only been here for a year and been able to sample three generations of mature organs, Dr. Havers. There's a fourth on its way and I've begun splicing seeds for a fifth—"

"But you're not a reliable worker." Dr. Havers shrugged and leaned his hip against my desk. The edge of his lab coat sent a pencil rolling for cover as his piggy little eyes pinned me in place as effectively as a nail through my instep. I bristled. "Your family has a history, and neither myself nor my supervisors are unaware of it. What am I supposed to think when there aren't concrete results?"

"You know this is a long term project — you knew that when I applied for funding and you endorsed my research!" My fists were clenched and I could feel the beginnings of an angry flush. "There hasn't been *time*! And my aunt has nothing to do with this—"

"But the Board won't believe that. Your early development included contact with your aunt, and I'm sorry, Zea, but you know as well as I do how radical ideas flow through families."

"That's not fair." I could say it as much as I pleased, but he was right. Familial conditioning was an embedded concept in psychology and sociology: we are a product of our environments just as we were built from our genes, and no word of mine would be able to shift current theory in my favour. Dr. Havers arched an eyebrow, and I couldn't meet his eyes so I stared at the dimple in his chin.

"Spin," he said.

"What?"

"It's all in how you perceive the problem. You have no results — yet." Dr. Havers' smile grew smug, and I wished again for a mint. "When I present your review to the Board, I can stress the lack of results. Or I can talk about the promise of results."

It was a neat trap, and I'd fallen into it before. I ran a hand over my face and attempted to smooth my expression

into something pliable, trying to erase the hate I felt for
him, for my stupid self. When I looked up, I was in control.
"What are you going to do?"

He pushed away from my desk and crossed the small
distance between us. His stomach brushed my own, and
he reached out to run his thumb over my lips. God, I hated
his thumbs. I hated all his appendages. "I don't know, Zea.
That depends on you."

"What do you want?" I was proud of the way my voice
didn't tremble.

He leaned towards me and his stubbled cheek brushed
mine. "I find you very desirable, Zea Reid," he whispered.
I felt my lip curl in disgust.

"No."

Dr. Havers grinned, but it was the smug grin of a man
who knew he'd won. He put a hand on my hip, ran his
palm up across the buttons of my lab coat and cupped my
breast. "I'm not an inattentive lover."

"You're married," I snapped. I turned on my heel and
retreated to the sanctity of the space behind my desk. There
was no greasy palm mark left on the pristine white of my
lab coat even though it felt as if there should be one. I
wished I'd told him, 'you're disgusting' instead.

Dr. Havers shrugged. "It hasn't bothered you before.
The ball is in your court, Dr. Reid. Good luck getting someone else to hire you after you've been slapped with a breach
of contract suit. And you can kiss your research goodbye."
He picked up the file and tapped its corner against the desk
and waited. I closed my eyes and said nothing, and after
a moment he left.

I don't know how long I stood there with my eyes closed
and my gorge rising. Giving the man a blowjob once in
a while was one thing: I hated the taste of it, I hated being
on my knees, and I hated myself for being so blasé about
it, and for having a price. But he was right — where else
could I go?

Eventually I left my office and returned to my lab. The
television in the corner was blinking rapidly through a

series of commercials: cars, restaurants, cars, lawyers. I turned up the volume, looking for something to distract myself, as I put on my gloves and opened the first of the terrariums. My tomatoes needed water.

It's surprising how attached one can get to a plant. I know each of my tomato plants by the shape of their leaves, the tilt of their stem, and the bloody smell of their sap. They lift their leaves toward artificial lights set beneath glass canopies, and my own, 100% human heart bleeds for them each time I have to infect them. I study heartworms. When we mutated tomato plants, nature mutated along with them and gave us *Helicoverpa hominidae*, a variation of the mis-named tomato fruit worm *Helicoverpa zea*. The adult moth is a bland little thing, an unassuming assassin who creeps into the heart of medical laboratories, past glass walls and through vents, to lay ticking time-bomb eggs inside mutated fruit. The larvae chew holes in the heart's chamber walls and if that doesn't kill the patient, then dead cocoons in the bloodstream will. Infection is almost undetectable unless the surgeons dissect the heart before transplant, which is costly and adds to the probability of heart failure. An infestation has a fatality rate of 87%, but there is only a 2% chance of a grown heart being infected.

The television changed from commercials back to the news, and once again the public face of M-Gen was thrown up on the screen. "The genetics companies M-Gen and Tri-Mark are attempting to push a revision of the current law through the International Parliament in the next three weeks. Theodore Banks is the president of M-Gen and has spearheaded the move toward closer regulation of the human body and the international gene pool," intoned the announcer, and the screen flickered as it returned to the bland face of the man I'd seen interviewed in Havers' office, replaying the same news clip over again.

"We do not claim ownership of the mind, or the soul — we only claim what our patents extend to — the genetic code and the body that houses it. We are protecting our property for the good of all humanity," said Banks. The screen cut back to the news announcers who began talking

about abandoned puppies and firemen, and I lost interest and turned back to my plants.

It's true what they say about my aunt. She did steal
seeds, and she modified them so that you could harvest
an ear of corn and plant any kernel from it, and it would
grow. When I was little, she'd given me a kernel of corn
and told me that we are the sum of our genetic heritage.
Humans, corn, tomatoes even, we're the result of our
ancestors. We reflect their loves, their lives, their hopes and
dreams, their desire to live and reproduce and be remembered into the next generation. We are the whole that comes
of a part, and if one cared to go back far enough, we're all
descended from the same thing, the same part, long ago.

I looked back up at the screen but it was still showing
firemen. *We are merely protecting our property for the good
of all humanity*, Theodore Banks had said, as if the abstract
idea of a human race was something you could physically
hold. M-Gen and Tri-Mark owned the patents for most of
the genes in the human body, and intellectually I knew that
they were within their rights as property holders to impose
laws that protected their investments. But I didn't *feel* as
though they owned my genes. I was nothing without my
genetic code. My body was me.

I gently closed up the terrarium and stood with the
watering can in my hand. I was the sum of parts, as was
Theodore Banks, as was Dr. Havers, as were my monstrous
sick tomatoes. Could the first living organism have imagined that the world would end up like this? This room, this
life.... Where did my DNA end and I begin? Where did I
end and my research, or Dr. Havers, or M-Gen begin?

If I didn't accept Dr. Havers' offer, I'd lose my lab, and
with it, my dreams. If Theodore Banks had his way, I'd lose
sovereignty over my body. There was only the safety of
my green lab and my green tomato-hearts locked away
behind glass that I was told was shatterproof.

My reflection and I eyeballed each other from our
respective reflected rooms, and I wondered how much of
the reflection really was me and how much of it was what
I imagined me to be.

+|+|+|+

I stayed late that evening, thinking about humanity and tomatoes and parts of a whole. I stayed until the lights went out and my heart was the only one left in all of the corporation's many rooms that beat. I felt alone, thrillingly sovereign and alive in the dark. It was liberating.

I knew Dr. Havers' code as well as I knew my own — once a month I'd stare at his liver spotted hands as he keyed it in and led me into the sanctity of his own laboratory, where I'd kneel and do to him what countless others have no doubt done and more will be subjected to. I'd stare at his hands again on the way out, chewing my gum furiously, desperately, as he released me from the locked inner rooms and I could run back to the green of my own, friendlier tomato plants.

I punched in the numbers — three, five, seven, one, nine, nine, one, four. My shaking finger slipped and the red light blinked as a message ran across the LCD display: Access Denied. I swore: that would be logged into the security records, a virtual fingerprint that might be traced. I wished I'd worn latex gloves: there was a box of them in my lab. Stupid of me. Stupider since I keyed in the code a second time with my bare fingers, correctly, and the light turned green. I reached out and twisted the door knob, and with a look over my shoulder at the sterile hallway, slipped inside.

It took a moment for my eyes to adjust. The air smelled like water and earth and stains on the armpits of lab coats and dress shirts. There was a dim corridor with doors to either side that led into small greenhouses where hearts quivered on tomato stems. Beyond that lay Dr. Havers' squash-and-kidneys, and oversized testicle-beans that I think he grows for his own amusement. It's the two doors off to either side that I'm interested in: in this facility, only Dr. Havers grows and tends to the organs that are destined for donor transplant.

I took a tentative step into the corridor and no alarm betrayed me, although the echo of my footstep made my heart leap and flutter like a moth's wing. I took another step, then a third, and then squinted at the clipboard that hung by the door to my left. A glass window that led inside framed several dozen tomato plants, all carefully labeled, peacefully photorespirating the night away. 'Banks, Theodore: L.h.-57263' was fourth on the list. I glanced over my shoulder to check for watchers and saw only myself reflected in the glass window opposite.

The bloody smell of sap and damp bone meal washed over me in a wave when I opened the door. The tomatoes, some hung heavy with pulpy hearts, others with their blood red blossoms furled against the dark, were lined up in neat rows inside individual cases to prevent cross-pollination and contamination. Instruments that regulated the damp of the soil, the humidity and ambient air temperature, the intake of carbon dioxide and exhalation of oxygen blinked and stared blankly with light bulb eyes.

My back felt exposed as I wandered down the aisle, taking my time in order to bolster my courage. The plant I wanted was tucked away by the back wall, quietly converting carbon dioxide to sugar, and I wondered if it would feel as peaceful if it knew in whose chest its fruit would beat. Theodore Banks' ripe hearts quivered as I opened the glass door that protected them, this time using the corner of my lab coat to shield my fingertips and retain what was left of my anonymity. The air that rushed out at me was as innocent as the summertime.

The syringe in my pocket slipped against my sweaty palm. God, I shouldn't be here.... I looked over my shoulder again, swearing I could hear someone breathing behind me, but I was alone. I shouldn't do this. I looked at the plant, then at the syringe I held in my hand. Theodore Banks might be M-Gen's president and the one who had proposed the stupid new genetics laws, but he was a person, too. He was probably married and lived in a nice house with roses in the garden, had a wife and a golf buddy and an aging mother he loved very much. He had a sovereign mind, a body... a heart?

I stood there for a long time. The sweat that slicked the syringe eventually dried and the machines that regulated the ambient air temperature clicked on to try to combat the draft from the door I held open. Using *my* hand. I stared at it and thought of corn, of tomatoes, of hearts and minds and of all the little parts that made us whole. I thought of living in suburbia and my aunt, wherever she was, running from the law but able to look at her reflection in the mirror. I thought about the choices I'd made — to go into botany, to do something that *meant* something, to give my boss oral sex once a month to keep my lab and erase the malevolent shadow my aunt had cast over my life. I thought about my genetic code, parceled out and sold as if I meant nothing. I wiggled my thumb and made a face at my shadowed reflection in the glass. The hearts hung ripe and full before me.

I uncapped the syringe, stuck a silver proboscis into the heart's soft walls, and depressed the plunger. Twice more I filled a tomato full of my worms' eggs as my own heart ached in sympathy. The plants looked no different but now they'd been damned, all because of a game I was playing. It was my cry in the night, my rebel act that drew a line between myself and the bureaucratic machine that was swallowing me whole.

Theodore Banks had made his choice — he let greed dictate his actions and used M-Gen as his weapon of choice. If he died then Dr. Havers would lose his job, and I would lose my blackmailer. My boss' vocal opinions, which ran counter to M-Gen's, would help bolster support for the brave souls who fought the corporation and their silly patents which tried to put a price on human life. The method of his death would make my work more important and I hoped I'd gain my freedom once I was in the media spotlight.

I returned to my laboratory with an empty syringe in my pocket and my heels tapping a staccato beat on the linoleum floor. The mirrors to either side reflected my face back at me, a face built from thousands of years of genes and mutations and the choices my ancestors have made along the way. Perhaps in the past there had been a woman with my dark eyes and pale hair who looked in the mirror and thought of the future. She'd imagine her grandchildren, and she'd smile.

I winked at my reflection, and smiled back.

Phantom Love

by René Beaulieu
translated by Sheryl Curtis

As he started up the stairs, he felt, as usual, deeply disgusted with himself. And, as usual, by the time he had reached the landing, his disgust had been almost completely transformed into desire. He crossed the hall and rang the bell. The door opened immediately.

"Good evening, handsome."

"Good evening, Sylvie."

The woman's long red hair floated over her shoulders. Her green eyes shone gently in the shadows. She was smiling. The low cut of her lace brassiere revealed firm, round breasts and the light from the hallway cast a wavelike reflection on her black silk panties.

The woman drew him into her arms, pulled him inside, and nudged the door closed with her foot. She rubbed gently against him, her pelvis against his, making small circles with her hips. He looked at her for a long moment, in silence, then pulled her to him and tried to kiss her on the lips. But she turned her face away with a smile, not quite as bright this time. He felt her irritation anyway.

"Not on the mouth. You know that," she said, looking out from under half-closed eyelids.

He glanced down and murmured, "Sorry, I always forget."

She slowly, but very deliberately, eased out of his embrace and took a few steps back. Her initial smile was back, even more brilliant this time.

"Would you like something?"

"No, thank you."

She moved towards the back of the room, slowly allowing her clothing to slip to the floor, as he undressed as well. She climbed onto the large bed, turned her back to him, and bent over on her hands and knees. She raised her hips a little, bent a little deeper, and started to slowly rub her breasts against the white satin sheets. Soon, a few brief sighs issued from her lips. He might almost have taken them for sobs if he had not been watching her. Her hand brushed against her belly, then slid down, between her legs. She gently opened the lips of her vagina and started to whisper softly, "Come... come..."

He walked over to the bed. With one hand, he placed two hundred and fifty dollars on the bedside table. She gave the money only a cursory glance. With the other, he grasped the woman's wrist and slowly, but firmly, removed her hand from between her thighs.

"Not like that."

She glanced up quickly, eyes suddenly filled with an almost savage light, in response to the change in the man's tone. She pulled her hand from his grasp, almost abruptly, then slowly rubbed her wrist.

"No need to get upset," she sighed, briefly glancing up with a weary, almost overburdened expression. But her brilliant smile gradually returned to her lips.

"I simply wanted to suggest a little change. I didn't know you were such a prude."

She moved closer to him, gently placing her hands on his chest. Her fingers played with the hairs there. She nipped him on the shoulder, not hard enough to cause any real pain. Just so that he could feel her teeth. Like a warning. Her hands started to roam, running up and down his body, as if she wanted to map out each tiny detail. Her green eyes moved down, towards the man's stomach, lingered a moment, her smile even brighter.

"And don't you try to tell me that you're not really frisky..."

Her hands slid slower, found his penis, and started caressing it gently. Then she bent down, kissed his belly, his thighs and, finally, took him fully into her mouth.

Their dialogue gradually became more horizontal. He kissed her, caressed her, prepared her for a long time before penetrating her. She came a first time, or faked it very expertly, then a second. Then it was his turn. Neither of them said a single word. They separated slowly, as if regretful, as if they had to exert their will over their bodies. They lay there, on their backs, on each side of the large, unmade bed, neither looking at the other.

After a moment, she reached over to the bedside table, on his side, stretching her fingers over the cover of the paperback edition of *Orpheus*, by Jean Cocteau, opened a small music box, releasing a well-known classical melody which he had never managed to identify. Next to the music box, lay a fine silver bracelet, the two well-known masks representing comedy and tragedy embossed in the metal. The man glanced quickly around the small room, astonished yet again by the number of books, CDs, tapes and videos that filled the overburdened bookshelves that literally covered the walls of the room.

She closed the box, a joint between her figures. She lit up and drew it slowly to her lips. She inhaled deeply, holding the first drag in for a long time, then exhaled the smoke as the sickly sweet odor filled the air between them. She held the joint out to him, negligently.

"No, thank you. You know that..."

She looked at him, amused, and smiled, eyes gently mocking as she remembers.

"Sorry, I always forget."

She laughed silently – she had used the exact same words he had – and puffed on the joint again.

They stayed there, looking at each other, taking in all the details, as if it were their first time. They had no particular reason to hurry. And, well, when someone paid her what he just had, then he could spend the night with her. He knew that.

"You want another go?"

He shook his head, pensive, no smile to match hers. She looked at him for a long moment then said, with just a trace of hesitation, "I've known men who were sad afterwards, but you beat all the records."

He managed a half-hearted smile, but took a long while to reply. Or rather, not to reply.

"How did a woman like you ever come to...?"

His voice trailed off in the motionless air as he continued to look her straight in the eyes.

"What? To practice the world's oldest profession?"

She didn't blink. She held his look without wavering, eyes filled with irony, but not really irritated.

"Don't get all bent out of shape. You all wind up asking the same question. It's just that I thought you were a little less predictable than the others in this respect. What do you want? Do you *really* want to hear my life story?"

He didn't answer, although his look never wavered. He simply waited, as one waits for mountains to crumble, for valleys to fill, for oceans to drain on their own.

She puffed on her joint again, thinking. Something flickered across her face, changing her expression, but he couldn't say just what. Finally, she opened her mouth again, allowing the smoke to escape slowly.

"Because you are who you are."

She took a deep breath, like a diver about to plunge off a diving board.

"I was born in the country and spent my entire childhood there, in a small village on the South Shore. A peaceful village, where nothing ever happens. My childhood was completely uneventful, and very boring."

She spoke in an expressionless, toneless voice, at a normal pace, as if talking about someone else, as if remembering something infinitely distant.

She had had good parents, loving, understanding parents and all that. Poor, but respectable. Too respectable. A little narrow minded, maybe. They were as they had been shaped, as they had been brought up. But she had loved them. As she had loved her sister, as well. Not the usual tragic, sordid tale. Nothing even the least bit traumatic for little Sylvie. So much for melodrama. All her parents wanted was the best for themselves and their children. What they *believed* to be the best of lives.

"Well, that was all fine and dandy... for them, and even for my sister. But not for me.... She fulfilled them. I discouraged them."

They all grew older, each growing a little more apart from the others, a little less able to understand the others. It was disappointing. The whole situation became difficult, then *very* difficult. And she started to blame them for it. She was convinced that she had been born for something, for something more. She felt no despair, just impatience and exasperation. There was so little time. And so many things to do. A life to live. And no one was able to understand that she could never be satisfied with that narrow life, without surprises, with no true joy.

As she spoke, she stared at him hard, almost challenging him to protest, to comment. Her look was a metallic green flame. Her voice had risen a little, her body had stiffened. She took another quick puff on her joint and coughed a little, practically spitting the smoke out. She looked at the joint, with pain and surprise, as you look at a friend that has betrayed you. Then relaxed a little, almost smiling.

When she spoke again, her voice was once again calm, distant.

"I had a life to live. I had my own projects. When I was twelve, I attended my first play, an insignificant little thing, in a small room in the community centre, with amateur actors. But... But it was beautiful, it was *magical*. The surprise, the revelation. It's something you never get over. In any case, that's what I thought. That's when I knew *who* I really was. I would be an actress. The best birthday gift anyone could have given me at that time would have been to put me on the bus to Quebec City or Montreal, with front row tickets snugly tucked in my pocket. I read plays all the time. I learned them by heart and played each role, one by one, in my head at night. Or sometimes with my sister, as we lay in our beds. She found it amusing, but she didn't take it – she didn't take herself – seriously.... It was just another game we played. But for me.... I exercised my voice. I practiced every little gesture. I'd pose in front of the mirror. I dressed 'like an artist.' I dreamed of the stage, the lights, the applause. I was Lady MacBeth, Miss Julie, or the Cat on the Hot Tin Roof. Nothing but sluts even then, as you can see..."

She laughed a little, a deep throaty laugh that ended with a hollow cough, which she quickly bit off. She raised herself onto her elbow, and pulled a bottle and a glass from a drawer in the bedside table, with one hand. She poured only one finger of alcohol, and threw it back in a single gulp. He wanted to tell her not to mix alcohol with pot, but there was no time. She put the bottle away and gave him a smile full of irony.

"Don't worry. I'm in complete control. It was just that my throat was dry, what with the smoke and all the talking."

She took another puff, then arranged the pillows behind her back, trying to get a little more comfortable before continuing.

"My parents didn't really understand. They thought I'd get over it. When I presented them with the *fait accompli*, they were distraught. It was no trade, no life. Reasoning, supplication, threats. Week after week after week. We all said things we should never have said. And one night, I emptied my bank account and left, cutting all my ties, burning all my bridges.

It wasn't easy. No doubt about that. She still loved them, as much as she disliked them. But once she'd made her decision, there was no going back. All alone, at eighteen, in the big city, that strange, dirty, sordid, worrisome world, full of possibilities. Bright lights, big city! How naïve and stupid she'd been. It was hard, but her will was strong. She spent the next three years washing dishes or floors, working in stores and restaurants by day, studying and working like a slave at the conservatory by night. A tight budget, no distractions, few outings, a few friends for sure, but no 'special' friend to get in her way and eat up her life, her time and her energy. She was serious. After the conservatory, she immediately got a lot of small roles. And a few big ones, everywhere, for months and months. She was constantly on the run, auditioning all the time, living on nerves, on uncertainty. But people knew she was willing to work for it. She performed. She learned. And that was normal. She had to prove herself. And then, roles were harder and harder to get, less and less interesting. Attrition.

A dry spell. She was worn out. Perhaps it was just a bad patch, a bit of bad luck. It shouldn't have lasted. She knew she should have gone on, but something inside had broken. She had started to fear. To cry over her beer at night, on the shoulders of friends. Some bored, others sympathetic. Work wasn't everything. Maybe she didn't have enough talent. Or maybe, she didn't want to meet those she should have met. Perhaps she just didn't feel like pleasing them, smiling at them, sleeping with them, doing photo shoots, commercials, television, movies. Compromise had never been her strong point.

She shrugged. Smiled, with a distant humor, overwhelmed.

"I didn't want to make concessions. I had to succeed on my own. With my own work. I wasn't ready to do just anything in order to become a good actress or even just a well-known actress. I had... *principles*. Gets to you, doesn't it? And maybe, just maybe, I was also coming to realize that if I had found myself in the theatre I would have been just as lost. So, finally, I gave up. I was fed up, probably."

The joint was almost done and could have burned her fingers. She butted it out, abruptly, in a deep, black glass ashtray, filled with gold and silver dust. She lit another. Neither of them spoke. Finally, the man made as if to say something, but Sylvie spoke first.

No, she hadn't gone home. Too proud. She had struggled hard to earn her independence and she would never abdicate. Besides, she still wanted to live life to its fullest, to experience something else. She wanted freedom. She was looking for space, for beauty in the world. Once again, she was interested in relationships with others. She still had her gang of friends, most as lost as she was. She still hung around with the same guys and girls, idealistic as people usually are when they're young, despite cries about the false cynicism of an adolescent despair. With them, she found a true camaraderie. She was able to find laughter, human warmth. And, then, there were the guys.... She had truly *discovered* sex, pleasure, sleeping around. Sometimes just as friends. They all had their illusions. One project even more unrealistic than another. Most of them finally decided to move to a farm in the country, purchased with the money they'd managed to scrape together. The ultimate cliché for the times. She went with them. They were idiotically happy, but they knew nothing at all. Yet, they worked hard. And produced almost nothing. The whole experiment had lasted two years. Two years of suffering and misery. In order to make everything better, she had suddenly thought that she had discovered love. She decided that she was happy. So, she married one of the guys. Reasonably good looking, he had a good voice, and he made her laugh a lot, at the start. But, really, maybe she had just jumped on him out of desperation.... In the end, he was unable to express his feelings. Or, maybe, he never had any. It hadn't even lasted a year. The few times she thought of him, she didn't know whether she felt pity or disdain. So, she found herself alone in Montreal, in the middle of winter, without a penny to her name. But, she was determined to change things.

She stopped talking for a moment, and looked at the forgotten joint, surprised.

"Look at the good pot I'm wasting..."

She took a drag before continuing.

"In fact there isn't a big difference between acting on the stage and what I'm doing now. I rent out my body. I fake it. But I earn an awful lot more and I manage to keep my soul. In fact, it may be more bearable as a way of life, even enjoyable, in some respects."

A brief silence. Then she abruptly waved the cigarette from left to right, in an almost vehement negation.

"I know what you're going to say to me, what it means for most women. I experienced that myself, at the start, just long enough to know what it's like. But I must have been luckier than most. No pimp, no hassles. I work alone, discretely, in 'nice' places. I have my own methods. They're efficient and satisfying. I choose my Johns. Or, well this doesn't happen too often, people recommend me to others. You'd be surprised to know how effective word of mouth can be in a situation like this. Men's sexual misery is very different from that experienced by women, but it's just as strong. And then, I also get a few women as well. It's very relaxing, often pleasant. I have a certain class and people

know it. There's a lot of demand for that. It took me a
while, but I've built up a good, steady clientele. Not too
much change. Quiet, reasonable people. No one complicated. Managers, bankers, judges, lawyers, doctors. 'Nice'
people. People who are doing 'nicely' for themselves.
Sometimes, I learn things.... I wouldn't trust them with
my money, or my health, but as far as our 'business' is
concerned... well, they're alright. Because it's in their
interests to be alright. They pay me well because I'm good.
It's a mutually profitable trade. My hours are great. I sleep
in late. I have a lot of hobbies and free time. I can organize
my life almost as I want to. Do you know many people
who can say the same? I go to the theatre a lot, to concerts, to galleries and art museums. You should get a look
at the faces of some of my clients when I meet them there,
by chance. Especially when they're with their wives. Most
of them don't know where to look. What hypocrites! But
I have to say that some of them greet me very politely,
like an old acquaintance or a business colleague.

She laughed deeply again, trilling a little this time. He
almost smiled openly.

"I still see my old gang of friends from time to time.
I have new friends. But they'd all be surprised if they
knew. Nowadays, I'm looking for beauty and I manage
to find it almost everywhere. 'Beauty is in the eye of the
beholder.' That's reason enough to live, you know. And
sometimes, although not that often I'll admit, I do a nice,
good-looking young man. Not for 'business,' just to keep
my hand in."

She laughed and then inhaled another dreamlike puff,
savouring it.

"Life could be worse, harder. I could be as miserable
as they come, leading a gray, sinister existence, married
to someone I've come to hate over the years, with the lies,
the deception, the disappointments, hanging on for dear
life, afraid of being alone, or poor, and burdened with
moronic, unbearable children that no one ever really
wanted. There are jobs that are worse, more dishonoring.
I could be walking around with a uniform on my back
that makes it my right, even my duty, to kill people, or

sell arms, or hard drugs to young kids who'll die of over-
doses. I could be wasting my life working for the civil
service, subjected to the whims of a petty little boss, learning to rob others legally – doing business, taking care of
business, wearing myself out working on an assembly
line in a plant, literally tied to my job there, spending my
whole existence washing hospital floors."

Her voice rose suddenly, "Or I could be washing dishes
in a restaurant I could never afford to eat in."

She stopped suddenly, as if she had run out of air, out
of rage, as if everything had spurted out all at once, and
there was nothing more to go back to. It was there,
hunched into a corner, where it would never stir again,
never haunt her again.

She looked sure of herself, but he didn't believe her.

"I don't even pay income tax. Officially, I'm on wel-
fare." She burst out laughing. "I set aside two weeks'
vacation each year, to travel. And since, apart from my
threads and... let's say various 'cultural products,' I don't
have to pay for anything other than my rent and a little
solid and liquid sustenance, within a few years from now,
before I get too old, I should be able to set aside a nice
little nest egg for my retirement. It's not a bad life, you
know."

He had listened carefully the entire time she spoke,
without once taking his eyes from her. But then, he looked
away. She didn't say anything for a long moment. He
finally screwed up the courage to look back towards her.
She wasn't looking at him either.

"That's the longest version I've ever told," she chuckled. "And probably the only true one, for that matter."

She looked at the light end of her joint, frowning
slightly. The smoke seemed to be coming from her fingers and it looked as if the fire were about to burn her
fingertips again.

"I talk too much. I should be more careful with dope.
And with you. I find you a little too sympathetic."

Without finishing, Sylvie methodically butted out what
remained of the joint.

"You needed to talk. That's normal."

Once again she laughed, the sound coming from deep within her throat, and winked at him.

"Say, maybe I should pay you. 'Psychiatrist: Five cents.'"

They both laughed this time.

Then she wrapped herself around him, pulled him to her. He caressed her a little, tenderly, nuzzling gently at her breasts, without any real passion. She noticed right away and pulled back a little.

"What now?" she said, almost softly.

"Do you know a place called the 'Ye Olde Shoppe of Your Heart's Desire'? Have you ever gone there?"

She thought for a couple of minutes, then smiled mysteriously, but with the secretly joyful expression of someone who believes they really do understand you, even if you're recounting a very personal dream, one for which you alone hold the keys that open the doors, even if you seem to be speaking in riddles, using abstract symbols or parables.

"Maybe we're there. What do you think?"

"Well, maybe.... Or it's somewhere else.... But you could come..."

He seemed to be a voluntary prisoner in some dream. It was powerful, appealing and overwhelming. Yet, it was also satisfying, definitely better than any dream that any drug, even the most powerful, so sought after by the mind or emotions lacking the resources to be re-born, lacking the hope to come back to life, to create and imagine an alternative of salvation, could provide.

A completely real dream.

Or a reality that was completely a dream.

He remained silent for a long time, then more intently than the first question he asked, "Why did you 'choose' me?"

She looked at him sidewise again, openly intrigued, this time.

"It's really 20 questions tonight, isn't it?"

Her voice didn't sound angry, harried or impatient. It was the voice of someone who really wanted to understand.

He didn't say a word.

"You should have seen how you were looking at me!"
She smiled at the memory. "You were there, at the table
beside the bar, below. You must have known I go there from
time to time. You also knew what you were looking for.
You tried not to show it, but your eyes never left me for
a second. You looked... fascinated. Like someone thirst-
ing after water in the desert, like a lost dog searching for
his master... something like that."

She caught herself, biting her lip, "Excuse me, it's not
because..."

"It's all right. And you're right..."

She smiled, shrugged gently, "You were so intense, you
almost frightened me."

It was his turn to smile, "Me too. I frightened myself.
But there's no mystery. I was very alone. And you're a
beautiful woman, a very desirable woman."

She raised two fingers to her forehead, as if she were
wearing a hat, and saluted him. The compliment had visibly
pleased her.

"And then, you've forgotten that you had the barman
send me a note. It was mysterious, seductive, nicely
worded. I hesitated a little. But it wouldn't cost me anything. The bar was filled with people. There was no risk
and you looked like someone who was sensible and reasonably well off. And you weren't exactly an ugly guy. I
trusted my instinct. You bought me a drink. You were a
little stiff at the start, but that's common with men who
aren't used to the business. We talked a little. Around,
above, below, subtly. But I could tell you knew. Recognition.
In both meanings of the word. And once it was clearly
established, we really started to talk. And kept on for a long
time. You weren't in a rush. Neither was I. You were pleasant, cultivated and intelligent. We even talked about books
and movies. Sometimes, you seemed to know what I was
thinking. It was as if we already knew one another. You
made me laugh. And I needed someone to make me laugh
that evening. I offered what you wanted. You offered what
I wanted. No problem. We went upstairs. You were *really*
very eager, weren't you? As for the rest, well you know
it all. What more do you want me to say?"

She laughed a little once again and lay back out, closing her eyes, stretching voluptuously, languorously, "You're good business."

He didn't reply. The silence dragged on a long, long time. He thought she had fallen asleep. But her eyelids suddenly flew open, a little alarmed, and she stared at him intently, with something akin to concern, maybe even pity.

"Good Lord, what's got into you? It's almost as if..."

"Nothing... nothing..."

He backed off, almost frightened, closed his eyes and raised his arms slightly, as if to protect himself from invisible blows. Then he opened his mouth wide, like someone desperately struggling for one last breath before drowning. Or as if he were about to speak for a long time, say something very important. Or cry out in pain. But he closed his lips over his intact, unchangeable silence.

Suddenly, he felt Sylvie's hand clasping his. He opened his eyes, panicked.

"What's wrong? Tell me!"

He shook his head in despair, struggling as if in a nightmare. She stood up, trying to catch him up, speaking quickly, as if to conjure away a wicked spell, even if it was too late.

"Come on. I don't like to see you like this. I'll buy you a drink. We'll talk over drinks, downstairs. Like the first time. As friends..."

Her voice was gentle, almost tender. In her attentive gaze there was.... No he couldn't stand that. Not that! He dropped her hand, stood up, turned his back on her and got dressed, quickly, clumsily.

"Another time, maybe," he murmured, his voice flat.

He walked out the door, without turning back.

＞┉╋┉╋┉＜

He drove through the night from Montreal to Quebec City, his foot almost constantly to the floor. At least half a dozen times, he considered just giving the steering wheel a good yank and driving into the ditch, into a hydro pole, a street light, or a cement wall. To make it all go away, the pain and the lies, the lies and the pain.

But finally, he did nothing of the sort.

When he walked into his place, he didn't even turn the light on. A pale dawn was already rising. A dawn and a light worthy of him. He threw his jacket on the floor, kicked off the shoes he could no longer bear, as if he could no longer bear himself, poured out a tall glass of Southern Comfort and collapsed into an easy chair, next to the table in the living room. He was still thinking about Sylvie, her desirable body, the look on her face when he left her. He thought about Sylvie's broken dreams. He was almost certain that Sylvie, like himself, like everyone else, was just pretending to live, to be happy. Or maybe they really believed it.

And somewhere, he still felt that kind of fear...

Fear of her. Fear of himself, above all...

Of dreams and reality, of hope and despair.

Of what his own mind harboured, or didn't. Of what existed, no longer existed, or perhaps had never really existed...

And who could know such things for certain? Not him. Not in the state he was in at that time, not in the state he was in today...

But that fear was no longer any more than the frayed edge of the vague memory of the previous. The real fear, as intense as it was, he had voluntarily, methodically and systematically identified it, chased it away, destroyed it during that long, endless night spent in a hotel in Lyon, during a wandering trip to a forgetfulness impossible to find, a few months ago, where he had understood that, if he had known before, just a few short months ago, if he had 'really' experienced that 'magic' that meant that two beings could really for moments that were far too brief, actually be one in love, he was now discovering that in this totally empty bed one being could become two, be born again as two through some very different, totally disturbing, totally upsetting, mysterious 'magic'.

That nocturnal fear, that fear had only grown after the heart rending emotion, the frightful shock and the troubled hope he felt in that improbable, dusty second-hand store, the 'Ye Olde Shoppe of Your Heart's Desire,' a fear that he had been unable to push aside to swallow up, after that sunburst flashing directly in his eyes, that sunburst that had drawn his glance, for just an instant, toward a table, that overwhelming joy caused by a simple reflection of light passing through a piece of glass set in what seemed to be a piece of spring sky casting its light on an impossible double smile, a smile that he knew had been and would always be unique in the world...

After paying the more than modest sum requested by the storekeeper for that object that could not, absolutely should not exist, he heard the man say, very quietly, "Everyone *always* finds what they're looking for, everything their heart desires, in my store. Believe me. I'm proud of that."

And he smiled a smile, strange, mysterious and ambiguous, like that of a man who had found happiness somewhere.

He sipped his drink, found it loathsome. But she wasn't loathsome. He was. And shame smothered him. Cowardice as well.

"Another time, maybe," he had murmured.

No, he'd never be able to tell her. Not now, not ever. It was too late. Never...

He wanted to weep, but he knew full well he was no longer able to.

He turned towards the table. Looked at the photos standing there in their frames. One of a beautiful woman with long, red hair, flowing in waves to her shoulders, at her brilliant green eyes, at her smile full of life and happiness. He reached out, delicately caressed the small black silk ribbon in the upper right-hand corner of the frame, then the smile of the woman in the photo.

That smile, so different from the one she wore in the few rare photos of her childhood, those taken in the orphanage.

No, he would never be able to tell her.

In the other photo, as if floating in the blue frame, as if in one of those 'fragment in a spring sky' paintings, two adolescents sat on a wooden fence, fields of golden wheat behind them, flowing in the wind, in the full summer sun, arms around each others' waists. They laughed as they gazed at one another. Two heads, with their long red hair, their brilliant green eyes. Two faces exactly alike, perfectly identical, peas in a pod. Yet two different hands had signed the photo:

Sylvie and Nancy, Forever.

Permission
by Mark Dachuk

Launa stands on her rickety porch, sipping a steaming cup of coffee. The only sound is the wind wheezing through the few trees around her small cottage. She can see it pulling the steam off her coffee, swirling with it like an invisible dance partner. The sun is low in the sky and she can smell the elusive scent of morning. Her gaze is drawn towards the edge of the sky, to movement on the horizon. A Jump-Shuttle pierces the blue and soars effortlessly towards the heavens. Its vapour trail seems to cut the sky in half along a beautiful arc. She wonders about the passengers, about how their lives will change now that they've been granted. Images of golden cities and carefree lives flutter through her mind.

She walks down the three steps onto the small stone path that curves around the house. Stopping, she breathes in the cool air, feeling the familiar pang of anticipation before she checks the fields. Her field of Permission spreads out around her, and from first glance it looks as if there are no blossoms today. But the field is large, and she'll have to check every plant to be sure. It has become a calming ritual, checking the field. She walks back into the house, takes a small bottle of water and grabs her steel clippers.

The Permission plant has to be the ugliest plant she has ever known. Brown like the colour of dead leaves, it crawls along the ground like a weed. It must be maintained con-stantly: trimmed, watered, fertilized. It must be protected from roaming insects, kept so that the sun can reach the base of the plant, yet not left so exposed that it can burn.

She steps out of her shoes before walking into the field. She loves the feel of the damp earth against her flesh and between her toes. It takes a full three minutes to walk to the end of the row, checking in and around every plant. The Permission blossom is the rarest thing on the planet and from what she's heard, the most beautiful too. She catches sight of a bright crimson vine lying limp against the ground. It's dead, and if left unclipped, it will rot and spread a virulent toxin to the rest of the field. She's lost more crops then she can remember that way. She kneels down and clips it three inches below the red. She places it in the bag on her back and continues down the row. Stopping at the end, she turns and wipes her forehead against her sleeve. A beetle crawls slowly across the narrow footpath. It's a nutrient beetle. In large numbers it can devastate a Permission crop. She picks it up between her thumb and forefinger and looks at it. Its legs wave frantically trying to grip the air. A droplet of sweat splashes onto her hand and she crushes the beetle. Its legs stop moving and a clear liquid spills over her thumb. She continues on, thinking only about tending her crop.

Launa drops the full bag of clipping on the porch and takes off her shirt. She sits with her back against the house and relaxes in the cool against her body. The sun is high in the sky now and the awning provides relief. She sips the cold coffee that she left on the porch. Today was like any other day, she thinks. No blossoms. Not even a hint of one, if there is such a thing. Her water tank is practically empty and she could've used a cold bath. Closing her eyes, she can feel herself falling into a deep sleep, but tries to fight it, knowing that she has to go into the city and buy more water and supplies. She pours some water onto her hand and splashes her face. The feeling is good as it runs down her body. Getting up, she wipes her feet on a small mat and walks inside. The heat is just as oppressive and it takes a moment for her eyes to adjust. She puts on a fresh shirt and a pair of sandals and walks out to her truck.

Near it is a small patch of knee high plants tied up with twine. Behind the leaves she notices a flash of gold. She runs over and spreads the foliage apart. It's a blossom. An

Anamnesis blossom. It's almost pure gold with crimson along the edges. It provides a rare opportunity; an eye into the past. The vines fall to their natural position, covering the beautiful flower. She should buy some more Anamnesis seeds today. The blossom releases a spore that kills the entire patch. It will be withered in a few days. Walking back towards the truck she thinks, there hasn't been a blossom in that patch for almost six months. She'll use it tonight. Tonight will be a night of memories. She runs her hand along the massive water tank behind the cab of her truck, and some of the rust peels off as she touches it. She drives down the gravel driveway and looks at the dirt road that leads towards the city. It's barren as usual. She has never seen anyone use the road except her. Towards the north, the road disappears over the horizon. She's driven north only once and only as far as a tank of gas would allow. The only thing she found was an abandoned farm with a beautiful green house behind it, and a field of dead Permission. The owner must've gotten a blossom, it's the only reason he would've left it. But that was before she made her home here. No one in the city remembers who lived there, it must've been years ago.

The city is desolate, just as it was the week before. Time torn shacks line both sides of the street. There's a supply shop, an inn for travelers, a tavern, each one held together by the will of the owner. There are a few trucks parked along the street, a station wagon and a large water truck. She parks her truck out of the sun.

The door to the supply shop opens easily and lightly brushes wooden wind-chimes. It sends a soft familiar sound through the store. A faint smell of filth and fertilizer haunts the air. Seed, the owner, is standing by the side entrance talking quietly to a man she doesn't recognize. They glance towards her for a moment, then resume their conversation.

Halfheartedly listening to the men talk about the price of water, she moves silently through the store, lightly brushing her hand over the equipment; rakes and shovels, clippers and hoses. She could tend such a superior crop if she had these tools. Only the people with these special tools ever grow blossoms. For a moment she loses herself in visions of Permission crops, extending as far as the eye can see, a blossom in every tenth plant; a magnificent sight.

"Launa. Launa!" The vision blows from her eyes like a creature of ash. Seed is standing in front of her, watching her with an intense curiosity. "You all right? Looks like we lost ya there for a sec."

"I'm okay," she says, smiling.

"Good." A smile cracks open his face like earth in need of a rainstorm. "Then what can I do for ya?" He limps back towards a small table that serves as a counter.

Launa smiles to herself, she's always admired Seed. He's been in this small store for as long as she can remember. The sound of his shoes on the wooden floor makes her feel safe. He turns and looks at her in a way that suggests honest concern. His face reminds her of an oil painting, thick and deep with a dark cast of crimson, and in his eyes there's a sparkle of passion. She's not sure for what though, life, his store, or maybe its something she can't even understand. He stopped trying to grow a blossom several years ago. Maybe it has something to do with that.

"So, what can I do for you today?" He says, sitting down in a small chair. "Well," she says, thinking carefully. "First of all, I need Anamnesis seeds."

"Ah, you got a blossom?"

"Yeah." She smiles. "First one in, I don't know how long."

"That's great Launa. I wish you good memories."

"Thanks."

"So, what else do you need?" He asks pushing the chair back onto two legs.

"Water, for the crops."

"Haven't you heard?" She furrows her brow at him. "There's a storm coming. Tonight. It's a mean one, Launa. This one's gonna break some crops, that's fersure." He gets up, walks to the back of the store, and scoops a load of seeds into a brown paper bag.

"I didn't know." The energy drains from her body. So much work. All to be ripped apart by a storm.

"Don't worry," he says, placing the bag of seeds on the table. "I got a feeling you're gonna be one of the lucky ones." He smiles and winks at her.

"Thanks." She reaches into her pocket for the money.

"Not this time." He gives her the bag of seeds. "I want you to have these. A gift from me." She closes her eyes, smiling.

"Thank you, Seed. I want you to know that... that I appreciate everything you've done for me. I..."

"No need to speak. I know." She walks over and kisses him on the cheek. His skin feels cold and hard. She can sense the layers of life stacked below that cheek.

"Thank you." She walks to the door.

"One other thing, Launa." She stops and turns. "Remember, if you ever get Permission, just go." She can feel the tip of a tear in her eye. She smiles tightly, nods and walks out.

She drops the seeds on the passenger seat and looks out towards the eastern sky. She can see the storm in the distance, as if someone smudged the sky with ink. It was only about three or four hours away. She would have to head back home soon, but first she walks towards the local tavern, called The Cell Wall, a dark and cool atmosphere. There's a gentle murmur of conversations around the room. A statue of a man strums a guitar in the corner. He seems unconcerned that people watch him. She sits at the bar. Pith, the bartender hurries over. He's a boy, no more then eighteen, but attractive and well built. He's always had a thing for her.

"Hey Launa, it's been a long time since I've seen you. Did ya hear about the storm that's coming?" He's jittery, nervous. He's always nervous.

"Hey Pith. Can I get a pint and two cigarettes?"

"Sure Launa, just a sec." He quickly moves away. She watches him pour the pint. His face is so different. So young. She wonders what it would be like to kiss that face. Her thoughts move to other places. Moments of passion flash in her mind. Quiet moments spent on the brink. Extended moments that lasted a lifetime. Peaceful moments spent under the protection of an embrace. A coldness brushes her face and neck. The sound of the glass on the counter tears the vision from her eyelids. She looks directly into the young eyes of the boy. Her face flushes. She's glad it's dark.

"So, how'vya been?" He asks.

"All right." She smiles and takes a long sip of the jade coloured beer. She picks up one of the two cigarettes sitting on the counter and places it carefully in her mouth. "You gotta light?" He jumps at the words.

"Sure." He runs down the bar, grabs something that rattles and runs back. He opens the small box of matches and snaps one alight. His face flashes crimson. His blue eyes intent on the tip of the match, guiding it towards the cigarette. She watches him watch the light, and pulls a drag. He shakes the crimson away as she slowly exhales smoke.

"Got an Anamnesis blossom today." She says, playing with the cigarette between her fingers.

"Really? That's fantastic. Good memories Launa." He stands there smiling at her.

"Thanks." She pulls another drag off the cigarette. She doesn't know what to say. Uneasy moments spent in silence. She can see that he wants to be there with her, but he doesn't know what to do. She finishes the pint and puts the other cigarette in her shirt pocket. "How much do I owe you?"

"Oh, nothing. This is on me." He stands there with his hands on the counter and a goofy grin on his face.

"That's okay," she says smiling. "I'll pay for this."

"Please Launa, let me buy you this drink and the cigarettes." He's trying so hard to pull this off. She feels so sorry for him.

"Okay Pith." She puts her hand on his. "Thank you." He smiles wildly. Walking out the door, she turns her head and waves.

The darkness covers the horizon like a chalk drawing. She climbs into her truck and starts it up, pushes the lighter into the panel and places her head on the steering wheel. It seems like a lifetime before it clicks back up.

She touches the white, hot tip to her cigarette and drives home, humming a song about a girl with brown eyes that someone used to sing to her, a long time ago.

Rolling up the windows on the truck, she can feel the first few drops against her face and arms. She grabs the clippers from the porch and runs over to the Anamnesis plant. Reaching inside the tangle of vines, she cuts the blossom free. Inside the house, she cleans all the green from the blossom until only the gold and crimson remain. With the burner set to high, she pours her last bottle of drinking water into a small pot to boil.

Leaning against the doorframe, Launa stares out the screen door. The blackness is halfway across the sky and she can already see the rain coming down in sheets in the distance. The leaves on the oak flicker with every drop, moving it like oil in water, paradoxically to a rhythm only it hears.

The small pot billows steam. She places the blossom carefully into the water and closes the lid tightly. It will only be a few moments now.

There is a long silent pause before she has the energy to move again. The darkness now covers most of the sky, creating an artificial night. It moves like a hunter stalking the light. The wind is stronger and it pulls at the great oak violently. It almost looks like the tree is in rapture, arms outstretched towards the heavens swaying back and forth like some demonic dance.

She pushes herself up and walks into the house. The heady vapours from the tea already hang in the room. She pulls out the limp blossom with a wooden spoon, its color completely drained, and drops it into the sink. Moving the pot off the stove, she leans down and breathes in the strong, earthy aroma of the tea. She pours the golden metallic liquid into a large mug and places it on the floor, then latches the door so it won't bang in the wind, returning to a small spot on the floor. She spreads a small blanket, and lights the candles. Watching the darkness overtake the light, she sips the tea.

Mending the fracture in her mind. A warm putty that slips into the cracks. A warm tear. A sad smile. Bright hair against a worn recliner. Criss-crossing patterns of tree branches through a window. Hot glass jungle house filled with the scent of citrus.

A young woman with red hair, slim with graceful, familiar features. Mother-mom. Mostly sad, caring-loving, called me Pumpkin. Hard hands holding open a book. Dirty fingernails. Tough, cold-sitting on the floor in front of the fireplace. Older man, calm-serene. Father-dad. Always building, loving-reserved, warm hugs like a bear. 'One time we were in the glass house, it was called a green house but I called it a glass house. Dad and me sat in the grass and ate oranges and mom said we looked like two baboons and then we started jumping up and down like baboons.'

Older. Father teaching me. Permission-clippers-sunlight-weeds. Hours spent with the crops. Sounds of footsteps on the porch while I lie in bed. Mother and father standing in my room while I pretend to sleep — watching me. Mothers whisper 'I wanted her to grow up among the stars.' Father's hand caressing my face 'I know honey.' Hands smell of earth. Mother yelling why. Father yelling why. Mother crying why. Father holding her why. I watch with one eye — face pressed against the wooden door frame.

Later-years. Mother-fever-burning up. Father gone-getting help. Mom's voice, 'the sky is watching us Pumpkin. There is goodness among the despair — I'm okay — I'm afraid Pumpkin.' I lie beside her in the sick bed — she smells of medicine. Father comes home with other men — I watch between legs as mother dies shaking. Father cries — a dirty hand touching her face.

More years. Father gets gray. Soft solemn years. Father quietly gets sick. I'm silently afraid — sitting with him as he sips his tea. He tells me he's not afraid — he's going to see mother. He dies gently in my arms. I cry for myself.

Familiar stranger. Building a house under a large Oak. Young-muscular-beautiful. Passing in the truck — through the passenger side window — lean-smooth-he turns to look-smile. Stomach burning in my throat — heart like a flutter-bird. Smile-talk-laugh-whisper. Love.

Child-tiny girl. My daughter. I hold her in my arms like a bundle of rose petals. I want her to grow up among the stars. I watch him play with her like my father played with me. The three of us sit on the porch and watch the sun set.

I am mommy. He is daddy. Our reason for living walks between us holding our hands, jumping up and swinging and yelling with joy as we hold her suspended in the air. We laugh and play and we teach her about the crops. I smile and listen as she tells me stories of the Princess that lives in the big Oak, and about the king and the queen that love and protect her. Her imagination and wonderment humble me. This child will be so much more then either of us.

One day she starts coughing and says that her tummy hurts. We take her to the doctor in the city and he gives us a tea that she should drink. It doesn't help. We go back and he says that her body is weak and has a problem fighting illness. Then he tells us something that stops my heart. We should be prepared. On the drive back I stare out the window, my insides burn. Flora sits between us coughing. I cry as quietly as possible, watching the wasteland that we call home fly by.

She gets paler by the day. Her laughter is now followed by a fit of coughing. I hold her in my arms as much as I can now- I can almost feel the warmth leaving her body. I sing to her and stare into those beautiful blue eyes — trying to remember every detail. She dies without warning and the house is plunged into cold and darkness. We cry for days. We bury her in the back yard near an outcropping of trees where she liked to play.

The house is silent. John retreats into himself. We hardly talk anymore. We move around the house like ghosts — I feel empty — there is no life left.

One morning I wake up alone. There is a note. 'Launa, I'm sorry — I can't stay. I will love you always. John.'

From black to gray to white she slowly opens her eyes to the early morning sun streaming in through a broken window. Pushing herself up and looking around at the damage her head sinks. Broken glass litters the floor and there are pools of water everywhere. She feels cold and damp — and the memories still fresh in her mind sting.

She moves as if she were waterlogged, and walks outside into the chirping of the birds and the smell of fresh,
clean air as if it were any other day. But there is destruction
everywhere. Her heart skips a beat as she stares at the crop.
It's entirely ripped up and torn. A tear rolls down her cheek
as she approaches the crops. It's completely destroyed.
Some trees are uprooted. The Oak is still standing. She takes
off her shoes and walks barefoot through the uprooted
Permission plants. She can't believe that she's going to have
to start over.

Launa sits for hours on the steps of the porch, listening to the birds and crying. She thinks about quitting,
maybe getting a job in the city. But so many years have been
invested in her crop, she wouldn't know how to do anything else. She walks back out into the field and begins
to pick through the dead Permission. Thick and wet, the
plants feel heavy going into the bag on her back. Reaching
the end of the row, she turns and wipes the sweat from her
brow. At her feet, between fallen plants, there is a small
burst of crimson. Thinking it's a dead vine, she reaches
down and picks up the plant lying on top of it. A blossom.
She kneels down and cradles it in her hands. She looks at
it, almost unbelieving that its there. This moment has
played and replayed itself in her mind a thousand times.
The colour is a vibrant gold, rimmed with fiery red edges.
The centre is touched with a gentle blue. She lifts it to her
nose and breathes in. The scent is a mixture of rose, cinnamon, and sharp pepper. Eyes clouded with moisture,
she runs back into the house, grabs a small box and runs
back out to the blossom. She clips it off and places it in the
box. She carries it about a hundred paces behind the house
to a small patch of trees. Then places the box on the ground
and kneels. Pushing the long grass and weeds out of the
way, she comes across a small wooden board stuck firmly
in the ground. She clears it from the rubble, sits down and
stares at it. Scratched into the surface of the board are the
words: 'Flora, My Daughter.' Tears come to her eyes.

"Flora my love. I'm so sorry I forgot you. I miss you
so much." She smiles. "I got it baby, I got that blossom we

were always talking about. I'm going to the stars — I'm coming to meet you. See you soon love." She kisses her fingers and presses them gently to the wood, then gets up and walks slowly back to the house. She walks through it one last time, then goes out to her truck and drives away.

She comes to the junction, where the road splits north and south. The city lies to the south, and she can just barely see it in the distance. She watches it for a moment then drives the truck onto the lightly travelled north road.

After an hour of driving, she comes to a vast open field. In the distance she can see three platforms. Two have huge shuttles on them, steam billowing out the bottom of each. The third must have been the morning flight. She drives into a large area where a scattering of people are leaving their cars and trucks. She parks the truck in the shade. The people around her look disoriented holding bags and boxes; holding their blossoms. Clinging tightly to her box, Launa awkwardly joins the cue.

The truck kicks up gravel as it drives towards the house with the big Oak. It pulls in to the driveway. The car door opens and a man steps out onto the still damp gravel. He walks up to the front of the house and knocks on the doorframe.

"Hello?" Pith yells. "Launa? Are you here?" He peers into the house, then carefully wanders around back. He looks at the Permission crop and flinches. On the ground at his feet, he notices a pair of shoes and a set of rusty clippers. He sighs and walks back to the truck. As he's about to get in, something catches his eye in the eastern sky. A Jump-Shuttle has just taken off. He watches it make a gentle arc across the sky, almost cutting it in half with its vapour trail. He watches it until it's gone, then gets in his truck and drives away.

Summer Silk
by Rhea Rose

"That's a wolf spider, not a tarantula!" Milo, my ten-year-old son explained, as I ran around the kitchen with the broom and tried to bat the huge beast out of the corner and down the heating vent. The terrified arachnid collapsed, crinkled its hairy legs and became as light as dust.

Milo bent to retrieve the carcass. "Don't touch it," I shouted, jumping backwards. Milo poked at the brown, inert pile; they always reminded me of a ball of discarded thread when they played dead.

"Toss it in the toilet now, before it wakes up," I ordered.

"I want to collect it," he pleaded; I caved. "Thanks, Mom," he said with such glee you'd think I'd bought him a video game. He ran off from the kitchen to a corner of the barn to find a jar to store the critter in.

"Make sure it has a tight lid," I hollered. No response. He hears everything, but never lets you know until one day he's repeated word for word all your gossip overheard during a phone conversation. Sometimes I could just kill that sweet kid.

As the weeks went by the webs around the kitchen window and doors thickened even though I worked hard to clean them away. The porch lights became killing fields. The bug blood from the midsummer slaughter stained the house's vinyl siding. The marks faded if I used bleach.

This morning I stepped onto the porch to catch a glimpse of the late summer sunrise over our fields of large, green and orange mottled pumpkins, I walked into a gigantic

web. It stuck to my neck; it stuck to the gloss recently
applied to my lips and snagged in my eyelashes; I imagined my reflection as it grimaced back at me eight glistening times as the spider scurried to take shelter somewhere in my long blonde hair. From the corner of my eye
I reluctantly observed the spider's miniature butt swing
round in mid scuttle and disappear. I squeaked in stifled
horror when I thought I felt the eight-legged weaver's
tiny tickle as it made its way down the canals of my inner
ear. Several small smacks to the side of my head didn't
seem to dislodge anything but my sunglasses. A frantic visit to the washroom mirror revealed nothing. Like
some great ape, I checked for fleas, brushed and parted,
combed and flipped my hair around. No spider. I picked
the remains of its web from my brow and felt the silk still
on my arms, still invisible except for its insistent tick-
ling presence.

>>I>>I>>I<<

Days later, the incident forgotten, I cleaned webs off
the windows around the house. The outdoor lights, thick
with layers and layers of soft white silk and bits of
tangled insect debris, took on the look of large glass eggs
in cocoons.

>>I>>I>>I<<

"Ted, do something," I said to my husband, then
stepped in front of the TV screen. He didn't flinch. A commercial for the latest Spider-man movie flashed.
"'Bout what?" He twitched his index finger, signaling
me to move aside. I noticed something odd about Ted,
odder then the usual odd things Ted had going for him.
A web. A spider's web hung between the lobe of his ear
and his shoulder. Small, delicate and still in progress,
the creature, no larger then the head of a pin, still spinning.
"It's that time of the year," I said, and gave him my
best you-know-what-I-mean look. He continued to stare
through my torso as if he had x-ray vision. He shifted
in his recliner.

"Time of the month? Already?"
I hit him with the tea towel.

➸╍╍➻

Spider season is a family affair for us. I hate the spiders.
Ted hates my project, and the kids hate both of us this time
of the year because no one is permitted to rest until every
breathing arachnid is gone.

At first, my plan of attack for this season seemed to take
on its own natural momentum. Ted faithfully sprayed the
owner of every web within reach. Then he used his new
feather duster to twist and noodle up the cobwebs like
twirling spaghetti on a plate. Once the duster, thick with
silk, was no longer useable he and the kids offered it to
me as cotton candy. Gratefully, I accepted these offers for
disposal. We'd usually light a fire in the evenings and watch
'em burn.

All was well, so I thought, and I relaxed to the voices
of the three kids yelling and teasing as they caught stray
spiders, "Pull off their legs," and "Throw a fly in."

Ted worked in the crawl space under the house.

"See anything in there?" I asked and handed him the
duster and sprays he needed "I'm hooking the latch, again,
Ted. No getting out 'till they're all gone."

"What's new?" he said, and I watched him follow the
flashlight beam into the darkness.

➸╍╍➻

Not until I started to prepare supper did anything
untoward present itself. Back in the farthest depths of the
cupboards, my fingers searched the corners for my jar of
black peppercorns. "Where's dada?" asked Tannis, my four-
year-old. The cool tin lid of the jar met my hand. With one
finger I pushed the dust from the lid.

"Dada? Oops," said I, as I considered her question,
patted her on her sweet corn yellow hair and ran downstairs to the crawl space. How long had I left him down
there? I calculated. Tried to figure out the ratio of time to

anger. Then I realized three hours had passed. *Shit.* I knocked gently, timidly. "Ted?" I called out to him. "Are you speaking to me?" *Of course he wasn't speaking to me. How did I forget? Trapped in that pit of spiders.* "Good God!" I said aloud, forgetting myself. *Therapy. He'll need it. I need it. We needed it.*

"Ted?"

Never before had I done anything as thoughtless. Well, I did back up over Ted's suitcase full of travel gear. A business trip called him away from home at the worst time of the year, pumpkin-picking time. He said I'd demonstrated my repressed hostilities toward him. Maybe this was the same thing.

"Ted?" I knocked again, gently.

"Just open it, Mommy," said Tannis. She'd followed me down from the kitchen.

"I can't, Peaches."

"Why not? Is Daddy in time out?"

"Sort of. Why don't you go find Mrs. Paisley for me," I said and tried to look really excited by the possibility that our old fleabag of a cat could help the situation.

"Sure," she said, and left me alone.

"Honey?"

"AAAHH!" I screamed and cracked my head against the low sill. For a moment passing out seemed like the only option. Then I looked at Ted and there were eight of him all spinning and circling around each other like some special effect from a bad horror film. Ted just grinned.

"When's supper?" he asked.

I gave him the silent treatment. *How the hell did he get out?*

In the kitchen I returned to making supper. I picked up the jar. The damn lid didn't budge. Thank goodness the magi-grip hung handy. The lid came off and out came the pepper — no, wait — not peppercorns, raisins — was my first thought. But no, they were actually dead flies. Legless, wingless; heads separated from the bodies. They rolled across the counter; some fell to the floor. Milo and his younger brother's joke, I imagined. My stomach growled as I selected a particularly fat juicy abdomen and placed it on my tongue. Damn, if it didn't taste good, but not as good as the next one.

Just as dinner reached its peak, food cooked, everything delectable and bubbly, table set, and all familial and cozy, a scream from the back yard halted us. We converged in the yard; only Tannis was missing. Assembled, we stared. Tannis looked fine. But great glistening tears like freshly deposited ova-sacs slid down her cheeks. "Peaches? Did you scrape your knee?" I asked, and knelt down to her height. I scooped her up in my arms; her heartbeat fast and hard and she felt very warm. The strangest sensation gripped me. As her blood raced through her it felt as if I sensed every red cell in her.

"It's Mrs. Paisley," she said.

"Did that nasty cat scratch you? I'll shave her fur off and put her in the freezer. I'll—"

"No!"

I nearly dropped her. Never had I heard Tannis speak in that tone.

Jason and Milo joined me.

"Tannis," Milo interrupted, "Where's Mrs. Paisley?"

"In the tree," she said, her voice small and doll like.

"In the tree?" Jason repeated her words as if she'd just said the lamest, stupidest thing he'd ever heard. He went to the tree.

"Holy shit. You've got to see this," he said.

Ted and I exchanged glances that accused the other of using bad language around Milo.

"What is it, Milo?" Ted asked, not moving.

"Mrs. Paisley all wrapped and twisted in a net or something. They look like they went through the wash together."

Ted and I looked at each other.

❖❖❖❖❖

We cut Mrs. Paisley down after dinner. We consoled the kids, rented a movie for them and got them settled into their rooms. Ted got the ladder and I got an old laundry basket that Mrs. Paisley used at times to sleep in. I changed into my jeans and they felt tight, which really pissed me off. They rode up into my crotch and I had to tug them out. Ted noticed. "You cheating on me?" he asked as he watched me yank on the seam at my crotch.

"Always," I said, his silly super-tooth grin lit up the twilight. I didn't want to alarm him but there was definitely weirdness going on with my jeans and, oh, yeah, the cat.

❖❖❖❖

In the kitchen we examined the dead creature. Mrs. Paisley didn't go through the washer with Milo's gym bag. Ted actually looked concerned. "Who would do a thing like this?" he asked me, as if I had the answer to his question.

Poor Mrs. Paisley. Ted retrieved his tin snips from the garage and cut through the thick net of gauze that bound our pet cat so tightly her eyes bulged out of her head. Thinking she'd be stiff as a board I tried to lift her out of the wrap only to discover that she'd turned into a furry beach ball of liquid, a waterbed kitty. Ted turned green and had to leave the room, which left me to deal with the situation.

There, alone in the kitchen, my stomach again gurgled. I too should have turned green, just like my husband. Instead, I dug through the Tupperware drawer, found one of those crazy curly kids' straws that loops back and over on itself and, and, — I needed something sharp.

Whoosh, the fricken SoyaKing cat-float geyser hit the ceiling. Cat innards, the sickly gray color of poi, leaked everywhere. It took me several hours to lick it all up.

❖❖❖❖

I caught Jason on the back porch the next day. At eight years he was the middle child, but older in spirit than all of us. He had this eerie wisdom thing.

"Whatcha doin', Jasie?" I asked as nonchalantly as possible.

"What did you do with Mrs. Paisley?" He asked, straight to the point. *Well, son, I stuck a straw in the pet cat and drank out her body fluids! How's that?*

"Dad and I found a shoe box and Tannis is decorating the lid and we're going to hold a funeral for her on the weekend. Will you attend with us?"

"That's four days from now. The maggots will finish her off," he said.

"Yes, dear, that's why we put her in the locked freezer. She's in a couple of freezer bags so that the fur doesn't touch the peas or anything like that." I thought that comment would go right over his spiky-haired little head.

"Your butt is fat!" he spat at me.

"Not nearly as fat as your head," I said, before I could stop myself. "Jason, what were you doing out here, just now and don't say, '*Nothing*'. "

I was concerned because from the kitchen window I saw him do something to his nose, and hoped he hadn't stuffed gum or some other small object up there. "Open your hand, Jason."

"You won't like it," he said.

I probably wouldn't.

In his dirt-lined palm squirmed a great huge furry moth. It rolled back and forth like a miniature rolling pin as it flapped its torn sail-like wings. It was legless. A single threadlike leg stuck to the end of one of Jason's fingers. Another whisker-like leg stuck to his upper lip. Speechless, I just stared at the helpless creature. Without a word Jason picked the moth up by the wings and held it tightly, pinched between his thumb and finger. He ran the long furry body over his top lip and under his nose back and fourth, gently, like it felt good. It did feel good. I saw it in his dark eyes; they watered and became glassy. Then as if in a trance he shut them while he spread gray moth dust across his face.

❖❖❖

"Ted! I need you, now. Ted!"

No answer. It really pissed me off when Ted made himself unavailable — and these jeans! I ran upstairs. I had to change out of these clothes. They were unbearable. In the bedroom with my jeans half off I caught my reflection in the mirrored closet doors. My tight body, always a source of pride after three children, looked, off. The symmetry lost. Even with all the lights in the room switched on something looked very, very odd. Several times I wiped the mirror and ran my fingers over it, checking for warps or dents and just when I thought I figured it all out my eyes itched, terribly. In the bathroom I splashed them over and over with water and grains of what looked like rice fell from them, from the lashes, like I had some weird major eyelash dandruff. And the pain in my abdomen! My tailbone ached. I'd hurt like this before, after giving birth. I donned a light, gauzy dress and felt much more comfortable. Maybe PMS caused my discomfort, but somewhere in the back of my mind I knew the truth.

Like a pending orgasm I was suddenly gripped with hunger. If I continued eating to stave off the hunger, I'd have to move into the garage to fit in the house. Milo found me upstairs in the bathroom as I swept up those strange bits of rice that had fallen from my eyes.

"They look like spider eggs," he said. He pointed at my face. "That's an interesting fashion statement," he said. I glanced quickly into the mirror. A few more grains of 'spider eggs' sat in the nest of my eye hairs. "Well, I walked into a web, earlier. How can you not walk into one around this place?"

"Look, they're hatching." He pointed into the dustpan and sure enough the little grains of rice exploded and out came the merest wisp of an eight-legged creature. I picked at the few grains that remained in my lashes.

Milo got to the point. He and the other two had taken a vote and decided they wanted a new kitten to replace Mrs. Paisley and Milo's best friend's cat just happened to have had a litter of kittens about six weeks earlier.

"How many?" I asked and dabbed a piece of toilet paper to the corner of my salivating mouth.

⊹⊱†⊰†⊱⊰⊹

On the freeway the traffic whizzed by me like crazy insects intent on beating me to somewhere. With the kids in the back seat, I found myself watching the pattern and flow of the cars around me, like an air traffic controller. In fact, tracking the four oncoming lanes and the four westbound lanes seemed a cinch. Strangely, I found myself able to sense the movements and whereabouts of approximately six cars per lane, in eight lanes. That came to forty-eight strands of movement that I seemed able to read with not just my eyes, but with my entire body. The unrelenting hunger in my stomach had an almost nauseating effect and caused me to drive faster than normal. I wished I could jump from lane to lane. The unavoidable happened next; what with my state, and the mood of the traffic, and three excited kids in the backseat, some guy cut me off. If not for the hypersensitive perception of my traffic observations he'd have killed us, I'm certain. Tannis screamed. Milo used the foulest language I'd heard come from his mouth to date. Jason said something that broke the slow motion spell cast when two cars are about to collide. The accident appeared in my mind's eye from eight different points of view. At the same time I glanced into my rearview mirror. Jason looked back at me.

"Eat him up, Mom."

I followed the car that cut us off. He took the next ramp. I followed until he finally pulled into a gas station.

"Mom," Milo said, "This isn't the way to Garret's house."

"I know, Sweety. I need the bathroom." And so did the idiot who cut us off in traffic.

⊹⊱†⊰†⊱⊰⊹

The speed at which I finished off the young guy in the bathroom amazed me. Thank goodness, I'd worn that long dress because the two retractable spinneret's that grew from somewhere between my, well, my private parts, were truly obscene — like a pair of short skis that extended between and yet at the same time behind my legs.

By the time the kids and I got to Garret's house, one kitten had already received a good home. But there were seven left! I let my three choose the one they wanted and when they piled into the car with the new family pet, I offered Garret's mom a hundred bucks for the rest of the kittens and the mother. She looked surprised but when I explained that we lived on this hobby pumpkin farm and we had a problem with rats she understood and sold me the lot. Momma cat had given birth to the litter in the family's washroom and so in the convenience of that privacy I went about my business. I had those critters wrapped in the finest silk in no time. That way they wouldn't squawk in the trunk on the way home.

→·I·•·I·•·I·←

Ted, of course, watched football in front of the T.V. Exhausted, I went upstairs to shower and contemplate the little snack in the trunk of my car. Stripped down in the shower I began to explore my new body. I shot out those spinnerets and exuded silk at various speeds. A little tricky, and I did end up giving the entire bathroom a wipe down. The only change that really disturbed me was the eyes. Small, discreet, more like six boils all over my head, but my thick blond hair covered them, which made it difficult to use them.

That night I awoke. Sleep became less of an option for me. I wandered around the house. Several times I went to the kids' bedrooms to check on them and make sure they slept soundly. The cat snack kept the hunger away most of the evening and the John Doe lunch in the gas station bathroom helped, too. But as the night wore on the pangs burned. I visited the fridge over and over unable to find anything to satisfy my craving.

→·I·•·I·•·I·←

Next morning I awoke to the sound of Ted's curses.
"What the fuck is this?"

Wow, Ted rarely spoke like that. *Did TSN get blacked out?*

"What's the matter?" I asked, overly sweet. He needed
to pee and headed for the bathroom down the hall. Snag-
ging my housecoat, I leaped from bed with the spinnerets
retracted as far as possible. The instant I stepped out of
our room I stopped.

The funnel of cobweb that filled the hallway made it
nearly impossible to see.

"Ted?"

"Right, here," he said, and sure enough not two feet from
me stood my husband, obstructed from my view behind
a curtain of webs.

"Don't move," Ted said.

"Why?" I asked in a whisper.

"Duh, clearly something made this stuff and — and—"

"What? You think Godzilla-spider broke in here last
night and did this?"

"Well, what then?" he asked, the perplexity in his voice
palatable.

"Ted, it's like this..."

✦◦✦◦✦◦✦◦✦

Ted was breakfast. He didn't struggle, much, in fact he
seemed to like it. The vibrations he sent through the webs
as I wrapped him were sexual. He went out with the biggest
erection he'd achieved to date.

Down in the crawl space I hid Ted's body still cocooned
in the extra special wrap I'd given him. I felt a little guilty,
especially for the kids. They'd miss him. A bit of a dishrag
as husbands go, but Ted did do great service as a father.
Responsible for three children all by myself, wished I'd
thought of that before succumbing to the incessant hunger
pain.

At first I told myself management of the kids only
needed some fine-tuning. A nanny, and when we tired of
her well, yum, yum. In the meantime, the vision of my three
children all snug and wrapped tightly in their beds filled

my head over and over. And I blame that obsession for my inability to remember what took place in the next couple of days. By now, the inside of our house, filled with tunnels of web made it nearly impossible for the children to move through. I showed them where to step so they wouldn't get stuck and tangled. The look of horror in their eyes whenever I felt their struggles and ran up the stairs, or around the corner to help, broke my heart. They feared me.

Eventually Jason cornered me. "It's nearly time to open the fields, Mom," he said, as I stood by the window gazing at a particularly beautiful Violin Back spinning.

"What do you mean?" Wondering how he thought we could possibly open the fields without their dad.

"The pumpkin fields, you know, our family business. The thing that pays the mortgage and buys food for us, which by the way you haven't done for awhile."

I looked away from the window to Jason. He looked small, but smelled so good. He smelled like cooked milk and my stomach rumbled.

"Jasie, if you really want to open the fields this year, you and Milo can do it."

"Me and Milo!" he said, and sounded so incredulous that I snapped out of my stupor. "Mom, Milo's wrapped and upstairs in his room. Asleep, or dead or whatever it is you do when you think you might eat. And even if he weren't, we're only ten and eight years old! You suck. You're losing it," he said, and left me. Yeah, I suck. I chuckled.

⇥·I·•·I·•·I·⇤

I never told Jason I'd already eaten his siblings. Their fate, I believed, was the best thing for them. Somewhere in my mind I knew that they'd be taken and the thought of them in the foster system made me crazy. Jason I left for last. He kept me in touch with myself. Without him I'd already be hidden in a dark corner waiting to pounce on whoever dared enter our house. And who would that be, I wondered time and time again, eventually a neighbor, the police, an ambulance crew. Really how long could I get away with this? Jason made me think things out. Like a pinch on the arm he kept me aware. And then an idea! Jason, the sweet peach, my instigator. Open the pumpkin fields. An endless supply of food awaited me there, if I were careful and selective.

In the next few days Jason avoided me. But he helped me out, self-preservation, I guess. He left me notes to remind me about how to prepare for the fields. Sweet kid. I guess he thought I'd lost my mental faculties but I hadn't. I let him think he hid from me but I knew where he went. He spent a lot of time in the crawl space near his wrapped up dad. I went down there one night to find that Ted, clear of all the silk I'd placed him in, lay curled in a fetal kind of position. If I touched him he sort of caved in at that spot, like flaky puff pastry.

Nearly pumpkin picking time and I eagerly awaited the weekend busloads of children, carloads arrived through the week. I even designed a cool, pumpkin maze for the kids to walk through while they made their selections, in the shape of a web of course.

That night before the fields opened, I lay in bed working out the details of my plans, changing my mind over and over, thinking it best to go for a parent rather then a child. Grandparents, older ones, would be least conspicuous. I'd forgotten about Jason over the last few days. I hadn't seen or sensed his presence anywhere.

Then he surprised me.

"Hey, Mom. Mom!" he called me from the house. Jason, I discovered later, took up residence in our little barn, really a converted detached garage.

I hurried out to see what he wanted and just to see him.

"Over here," he said and waved me into the barn.

When I entered I blinked. No lights lit the interior, only a single small window and of course spiders' webs cut off most of the light from it.

"Jason?" I called out.

"Mom, I'm hungry," said a voice, that of a very young child, not Jason's. " I want some candy," said the same voice. Something odd about the voice stopped me in my tracks. He stepped out from the shadows.

"I brought her in here for you," he said. And I turned to look. He stood near the barn door.

"Brought who in for me, Jasie?"

"A little girl," he said. "I brought her from the pumpkin field."

I didn't know what to say, but my stomach hurt with the hunger pang that hit me. "Why don't you go back into the house, Jason and I'll take care of her."

"She's hiding in the big cement drainpipe dad took from the construction site on the Tanner's farm," he said. Nodding, I slowly stepped in the direction of the pipe and recalled that Ted brought the pipe in here a couple of years ago. He'd intended to dig a well and use the cylinder to line it. Just another project he never got round to. As I moved deeper into the barn, Jason closed the door behind me. I heard him fix the two by fours across the doors. That struck me as odd, locking me in. And I wondered what my little Jason might do next. The drainpipe lay down on its side. I hadn't heard a sound since the last request for candy.

"I have candy for you. Would you like some?" And approached the pipe with caution. A light shone at the other end. Down on my hands and knees I crawled closer. One of Ted's extension lights hung on the outside perimeter of the pipe. I crawled in. The tunnel appeared to be sealed at the opposite end. Inside a doll and tape recorder sat propped up against the board. Tannis' doll, and it talked. Jason had recorded a couple of her phrases and set them up for me to hear. Did he hope to make me feel badly about his sister? There inside the pipe, on my belly, I pulled the doll toward me and revealed a huge mud dauber nest. Several of the nasty wasps flew out and into my face. I backed up quickly and got out of there. But not before those damn wasps got me. They didn't want to let go of me and clung with those damn long legs and drove their stingers into me. Furious, I scrabbled around in the dark barn for quite awhile. I got the light from the drainpipe and carried it. Breaking the glass on the barn window was easy enough but the small window couldn't accommodate my rear end. For the moment I was stuck.

Knowing Jason, he'd come and look and see if his plan worked. If it were me I'd look through the barn window first, so I cleared it of all its webs and dirt and then lay beneath it and feigned my demise. Sure enough he entered the barn and crept over to me. I didn't move. And I kept my eyes closed because I didn't want him to run.

"Jason," I spoke his name quietly. A long pause. "Jason, I'm here."

"Mom, are you OK?' he asked, I could hear the fear in his voice.

"I need a hug, Jason." I just waited, motionless. Then, I slowly sat up and we embraced, for the last time.

I didn't have the heart to eat him, nor the courage to just let him go. What else might he be capable of? I put him to sleep and wrapped him in a nice warm cocoon made of mother's silk. I carried him inside his silk papoose on my back. It felt perfectly natural.

I felt closer to Jason for some reason, than the other two. Eating him wasn't an option. I loved them as much. I know I did. In fact, Jasie was my most difficult child. These thoughts disturbed me as I went through my days, Jason next to me; his heart quietly beating through my back, to my heart.

Something else was happening to me. My abdomen and butt distended daily and I knew from having done it three times before that my body prepared itself for birth. My strong urge to keep Jason with me on my back started to make sense to me. And I wondered how many hundreds of tiny replicas of something like me I'd carry under my skirts and for how long until they made their own way into the world?

Canadian SF
Comes of Age
by Edo van Belkom

Tesseracts TEN.

Ten. Such a nice round number. But while this is the tenth volume in the *Tesseracts* series (okay it's really the eleventh, counting *Tesseracts Q*, but let's not let facts get in the way of a cogent argument), it's been more than twenty years since transplanted American, Judith Merril edited the landmark first anthology. In a way it was appropriate that someone from outside was the one to get the Canadian science fiction ball rolling. With the exception of Phyllis Gotlieb — an excellent writer who for the longest time had to bear the cumbersome label of Canada's only science fiction writer — the vast majority of early "Canadian" science fiction and fantasy writers hailed from somewhere else.

Americans led the initial charge with Spider and Jeanne Robinson making the move north in the 1970s and became Canada's first winner of the Hugo and Nebula Awards — the pinnacle of science fiction writing the world over. Another American expatriate, William Gibson, actually came to Canada in 1968 but wouldn't make his mark in science fiction for another dozen years with the publication of several short stories in *Omni* magazine and his first novel *Neuromancer* redefined the genre.

Considering Canada's origins as a British and French colony, it's not surprising that Great Britain and France also made significant contributions during the formative years of Canadian science fiction. Young adult author Monica Hughes came to Canada in the 1950s with her first book for young readers being published some twenty years later. Michael Coney settled in Canada in 1972, the same year his first science fiction novel was published. And Dave Duncan settled in Canada in the mid-fifties and began writing after 30 years in the oil and gas industry. And finally, Élisabeth Vonarburg emigrated from France in the mid-seventies, publishing her first efforts in the genre just a couple of years later.

An auspicious start indeed. But once the outside force got the once immovable object rolling, Canadian SF began to take on a life of its own. Sure Canadian SF was still infused every so often by outside sources — Robert Charles Wilson, Lesley Choyce, Nancy Kilpatrick, are all American born, Charles de Lint was born in the Netherlands, and Andrew Weiner is British — but the genre was started to show signs of becoming a sustainable, indigenous art form. Volume two of the *Tesseracts* series was edited by Canadians Phyllis Gotlieb and Douglas Barbour in 1987, and Canada's own SF magazine, *On Spec*, took flight just two years later. These publications continue on to this day, and during the interim, Canadian SF has blossomed into a vital and vibrant Canadian literature with countless Canadian-born authors publishing in Canada, the United States and all over the world.

Robert J. Sawyer tops the list with Hugo and Nebula award wins, but he's by no means alone. Other Canadian science fiction and fantasy authors who have emerged over the past two decades include the likes of Guy Gavriel Kay, James Alan Gardner, Tanya Huff, Julie Czerneda, Joel Champetier, Donald Kingsbury, Terence M. Green, Peter Watts, Jean-Louis Trudel, Karl Shroeder, Ed Greenwood, Candas Jane Dorsey, Alison Baird, Daniel Sernine, Nalo Hopkinson, Fiona Patton, Michele Sagara West, Scott Mackay, Kelley Armstrong, Yves Meynard.... Well, the list is long and continuously growing.

But the best thing about all of these authors is that scant few of them were around when Judith Merril put together the first *Tesseracts* anthology. That means that in the twenty years since, Canadian science fiction and fantasy has grown by leaps and bounds since the early 1980s.

This volume continues that tradition of growth and freshness. The nineteen names in this anthology might not be familiar to SF readers, or perhaps even fans of the Canadian variety — yet. Just give them time, Canadian science fiction is still growing. If Judith Merril's original *Tesseracts* anthology marked the birth of Canadian SF, then after ten volumes and twenty years, that child is coming of age and entering adulthood with its best and most fruitful years lying ahead with only the sky serving as the limit to their creativity and ambition.

Just think, in another twenty years, you'll be able to say of the new authors appearing in this volume, "I remember reading them, when..."

Biographies

René Beaulieu is a writer, anthologist, critic and translator (works by De Lint, Moorcock and Sturgeon), René Beaulieu is also a library technician and has been actively involved with SFQ since the early 1970s. He is the author of three collections of short stories, including *Légendes de Virnie* (Prix Boréal). His short story "Le Geai Bleu" won both the Dagon and Boréal awards. René is a former radio host, specialized librarian, and literary director (PTBGDA, L'ASSFQ), and member of the Board for the Grand Prix de la SFFQ. A half dozen of his short stories and articles have been translated and published in English. Recently, he has published articles and reviews in *KWS*, *Bifrost*, *Solaris* and elsewhere, but has never forgotten his love for short fiction. Upcoming publications include: "Sandra" (*XYZ*), a new version of "Un Fantôme D'Amour" (*Solaris*) and a new version of "Cendres" dans *Les Anges Électriques* (Les Moutons Électriques, A.-F. Ruaud). He has a blog: http://geaibleu.joueb.com/

Greg Bechtel's stories have appeared in *Prairie Fire*, *On Spec*, *Challenging Destiny* and *Qwerty* magazines. He has recently moved to Edmonton, where he is pursuing a PhD in English literature and attempting to resurrect his first novel, which saw its original incarnation as his MA thesis in creative writing at the University of New Brunswick. At the moment of drafting this bio, "Blackbird Shuffle" has been nominated for the Journey Prize, a National Magazine Award, and a Western Magazine Award.

Stephanie Bedwell-Grime is a five-time Aurora Award finalist and the author of eight novels and over fifty short stories. Stephanie welcomes visitors to her website at www.feralmartian.com

Nancy Bennett is an essayist, poet and fiction writer. Her work has appeared in such places as *Tales of the Unanticipated*, *Tesseracts*, *Flesh and Blood* and *Not One of Us*. She has made the recommended reading list for the *Year's Best Fantasy and Horror* three times. Her latest achievement, a cinquain poem, appeared in *ìIn Fine Formî* alongside the works of P. K. Page, Robert Service and Margaret Atwood.

Jason Christie is considered to be one of Canada's cutting-edge poets and is, perhaps, one of the most important poets of the late 20th and early 21st centuries. His avant-garde style challenges the status quo and questions what a poem may be. The robot poem included in this collection, from his *i-ROBOT Poetry by Jason Christie* collection, illuminates his unique and somewhat whimsical, alternative style.

Sheryl Curtis. With undergraduate and graduate degrees in translation from the Université de Montréal and a doctorate in interdisciplinary studies from Concordia University, Sheryl Curtis is a certified member of the Ordre des traducteurs, terminologues et interprètes agréés du Quebec (OTTIAQ) and works as a professional translator. During the course of her career, she also taught translation over a period of 20 years as a member of the part-time faculty at Concordia University, in Montreal, Quebec. She is also a member of the Literary Translators' Association of Canada and is devoting more and more of her time to literary translation. Since 1998, her translations of short stories have appeared in *Interzone*, *Year's Best Science Fiction 4*, *Year's Best Fantasy and Horror 15*, *On Spec*, *Altair*, *Tesseracts8*, *Tesseracts9*, and elsewhere.

Mark Dachuk is a lifetime resident of Toronto, and makes his living as a carpenter. He is also a raging gamer, often pitching multiple card and board game ideas to friends, or boring them with various exploits in his online universe. He is currently in the process of forming a game company with a group of friends. "Permission" is his first published short story. Serious inquiries can be sent to Mark Dachuk at: markdachuk@gmail.com

Victoria Fisher was born in England but now divides her year between Ottawa and Toronto, where she is currently studying English, History and Politics at the University of Toronto. She is distracted from her studies by her first love — a fascination for stories of all kinds.

Susan Forest's first novel for young adults, *The Dragon Prince*, (Gage Educational Publishers) was awarded the Children's Circle Book Choice Award, and was chosen by Gage as one of two young adult novels to represent the company at a book fair in Berlin. Her short story, *"Playing Games"* appeared in the Winter issue of *ON SPEC* magazine, and her story, *"Immunity"* will be included in the December 2006 issue of *Asimov's Science Fiction*.

Matthew Hughes writes science fiction and science-fantasy. His alter ego, Matt Hughes, writes suspense fiction. He has published four novels, thirty short stories, one collection and two non-fiction books.

His latest sf novel is *Majestrum* (Night Shade, 2006), the fourth set in the Archonate universe. The first three were *Fools Errant, Fool Me Twice* and *Black Brillion*. His short sf stories have appeared in *Asimov's, The Magazine of Fantasy & Science Fiction, Interzone* and *Postscripts*.

His web page is at http://www.archonate.com/

Matthew Johnson is a writer and teacher who lives in Ottawa with his wife Megan. He has published stories in *Asimov's Science Fiction, On Spec*, and *Space and Time*, as well as the anthologies *Time for Bedlam* and *Deathgrip: Exit Laughing*. He has written two novels, both of which reside currently in Slush Pile Limbo, and is at work on a third. "Closing Time" was workshopped in its early stages by the Stone Stories workshop group at Queen's University, to whom many thanks are due.

You can find more information on his website: www.zatrikion.blogspot.com.

Sandra Kasturi is the co-creator (along with Jason Taniguchi) of the animated children's TV series, *Adventures of the Sinister Horde*. She recently won the prestigious ARC magazine annual Poem of the Year award for her poem "Old Men, Smoking." Sandra edited the SF poetry anthology, *The Stars As Seen from this Particular Angle of Night*. She has three chapbooks published and her work has also appeared in magazines (Prairie Fire, ON SPEC, TransVersions, Star*Line and others) and anthologies, including several of the Tesseracts series, 2001: A Science Fiction Poetry Anthology, Northern Frights 4, and Girls Who Bite Back. Her first full-length poetry collection, tentatively titled *Animal Bridegrooms*, will appear in 2007 from Tightrope Books. Sandra is the grant administrator and a judge for the Speculative Literature Foundation's Older Writers' Grant, and is a founding member of the Algonquin Square Table poetry workshop. She runs her own imprint, Kelp Queen Press, and has won a Bram Stoker Award for her editorial work at the on-line magazine, *ChiZine*. During the day, Sandra works as a production coordinator at YTV.

Michèle Laframboise. A science-fiction lover since childhood, Michèle Laframboise juggles her time between drawing comics, writing stories, and caring for her family.

With an academic background in geography and civil engineering, she began to draw and write SF. She has published six SF books so far, two of which have won awards: *Les Nuages de Phoenix*, a YA novel, received a general literature award in Québec and *Les Mémoires de l'Arc* was awarded a 2005 Aurora Award. She has published several short stories. She is currently working on two comic book projects and one YA novel, in addition to translating her novels into English.

Scott Mackay has published over forty short stories in magazines such as *Science Fiction Age*, *On Spec*, *The Magazine of Fantasy and Science Fiction*, *Interzone*, *Ellery Queen's Mystery Magazine*, and *Alfred Hitchcock's Mystery Magazine*. He's winner of the Arthur Ellis Award for best mystery short story, as well as the Okanagan Award for best literary short fiction.

He's the author of nine novels, including *Outpost* (Tor 1998), *The Meek* (Roc 2001), *Orbis* (Roc 2002), and *Omnifix* (Roc 2004), which was listed at Number 6 on the Locus bestsellers list. *The Meek* was a John W. Campbell Memorial Award finalist for best SF novel of 2001. Prometheus Books published his latest SF novel, *Tides*, under the Pyr imprint in fall of 2005. Recently, he sold two new novels to Roc: *Phytosphere*, which will appear in 2007; and *Omega Sol*, which will appear some time after. His books have appeared in six languages.

Colleen McDonald is a graduate of the Alberta College of Art & Design. She is a fine artist, illustrator and creature designer. Born in Vancouver, British Columbia, she now lives and works on her designs in Weymouth, Nova Scotia. Examples of her work can be seen on: www3.ns.sympatico.ca/colleen.mcdonald

Allen Moore worked for two decades in high technology. He designed laser writing equipment for the printing industry and instrumentation for astrophysics. Allen is now a volunteer in his community, providing support to people with life-threatening illnesses. He also tutors both math and physics to street youth in downtown Vancouver.

Yvonne Pronovost is a twenty-something living in Edmonton, Alberta, whose work has appeared in *Neo-Opsis Magazine*, *NFG*, *Beyond Centauri*, and the *Darkness Rising 2005* horror anthology from Prime Books. She likes tea, pina coladas, and getting caught in the rain, but isn't very fond of onions. Neither of her thumbs are green.

Rhea Rose was born in Etobicoke, Ontario and rode the CN rails for 3 days to move to BC when she was twelve (she took her parents with her), writing almost continuously before and since then. She nearly didn't attend Clarion West in Seattle in 1984 when, at the US border, they asked her if she had a student visa to study at Seattle Central College? She said no and so did they. So she promised that she would just go shopping in Bellingham and they let her in. Six weeks later, she was a born again SF and F writer. She also writes nonfiction and fiction. Her speculative short stories have been published in *Northwest Passages: A Cascadian Anthology*, *TaleBones*, *Tesseracts*, *Tesseracts 2*, *ON SPEC*, and *Christmas Forever*, edited by David Hartwell. Stories from both these latter publications made the preliminary nebula award list. Her speculative poetry has appeared in *Tesseracts 9*, *Tesseracts 6 (poem nominated for a Rhysling award)*, *TaleBones*, *Transversions*, *Mythic Circle*, *Olympic View* anthology, and *T.S. Elliot Remembered*. She is an active member of The Lonely Cry (a writers' performance group) and the Helix writers' group. She has organized many local writers' workshops, has had the opportunity to do extra work in local movies, and has participated in the Vancouver Fringe Festival. To support her writing habit she teaches senior English at an alternate school in Coquitlam.

Lisa Smedman is a writer and game designer, with a dozen novels published to date. She has designed adventures for the Advanced Dungeons and Dragons game, as well as a number of other roleplaying games. She wrote *The Apparition Trail*, an alternate-history science fiction novel, is the creator of three one-act plays, and the author of numerous short stories. A journalist for more than 20 years, she currently splits her week between her "day job" as an editor and historical columnist at a Vancouver newspaper and writing fiction. She facilitates a bi-weekly writers' workshop and has been active in organizing science fiction conventions. Lisa Smedman's website is located at www.lisasmedman.topcities.com.

Sarah Totton has sold stories to *Realms of Fantasy*, *Polyphony 5*, *The Nine Muses* (Wheatland Press), *Tesseracts Nine*, and *Tales of the Unanticipated*. She is a Third Place winner in the 2005 *L. Ron Hubbard's* Writers of the Future Contest.

Edo van Belkom has won both the Bram Stoker and Silver Birch Awards and is a three-time winner of the Aurora Award, Canada's top prize for speculative writing. Among his novels are *Scream Queen*, *Blood Road*, *Martyrs* and *Teeth*. In addition to *Tesseracts 10*, Edo is the editor of four other anthologies including *Be Afraid!* and *Be Very Afraid!* His most recent work is a series of novels for young readers, *Wolf Pack*, *Lone Wolf*, and *Cry Wolf*. Born in 1962, he graduated from York University with an honors degree in Creative Writing and has worked as everything from school bus driver to security guard, newspaper reporter to television horror movie host. The author of well over 200 short stories, Edo makes his home in Brampton, Ontario with his wife and son. Feel free to visit his website at www.vanbelkom.com

Wendy Waring is a translator, editor, lecturer and writer who lives in Sydney, Australia whenever she gets the chance. She's currently finishing a fantasy novel, *Empire of the Pure*. A survivor of Clarion South, "*Au pays*" is her first specfic publication, and her second, "*Stonework*", will appear in *Interzone*.

Robert Charles Wilson is the author of many short stories and twelve novels. His work has appeared in such publications as *Realms of Fantasy*, *F & SF*, and *Tesseracts 3, 4 & 6*, and his short story "The Inner, Inner City" was a World Fantasy Award finalist. His latest novel, *Spin*, now in paperback, won the 2006 Hugo Award. He has also received the John W. Campbell Award, three Aurora Awards, and the Philip K. Dick Award. Robert Charles Wilson was born in California in 1953, but moved to Canada when he was nine years old. He currently lives near Toronto.

Copyright Notices

Our titles are available at major book stores and local independent resellers who support Science Fiction and Fantasy readers like you.

Alphanauts by J. Brian Clarke - (tp) - ISBN: 978-1-894063-14-2
Apparition Trail, The by Lisa Smedman - (tp) - ISBN:1-894063-22-8
Black Chalice by Marie Jakober - (hb) - ISBN:1-894063-00-7
Blue Apes by Phyllis Gotlieb (pb) - ISBN:1-895836-13-1
Blue Apes by Phyllis Gotlieb (hb) - ISBN:1-895836-14-X
Children of Atwar, The by Heather Spears (pb) - ISBN:0-888783-35-3
Claus Effect by David Nickle & Karl Schroeder, The (pb) - ISBN:1-895836-34-4
Claus Effect by David Nickle & Karl Schroeder, The (hb) - ISBN:1-895836-35-2
Courtesan Prince, The by Lynda Williams (tp) - 1-894063-28-7
Dark Earth Dreams by Candas Dorsey & Roger Deegan (comes with a CD)
    - ISBN:1-895836-05-0
Distant Signals by Andrew Weiner (tp) - ISBN:0-888782-84-5
Dreams of an Unseen Planet by Teresa Plowright (tp) - ISBN:0-888782-82-9
Dreams of the Sea by Élisabeth Vonarburg (tp) - ISBN:1-895836-96-4
Dreams of the Sea by Élisabeth Vonarburg (hb) - ISBN:1-895836-98-0
Eclipse by K. A. Bedford - (tp) - ISBN:978-1-894063-30-2
Even The Stones by Marie Jakober - (tp) - ISBN:1-894063-18-X
Fires of the Kindred by Robin Skelton (tp) - ISBN:0-888782-71-3
Forbidden Cargo by Rebecca Rowe - (tp) - ISBN: 978-1-894063-16-6
Game of Perfection, A by Élisabeth Vonarburg (tp) - ISBN:978-1-894063-32-6
Green Music by Ursula Pflug (tp) - ISBN:1-895836-75-1
Green Music by Ursula Pflug (hb) - ISBN:1895836-77-8
Healer, The by Amber Hayward (tp) - ISBN:1-895836-89-1
Healer, The by Amber Hayward (hb) - ISBN:1-895836-91-3
Hydrogen Steel by K. A. Bedford - (tp) - ISBN-13: 978-1-894063-20-3
i-ROBOT Poetry by Jason Christie - (tp) - ISBN-13: 978-1-894063-24-1
Jackal Bird by Michael Barley (pb) - ISBN:1-895836-07-7
Jackal Bird by Michael Barley (hb) - ISBN:1-895836-11-5
Keaen by Till Noever - (tp) - ISBN:1-894063-08-2
Land/Space edited by Candas Jane Dorsey and Judy McCrosky (tp)
    - ISBN:1-895836-90-5
Land/Space edited by Candas Jane Dorsey and Judy McCrosky (hb)
    - ISBN:1-895836-92-1
Lyskarion: The Song of the Wind by J.A. Cullum - (tp) - ISBN:1-894063-02-3
Machine Sex and other stories by Candas Jane Dorsey (tp) - ISBN:0-888782-78-0
Maërlande Chronicles, The by Élisabeth Vonarburg (pb) - ISBN:0-888782-94-2
Moonfall by Heather Spears (pb) - ISBN:0-888783-06-X
On Spec: The First Five Years edited by On Spec (pb) - ISBN:1-895836-08-5
On Spec: The First Five Years edited by On Spec (hb) - ISBN:1-895836-12-3
Orbital Burn by K. A. Bedford - (tp) - ISBN:1-894063-10-4
Orbital Burn by K. A. Bedford - (hb) - ISBN:1-894063-12-0
Pallahaxi Tide by Michael Coney (pb) - ISBN:0-888782-93-4
Passion Play by Sean Stewart (pb) - ISBN:0-888783-14-0
Plague Saint by Rita Donovan, The - (tp) - ISBN:1-895836-28-X
Plague Saint by Rita Donovan, The - (hb) - ISBN:1-895836-29-8
Reluctant Voyagers by Élisabeth Vonarburg (pb) - ISBN:1-895836-09-3
Reluctant Voyagers by Élisabeth Vonarburg (hb) - ISBN:1-895836-15-8

Resisting Adonis by Timothy J. Anderson (tp) - ISBN:1-895836-84-0
Resisting Adonis by Timothy J. Anderson (hb) - ISBN:1-895836-83-2
Silent City, The by Élisabeth Vonarburg (tp) - ISBN:0-888782-77-2
Righteous Anger by Lynda Williams (tp) - ISBN-13: 978-1-894063-38-8
Slow Engines of Time, The by Élisabeth Vonarburg (tp) - ISBN:1-895836-30-1
Slow Engines of Time, The by Élisabeth Vonarburg (hb) - ISBN:1-895836-31-X
Stealing Magic (flipover edition) by Tanya Huff (tp) - ISBN:978-1-894063-34-0
Strange Attractors by Tom Henighan (pb) - ISBN:0-888783-12-4
Taming, The by Heather Spears (pb) - ISBN:1-895836-23-9
Taming, The by Heather Spears (hb) - ISBN:1-895836-24-7
Ten Monkeys, Ten Minutes by Peter Watts (tp) - ISBN:1-895836-74-3
Ten Monkeys, Ten Minutes by Peter Watts (hb) - ISBN:1-895836-76-X
Tesseracts 1 edited by Judith Merril (pb) - ISBN:0-888782-79-9
Tesseracts 2 edited by Phyllis Gotlieb & Douglas Barbour (pb) - ISBN:0-888782-70-5
Tesseracts 3 edited by Candas Jane Dorsey & Gerry Truscott (pb) - ISBN:0-888782-90-X
Tesseracts 4 edited by Lorna Toolis & Michael Skeet (pb) - ISBN:0-888783-22-1
Tesseracts 5 edited by Robert Runté & Yves Maynard (pb) - ISBN:1-895836-25-5
Tesseracts 5 edited by Robert Runté & Yves Maynard (hb) - ISBN:1-895836-26-3
Tesseracts 6 edited by Robert J. Sawyer & Carolyn Clink (pb) - ISBN:1-895836-32-8
Tesseracts 6 edited by Robert J. Sawyer & Carolyn Clink (hb) - ISBN:1-895836-33-6
Tesseracts 7 edited by Paula Johanson & Jean-Louis Trudel (tp) - ISBN:1-895836-58-1
Tesseracts 7 edited by Paula Johanson & Jean-Louis Trudel (hb) - ISBN:1-895836-59-X
Tesseracts 8 edited by John Clute & Candas Jane Dorsey (tp) - ISBN:1-895836-61-1
Tesseracts 8 edited by John Clute & Candas Jane Dorsey (hb) - ISBN:1-895836-62-X
Tesseracts 9 edited by Nalo Hopkinson and Geoff Ryman (tp) - ISBN:1-894063-26-0
Tesseracts 10 edited by Edo van Belkom and Robert Charles Wilson (tp)
    - ISBN-13: 978-1-894063-36-4
TesseractsQ edited by Élisabeth Vonarburg & Jane Brierley (pb) - ISBN:1-895836-21-2
TesseractsQ edited by Élisabeth Vonarburg & Jane Brierley (hb) - ISBN:1-895836-22-0
Throne Price by Lynda Williams and Alison Sinclair - (tp) - ISBN:1-894063-06-6

EDGE

EDGE Science Fiction and Fantasy Publishing
P. O. Box 1714, Calgary, AB, Canada, T2P 2L7
www.edgewebsite.com
403-254-0160 (voice)
403-254-0456 (fax)

WHAT SHOULD I READ NEXT?
Selected books published by EDGE . . .

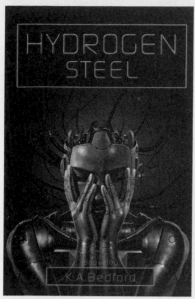

Hard Science Fiction

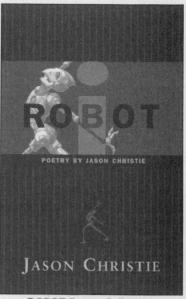

ROBOT Poetry Collection

Science Fiction

Science Fiction

WHAT SHOULD I READ NEXT?
Selected books published by EDGE . . .

Science Fiction

Fantasy Short Story Collection

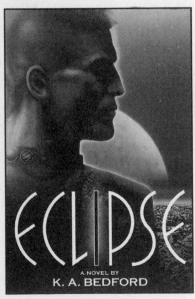

Science Fiction Psychological
Thriller

Science Fiction Space Opera

WHAT SHOULD I READ NEXT?
Selected books published by EDGE . . .

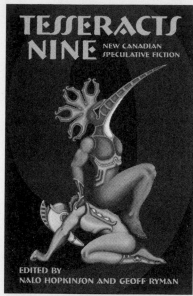

Speculative Fiction Short Stories

Historical Science Fiction

High Fantasy

Science Fiction